Sadie's Wars

By

Rosemary Noble

To Pat

with thank

Rosemary

Edited by J L Dean

Cover by German Creative

Chichester Publishing

© 2018

For the descendants of Joseph Timms

Be Proud

Also, for the brave men of Bomber and Coastal
Commands, including the uncle I never met, who died
aged 18.

Chapter One

England
Cleethorpes, June 1940

Sadie awoke with a jerk. A dream skittered around the back of her mind and then faded. All she remembered was her papa's smiling face, enough to get the day off to a good start. She lay in the dark, luxuriating in having her boys all under one roof for a change. A loud, abrupt snore from Henry in the next room left her wondering what time they had returned from the *Café Dansant*. She imagined her two older boys wowing the girls in their RAF uniforms and smiled. Glen must have been miffed, but it would be his turn next.

Today's the day, she thought. A sense of unease had been building for weeks in her stomach. The churning inside her brought the taste of bile to her throat. Sleep finally fled. Rousing herself, she walked to the window and lifted the blackout to let the June sunshine flood the room with light. She glanced at the clock on her bedside table. Nearly eight o'clock, she would let the boys sleep on while she washed and dressed.

'Eggs and fried bread for breakfast, I think. Shame there's no bacon, but there's a war on.' She grimaced with acceptance. A small sacrifice in the scheme of things.

Glen was first down.

'How do you feel?' Sadie asked.

'Excited, nervous. It was good to talk to Henry and Dale last night. They reassured me a little. I just wish I knew whether I am going to pass selection as a pilot. You know that's what I want.'

'Does it seem greedy to have three pilots in the family? Wouldn't a navigator, or flight engineer be good too? You're good at maths.'

'I suppose. You know they may send us overseas for training?'

She nodded. 'You'll get to see something of the world then.'

'I can't remember our life in Australia at all, not the slightest thing.' He looked rueful.

'Maybe you'll be sent there for training.'

'Too far I think. Rhodesia or Canada perhaps.'

Dale poked his head into the kitchen.

'Can I smell fried bread? I need a ton to mop up the beer I drank last night.'

'Go and sit down both of you, I'll bring it through. Help yourself to tea. It's on the table.'

After breakfast, she set about preparing a mountain of vegetables for dinner. She would have to fill them up somehow. A cottage pie, more potato than meat with a liberal crust of baked cheese wouldn't satisfy them, especially Glen, who liked to graze the pantry after school. Empty legs she called him, but he was still growing and almost as tall as Henry. She supposed the RAF would feed him well.

The boys were helping Glen fill his suitcase. They knew what was needed by now; she was happy to leave them to it. Glen didn't want his mother fussing. She pretended it was the onion making her eyes water, but a deep sense of her future loneliness was settling over her. Glen's still a child, she thought; his eighteenth birthday only a week before. Tears ran down her face. She grabbed a tea-towel to mop them and glanced at the kitchen clock. Could she give Chapel a miss this morning?

Henry answered her question. 'It's a glorious day. We fancy a stroll down on the prom and then a drink at the Dolphin.'

She looked up and smiled. 'You'll enjoy that, and I'll have dinner ready for you when you get back.'

'No, Mother. You're coming too.'

'Me in a pub bar, no.'

'There's a war on. You're coming, no excuses.'

'But the meal?'

'How long will it take to cook?'

'An hour, no more if it's all prepared.'

'Well then. It's settled. You're coming.' He picked her up, knife and all, and kissed her on the cheek. His violet eyes, her mother's eyes, always knocked her sideways.

'Henry, you will take care, won't you?'

'I'll do my best. We all do. Now let me have the knife, and I'll peel potatoes while you go and get ready. We want you looking tip-top if you're going out with us handsome fellows.'

She laughed. 'I'll do my best too. I don't want to let you down.'

'You'll never do that.' He took her in his arms again and hugged her.

She felt skittish as she swapped her Chapel suit for a summer dress. Did it look too young for her? Who would care? Blue and white polka dot with a broad white collar and cuffs, and a royal blue jacket, she had last worn it for her niece's wedding. It deserved another outing. After a quick twirl in front of the mirror, she grabbed her best hat from the cupboard, fixing it with a hat-pin in case of a breeze on the sea-front. Finally, she picked up her gloves to join her sons waiting below.

'Strewth Mom, you look like Vivien Leigh!' They chorused, grinning. They'd practised that line. It was the kind of thing she would miss.

'Get away with you. She's twenty years my junior, and my nose is too long.' She laughed with a schoolgirl's giggle.

'Frankly, Mother, I don't give a damn.' Henry bent to kiss her on the cheek. She wanted to ruffle her fingers through his dark hair, but it was slicked down with Brylcreem.

As they walked up the hill towards the seafront, it dawned on her that they had conspired to make their last day together memorable. Henry and Dale each took an arm. Pride lit her eyes as people stared or stopped to wish them well. At the top of the hill, they let Glen take a turn, and her pride did not dim. The next time she saw him, he would also be in uniform.

They surprised her by marching over the road and turning left towards the station and not the pier.

'Not Wonderland!' She cried.

'Wait and see.' Glen replied grinning. Her heart flipped. What mischief were they planning?

They joined the dozens of day-trippers arriving from nearby towns and villages, all walking along the promenade to the funfair. But they passed the shed-like entrance to Wonderland and carried on walking. The Big Dipper, no less. She shivered with anticipation. For how many years had they threatened her with the monster roller coaster? This time she could not gainsay them. If they could fly bombers, what right had she to refuse the Big Dipper? Despite her drying mouth, love overcame her fear as the attendant placed the bar across her middle. Henry sat with his arm around her shoulders. Glen and Dale sat in the car behind as they slowly moved away and began to climb up into the sky. All Cleethorpes lay before her, a stunning view of the sands and the pier in one direction, with Grimsby Dock Tower in the other, the skating rink below. Chapman's Pond sparkled to the right as the car suddenly began to fall. Her stomach catapulted. She heard herself squealing as she held the bar tight, while Henry gripped her waist, laughing and screaming with her. They swooped lower and lower, then climbed again and fell once more.

A line from Othello bubbled into her mind.

If it were now to die, 'Twere now to be most happy.

She surrendered herself to the whim of her sons, knowing this day would have to sustain her for the duration of the war.

Hours later, Sadie waved them goodbye on their motorbikes. Dale left first with Glen riding pillion down towards Grimsby Station, where he would drop off his brother before heading to the Humber Ferry. Henry followed, driving down Clee Road towards Lincoln. When would they be together again? She turned back to the house where the dog next door was barking madly at the roar of the bikes. Mr Brain waved and pulled him away from the open sash-window.

'Sad to see them go, Mrs Tinsdale. They're fine young men.' She nodded, eyes too full of tears to speak as she stepped back inside the empty house.

She wandered around their rooms, picking up clothes, sitting on beds, staring into space with her memories of moving into this house fourteen years before. Sadie had been newly divorced, having escaped her former life in Adelaide. It had been a leap into the unknown.

Children are resilient, she had reasoned. Given love and security, they will thrive. With only occasional whines about the lack of sunshine as that first cold, wet winter kept them indoors, they had adapted. They learned to play football in winter, cricket in summer and fished in all weathers.

She had chosen this house well, five minutes from the beach, their primary school in the street behind, a good boys' grammar school a cycle-ride away at Old Clee, and a bus stop across the road. Money stretched further than it did in Australia and she had given them the best childhood possible. All that was left was to pray they would stay safe and maybe bring her grandchildren one day. She lay on Henry's bed, hugging his pillow to her, breathing in the smell of Brylcreem and tobacco.

Nancy, her niece, called a few days later. Sadie was drying her hands on the tea towel as she opened the door to her knock.

'You're up early. Wouldn't she sleep?'

Nancy jiggled the pram holding her baby daughter. 'Do you fancy a stroll on the prom? It's such a beautiful morning. Mother's busy, and I feel as though I've been stuck inside for too long.'

'Betsy Ann getting you down with her carping and criticism is she?' Nancy gave a rueful nod. 'Just like my Grandma Jane. What is it about those old women? They think they know best, but really! They get on your nerves. Do you remember your Australian grannie?'

Nancy shook her head. 'Hardly at all. Was she short, thin and spiky?'

'Spiky, that's a great way of describing her. Fearsome – you didn't cross her, that's for sure. I shouldn't speak ill of the dead. My grandpa on my mother's side, he was a darling, it's a shame you never met him.' Sadie smiled as she stroked baby Anne's reddened cheek. 'Have you tried oil of cloves on her gums?'

'I have, but she hates it.'

'Wait here; I'll grab a jacket and my handbag. I wonder if the café has choc ices, you could give her a spoonful and it will do us good to have a treat.' She turned into the hallway and took a navy jacket and handbag from a hook, shook off her slippers and moulded her feet into matching court shoes before grabbing her gas mask.

'Let me push her. It's been so long since my boys were this age,' Sadie said, as they set off up Isaac's Hill past large, brick villas. She took the handle of the battered family pram, passed down over the years. 'It's amazing what a walk outside will do to get a baby to settle, look at her now. So peaceful! Have you any news of Jimmy?'

'He wasn't in France, thank God. He's somewhere further south.'

'Let's try and forget about our troubles on this glorious morning. I spend every night sick with worry, as you must be for your husband. I'd rather enjoy this gorgeous sunshine right now.'

Nancy nodded in agreement. 'Can we nip into Woolworths? I need a few things for Mother.'

Watching out for trolley buses, they crossed the road at the top of the hill by the library, before walking towards the former art-deco cinema. Taped-up shop front windows added to its desultory air. Sadie's high heels clacked on the creaking, wooden boards as she trundled the pram down the aisle to the haberdashery section.

With a brown paper bag containing different coloured threads stowed in the bottom of the pram, they carried on towards the seafront then turned right on to Alexandra Road. The wide Humber estuary lay before them. The tide was in, and for once the water looked inviting, though never aquamarine like the water around the coasts of her Australian youth. It shone like a sheet of blue-edged steel.

'Shall we walk as far as the boating lake? We can stop at the *Bird's Nest Café* for a cup of tea.'

'That sounds delightful.' Sadie agreed. 'There's nowhere I have to be, no one at home now to consider.'

Nancy patted her gloved hand. 'I know how you feel, Aunty.'

What a sweet girl she was, Sadie thought, thinking of her aunt rather than her own troubles. Almost twenty-three, living in a house full of disappointed women and her husband away in the army, facing years at war, unless... Could it be possible that even Britain would capitulate? No, unthinkable, she shoved the idea to the back of her mind.

At the *Dolphin Hotel*, they turned down past the pier gardens where it looked like Jimmy Slater's Follies would be entertaining the crowds that afternoon. Perhaps she would go. They were always lively and fun.

'Will they put the middle section back once the war's over?' Nancy asked.

'Who knows? It's sad to see the pier broken in two; the pavilion seems to be pining for its other half. My boys would find it harder to fish out there now.' She must not get maudlin.

The warm weather brought people out in droves. Children skipped alongside their mothers. Some were carrying knitted bathing costumes and trailing thin, stripy towels. At least the bathing pool remained open. Sadie hated to see the sandy beach disfigured with rolls of barbed wire and tank traps. Her boys had lived on the beach in the summer. She missed the days when they came home hungry and tired, their clothes spattered with mud from cockling, hair gritty with sand but with happy, shining faces.

Before they reached Ross Castle, they sat on a seat to admire the unspoilt view. No barrage balloons interrupted the vista. The opposite side of the river appeared closer with the tide in, as did the forts protecting the mouth of the river. Seagulls soared, silent for once in the still, clear air. Above them, a trio of swifts swooped after insects. It looked to Sadie as though they were playing tag, one in front and two behind. As the swifts cavorted and darted through the air, the two women sat enthralled at the chase.

'You know that's one of the things I miss about home. The birds. The brilliant colour and plumage of the parakeets and the warbling of the Australian magpies, so different from their namesakes here. You know, Nancy, I have a magpie in my garden, and it sounds like a machine gun when it squawks, frightens me to death.'

As they began to walk again, Sadie turned and took one last look at the swifts flying north in the direction of Grimsby. She felt a hand on her arm.

'See that?' Nancy said, pointing to the east. A dot on the horizon appeared to be moving towards them, a distant hum disturbing the air.

'An aeroplane, they're always practising around here.' The drone of the engine too familiar for concern, until the unmistakable wail of the air raid siren assaulted their ears. Shots burst from one of the forts, and Sadie's mouth dried. Screaming women and children scattered. Nancy grabbed Anne from her pram and began to run up the sloping path towards Ross Castle. The siren reverberated at her heels, mixing with the sound of the ack-ack guns from beyond the bathing pool.

11

Sadie kicked off her shoes, panting her way up the small hill. She followed her niece to the safety of the walls of the tiny folly. Once there, they threw themselves against the stonework at its base. Others followed until it became crowded. Nancy struggled to get the baby's gas mask out of her bag.

'Let me help.' Sadie eased the steel mask over Ann's head, tying the canvas straps beneath her bottom. Poor thing, she looked like an alien enclosed in the ugly suit. She tried to remain calm for Nancy's sake, but her heart hammered in her chest as she dug out her own mask.

The noise of the engine throbbed in her ears and seconds later the plane roared overhead, low enough to see the pilot. They watched it disappear over rooftops, flying northwest, the cross on its side and a swastika on its tail fin. Sadie caught her breath, glanced at her ruined stockings, before feeling the ground shake as a booming sound hit her ears. A distant black plume of smoke rose in the sky.

The baby woke and began to scream, the sound muffled, her tiny hands batting against the mask over her nose and mouth. Across the road, stragglers still ran for the safety of shelters. Sadie sucked in her breath, bloody Germans! In her sight line towards the right was the triangular roof outline of the rebuilt Baptist church.

Further in the distance another smaller boom. Nancy tore off her mask.

'What should we do? Maybe that's only the first plane. Do you think there are more on the way?'

'Sit tight Nancy. We're as safe here as anywhere.' Unless they bomb the castle, she thought. Nancy held the screaming baby against her shoulder, rocking her, trying to soothe her, but Nancy's face grew pale.

'Nancy dear, we've escaped the Jerries again. God or Lady Luck must be looking down on our family, don't you think?'

Nancy looked puzzled.

'See over there, that's the Baptist Church where the Manchesters were billeted in the last war. Your father escaped the bomb that night, and we've escaped them this time.' As she spoke, the all-clear sounded. A collective sigh of relief rippled around them as gas masks were torn off and people rose shakily to their feet.

'I must get back to check on Mother.' The question of where the bombs fell lay between them.

'I'll get the pram and meet you in the Market Place.'

Sadie began to retrace her steps, a throb in her heel where a stone had lodged in her laddered stockings. She recovered her shoes on the way down the steep slope, but by the time she got to the pram, she was shaking uncontrollably, tears spilled from her eyes, smudging her makeup. She forced herself to keep walking, the morning ruined, the promenade, no longer a place of beauty, of joy and children's laughter.

She'd sat out the last war in Australia, cocooned in her family home, but all too aware of what Nancy was going through now. News, it was all they lived for, devouring the newspapers, letters like gold dust but dreading the sight of a dog collar. Priests bore bad news. Those feelings had trebled now that she was the mother of boys, rather than a sister and a wife.

Chapter Two

England
Cleethorpes, June 1940

Gaggles of women clustered in the Market Place, their talk animated by gestures and pointing fingers. Nancy stood outside the *Yorkshire Pie Shop* amongst a group of women Sadie recognised from the Methodist Ladies' group. She pushed the empty pram over to join them.

'Mrs Johnson said she saw a fire engine rushing down Clee Road. Don't worry about your house. It carried on past Brereton Avenue.' Nancy knelt to put the baby back into her boxy pram and tucked a sheet around her. 'I hope the schools didn't get hit.'

'Thank goodness it's a Saturday. And anyway, they've got good shelters there.' Sadie's insides writhed at the thought of bombs falling on the schools on a weekday. Glen had left school after his final exams only a fortnight before. 'Let's get both of you home. There's nothing like a good, hot cup of tea for shock.'

As they were walking towards St Peter's Avenue, they passed a policeman on a bicycle.

'Hello, Nancy.' He skidded to a stop.

'Eric, do you know where the bombs fell?'

'Love Lane Corner, in those fields by Old Clee Church. Not so much as a cow been hit. No real damage. The other one fell near a bridge in Grimsby; no one was hurt. We've been lucky this time. Regards to Jimmy when you write. Tell him we miss him.'

'Thank you, Eric. Will do.'

He pedalled off.

This time; there were going to be more times, perhaps many more times, Sadie shuddered. Lots of air raid warnings over the last year, but without so much as a firecracker dropped. Were they in for it now?

Crossing the road by Broadburn's Chemist Shop, they entered Bentley Street. Sadie looked at Nancy knowing what was going through her mind. She recalled how she felt holding Henry in her arms for the first time. Something changed. She remembered the sense of responsibility that threatened to overwhelm her when she looked at her new-born. How much worse in a country under attack? For her, that feeling had never gone away, had grown worse as her sons became older, and with good reason. She put her arm around Nancy's shoulders giving her a gentle squeeze.

'We were lucky too, weren't we, Auntie? He could have gunned us down like those poor people trying to escape from Paris. Don't tell Mother we were on the prom.'

'Your mother's stronger than you think. She's needed to be with your father running off prospecting in the outback or wherever he is.'

'I know. Dad dreams of making a fortune like his father. But for that, he's left his family all these years. Somehow, he can't see that he's thrown us away instead. We should have been enough, don't you think?'

Sadie squeezed her tighter. Nancy thought that her grandpa had left all his money to his fourth wife, a tale told to save face. Sadie sighed. Should they have lied? Once told, those lies developed a myth of their own.

Women scrubbed their doorsteps while gossiping about the raid with their neighbours. Small boys ran around the street, their arms like flailing wings, pretending to be aeroplanes.

One stopped her, 'Did you see the Heinkel, Missus?' Sadie nodded as he careered away making stuttering engine noises, others chasing him. Children saw excitement rather than fear in war, thank goodness.

They turned into the small front garden of her sister-in-law's terraced house; the prams wheels scraping on the iron gateposts.

Leaving the pram outside, Nancy opened the front door. The bucolic scene on the face of the ticking grandfather clock spoke of peace and tranquillity. Sadie's heartbeat began to slow. Maybe there's something to be said for refusing to change, she thought. Even on a good day, this house depressed her. She had some sympathy for her brother.

While Nancy rushed to tell her mother they were safe, Sadie poked her head through the door of the middle room, Betsy Ann's domain. The old lady sat by the window, heavy drapes allowing minimal light into the room. She was dressed as always in a floor-length, black dress, her white lace collar, the only adornment. Knitting lay in her lap, thin grey hair scraped up in a bun, and her face immobile, but for the constant grinding of teeth. Sadie shuddered as she said, 'Hello, how are you?'

Walking down the dark corridor to the back room, it never ceased to amaze Sadie how all life went on in this dark, narrow space, while the front room was rarely used, except at Christmas. How could they bear the suffocation? The high wall between the houses cast a continuous shadow, adding to the gloom. She knew her brother found it claustrophobic.

What about his wife? Did she not miss the airy bungalow and wide verandas of her home at Nelyambo? The uninterrupted sky changing from purple to cobalt and then vermillion between dawn and dusk, the gum trees shimmering in the heat, as the kookaburras' laugh competed with shrieking parakeets and the lazy Darling River glided by only yards from her door?

The incessant fire heated the black-leaded range, infusing the house with the smell of coal dust. A sooty kettle hung by the fire, steaming. Tea was always on tap.

'Thank goodness you're back Nancy. I was that worried when the siren went.' Jane, Sadie's long-suffering sister-in-law, greeted her daughter with a kiss, taking Ann from her to cuddle.

'We weren't in any danger. We met Eric, and he told us the bombs fell in fields near Old Clee. No one's hurt.'

'Did you get out to the Anderson Shelter?' Sadie asked.

'We'd just opened the back door to run out when that plane was flying over, so we got under the table. Was it only one plane?'

'Yes. Don't you think that odd? One plane in broad daylight dropping bombs in a field. Why would the pilot risk the anti-aircraft guns?' Sadie said as Nancy poured tea.

'No sugar, I'm afraid.'

'I'm just about getting used to that.' Sadie accepted the tea with a smile. 'It's the bacon I miss. And the butter, of course.' Just thinking of a slice of bread, thickly buttered with salt bacon wedged between it, made her mouth water.

'They're saying margarine's next, even tea.'

'What about tea?' Betsy Ann demanded. The old lady stood in the doorway leaning on her stick, her hand cupping an ear.

'It may be rationed, Mother,' shouted Jane.

'Over my dead body!' Betsy Ann settled herself by the fire, watery eyes demanding her tea.

The women cast their eyes to the ceiling, followed by a quick grin at Betsy Ann's expense.

'We won't have any choice. The government's not going to listen to you. Nancy, there's a letter from your brother. Brian's shipping out to India and has three days leave next week.'

'That's wonderful news. He'll be safe in India, won't he?' Nancy's shoulders began to relax for the first time since the plane appeared in the sky, an hour earlier.

Sadie sipped her tea, considering how quickly she could leave this oppressive house. Her eyes drifted to the Staffordshire dogs on the mantle-piece, their spiteful eyes reminding her of her granny's chihuahua, and then settled on the radio. Stanley had bought it on his last visit.

'Do you mind if we have the radio on?' Sadie asked. Some light music would lift her spirits.

'Good idea.' Nancy got up to turn it on.

Dance band music. That's more like it, she thought, relaxing into happier memories.

Jane's elder sister, Nibby, came through from the scullery carrying a pie to put into one of the drawers in the range oven.

'Hello, I wondered where you were.' Nibby did everything around the house, cooked, cleaned, washed, baked bread, a role she had settled into and never relinquished after her fiancé died in the previous war. Did she ever feel hard done by? Sadie never heard a word of complaint from her.

'Are you staying for lunch? There's enough.'

'No thank you, I've things to do.' A polite mistruth but Sadie itched to go. The music stopped, and a cultured, male voice began to speak.

'It has been announced that France has signed an armistice with Germany in the forest of Compiègne. France is out of the war, ladies and gentlemen.'

The Marseillaise began to play. Jane switched off the radio. 'Well, that's it, we're on our own.'

'We knew it was coming. What now?' Nancy's concern expressed what they all felt.

'You're forgetting the Empire, and at least we got our troops out of Dunkirk. We still have an army, a navy and our flyboys.' Sadie attempted to reassure them. Jane grasped her hand and squeezed it. Now more than ever they needed the Empire's troops. Like the last war all over again; images of men in slouch hats marching to Waltzing Matilda flashed through her mind. She had to leave before the tears of homesickness and sadness overtook her.

'Time for me to make a move, Jane dear. Bring the baby to see me again, Nancy.' She stood and made her goodbyes.

Leaving the house, she walked towards Woollaston Road. On the corner of Fairview Avenue, she saw an acquaintance, Mrs Fields, dressed in her Petty Officer's uniform. As she approached, Sadie noticed that beneath her black-edged hat, lay eyes tinged with pain.

'Rosie dear. I was so sorry to hear about your Tony.'

'Thank you for your letter, Sadie. It's been a difficult time. We're still stunned. He had such a wonderful future ahead of him. My only consolation is that we were able to bury him, and he wasn't shot down somewhere over France. His funeral was on my birthday.' She took a handkerchief from her pocket to dab her eyes. 'And your boys? They're in the RAF too, I believe.'

'Henry is flying out of Scampton; Joseph is at Driffield and Glen is at flight school.'

'I will pray for them, Sadie. Look, I've got to go, duty calls.'

'Call round for a cup of tea sometime. Bring Shirley with you. What is she now, fourteen?' Rosie nodded and smiled, before walking away.

How can life be so cruel as to take away your only son? Was Tony eighteen or nineteen? Such a lovely boy too. It sent shudders down

Sadie's spine to think of it. She hardly dared imagine how she would react in the same position. Could she ever recover from such a loss? But there was Mrs Fields carrying on with her war duties, despite her son's death. As Sadie walked home, she knew something needed to change. For a start, she ought to keep busy to stop herself from dwelling on possibilities too awful to contemplate.

Arriving at the house, she found an envelope on her doormat. Sadie picked it up without looking at it while she took off her jacket and shoes. Making her way to the kitchen, she placed the envelope on the table to read while she ate her lunch. She assumed it would be from Glen telling her where to send mail. Her boys were not big letter writers. If she was lucky she received a few lines saying they were well, had been to a dance and were enjoying life on camp. To know they were alive and unhurt was enough.

Her house mirrored her sister-in-law's house in many ways, but all the rooms were bigger, lighter and airier. She had covered the walls with pretty paper and the skirting boards in white, rather than brown paint, after having the gas mantles removed and electric light installed. Cosy and clean gas fires provided her heating, and a gas cooker in the kitchen had replaced the range. It might not compare with the homes of her childhood, but it would do. She had arrived in England never having cooked so much as a piece of toast, but she had learned. At first, her sons used to laugh at her disasters, burnt macaroni cheese, meringue which sat soft and oozing on its lemon pie base, and boiled potatoes reduced to liquid, fit for nothing other than adding to soup. Times of plenty, unlike now.

She sat at the table by the window to eat a sandwich, grimacing at the unpleasant, cloying taste of margarine, only thinly disguised by the filling of potted fish paste. Picking up the letter, she turned it over, and her eyes were drawn to the stamp, unmistakeable the three standing figures with a digger in the centre. Who was writing to her from Australia? Only Stanley knew her address, and he would have written to his wife and children, not to her. She turned it over and over, sick to think it might be from her ex-husband, but how could he have found her?

Steeling herself, she tore it open, her precious tea cooling beside her, then turned to the signature at the bottom of the second page and quickly fell back into the glorious days of her carefree childhood.

Dear Sis,

Well, long time no see. Where's the time gone? I've been travelling around working on stations, sheep shearing, that kind of stuff, when who should I bump into but Stanley! He was in Dad's old hotel in Katherine, on his way to Darwin. Stopped for old times' sake, he said, but I think he came looking for me. We talked about the old years in Freeo (not that I remember much about Riverview) and Yarra Glen. The good times, hey! Do you remember our fishing jaunts or the day we let the pigs into the vineyard? Those were beaut! If only it had stayed like that. Didn't we have fun?

Anyway, Stanley told me that he's off to some island off the coast of Borneo. Pops bought a teak forest there, and Stanley found the title; it had never been sold, not worth a cent at the time. He's persuaded me to go fossicking with him. I thought, why the hell not? Who knows, it might be a winner. So tomorrow, we are on our way to Darwin to board ship.

Love to your boys, Stanley tells me Henry's in the RAF. You must be proud. Good on him. I haven't seen my son since – shucks, you know when. Sis, you did good to leave and take your boys with you.

Your little brother,

Eddie

Chapter Three

West Australia
Cannington, 1902

Papa picked them up from the station in his trap. He had been overseeing the move of their furniture since dawn, but now the summer sun shone bright and fierce in the brilliant, azure sky. His eyes twinkled with excitement as he helped the younger ones climb up.

'Just you wait children. You're in for a treat.' He turned his smiling face to Mama, and she planted a kiss above his whiskers.

'You must be tired, love.'

'No, I've had much longer days than this,' he laughed. 'And I could never tire of this house. We've made it Bella.' He caught her face in his hands and kissed her on the lips. Pride swept his face.

As the trap turned onto the sweeping drive of their new home by the Canning River, the children gasped in delight. Sadie caught the strong perfume of the roses, red, orange and yellow blooms competing with each other for vibrancy. Mama sucked in her lips, muttering 'too showy by half' under her breath, but her smile returned as Flora, their cook-housekeeper, greeted them at the door.

The horse came to a halt next to the portico, Stanley and Bruce hopped down and ran into the garden to explore.

'Choose your bedroom, Sadie, while you have the chance,' Mama whispered, with a conspiratorial wink.

She needed no further encouragement, running into the house without a backward glance, pausing only to find the direction of the sun in the late afternoon. Sadie opened three doors on the right-hand corridor before finding the perfect room. The pink blush of the walls reminded her of the dawn just before sunrise, her favourite time when she rose early on school days. Even before breakfast, she liked to stand on the veranda with bare feet, before the sun had a chance to burn into the brick, smelling the new day like a thirsty plant welcoming the morning dew.

'This one please,' she said after her mother poked her head around the door.

'A perfect choice, my love. Off you go now and join your brothers while Flora and I unpack.'

Sadie ran to find them, hearing laughter near the river. Barely breaking stride, she grasped at the lowest hanging oranges which she gathered in her pinafore before sinking onto the bank. Her toes dangled in the warm water while she peeled away orange skin. Lifting the fruit to her nose, she drank in the fragrance before biting into the ripe flesh, the juice coating her face and hands.

'Can we stay here forever?' She lay still, staring at the cloudless sky until black flies gathered on her sticky hands. Her brothers had already stripped off their clothes and were in the water showering her with splashes as they shrieked with laughter. Please let's stay here forever, she thought, as she shrugged off her clothes down to her knickers and joined the boys in their frolics.

'I love it here. I never want to leave,' Sadie told her mother as she snuggled down into her bed, a cotton sheet all that was needed in the January heat.

'Do you dear? I do too.' Her mother's tinkling laughter soothing as she tucked Sadie in.

'I'm proud of Papa, but I wish we didn't have to keep moving. Riverview is much nicer than our other houses.'

'I have to agree with you, but Papa's work takes him all over, and we'd miss him so much if we stayed here, don't you think?'

Sadie nodded, she loved her Papa, but crisscrossing the country almost every year meant she had to keep on making friends all over again. As the only girl in the family, she found it hard to keep changing schools.

'I'm sure you'll make new friends,' said her mother, reading her mind before one last kiss and turning out the light.

22

Tomorrow, she would write a letter telling Julia, all about her new home. She fell asleep painting in her dreams, the white house with its wide verandas, surrounded by orange and lemon groves.

'I want to learn to fish,' said Stanley, early next morning.

Papa put down his pipe and said, 'Of course you do.'

'Me too,' said Bruce.

'Can I fish, too?' Sadie joined in.

'Why don't we take a picnic down to the river and we can all go fishing,' said Mama.

'Even Eddie?' Stanley looked affronted. 'He won't sit still; he'll frighten the fish.'

'Me go too,' Eddie lisped.

'While Sadie and I prepare a picnic, Stanley, you and Papa can find some poles for fishing rods for the boys. Have you any hooks, Joe?'

Sadie danced on the way to the kitchen. To spend a day with Papa was unheard of. Days went by with him out at dawn and back long after night fell, if at all. On Sundays, he caught up with paperwork, rarely accompanying them to church.

'Your Papa works hard so that we can have the good things in life,' Mama told them when the children complained that they scarcely saw him. But occasionally he would throw up all his work and spend a day with them. Today was one of those days.

Flora stood in the kitchen with a batch of fresh-baked scones.

'They will be perfect for a picnic,' said Sadie, throwing her arms around Flora and being rewarded with a floury kiss on her dark curls.

'I'm glad you moved with us, Flora.'

'I wouldn't have missed moving into the Brookman house for all the tea in China, girl. My friends in Freemantle are agog to hear all about it.'

'It's wonderful, isn't it? Have you seen the oranges?'

'I'm more interested in those Axminster carpets; so thick, they'll last a lifetime. And the size of that ballroom! You could fit in half of Perth, I'm sure. The parties he must have held here when he was Lord Mayor.'

'All well and good, Flora,' said Mama, coming into the kitchen. 'But let's get this picnic started, or we'll lose the best of the morning. What's in the Coolgardie?'

23

'The remains of last night's chicken pie and some ham, Ma'am.'

'Maybe not the chicken pie. Sadie, fetch the ham, please. Look for some cheese for the scones too, while you're there. Flora, hard boil enough eggs for us all. That should do us.'

Sadie ran out onto the veranda to collect the ham and cheese. She was always struck by how cool it was inside when she stuck her hand in the Coolgardie to take out food. A vague recollection lodged in her memory of being in Menzies when the first safe arrived and Mama, at first doubtful, but completely won over when meat did not turn rancid overnight.

Mama packed all the food in a dampened hessian sack before asking Flora to make some lemonade.

'Bring it down to the river when it's ready, please, along with a bottle of beer for the master.'

Papa had found some poles and hooks. He carried a spade and his rifle down to the river with the children marching behind him, singing 'One! Two! Three – four – five! Once I caught a fish alive.' Mama, all hatted up, brought up the rear, carrying her hessian sack and a rug to sit on.

Papa showed the boys how to dig for bloodworms in a dried-up patch of riverbed. When it came to Sadie's turn to try and fix a worm on the hook, she gritted her teeth before picking up the wriggling creature, hooking it firmly.

'Cobblers feed along the bottom,' Papa told them as he tied a stone to their lines. 'This will help your hook stay there. The first one of you children to catch a fish will receive a shiny new florin.'

They needed no encouragement, each child casting their fishing line into the water with varying degrees of success. In the meantime, Mama had hung the hessian sack with their food to a branch, trailing the bottom edge into the water to stay cool in the mild breeze.

Sadie sat on the rug next to her mother, keeping her eyes glued to the line to see if it suddenly bobbed down. Insects buzzed lazily over the water, an occasional plop as a fish came up to feed.

'Did you ever come to one of Mr Brookman's parties, Mama?'

Why yes, we did.'

'What were they like?'

'Extravagant. I'm afraid he liked to show off too much for my liking.'

24

'Did Papa buy this house so that you could have parties?'

Her mother looked at her in amusement. 'You're a sharp little thing. Yes, he will give parties. People expect it when you're in business, but they will not be on the scale of Mr and Mrs Brookman's.'

'Can I watch?'

'No Missy. You'll be in bed. You need to be sixteen, not eight before you can watch.'

A shout from Stanley interrupted the conversation as he swung his pole onto the riverbank, an ugly, whiskery fish writhed and flopped on the ground.

'Careful of his barbs, boy. They can give you a nasty sting. Yes, that's right, unhook it. Now put it out of its misery.' Stanley smashed a rock down on its head. 'Good effort, now a few more cobblers like that and we will have a feast tonight.'

By midday, they had caught three good-sized fish. Papa and Eddie caught the second, much to the three-year old's delight, and Stanley shouted in triumph at his second fish. The overhead sun, dappled by the trees, shone fiercely along the riverbank. Mother distributed the picnic after Flora brought down cool lemonade and beer, returning with the fish to prepare for tea.

Father showed the boys how to net prawns and mussels as he waded in the river, his trousers rolled up to his knees. Even Mama dared to remove her stockings and dangle her feet in the water.

'We must get some rubber shoes for the children, Bella. One of them is bound to tread on a cobbler. I will bet my last pound that they'll be in here every day until school starts unless we have a gully blow.'

'What's that, Pa?' Stanley asked.

'You'll hear it before you see it. The easterly winds from the Nullarbor Desert funnel through the gully, and it sounds like a train is coming. Go straight inside if that happens.'

Bruce and Stanley needed no further encouragement but ran around pretending to be a storm, arms flailing and knocking over the empty lemonade jar. Soon all of them, even Mama and Papa joined in amid shrieks of laughter.

'Remember Stanley, always bring a rifle with you. If you see a snake or a rabbit, shoot first and ask questions later. Not that there should be any rabbits this far west. But be on the lookout for them. They're building a fence, but the blighters get everywhere. You too Sadie, keep an eye out.'

Sadie thought that no day could ever be as perfect as this one.

'Why did Mr Brookman sell this house, Flora? I can't ever imagine wanting to live anywhere else.' Sadie asked as she helped Flora clear away the dishes after tea.

'He lost all his money, Pet.'

'Oh!' Sadie wondered how. 'Did he bury it and forget where? That would be stupid, wouldn't it? Perhaps we could go searching for his buried treasure.'

Flora chuckled. 'No, Sadie. He bought something called stocks and shares, and he lost it all. Don't ask me how or why because I don't understand it. But you'd never catch me putting my money in a bank.'

'Does Papa put his money in the bank, Mama?' Sadie asked that evening as her mother was tucking her in.

'What a strange question.'

'But, does he?'

'Yes, some, but he prefers to buy land with his money.'

'Like this land, you mean?'

'And some in Victoria. When he's finished his work here, we'll move there. I promise you'll see a lot more of Papa then. The farm is in a beautiful valley; you'll love it. Now go to sleep.'

More than here, Sadie doubted that. But land, you could never lose land. Sadie settled down, comforted that Papa was a clever man.

Chapter Four

Australia
Yarra Valley, 1904

Two years later they were packing up again. Furniture sold, friends said goodbye to, and this time a tearful farewell to Flora, their faithful housekeeper. She had no wish to move to Victoria with them. Only one thing remained to be done, the grand opening ceremony of the new railway line.

Sadie loved to watch. It was not the first opening ceremony she had witnessed. A besuited man with a chain around his neck would pump Papa's hand, and Mama would wear a new dress, sun-shading hat and long gloves. Everyone would smile to see the bulky, gleaming locomotive arrive or depart, steam pouring from its smokestack as people cheered and men waved their hats in the air. As dusty and scorching as the air might be in the outback, Sadie's heart filled with pride to observe the event which meant these little mining towns were no longer cut off from the rest of the continent. She could see the relief in the sun-narrowed eyes of the watching wives, a brood of barefoot, raggedy children excitedly running around their feet; just knowing another town and a hospital were now only a train ride away must be wonderful, and it was Sadie's Papa who had made this happen.

He had been working away for the best part of the year linking that goldfield town to its closest railway, but now they were on their way east again. Uncle Jonnie, Papa's brother, was getting everything ready for them. Sadie tried to imagine the land the way it had been described to her by Papa. Rich grassland and vineyards as far as the eye could see, framed only by majestic mountains, and if you were lucky, snow-tipped peaks in winter. A white house, not as grand as Riverview, but with the sparkling Yarra River a mere stone's throw away. Best of all, he had promised her a pony. It seemed as if Papa was all set to become a farmer.

Chateau Yering had an upstairs. Sadie had never lived in a house with stairs. The grand sweep of the mahogany staircase looked like something out of a fairy tale. Eddie galloped up and slid down the bannisters in delight. Sadie now ten, and soon to be a young lady, practised walking down as Cinderella or a princess would. Her sketchbook perched on her head to ensure she stood straight, she tried gliding from step to step. As soon as the book began to slip, she ran back to the top to begin again.

'Is it a real Chateau?' She asked her mother. 'I thought they only had Chateaux in France.'

The man who built this was Swiss. Switzerland's next door to France.'

'I live in a castle,' shouted Eddie, pretending to fight with a sword.

'Outside!' Papa boomed, lifting up Eddie. 'Go and find your brothers. Sadie, help your mother unpack.'

She needed no encouragement. Two square rooms lay to the left of the staircase and a long, airy sitting room to the right. A Chilean palm tree had been planted years before, close to one of the windows at the back. In the front lay the sweeping drive surrounded by flower beds. To Sadie, the road from Lilydale confirmed everything her Papa had told her about the Yarra Valley. Was there anywhere more beautiful on earth?

Her mother clucked with delight as she and Sadie walked around the house, deciding where things should go. 'Now this is a house I never want to leave.'

'Do you think Papa will settle here, forever, I mean?'

Mama placed her hand on the top of Sadie's head. 'God willing. You know Papa. He needs to keep busy. If he's going to be a dairy farmer, he'll have to be the very best one there is. And when he's achieved that?' The question hung in the air around them.

Her father worked as hard as ever, but he was at home which was a novelty, as was having her half-brother Joe Junior around. At eighteen, he had worked with his father for the last few years, and the family rarely saw him. Sadie thought him handsome. He must take after his late mother, Agnes, with his thick brown hair and dark eyes set in an open, square face.

With Stanley attending Scotch College in Hawthorn, Bruce, her next brother, was her closest ally. When not at the local village school, they saddled up their ponies and rode all over the valley, through pastureland grazed by black Ayrshire cattle, along the river bank, past rows of vineyards, carefully pruned and now hanging with tiny, green grapes. Workmen were cutting a new road through her father's land. The old one ran across the flats to Yarra Glen and was liable to flood every winter. Sometimes they stopped to watch the men wielding their picks as they cut through the rich, black earth.

Sadie most liked it on autumn weekends. Rising early, when the river valley was swathed in mist, she and Bruce rode up towards the Coldstream Hills to look back over the valley, ethereal and magical, as the sun burnt back the mist revealing the riches of the land.

Mama gave her chores too. 'All ladies must know how to run a household,' she said. 'Silver tarnishes, and it requires frequent cleaning.' They polished their way through a table full of dishes and a decorative tea service.

Sadie loved to help her mother get the house ready for guests, arranging flowers in vases, overseeing the food preparation, ensuring that beds were made up with fresh, crisp linen. Her favourite guest of all was her mother's father, Grandpa Bill. When he arrived, he would swing her around and say in his broad, Irish brogue, 'Look how ye are growing. Sure, aren't ye just the image of your Mammy.'

Sadie knew her mother to be beautiful with her dark hair, violet eyes and a flawless complexion, always graceful, always smiling. The thought of being her mother's image enchanted Sadie.

Grandpa's grey whiskers tickled her face, but she didn't mind. His blue eyes twinkled with a ready smile, seeming to gather everyone to share the playfulness of his mood. All his efforts went into enjoying himself, never caring that his shirt may have lost a button, or his socks may have holes in them. Whenever he came, Mama would take him in hand and cut his hair and mend his clothes.

Such a contrast when Grandma Jane came to visit. Skinny, ramrod straight, her hooded eyes cast around, taking everything in. She used to own hotels and could not abide sloppiness or slovenliness and was more than happy to criticise at any opportunity.

'Your boots aren't clean, young man. Children should be spoken to, not heard,' if any dared interrupt. 'Sadie, sit straighter. Why are you looking at yourself in the mirror? It won't make you any prettier.'

Sadie could tell how her mother dreaded Grandma's visits. The house would get an even more thorough cleaning; the silver polished within an inch of its life; the duster run up and down the wooden bannister until the wood gleamed, and you could see your face in it. Her mother would be on edge until Grandma left to catch the train home to Hawthorn.

A year after they arrived, Sadie woke up one morning to a scene so magical it took her breath away. Snow lay thick along the ground, covering all the grass and Sadie itched to walk out in it. Eddie bounded into her bedroom like a puppy eager for its walk.

'Sadie, come on, help me build a snowman.'

This is what snow feels like, Sadie thought, as she stepped out into the glistening new world of their garden. Her boots crunched along the driveway, sinking and compacting the snow. She could almost taste the cold air on her face. Bird tracks underneath the richly scented mahonia bushes, and footprints from a mammal, maybe a fox, the only evidence of life in the silent morning. Alas, it could not last as her brothers screeched out of the house. A snowball hit her between the shoulders; she did not turn at first, wanting to capture one last image of the beauty before the boys messed it up with their boot prints and scattered snowballs. Seconds later she was joining in the game, the thick snow coating her woollen gloves as she pressed it into a ball before throwing it, laughing as her brothers dodged and hurled their own.

A day later, with snow still on the ground, her father was contemplating the amount of hay in the barn. 'If we build up the herd of dairy cows to three hundred, we're going to need more hay for times like this. We need more acreage.'

Halfway through the year, Papa bought the Saint Hubert's Estate from Mr Mitchell. Mama told Sadie that he was Dame Nellie Melba's father. The name meant nothing to Sadie until Mama told her that she was an opera singer famed throughout Europe. It sounded terribly glamorous.

Owning five thousand acres of land gave Papa status, which was evident in the way people addressed him and sought his opinion. He began to work on his latest project to help set up a refrigeration unit allowing produce and milk to be sent by train to Melbourne, arriving fresh even in the hottest of summers. Sadie passed around tiny sandwiches and cakes, listening to the admiration in ladies' voices as they sat around the tea table with her mother.

Her father began to allow the hunt to set off from Yering Station, with all the riders looking splendid in their red hunting coats. Mostly they would lunch at a nearby hotel, but one day Sadie assisted her mother to prepare a cold buffet at the Chateau. Grandma Jane came to help, and they all stood to wave off the hunt with Mr De Pury blowing the horn, the excited hounds yapping and streaming out over the fields.

'I don't know whether my mother would laugh or cry to see her grandson as part of the hunt.' Grandma said, under her breath.

'Why's that, Grandma?' Sadie asked.

'Little Miss Sharp Ears, never you mind. Go back to the house.' Sadie felt her grandmother's hand on her shoulder giving her a none too gentle shove.

The only blight on that perfect year came with the grape harvest.

'It's no good winning prizes in Paris or Melbourne if we can't make money from it,' Papa declared at the dinner table. Too much production means low prices, and it doesn't pay to ship the wine to Europe.'

'It seems such a shame. Why else did you buy St Hubert's?' Mama asked.

'We'll get more money in dairy, or I can rent out the land to other dairy or beef farmers. There's money in grass. More so than there is in grapes. But the agreement is that we keep the grapes for five years. David Mitchell wants to stock up his cellar.'

They let the pigs into the Chateau Yering vineyard. Neighbours were shocked at the sacrilege. A reporter came from a Melbourne newspaper. Papa, however, had no regrets.

'The vines may have been fifty years old,' he told the young man busily scribbling in his notepad. 'But people want good quality meat at low prices, not expensive wine. How is that going to help hardworking men put food in their children's bellies?'

Two days later, Stanley ran to tell Pa there was something wrong with the pigs. Being a Sunday, all the family ran to see what was wrong.

'Oh, my Lord,' said Mama. 'You must call the vet.' Each pig staggered drunkenly around what remained of the vines.

'No, I know what's wrong,' Papa said. 'The grapes have fermented in the pigs' stomachs.'

'Papa! Look at that one,' Eddie squealed, as one of the biggest pigs wobbled on its short legs and then fell senseless to the ground. Another grunted in surprise, its legs refusing to obey its body. One by one they watched as the pigs keeled over until all lay in a fat heap, panting, eyes rolling.

'Go and fetch rifles Stanley. I'll find that camera. We have to take a photo of this,' shouted Papa.

He poised Stanley and Bruce so that they stood each with a foot on a collapsed pig's back, their rifles pointing towards the pigs' heads.

'Our great hunters,' he said, laughing at the sight. 'Keep that pose while I take the photo. Don't move. I wonder if we'll taste the wine in the bacon? Maybe it will attract a higher price.'

'Can you take my photo, Papa?' Sadie jumped up and down in excitement.

Her mother's hand on her arm was gentle but insistent. 'No, the photographic plates are expensive.'

'But Papa took the boys' photo. It's not fair.'

'Sadie, a young lady does not pose in such a way.' Her mother's brow furrowed in annoyance.

Her rebuke was like being thrown in the Yarra River on a winter's day. The shock of cold water rinsed away her dreams. Her life would be different, less adventurous, more restricted. Her brothers would have freedoms denied to her. Maybe she had always known that, but this was the first time she had been forced to face the reality. She turned her face away from the scene, all pleasure in it erased.

By the spring, where grapevines once grew, two hundred Ayrshire cows grazed the new grass, but Papa soon found that this brought its own problems. However widely he advertised, he could not get the labour to milk them.

'We need a modern dairy with electric milking machines,' he declared at dinner one evening in July.

'But that will take months to build. What are we going to do in the meantime?' Joe Junior was doing his best to organise what men they had, even helping out with the milking, and drumming up his brothers to give a hand before school.

'I see no option but to divide the property into lots and auction it. That will pay for the dairy, and we can think about opening a farm shop in Melbourne for all the beef and pork products.'

Mama's face fell in disappointment. 'Do you mean to sell the Chateau?'

'Yes, we'll move into St Hubert's.'

Only two miles away, but Sadie was forlorn at the thought of moving. The homestead at St Hubert's lacked the elegance of the Chateau. Other than a few scrubby roses, the gardens were merely grass rather than flower borders. But most of all, there was something about the Chateau which drew her in, making her feel safe and warm inside. Her mother felt it too.

'When is the auction, Joe?' Mama asked, still frowning.

'At the end of August. That should give you time to pack for moving in late September.'

The land and the house were divided into seventeen lots and snapped up on auction day. Sadie was thankful she was at school. She could not bear to be present when the crowds descended on the house for the sale. A hollow feeling made her stomach clench when her mother told her afterwards that Mr Towt had bought the house. She hated to imagine his family taking over the chateau, his daughter sleeping in her room, his wife holding sway in the parlour.

The day of the move arrived far too quickly for Sadie. Something niggled at her. Nothing she could put her finger on, but a gloomy feeling settled on her as she helped her mother wrap ornaments for the tea chest. The eighteen months at Chateau Yering had been the happiest Sadie could remember, and she wandered around the emptying rooms trying to imprint happy memories on her brain. She walked in the garden, trailing her hands on the burgeoning yellow flowers of the feathery wattles, regretting she would not see the myrtles in flower. She looked back at the house, the Chilean Palm peeping above the roof, the last daffodils in the border, the fat buds on the peonies, a sign of the summer to come. Her mother, dark hair bound up in a turban, was bent over a box in the long salon facing her. She caught sight of Sadie as she stood up and waved. That's the memory that will live with me, she thought, a sudden pang lodged in Sadie's heart.

St Hubert's had a European feel to it, most probably evoked by the look-out tower to one side of the house. Her mother was delighted with the wisteria-covered veranda. The scent of the flowers invaded the house that spring.

'I could be in Italy or Spain,' she said. 'I've heard of balconies overlooking the sea with ancient wisterias to sit under and enjoy the view. One day, I'd like to see for myself.'

'But the rest of the garden's so dull,' Sadie complained. 'Where are the flower beds?'

'We can plant it up together. I'll get Papa to ask one of the men to dig some flower beds, would you like that?'

'Won't they take years to grow?'

'Two or three. Gardening is a good pastime for a lady, Sadie. You'll enjoy it.'

'I'd rather go riding with Stanley and Bruce.'

'You can ride too, but it's time for you to learn other skills. One day you will be a wife and a mother. Your husband will expect you to entertain and keep an efficient house. Stanley and Bruce have their chores too, but they're dirty jobs and hard work, not fit for you.'

As Sadie knelt on an old mat next to a freshly dug border that Spring, her heart was torn as she watched her brothers gallop off up to the hills to help haul logs for the new dairy floor. Her mother patted her hand to encourage her to plant the seedlings she had brought with her from the Chateau.

Papa always began the day with a trip to the tower and Sadie joined him whenever she could. In high summer, she observed the orderly rows of vines as though looking through his approving eyes. Pastureland lay beyond, the grass greenish yellow in the early morning light. Papa held her hand as he checked for any signs of swirling smoke from the surrounding hillsides, a satisfied puff on his pipe when he saw none. He owned acres of forest and a sawmill up on the north-eastern road to Alexandra. There had been a bushfire the previous summer near Dixon's Creek, a little way to the north-west, and Sadie knew it was his biggest dread that a fire could take hold, decimating everything in its path. She'd overheard him talking with Joe Junior about it, warning him to be constantly on the look-out for signs of smoke.

Sadie treasured the few moments Papa stood with her in the tower each morning. It was the only time he spent with her, alone. Now that they had left Chateau Yering, it was being with her father that made her feel safe. She couldn't shake the sense that something was wrong. Stanley told her she was an idiot when she tried to explain it.

'It's as though I'm about to lose something very precious,' she had told him.

'Why are girls so silly?' He had answered, before throwing a pillow at her.

It was strange how tongue-tied she felt in Papa's presence. In stature, he was not a big man, but success gave him a powerful aura. It made her slightly afraid of him, although he never raised his voice to her. She loved the feel of his hand as he patted her shoulder and pointed something out to her, maybe a mob of wallabies by the river or a king parrot flying amongst the trees, a quick flash of scarlet amongst the green. The need for his approval overwhelmed her. That he noticed her at all, amongst his brood of favoured sons, was reward enough.

Chapter Five

England
Cleethorpes, June 1940

Sadie smoothed out Eddie's letter, imagining it passing between Nancy and her mother, curious to know anything about Stanley, although they pretended indifference. Fancy her brothers meeting in Katherine. None of them had heard from Eddie in years. The thought of him not seeing his son, Jeff, again brought tears to her eyes. Guilt gnawed away in her stomach until she squashed that memory back in its box; opening it was too painful.

But now her two brothers were setting sail for Borneo to become teak foresters on some remote island plantation in the Dutch East Indies; another of Stanley's attempts to recover his wealth. Well, good luck to them.

In her heart, she knew what Stanley's wife would think; yet another hare-brained scheme when he should be back in England supporting his family. But Sadie understood her brothers' yearnings, their restlessness. She'd tried to tame it in herself, but they were their father's sons, always seeking an opportunity to make a fortune but, unlike him, never able to follow it through. More than that, none of Papa's children measured up to him. They had clung to his coat tails as he reaped success upon success, but when his fortune turned, they had nothing to fall back on, their goose well and truly cooked, as Grandma would say. Poor Grandma, she must have been beside herself with disappointment the way things turned out. Sadie had not stayed to find out.

'Papa, we let you down, didn't we?' Sadie murmured. 'You worked yourself to the bone for us and what did we ever do in return? It's up to your grandsons now. Perhaps they will inherit your luck.'

Bringing up a family of three sons had been enough work for her until they flew the nest. She thought of Mrs Fields in her uniform. No one could doubt her contribution to the war effort. Sadie had wanted to do something other than fundraising for the last war, but it was not allowed. Most Australian girls sat at home, twiddling their thumbs, while British girls volunteered.

'Not this time. I can't sit out this war on my backside when my sons are fighting.' Speaking aloud helped to stiffen her determination. 'I will join the Women's Voluntary Service, yes, that's what I'll do. And there's no time like the present.' She took a swig of her cold tea and grimaced before clearing away her dishes and rinsing them in the sink.

Standing at the door with her jacket and hat on, she had a momentary fit of nerves, remembering her last jaunt outside. She steeled herself and opened the door to a deceptively peaceful afternoon. The sun shone on the white rose blooming in her tiny front garden, planted in remembrance of her mother's favourite flower. Heat rose up through the concrete paving slabs into her leather shoes. Not the shimmering, humid heat of a Melbourne summer's day, nor the dry heat of the bush which sucked the breath from your body. A normal, English summer's day. Only nothing seemed normal anymore. Sadie saw it in the faces of everyone she passed, a forced smile, a slight narrowing of the eyes, a wince as a car backfired.

She crossed the road to catch the bus from outside the Art Deco electricity showroom, built at a time of optimism. Was it only three years ago? She would be surprised if they had many customers other than bill payers these days.

She watched as a bus travelled up Grimsby Road toward her, passing Beaconthorpe Chapel, it stopped outside the little row of shops for a minute then set off again. The bus drew to a halt, and she climbed on for the short ride retracing the walk of the morning.

While more people strolled along Alexandra Road and down to the promenade, it was nothing like a warm Saturday in June should be. Pre-war, locals knew better than to compete with the hordes disgorging from the trains from the south Yorkshire mill towns. Whole towns decamped to sample the delights of Wonderland and the miles of sandy beaches for their annual Wakes Week holidays. The sickly smell of candyfloss and the vinegary smell of salt-laden chips competed as far as High Cliff, where the shops dwindled, and hotels took over. How were the shopkeepers and boarding house landladies coping with the loss of all that trade, she wondered?

Just before the bus reached Ross Castle, she stood to get off. She walked down Knoll Street, past the town hall towards Cambridge Street and the WVS offices on the corner.

A short queue had formed with several other ladies having the same idea.

'Where were you when the plane came over?' They asked each other. It broke the ice, and by the time it was Sadie's turn to speak to the lady on duty, any nerves had disappeared.

'Name?'

'Sylvia Tinsdale.'

A sharp look up. 'Don't recognise that accent. New Zealand is it?'

'Australian.'

'Hmpf! Address?'

'15 Clee Road.'

'Skills?'

'Skills?' Sadie was confused.

'Driving, cooking, office, you know. What job did you do before you married?'

'I've never worked. I can drive, but not since I came to England. Plain cooking only.' Sadie's heart sank. She sounded feeble.

'Never mind, you can pour tea and hand out clothes no doubt.' Sadie nodded in relief.

'Next of kin?'

'Um, my eldest son, Henry, he's based at Scampton.'

'Widowed, are you?'

This was why Sadie kept to herself. She hated revealing anything about her personal life. 'Divorced,' she mumbled.

The woman raised a speculative eyebrow. 'Rotter was he?'

Sadie did not answer, but for the first time felt a measure of sympathy from this no-nonsense woman.

'Right you are. Take this wristband until you get a uniform. Next first-aid training session is on Tuesday at ten a.m. Don't be late.'

That was it. Sadie was now a member, presumably. She wondered what it would mean.

'Do you fancy a cuppa, love?' A lady in a bottle-green, WVS belted dress asked her as she turned away. 'Come and sit down dear; we can stretch to tea and a fig roll.'

Sadie found herself sitting next to a woman around the same age as herself, she guessed, but double her girth. Her round, cheerful face sat above wobbling chins, a brightly patterned headscarf not quite hiding a greying blonde perm.

'Hello, I'm Lucy, but everyone calls me Lu.' She stuck a podgy hand out to shake. 'What's the matter, dear? You look as though someone's walked over your grave.'

Sadie swallowed hard, 'Just a memory.' She forced a smile back to her face. 'I'm Sylvia, but everyone calls me Sadie.'

Chapter Six

Australia
Yarra Valley, 1905

One morning in December, shortly after the move to St Hubert's, Sadie's mother received a letter. As she read it, her eyes lit with excitement.

'Listen to this Sadie; a place has come up in the senior school at Stratherne Ladies College. The headmistress says you can start in February.'

Sadie's heart sank at the thought of another new school, but her parents were so overjoyed she knew that there was no chance of changing their minds.

Mama took her into Melbourne on the train and kitted her out in her new uniform; half a dozen long-sleeved white blouses, two navy full-length skirts, a broad necktie in the blue and green of the school colours. Then there was sports-wear; so much expense, Sadie thought, worried that she might hate the school, or they dislike her. They visited the college on the return journey. Miss Dare, the headmistress, greeted Mama warmly and assured her that Sadie would be happy and do well. As they walked around the school, Sadie changed her mind, and by the time they left, she could not wait until February.

'What did you think?' Papa asked that evening.

'I loved it. They teach art and music, and they're building tennis courts.'

Stanley was to accompany her there and back on the train as Scotch College for boys was nearby. Excitement gripped Sadie for weeks. How many times had she tried on her uniform? At last, the day arrived. A bright, cheerful day but one that promised a little relief from the parching days of summer. There was almost a nip in the early morning air.

Mama appeared fraught at breakfast but kissed her goodbye, her lips cool on Sadie's cheek. 'Have a wonderful day sweetheart.'

She said it with a smile, but Sadie thought she looked tired and her violet eyes unusually dull. Sadie threw her arms around her neck and kissed her cheek. Her mother shivered, drawing a shawl around her shoulders. Sadie waved to her as she walked down the drive with Stanley to the waiting trap.

During the train journey, butterflies fluttered in Sadie's stomach. Stanley was not much help; he was deep in chatter with friends who boarded the train in Lilydale. He did his best to ignore his sister.

This time, this school, Sadie's hopes were high. In five years, she had changed school four or was it five times already? She looked across the compartment to Stanley who was describing his latest hunt. She knew he itched to leave school and join Papa in his business, just like Joe Junior and Papa's brothers. 'It's a family firm,' Papa delighted in saying, 'there's room enough for everyone.' As long as you're male, thought Sadie. She knew that by sending his children to the best schools in Melbourne, Papa expected them to mix with people of quality. It was part of his plan. He never did anything without considering the possibilities for business.

Once off the train at Glenferrie, Sadie joined a throng of young ladies walking towards the school. She watched them with longing as they walked arm in arm, gaily laughing and chatting. Shyness overtook her as she trailed in their wake through the school gates. She chose a tree to stand under and observe friends greeting each other after the long summer break. Another girl joined her, white-blonde hair beneath her boater, a sprinkling of freckles across her pert nose.

'Are you new too?'

Sadie nodded.

'I'm Lucy St Vincent.'

A bell rang. A mistress stood in the cloisters, swinging it in her hands.

'Hurry up girls, line up, no talking.'

'I'm Sadie Timmins, shall we go in together?' Lucy grinned and nodded. Ice broken.

A chatty, happier Sadie joined Stanley on the platform for the return trip home; first day nerves out of the way.

'We had French,' Sadie told her brother. 'Je m'appelle Sadie and I made a friend. Elle s'appelle Lucy.'

'French, I hate it. Why on earth do they insist on teaching it to us? It's hardly likely that I'll ever go there.'

Sadie had enjoyed the lesson. She liked pulling her mouth into different shapes to create new vowel sounds. She insisted on practising them to annoy her brother until the train arrived.

Stanley used the journey home to do his prep. If he finished it in time, he could go riding. Sadie stared out of the window, replaying the day in her mind, considering how she would describe it to Mama. Her mind brimmed over, but Lucy stood out most of all. Papa would be impressed that her new best friend was the granddaughter of a baronet.

Joe Junior was waiting at Yering Station with the trap, a subdued expression clouding his face.

'I made a friend Joe; I can't wait to tell Mama all about it.'

'Hurry on to the trap, both of you.' Something in his voice perturbed Sadie. Joe looked unusually dour.

'What's wrong, Joe?' Stanley cut in.

'Mama's ill; the doctor is with her.' He bit his lip, refusing to be drawn further.

Stanley and Sadie shot him a puzzled look. He looked away, avoiding their faces. They sat in the trap for the short journey; an unbidden instinct made Sadie grasp Stanley's hand, as clammy as her own. Despite the heat of the late afternoon, she shivered. As they drew into the driveway of St Hubert's, a lone workman raking leaves took off his hat and bent his head as they passed. Her chest tightened in panic.

Papa stood by the door as they dismounted. Instinct again forced Sadie to run into his arms.

'She's gone. Mama's gone.' He groaned through her hair.

'How? She was fine this morning?' Disbelief curdled Stanley's voice.

'Blood poisoning.' Papa's shoulders heaved as he fought to stay calm for his children. 'Mama cut herself a day or two ago, and it must have turned septic. She said she felt a little dizzy this morning after you left. She thought she was coming down with something and went back to bed. I checked on her at midday and found her,' he broke off. His sobs shocked

Sadie. He turned up a tear-stained face. 'She was unconscious. The doctor tried his best but...'

'No, I don't believe it.' Stanley's voice rang shrill in Sadie's ears.

Papa let her go and turned to Stanley. 'It's true son. The doctor could do nothing for her. She was peaceful at the end.' Stanley clung to his father. Sadie had never seen Stanley cry, but his whole body shook. Joe Junior put his hand on Sadie's arm; she looked up at his face, tear-wracked for the only mother he could remember. She let him guide her into the house before she too dissolved into a whimpering ball of grief.

At least she got to kiss her mama goodbye, Sadie snivelled through the onset of her tears. She began to shake, holding on for dear life to Grandpa Bill's hand in the Yarra Glen Cemetery. It was near enough for her to ride to, and at first, she imagined spending hours by her mother's grave. Now, she wondered if she could ever bear to come here again. Believing Mama had gone from this life was too hard, too raw. Grandpa squeezed her hand, tears rolling down his cheeks. She turned away from the deep hole as they lowered the coffin, choking with emotion, and buried her head in his coat.

'No father should have to lose his only child, and no daughter should lose her mother,' Grandpa told her. 'So unfair, so senseless, but we'll help each other through this dreadful day,' he promised. He needed her as much as Sadie needed him.

Grandpa's arrival had been the sole bright spot after the last few days. Grandma Jane, summoned by telegram, arrived on the evening of Sadie's mother's death. Cool efficiency might be what her father needed, but Sadie resented the way Grandma took over her mother's household, changing the way she had done things, ordering Sadie to sit up straighter, or eat up when she had no appetite, and refusing to allow her to ride away her pain on her pony.

'But Mama let me ride when I'd finished my chores,' She complained when Grandma caught her trying to sneak out of the house.

'It's not fitting. You have no black riding outfit, and people would think it disrespectful so soon after your mother's passing.'

'But the boys are out riding.'

'They're out working for your father. They happen to be on horseback.'

'But...'

'No buts! What a disobedient girl you are. Go to your room until you can learn to behave as a young lady should.'

Sadie burst into tears, flinging her riding boots at her grandmother's feet, before rushing upstairs to hide in her room.

The boys, apart from Eddie, who went to live with Uncle Jonnie and his wife until the funeral was over, wandered around in a daze and escaped outside as often as possible. Papa could not bear to be in the house and threw himself into work and plans for Mama's memorial statue.

However, when Grandpa Bill arrived the morning before the funeral, he extracted Sadie from her grandma, taking her into her mother's new garden to walk, despite the threatening sky. What were a few drops of rain when their world had collapsed?

They found a seat, and he held Sadie while she let out all the pain which Grandma previously had told her to bottle up, saying, 'It does no good to cry. You need to get on with things. Work through it Sadie, like your Pa.' Why did everything that came out of Grandma's mouth sound like a rebuke?

Grandpa Bill cried as much as Sadie. His arm around her shoulders, shaking, his tears dripping onto her neck, while his shuddering breath matched hers.

'Let it out, Sadie dear. Sure, we'll never see her like again. Too beautiful, too young to die. Your Mammy was the apple of my eye.' He dabbed his handkerchief at her eyes while stroking her hair. 'You're the image of her. I wish your dear old granny could see you; she would have loved you to bits.' His Irish accent, never diluted for all the years lived in Australia, comforted Sadie.

She leaned against him, breathing in the dampening wool of his jacket, too sad to speak. Would she ever feel happy again? Mama should have asked for the doctor earlier. But she didn't look ill when she waved goodbye, paler than usual perhaps. If only! If only! Fresh tears poured from her eyes.

'I knew we were wrong to move here,' Sadie told her grandfather. 'I always had a bad feeling about it.'

'Did you now. Maybe you have inherited my mother's curse.'

'What's that?' Sadie asked.

'She always said she could foretell death.'

Sadie shook with horror. 'No, I don't want such a thing. Take it away.'

'It's a gift or a curse of the Irish. But I'm a stupid, old man. Don't listen to me, child. Trust in God, Sadie, He'll see you right.'

Once spoken, he could never take that back, and Sadie knew she would live in dread of that fear returning. If it ever did, she would recognise it as something evil. It was no gift. She let her grandpa hold her tight, seeking safety in his arms.

How long had they sat there? Sadie could feel Grandma's eyes boring into her back through the window, disapproving of such emotion. What did she care? Grandma would be gone soon enough. Papa had hired a housekeeper, so there was no need for her to stay once the funeral was over.

The reception after the funeral was an opportunity for Sadie and Stanley to escape upstairs. Their absence would go unnoticed amongst the throng of Papa's neighbours and business acquaintances. They sat looking out over the fields behind the house, wondering what was going to happen.

'Do you think Papa will want to leave here? I hate this house. I wish we were still at Chateau Yering.'

'You'll get used to it. No matter what, Papa will be guided by what's best for business.' Stanley said.

Sadie wondered how he could be so calm, so matter of fact. Her nerves were still jangling from standing over her mother's grave. Grandma had told her father she shouldn't be there, but she had begged and begged until her father gave in. Perhaps Grandma was right. The memory of that yawning hole and then the sound of her voice uncontrollably sobbing into Grandpa's lapels, shamed her.

After the guests departed, Sadie crept downstairs, her stomach rumbling. On the hunt for leftover sandwiches and cake, she heard voices in the room Papa used for his office. She did not mean to listen until she heard her name.

'Sadie needs a woman's guidance. She's nearly twelve and the next few years will be difficult.'

'Do you think so? I suppose you're right.'

'Just until you marry again.'

'It's too early to think about that, Mother.'

'Quite! But you will remarry. You're not yet fifty, and you need a hostess.'

'Bella was more than just a hostess, Ma.' A catch of anger in his voice.

'I wasn't suggesting otherwise. Son, I know you loved her. Maybe you'll never find anyone you love quite as much, but you will remarry. You know it, and until you do, the girl is best off with me. She needs a firm hand. Bella, maybe you as well, spoiled her. One minute she's an unruly hoyden and the next an overwrought, emotional wreck.'

Sadie shrank back with horror. Papa would never agree to that, would he?

'I'll think about it. Let it be for now.'

Sadie raced back upstairs, throwing herself onto her bed. Fresh sobs. I won't go with her. Papa won't make me do that. Grandpa Bill will tell him I need to stay at home. Fancy talking to Papa about a new wife. How could she? I hate her. Sadie's mind grappled with distressful images of a shadowy, faceless woman standing in her mother's place, pouring tea, standing beside Papa with her hand outstretched to greet someone. No one could ever replace her mother. Sadie's mind twisted into knots, pain burning in her chest as she fought to breathe, but she could not dispel the image of someone else in her mother's place. The thought of living with Grandma added to her panic, and that was the most imminent danger.

I have to talk to him, make him understand I can't live with her. She forced her breathing to slow, slid from her bed, then splashed some water on her face to hide the tell-tale streaks of tears. Blowing her nose, she left her room to find her father.

He was still in his office, staring out of the window. Sadie sat beside him; he turned his face towards her. His grey eyes barely acknowledged her; his face drained of colour. He rubbed at his eyes as though trying to bring life into them. Although his beard was neat and trimmed, there were flecks of grey in the whiskers nearest his ears that she'd never seen before. His usual energy seemed now like an unwound clock, its ticking and chimes silenced. Her heart skipped a beat, she saw his mortality, and it frightened her.

'What do you want, Sadie poppet?' Even his voice sounded defeated.

'I love you, Papa.' She moved towards him, wanting to sit on his lap and clasp her arms around his neck. He let her, but normally he would have squeezed her tight in response. This time his arms felt slack and half-hearted. He rested his head in her hair for a second and then choked back a sob. She clasped him tighter only to feel him withdraw and set her down on the floor.

'Leave me, pet. I've things to do.' He turned back to his desk, his eyes sliding away from hers.

She stood for a second or two before saying, 'Papa, there something I need to ask.'

'Don't you think you've asked me enough for today. I should never have taken you to the grave. Your grandmother was right.'

Trembling, she turned to leave the room, not daring to say the words she had practised. Had he already decided to make her go with Grandma? If so, it must be her fault for making such a scene.

Disconsolate, she wandered into the garden and found Grandpa Bill standing on the riverbank, staring across the water towards the northern mountains.

'Are you really going home tomorrow?' Sadie asked in a sad voice.

'I've thought about this long and hard over the last few days.' He turned his face towards her and smiled. Such longing in his eyes. 'I'm going to give up my house in Molong and move to Melbourne. I want to spend as much time with you as I can. Who knows how long I have left? I didn't get to see my only child as much as I liked with you always moving around. But your Papa seems settled in the valley now.'

Sadie threw her arms around him. 'That's wonderful, Grandpa. But Papa's thinking of sending me to live with Grandma.'

'He's never mentioned it to me.'

'I overheard them talking.'

'Do you want to go? It will be nearer your school.'

47

'No, I want to stay with my brothers.' She raised a tear-stained face towards him. 'Please, will you tell him I don't want to go. If you move to the valley, I can ride over to see you every day.'

'You don't want to promise something you'll regret. I'll have a word with your Papa, but maybe I'll move near to your grandma, and you can visit after school sometimes.'

Her grandmother left without her on Sunday morning. All through the previous day, Sadie lived in fear of a summons to her father's study. It did not happen. Perhaps Grandpa Bill had succeeded in persuading him to let her stay, but he had left early on Saturday morning without Sadie having an opportunity to speak to him alone. When Papa took Grandma to the station. Sadie waved her goodbye with her broadest smile and received a brief peck on the cheek in recompense, together with an instruction to behave well for her father.

'Of course, Grandma. I'll never misbehave again.' Sadie could almost see the smirk on Stanley's face.

The house felt empty without Eddie running around or her mother humming a song as she worked. It was left to Sadie to pour tea the following afternoon as they gathered after lunch. Once she would have been proud to have that responsibility, now the reason for it left her desolate.

'We must do everything we can to make your mother proud,' Papa said, as he took the cup from her. 'Eddie will be coming back from Uncle Jonnie's this afternoon, and he's going to find it hard without Mama. Sadie, you must be a mother to him, as much as you can.'

Sadie nodded, 'I will Papa. Thank you so much for keeping us together.' She burst into tears of relief.

'Come here sweetheart,' Papa pointed to his lap, and Sadie scurried to sit in it, leaving Joe Junior to finish pouring the tea.

'We've all been hit hard by your mother's death, but we have to move on for her sake. Remember her with joy; try not to let your sadness win. We'll stay together and be strong for her, for our Bella. Most of all, we're a family that sticks together. While there's breath in my body, I will work hard for you all, and I expect you to do the same. In a couple of weeks, we are up for the best dairy farm award. Let's win it for Mama.'

Chapter Seven

The WVS was like being back at school again; the camaraderie, the gossip, a mixture of mind-numbing and interesting tasks. Fun and laughter too, the best medicine Sadie could wish for. She fell asleep exhausted after days rolling bandages, sorting through donated clothes to see what could be salvaged and remade into something useful.

The first-aid training cemented new friendships. Try tying Muriel's arm in a sling or applying a tourniquet to Gladys's meaty arm without falling into fits of laughter. They all baulked at attempting to kiss each other's mouth to bring life back to deprived lungs, and it was a huge relief when Edna produced a battered, practice model. As they each knelt on the floor to kiss and pummel the chest of the dreary looking puppet, they encouraged each other on, hoping they would never have to do it for real.

After years of bringing up her sons, her only friendships being with her sister-in-law's family and a few chapel ladies, the WVS filled a void of loneliness she knew existed but managed to bury while her sons were at home. Memories of her childhood and her mother began to resurface. The more she thought about it, the more she realised that everything had changed the day she lost her mother. The seeds cast by her death had grown into twisted vines in her soul. It was the same for her father and her brothers. They had all lost their compass that day, veering off along some uncharted course, feeling their way through life, as though blindfold. But now, Sadie found something to fight for, a sense of renewed purpose.

Whereas the first bombing raid appeared random, the next one was not. Several planes targeted the docks, but all the bombs dropped into the sea. Despite this failure, concern was growing. 'It's just a matter of time.' Everyone knew it, everyone said it, her sons wrote it in their letters. Sadie likened it to a rope being twisted; one turn every day.

'We need to be prepared for everything and anything,' she was told that first day of training. 'Whatever is required, we will do. However tiresome, however small; we must do it with a smile. Our job is to support civil defence, our soldiers, sailors, airmen, their wives and families, everyone in fact.'

Sadie was given an armload of socks to darn for the soldiers stationed in the town. She took several pairs home to work on while she listened to the radio in the evening. War and socks, women and socks, she'd done enough of knitting socks in the last war. She remembered entering a pair of her socks into a competition for the Red Cross Fair in Glenelg. She hadn't won, hers were passable at best. Each sock darned now, she imagined was for one of her sons.

Sadie received a letter from her youngest son, Glen, telling her he was being shipped to RAF Seletar in Singapore. He was hoping to spend any leave he accrued in Australia. 'Who should I look up?' He wrote? Who indeed? Not his father, he had not asked for Frank's address. As far as she knew, he was in Sydney, but he had never shown any interest in his sons, not even when he lived with them. She would get her address book out, but it was all so long ago; how many of the entries there were still accurate; how many of her relations were even alive? Apart from Eddie, no one had written in the last dozen years. What a relief at least, she thought, to have one of her sons safe from the action.

A programme of American dance band music began. Sadie turned up the sound to hum along, her heart lighter than it had been for months. She smiled, remembering Christmas eighteen months before when they all cavorted around her front room trying out the Lindy Hop.

Hard upon Grimsby's first bombing casualty in August, Henry arrived home on leave for a weekend bringing his friend Simon. Her son noticed the card in the front room window immediately.

'You've joined the WVS, good for you Mother.'

'They tell us to put the card up; I'm not sure if it's to prove I'm working for the war effort, or to let people know they can knock on the door if they're in trouble. No one's called as yet. I'm not sure I would know what to do. It's still early days.'

'But you're doing something, Mrs Tinsdale, that's important,' said Simon.

'You're going to need your windows taped up. That's something we can do tomorrow.'

'Are you sure that's necessary?'

Her son nodded. 'I've seen the damage glass splinters can do to a body. A small one alone can take off a child's arm.'

She hated the thought of her sons experiencing such horrors but supposed it was inevitable. To lighten the sudden chill in his voice, she said, 'Enough about me, how are you boys doing? You both look done in. Are you getting enough sleep?'

'So far we've just been laying mines around the coast. But we think that's going to change. I can't tell you more, but this war is going to be bloody, damn bloody. If I had any sisters, I would tell them to move away. Grimsby's going to be targeted, maybe not as much as other towns, but anywhere with a port or factories is at risk. Civilians are going to suffer too.' Henry's tone was insistent.

'Nancy's gone up to Elgin with the baby. Jimmy insisted she stay with his sister, Kitty, after that first raid. She left a month ago. I miss her and little Anne. Aunt Jane is bereft.'

'It's the best place for them. The next few months will be telling. It's vital we stay strong and grit our teeth. I don't envy the fighter boys. They'll have their work cut out. But the Spitfire's a winner. The best. What I wouldn't give to fly one rather than my old Hampden; they say it almost flies itself.'

'So we've heard. Grimsby is raising money to buy one for the war effort.'

'Thank goodness Glen is going to be out of the action. I remember Singapore, hot steamy, all those junks in the harbour and the coolies carrying those huge loads.'

Simon yawned. Both boys looked dead on their feet.

'I've made up the back bedroom for Simon. Go up when you're ready. I'll make you some hot milk.' She bustled off to the kitchen, pleased to have Henry home, but his words reinforced her anxiety. What terror would the next few months bring? How many mothers would lose their sons?

In some ways, Henry reminded her of Rob, although she remembered Grandma Jane saying Henry took after her father, Thomas. On that, she could not comment, but Henry strangely resembled Rob with his square jaw and strong face; how different her life should have been with Rob. Over the years she had learned to accept what she had done. One stupid decision changed the course of her life. But her boys made up for it all. The pride she felt in them added justification to her regrets.

She had begun to dream of her first love. Strange how those dreams left her with such longing when they had done little more than kiss. Unrequited love, the stuff of cheap romances. Real life was more complicated.

Sadie poured hot milk into cups and carried them through to the boys. 'Thanks, Mrs Tinsdale.'

'You are very welcome Simon. Tell me, where are you from, I've not heard that accent before.'

'Birmingham, Erdington to be precise.'

'I remember my Grandmother saying her father was from Birmingham, so that's what he would have sounded like.'

'You've never mentioned him before Mother. What did he do?'

'We learned never to ask questions. If Grandma let something slip, you let it go, or you would have felt the sharp side of her tongue. All I know is that his surname was Dugmore.'

'There was a boy named Dugmore in my school in Aston.'

'Strange to think we may have lots of relatives in England and Scotland. With everyone moving around in this war you could bump into them and never know. Thanks for the milk. I'm going to turn in.' Henry stood up, yawning.

'I'll take your cups. I won't be long myself. Let's hope the Jerries leave us alone tonight. Goodnight boys.'

'Goodnight, Mrs Tinsdale and thank you for having me.'

As Sadie washed the cups, she thought about her Grandma. What no one ever said because it was taboo, was the question of having convicts in the family. Grandma was born in Tasmania. It was more than likely one or both parents were convicts, her secrecy suggested it. For the first time,

Sadie felt sympathy for her. She had not mourned her when she died less than ten years before, but Grandma had strength and purpose which, seen from this distance, became admirable. How sad that she had to guard her tongue and disavow her parents. To have given the middle name Dugmore to two of her children meant that she had been fond, even proud, of her father. Sadie sighed. What good did it do to think back in time? Maybe it was because the future now seemed uncertain, so fraught with danger. At this moment, Australia looked the safer option.

Time for bed, with Henry safe at home she hoped to sleep and maybe Rob would appear in her dreams. Where did that thought spring from? She hadn't dreamt of him in years.

Chapter Eight

Australia   -
Yarra Valley, Winter 1910

'Come on!' shouted Sadie. The drizzly rain did not appear to dampen anyone's spirits, not when the daffodils were about to reappear with the promise of spring around the corner.

The riders were back in view. 'Come on!'

'What's that, a rider down? Who? Is he hurt? No, he's up. Who was it?' The chattering crowd of horse lovers and gamblers kept up an ongoing commentary.

This was Sadie's favourite day of the year, the Yarra Glen and Lilydale Point-to-Point and Steeplechase. Crowds of race lovers came out from Melbourne by car and train, until the whole valley from Healesville to Yarra Glen choked with onlookers.

'It's St John and Sligo in the lead,' a voice announced over the loudspeaker. Everyone was shouting as the horses leapt over the last fence. Sadie jumped up and down in excitement while the two horses battled it out. 'Sligo has it, ladies and gentlemen and it's a record time of eight minutes and fifty-three seconds.' Cheers and groans as the winners and losers counted the cost.

Papa did not have a horse running; so Sadie, although cheering the horses on, did not mind who won that much. Everyone but Papa was there; he was still tied up in New South Wales with another railway contracting job. Sadie saw less of him than ever. He had stayed in the Yarra Valley long enough to conclude that his dream of owning a three hundred strong herd of dairy cattle was impossible without labour on hand to milk them. Instead, he must build a new dairy with the latest Thistle milking machines from Scotland and refrigeration units for the farming produce. To pay for it, he took on the contract to build a railway north from Newcastle and a tram system in Adelaide.

Would he ever stop driving himself to do more and more? The last year had seen him travelling backwards and forwards between Adelaide and Newcastle, almost a thousand miles distant, with an occasional visit home. Each time Sadie saw him, he had grown greyer and more fraught with worry about the weather, overdue contracts and the latest thing was a strike up in New South Wales. Why couldn't he have been satisfied with a small dairy farm? She didn't care about the money. It was him she missed.

They were back living at Chateau Yering. Sometimes, Sadie felt like a parcel passed back and forth like the land she stood on. She lost count of the times Papa bought and sold land in the valley. Nominally, Joe Junior was in charge of the farm and the produce shop in Melbourne, but Sadie detected a tension. She heard loud voices through the study door, and once, Joe Junior slammed out of the front door with his new wife, Olive, casting upset glances at Papa. Was he harder on his sons than on his workers? She knew his men looked upon him with respect and affection. It was as though Papa could never quite trust Joe Junior to manage.

The loudspeaker announced the novelty races, breaking her reverie. Much to Sadie's chagrin, girls weren't allowed to enter, but Stanley had. Sadie hovered as close to the finishing line as she could to cheer him on. Each competitor must hold three eggs, mount their horse and then race to the finish without breaking them. Finally, the balloon race ended with Stanley nowhere near the placings in either. Sadie picked her way through the churned-up grass to commiserate.

'This is my sister.' Stanley introduced her to the rider who had trailed the field but was now beside him.

'Rob Fraser.' He held out a mud-spattered hand. Sadie shook it, the warmth through her gloves creating an instant shyness. How pleased she was that her hair was pinned up beneath her straw hat making her appear older than her sixteen years.

'Why don't you join us in the refreshment tent once we've cleaned up,' Stanley said.

'Please do Miss Timmins,' Rob's smile lit up a serious face. His warm brown eyes held hers before she glanced away in confusion.

Her heart gave a little leap, a reaction to one of Stanley's friends that she had never experienced before. Mr Fraser was no horseman. She wondered why he had volunteered to enter that last race, chasing the galloping riders at an unsteady canter. With his stiff posture, he sat uneasily on the nag Stanley had chosen for him, despite its elderly gentleness. His legs had gripped the horse's flanks for dear life as he'd bobbed up and down in the saddle. Normally, she would have laughed, but was surprised to admit to a sneaking admiration for his desire to give it a go in front of such a critical crowd. She couldn't help liking him for that alone.

A feast of St Hubert's baked hams, roast beef, cheeses and wines lay spread out in a tent for guests on gleaming white cloths. Before making her way there, she ducked into the house to find a mirror to inspect herself. Horrified, she saw a splodge of mud on her chin. After wiping it away, she tucked one loose strand of hair beneath a hairpin, patted her cheeks and bit her lips in the hope they would attain more colour.

On the journey to school the following day, Sadie attempted to wheedle some information out of Stanley.

'How long have you known Rob?'

'A year. He moved here from Ballarat.'

'What does his father do?'

'He runs a bank or a store, I think. Why so curious?'

'He didn't seem too comfortable on a horse.'

'Ah, he did that for a bet.'

She snorted. 'Why does that not surprise me? You boys will bet on anything and everything.' She paused. 'Out of interest, what was the prize?'

'That would be telling?' Stanley tapped his mouth, smirking.

'Go on, tell her.' Bruce said. 'Or I will, she's obviously interested.'

Stanley considered it for half a second. 'The bet was ...' He waited, grinning like a Cheshire Cat. 'The bet was that he had to ride a race before I would introduce him to you.'

Sadie did not know whether to be infuriated or pleased. She allowed herself to smile.

'See, I told you she was interested.' Bruce said.

'How does he even know who I am?'

'He saw you walking to school and asked one of his friends who you were. Ever since he's been on at me to introduce you. He even took riding lessons last month to try and avoid falling off in front of you.'

Sadie's heart leapt again, her first admirer. 'What do you know about him?'

'He's a clever so and so; scholarship boy, wants to be a lawyer. Office job - couldn't stand it myself.' Stanley resented that Papa had made him stay at school for a further year, too busy even for his own son.

'I'd rather take you on at the start of a contract, not when I'm in the middle of three, and each of them causing me headaches,' Papa had said when the school year finished last December.

Sadie remembered the conversation. How could she not? It was the day she got to meet her latest stepmother. Janet, the one before, the sweetest person one could imagine, had died of a burst appendix only nine months after marrying Papa.

Now there was Caro, half her father's age, younger even than his eldest son. The bride's family attended the wedding, as did Joe Junior and Olive, who were on honeymoon in Sydney. Sadie begged for details when they returned, but little was said, other than Olive's description of the bride's dress. What was left unsaid, disturbed Sadie. There was no 'how delightful', as was said of Janet, nor 'how charming or loving or friendly'.

Grandma Jane had at first been impressed that the marriage was in St Andrew's Cathedral in Sydney. Less impressed at the note she had received from the bride, thanking her for the gift of a silver teapot. 'It's too formal,' she complained. 'Not so much as a how she is looking forward to meeting me. I hope she's not uppity.'

Uppity, a good description, thought Sadie, after kissing her new Mama on the cheek. Elegant, beautiful, cool, Caro's gold-spun hair and cat-like green eyes made her an alien species amongst Sadie's dark-haired kin.

Grandpa Bill, normally the person to see the good in everyone, told Sadie in a quiet moment, 'She's married above herself, married into money. It may take time for her to unbend, feel at ease with all of you. Right now, she's enjoying the attention and is maybe a little jealous of you all. Give her time.' But anyone with half a brain could see that Papa was besotted.

'There's nothing so pathetic as an old man panting after a young woman,' Grandma muttered under her breath later. Sadie had never thought her father old. Four years ago, her Grandma described Papa as young. Could fifty be described as old? He possessed the vitality and energy of a man far less in years.

Immediately after Christmas, the new Mrs Timmins scurried back to Sydney to spend New Year with her own family, Sadie's father in tow. Caro had not been seen in the Yarra Valley since.

Sadie received two tellings-off in school that day for daydreaming, as she tried to recall her conversation with Rob. Her cheeks blushed to think of it. Was she sufficiently poised and grown up or did he now think of her as a silly child? He was a head taller than herself and her brother, who had the physique of a jockey, obliging her to gaze up at Rob's liquid eyes. Remembering the way he inclined his head to reply to her question, made her smile and added a glow to her heart. Rob's height gave him a quiet confidence. She could imagine him in a courtroom, holding forth with assurance and dignity.

If only Lucy, her friend and confidante since she began at Stratherne, had not left for England the previous month. Now a letter would have to suffice. They used to be inseparable, and she missed her lively, forthright chatter. The only other person she could talk to was Grandpa Bill. Every time he saw her, he asked her if she had a beau and laughing she always said no, perhaps next time she could say 'yes.' The thought thrilled her.

The telegram that evening hit her like a hammer blow. Her beloved Grandpa was in hospital following a heart attack.

'I have to see him,' cried Sadie.

'It's too late now. We'll go in the morning,' Joe Junior tried to calm her.

She hardly slept. All thoughts of Rob fled from her mind. She adored Grandpa Bill, loving his tales of Old Ireland and his stories about her mother's childhood. No one else in the family talked about Mama as easily. In fact, they mostly avoided mentioning her.

'The hospital allows only two visitors at a time,' Joe Junior explained the following morning. 'I'll take Sadie and Stanley.

All the way on the train into Melbourne, Sadie was on tenterhooks, remembering the carriage ride from the station to St Hubert's on the day of her mother's death. Was it an omen that the same three people were on that journey?

She had never been in a hospital before, the strong smell of antiseptic unsettled her as they walked down a seemingly endless corridor to the men's ward. There was Grandpa Bill in the end bed.

'I'll stay outside,' Joe Junior told them, pushing Sadie forward. 'When you've finished, I'll go in.'

Sadie approached the bed with trepidation; Grandpa appeared to be asleep. Stanley told Sadie to sit in the only available chair. She drew it close to the bed, noticing Grandpa's whiskery stubble and his sunken mouth. Her mother would have had something to say about that. Tears filled her eyes. She grasped his hand, whispering 'It's me, Grandpa.'

His eyes opened, 'Bella?'

'No, Grandpa. It's Sadie.'

'Sadie, love.' He attempted a toothless smile. 'Don't be sad.'

'Hello, Grandpa.'

He turned his head, 'Stanley too. Always look out for Sadie, promise me, boy.'

Stanley nodded.

He turned his watery eyes back to Sadie. 'I'm ready darling. Ready to meet your lovely Mammy and my Lizzie again. I wished I could have waited for your wedding, but the Dear Lord has other ideas. Don't you grieve, you hear me. Your Mammy's calling me. She sends you her love, both of you, and Bruce and Eddie too. Believe me. Last night she came to me in a dream.'

Sadie attempted a smile. She so wanted to believe that.

'Kiss me, darling, then tell Joe Junior I want a word.' He began to wheeze with the effort of talking.

Sadie bent down and placed a lingering kiss on his cheek, then stood to allow Stanley to do the same. Stanley put his arm around her as they walked from the ward.

'He wants to talk to you, Joe.' Stanley said as Sadie took out her handkerchief to wipe away her tears.

The two of them watched as Grandpa gave Joe a scrap of paper from his pyjama pocket. Joe Junior read it and nodded. He kissed the old man too. A nurse approached and laid a hand on Joe Junior's arm as she spoke softly to him. He nodded and with a final glance at Grandpa, walked back towards his brother and sister.

They were mostly silent on the way home, wrapped up in their thoughts. Sadie realised how lucky she had been to have Grandpa nearby for the last four years. He was always there for her, always knew the right words to cheer her up when she missed her mother. They shared that loss between them. Where Stanley and Bruce took to their horses when the pain got too bad, Sadie turned to their special bond which had grown stronger over the last few years. How hard it would be to lose that. A double loss. But there was comfort in his words that her mother was waiting for him. She should not be selfish, and she was grateful that she had had no inkling of his final illness. Perhaps the curse was lifted.

Papa came for the funeral. He called her into his study after they returned from the church.

'You're quite the young lady now.' He studied her before kissing the top of her head. He did not have to bend far these days. None of her brothers was tall, and she wasn't far behind Stanley.

'Sit here.' He patted the seat next to his. 'I'm sorry that I'm not home more often,' he said, as his hand swept through his thinning hair. Tiredness had etched lines in his face.

'Do you need to work so hard, Papa? We miss you being here.' His face softened, and he patted her knee.

'I know, I know. But there's work to be done, and I would hate to be idle. Caro says the same, but she doesn't complain when I buy her a new necklace or take her to the races. Shall we go to Flemington for the horse racing next year? You'll be seventeen. Would you like to go?'

'I would love to Papa. Please take me.' Sadie almost jumped from her chair to hug him. But the thought that she was no longer a child stopped her.

He looked wistful. 'You're the image of Mama.' He shook his head trying to dispel the thought. 'Now, before he died, Grandpa Bill wrote this.' He picked up a torn scrap of lined paper from his desk and gave it to her.

'I leave all my worldly possessions to my darling granddaughter, Sadie.' She read it and looked at her father in astonishment. 'He left everything to me?'

'It may not be a legal document. There are no witnesses, but his intention was clear. Joe Junior spoke with him after all. We have agreed that we will carry out his wishes, which makes you a wealthy young lady when you reach twenty-one. Not rich, but if you are sensible, you'll never have to worry about money.'

'But what about my brothers?'

'You don't need to worry about them. 'They'll have land and a business to inherit.'

Chapter Nine

Australia
Yarra Valley, Summer 1910

Stratherne College planned an end of year dance for the senior girls. Young gentlemen were invited from Scotch College, marking both the end of Sadie's and Stanley's schooling. Everyone was talking about it at school and discussing what they would wear. Sadie listened with jealousy as her fellow students discussed shopping trips to the best shops in Melbourne with their mothers. Olive declined to take Sadie, not wanting to fight the pre-Christmas crowds on Saturdays leading up to the busiest social season of the year. However, she rummaged through her wardrobe to find Sadie a suitable gown, and Sadie had to admit that the selection was as wide as she could wish. Olive's taste veered towards the sophisticated, and while their colouring differed, several dresses drew Sadie's eye. She picked out a turquoise ball gown edged with gold.

'Oh no, Sadie. That won't do at all. It should be white or perhaps lemon at a push. I think I may have something here I wore a few years ago. I was fond of it, but I should have thrown it out. I'll never wear it again.'

Sadie's heart sank, remembering the pink taffeta, Bo-peep bridesmaid dress she was forced to wear to their wedding. She had hated it from the moment she saw it, but Olive's mother, would not listen to her protests.

'I'm fifteen, not six,' Sadie had complained.

'It will be perfectly charming, my dear. You'll carry a little basket and scatter autumn leaves along the aisle.' Olive's mother did not mention the silly crook that she would also have to hold for the photographs. For days after, whenever she walked into a room, Bruce and Stanley began humming the nursery rhyme. When they started singing the song on the train to school too, she flew at Bruce with her fingernails until Stanley caught her and called a truce.

'Ah yes, I knew it was here.' Olive picked out a skirt of pale yellow crepe with a cream chiffon overskirt, a wide, gold silk ribbon for the waist and an embroidered blouse top.'

'It's gorgeous, Olive.' Sadie sighed entranced as she imagined herself twirling around the dance floor.

'Yes, it is. I had all the young men vying to dance with me if I remember. It needs a string of pearls or perhaps a gold chain to set it off. I'll speak to Joe because I'm sure your mother's jewellery has been put aside for you. No doubt there's a pearl choker.'

Sadie caught her breath. A cold finger of sadness crept up her spine.

Olive saw her distress. 'Oh, my poor dear.' She took a lace handkerchief from her pocket, handing it to Sadie. 'It should be your Mama helping to dress you, I know. As you're leaving school, you will need a whole new wardrobe. Perhaps I'd better speak to Grandma Jane about it.' A look of horror passed over Sadie's face at the thought. Olive giggled. 'Honestly Sadie, she's not that bad, and she likes nothing better than shopping for clothes. Behind that austere façade is quite a vain woman. You need to catch her in the right mood.'

Later that evening, Joe Junior set before her a box she knew. 'Take a look through and choose what you want for the dance, then I will put it away for safekeeping until Papa says you can have it.'

Sadie stroked the silver box, remembering the Christmas Papa gave it to her Mama. She gazed up at her half-brother and offered him a small, tight-lipped smile which mirrored the pain on his face. Moments like this brought their loss to the fore.

'Do you mind if I take it to the library?' He shook his head, understanding her need for solitude.

She lifted the small casket and walked to the room her Mama had loved best. Sadie set it down on a Chinese lacquered table, staring at it for several minutes, steeling herself to turn the key. She wondered what memories would be triggered by opening the box. She traced her hand over its decorative swags and tiny balled feet, before turning the key and lifting the lid. The jewels looked as though they had been thrust into the box, rings, brooches and necklaces lay jumbled on the red velvet lining. Sadie could see her father or maybe even Grandma, sweeping items hurriedly away from her mother's dressing table. Just the sight of them brought tears to her eyes. She emptied the box on to the table, determined to bring order to it. There was less than she had imagined. It was possible to put it in order of purchase by the quality alone. First her mother's engagement ring, a tiny solitaire diamond, next her simple wedding band. Papa had been working for other contractors then. A string of glass beads, worthy now only of a child's dressing up box. A gold locket which her mother often wore. Sadie prized open the clasp to look inside. There lay a heart-shaped photo of Sadie as a baby, with a lock of her baby hair. A present to Mama following her daughter's birth, no doubt, when Papa had delivered his first successful contract for the West Australian government. Sadie gulped with emotion before looking through the rest,

A garnet brooch in the shape of a bee; a pearl choker with drop earrings to match; another brooch – a butterfly set with diamonds; a thick gold chain and last of all, an opal ring, surrounded by diamonds. This last from the profits of the Menzies railway line. A small blue velvet bag tied with cord was the only thing she did not recognise, its contents – another wedding band and a ring of tiny ruby chips. Her own mother's rings, the most likely possibility. Sadie slipped on the ruby ring; it fitted her middle finger. No one could object to her wearing such a small, unshowy item. Somehow it brought her closer to Grandpa Bill, to think that he bought it for the grandmother who died before she was born.

One by one, she placed the other jewels back in the box, leaving only the gold locket. It would look perfect with the dress, and the one item which held sentimental attachment. She closed her eyes, imagining herself dancing in Rob's arms, while cocooned in her mother's love.

The school staff made valiant attempts to decorate the hall on the evening of the dance with paper chains and bunting. Dusk was falling, as Stanley escorted his sister into school. He passed his hand around the neck of his shirt, already moist from the December heat. Sadie cast aside her wrap, a tiny booklet hanging from her wrist. Would her dance card fill up? She dreaded sitting watching everyone else have fun. The headmistress and her sister greeted all the young ladies and gentlemen, making it plain that no one was allowed to sit out a dance, nor wander off into the grounds for any purpose whatsoever. Twenty couples would dance or none at all, and no more than one dance each pair.

Sadie's card filled up in next to no time with Rob demanding the final dance. Why the final one when she longed for it to be the first? By the end of the evening, her dress might be mussed, her hair loosening from its pins, her feet sore and horror of horrors, she may be glowing with perspiration.

As each dance began, she looked for Rob. Was his partner prettier than her, did they appear to be enjoying themselves too much, talking nineteen to the dozen, laughing, did his face lean down to whisper in his partner's ear? Jealousy pricked her. She tried her best to smile and chat with each partner as she had been taught ladies do, but she disliked each clammy hand around her waist. Few partners were as good looking as Rob; some were pimply, a couple podgy, one smelled of beer and another of stale tobacco.

When they stopped for a supper of cold meat and salad, Rob made his way over to her. Why did her heart beat a little faster and a blush coat her cheeks? What was it about him, in particular, that had that effect on her?

'Can I fetch you a drink, Miss Timmins? Some cordial perhaps.'

Sadie nodded, suddenly tongue-tied. This would not do. She wanted to sparkle, longed to have him hang off her every word.

'I must say you look very fetching in that dress.' he said, handing her the drink.

'Thank you, Mr Fraser.'

'Please call me Rob.'

'Rob.' The colour rose once again in her cheeks. 'Have you done any more riding?'

It was his turn to blush. 'You found me out, didn't you? Me and horses, well, they're not really my thing. Does that upset you?' A mischievous grin settled on his lips.

'I could not imagine living without horses. Do you not think with a little more practice, you might come to enjoy riding?'

'Are you offering to teach me, Miss Timmins?' The grin widened.

65

Colour now flamed her cheeks. She stumbled over her words. While there was nothing more she would rather do, she could not appear forward.

'Take your partners for The Dashing White Sergeant.' She was saved by Miss Dare's announcement.

'I will look forward to your answer,' Rob whispered in her ear. before departing to find his next partner.

A young man, a friend of Stanley's and not without charm, offered his hand for the dance. She tried to concentrate, but her heart fluttered with anticipation. How should she answer?

Rob knew what he was doing when he insisted on the last dance. When Miss Dare declared it to be a waltz, a shiver ran up Sadie's spine. The entire dance would be spent in Rob's arms, just as she had imagined. When he came over to her, she drifted towards him, and he grasped her firmly around the waist. Her gloved hand clasped in his; she felt the strength in his body and purpose in his movement. Maybe not a natural dancer but he did not tread on her toes, and he kept to the rhythm of the music. He led her around the dance floor, and she floated on a bubble of happiness.

'Have you decided? Will you teach me to ride?'

'I doubt that my father will allow it,' she said. It was the only proper answer.

'I would like to meet him.'

'He is coming home for Christmas.'

'What a shame. I will be staying with my parents until the day before New Year.'

'We are having a New Year's Eve Party. Perhaps you could come? Stanley will invite you.'

'I would love to. You know I will miss my glimpses of you now that you're leaving school. I have another year at Scotch College. My mornings will not be the same without watching you walk by.'

Sadie wanted to tell him she would miss him too. 'Will you stay in touch with Stanley?'

'Yes, but isn't he going to work in Adelaide with your father?'

'He is. I will miss him. We depended on each other after Mama died.'

He drew her tighter into his arms. It felt safe, secure and then the piano stopped playing. Rob lingered a moment before taking a step back and bowing. Sadie bobbed a curtsey, suddenly bereft. The end of a chapter of her life. Time stretched before her. Would Rob be in it or would this be the last time she saw him?

'We will meet again, Sadie.' She clung to the promise, noting that he had dropped the Miss.

'I would like that, Rob.'

Chapter Ten

Australia   -
Yarra Valley, Christmas 1910

Sadie eagerly awaited her father's arrival. It seemed like months since he had last paid more than a fleeting visit. She blamed it on the birth of his newest son, Oliver. Part of her longed to make a fuss of her baby brother, a small part because mostly she was jealous of the amount of time Papa spent away from the rest of his family. The lack of him in their lives grated on her brothers too. Her eldest brother, compensated by his wife and daughter, received copious instructions by telegram or letter regarding the running of the farm. If anything, Sadie detected nervousness in Joe Junior, that his father may find fault with his management.

How Papa kept all his plates spinning in the air mystified Sadie. A family in both Sydney and Melbourne, a railway contract north of Newcastle, railway contracts in Adelaide and Western Australia and tram contracts in Adelaide. Goodness knows how many miles he covered in a year. It made her head ache to think of it.

The day arrived. A telegram informed them that Papa would arrive by late afternoon and there was no need to meet them at the station, which must mean that he was travelling by car. Stanley's and Bruce's eyes lit up with anticipation. Their afternoon was spent discussing the relative merits of various cars which soon tested Sadie's boredom threshold, but even she looked forward to a spin in whatever turned up in the drive.

No one had bet on a Rolls Royce. Stanley's long whistle of admiration competed with the squawking cockatoos in the late afternoon sunshine, as the red car made its stately entrance. Bruce ran towards it and jumped on the running board as the car slowed to a halt.

Everyone ignored Caro and the baby until she emitted a shriek of annoyance and the baby began to howl its displeasure at being woken so abruptly.

Remembering his manners, Stanley walked round to the passenger door and opened it. Sadie ran forward to take Oliver while Caro climbed out, her face dusty from the untarmacked roads and a grimace on her face.

'I hope you have plenty of hot water; I need to soak away all the dirt.' Her voice petulant.

'I'm sure we will have,' Sadie hastened to reassure her. 'Won't you have a refreshing glass of lemonade first? We have some cooling for you.'

Caro took the baby and marched into the house.

Sadie, momentarily taken aback, rushed to her father and received a hug and a kiss.

'Why Sadie, you're all grown up my darling girl.' He took a step back to admire her, and she drank in his admiration.

'Pa, you didn't drive all the way from Sydney, did you?'

'No Stanley, we sailed from Sydney, and this gorgeous beast was waiting for us at the docks, fresh from England. What do you think?'

'It's a real beaut! When can we go for a drive?' Stanley rubbed away at some of the dust to see the red paintwork gleaming below.

'Tomorrow, I have a mind to drive over to Traralgon to see my sister Hannah. I can't remember when I last visited. Caro says she wants to rest, so we could all get out of her way. What do you think?'

'Yes please,' they shouted as one.

'Well, how about you boys give the car a good wash now while I talk to Sadie.' He took Sadie's hand and led her indoors, leaving the boys to pore over the car with delight.

Sadie wondered what her father wanted to talk about with her. Perhaps it was about her legacy from Grandpa Bill. She knew that the house in Carlton was now hers. Papa had mooted renting it out until she married, which made some sense, although she missed going there. But it was not that at all.

'How would you like to come and live in Sydney?'

It was such a bolt from the blue that Sadie was at a loss. 'Do you mean permanently?'

'Until my contract finishes. I'm away during the week, and I think Caro could do with the company and some help with the baby. We have a lovely house in Manly right on the waterfront. I'm sure you'd like it.'

Sadie did not know what to say. Would Papa take offence if she declined? Was this why he said she could leave school. There was no way she wanted to live with Caro and be a nursemaid to Oliver.

'But my life is here,' she stumbled. 'My pony, my brothers.' And Rob, would she ever see him again?

'Stanley will be working with me, and I will enjoy showing my beautiful daughter off to Sydney society. Now I must speak to Joe about the farm.' She was dismissed.

All that evening Sadie watched Caro. When Sadie's brothers talked about the business, boredom creased Caro's forehead. She pecked at her food, staring into space. Olive tried to engage her in conversation. Only when the discussion moved onto clothes did Caro's eyes light up. Sadie cast her mind back to family meals with her mother, when dear Mama would talk about anything and everything. She had a particular knack for engaging people in conversation, no matter who they were. Sadie saw her father glance at Caro. Seeing the glance, Caro smiled coquettishly at him, but as he turned his face back to speak to his eldest son, a frown of tedium settled once again over her too perfect features.

Sadie wondered what kind of marriage it was, where the wife sat like a trophy at the table, unwilling to share her husband with his family. How could she bear to keep this woman company? Olive tapped her on the shoulder.

'Sadie, pay attention. I have just suggested to Caro that she take you shopping for clothes tomorrow. You seemed reluctant to go with Grandma Jane.'

'But Papa's taking us out in the car.'

'Don't be ungrateful, Sadie. If Caro has made the offer, you should accept with good grace.'

'What about the baby?'

'My nursemaid is perfectly able to cope with two small children.'

Sadie looked across at Caro. 'Are you sure Caro? Papa said you were tired.'

Caro managed to look vaguely interested in the project. She inclined her head to show acceptance.

'Thank you, Caro.'

'I would prefer that you call me Belle Mère. It shows respect, don't you think? My mother is French, and it's much more sophisticated than step mama.'

Sadie bit down on her tongue. 'Thank you, Belle Mère.' Sadie dreaded the next day. Out of the corner of her eye, she could see Stanley sniggering.

'Beautiful horse, what an idiot?' He said later, as they made their way to bed. Sadie giggled at his deliberate misunderstanding of French. 'Let's call her the old nag.'

She felt better having Stanley on her side.

Caro insisted on a lift to the station in the Rolls, so at least Sadie got to drive in it before her brothers, but the short distance left her wanting more. They barely got up to twenty miles an hour before the station appeared. The sensation of speed left Sadie exhilarated and envying her brothers.

Papa handed Sadie an envelope containing enough money for several outfits. 'An early Christmas present for you, my dear.' He pecked Caro on her upturned cheek, leaving a lingering hand on her arm which she gently shrugged off. Sadie caught a fleeting look of sadness in his eyes as he bid them a good day's shopping. She longed to run back and throw her arms around him as she had done when she was younger, but Caro hurried her along the platform to where the train waited.

Once settled in an empty compartment, Caro smiled at Sadie. It reminded Sadie of a snake eyeing up its prey. 'Let's be clear at the outset, Sadie dear,' she hissed. 'I do not want you in Sydney. You must make any excuse you want but I will not have it, do you understand?'

Sadie sat dumbstruck. She opened her mouth to speak, but nothing came out.

'I can see that you are wondering what to say. But you need say nothing. You will not tell your father about this conversation. He will not believe you. I have already told him how much I am looking forward to your stay. But it's not going to happen. Am I clear?'

Sadie nodded. 'I don't want to go to Sydney anyway,' she spoke quietly. Her mind racing, what was going on?

'Then we are both happy. We'll now have a very jolly day spending your Papa's money.' Caro took a lady's magazine out of her bag and proceeded to ignore Sadie for the remainder of the journey.

Guilt became the overriding memory of that day. To lie to her father seemed unforgivable. That his wife would stoop so low, made Sadie angry, but what was she to do about it? There remained the niggle of relief that she would not have to leave her home for Sydney, but how was she to refuse her father's bidding?

Once off the train, Sadie guided Caro to the shopping area in Bourke Street. Where, far from Caro taking her shopping for a new wardrobe, Caro left Sadie to her own devices while she went to examine what each shop had to offer. It was left to shop assistants to advise Sadie. They knew their job.

A young woman about to enter society. 'Oh yes, Miss. Let me show you the very thing.' Both in Bussell's and in Buckley and Nunn, Sadie accepted their help with gratitude. Strangely, she had a feeling that her mama was guiding her to make the right choices, while her stepmother was nowhere to be seen.

They met for tea in Buckley & Nunn's refreshment café. A glow of pleasure suffused Caro's face.

'There's nothing like shopping to make a lady happy, don't you find, Sadie?'

Sadie flushed. This was her first attempt on her own, and she had found it nerve-wracking.

'I suppose I will have to inspect what you bought before we leave. Never let it be said that I failed to do my duty.'

'There's no need, Belle Mère. The lady assistants helped me. I am sure everything is suitable.'

'There's every need dear. How else will I describe it to your Papa.'

Caro's eyes appeared to glitter with triumph or menace. Sadie was not sure which. She longed for the shopping trip to be over but found herself trailing after Caro, her face crimson with embarrassment as Caro commented on each item before it was packed for delivery.

'I wouldn't have chosen that shade myself darling, but it may go with your colouring. Are you sure that won't be too small? You're quite full in the bosom department. Oh, I like those shoes, but they would look better on me. They're a mite sophisticated for a girl your age.' Every barb spoken with sugary sweetness.

Sadie watched the expressions on the sales assistant's faces. Pity. Humiliation turned her stomach into bile. Nausea threatened to choke her. Sadie understood what Caro was doing. She was making a point of how her life would be if she dared to come to Sydney. How could her father love this woman?

Grandma was there when they arrived home. For the first time, Sadie wished she could throw herself onto the old lady for protection. She caught the wariness in her eyes as Grandma observed Caro. Surely, she would understand and intervene on Sadie's behalf. Sometime over the holiday, she would try to catch her in a good mood. If Grandma could be persuaded that Sadie should not go to Sydney, it would be less difficult to persuade her father.

At dinner, Grandma asked what clothes Sadie had bought. Caro did not give Sadie a chance to reply, describing everything down to the last detail.

'What about the gown for New Year's Eve? Presumably, you have bought a dress for that evening?'

Caro floundered for a few seconds, looking towards Sadie for help, a whisker of panic in her eyes. Sadie was about to say that Caro hadn't been there when she chose the material and pattern, hoping that her story would start to unravel.

'It's a surprise, isn't it, Sadie dear?' Caro recovered herself.

Grandma gave Caro a sharp look but let it go. The chance lost.

When the parcels arrived the following day, Sadie took no pleasure in unwrapping or hanging her new skirts and blouses in the wardrobe. The evening gown, still being made for New Year's Eve, was the sole item not to have been dismissed with distaste by Caro. At least Sadie would wear it to dance in Rob's arms, free from the mockery of Caro, who having lied, would not dare criticise it.

Christmas came and went without too much upset, other than Sadie's peace of mind. She was surprised to receive another present from her father, a gold filigree bangle for her wrist, set with tiny sapphires.

'It's beautiful, Papa. I love it.'

'Do you? Well, Caro chose it for you. She has excellent taste, don't you think?'

Sadie's heart sank, the present ruined. She felt her stepmother's smirk before she saw it.

'Thank you, Belle Mère,' she said through gritted teeth, attempting to raise a smile.

After a sumptuous dinner of roast pork, crispy crackling and applesauce, Sadie took the opportunity to speak to her grandma, who was taking a rest in the library.

'Did you know Papa's asked me to go back to Sydney with him and Caro?'

'Yes.'

'I really don't want to go. Belle Mère has made it plain to me she doesn't want me there.'

Grandma sucked in her cheeks. 'I'm sure she doesn't.'

'You are?' Sadie said in surprise, but also with the hope that Grandma would be on her side.

'But that is exactly why you need to go, Sadie.'

'What, I'm sorry, pardon?'

'I don't trust that woman and perhaps deep down your father doesn't either.'

'You mean, I should be a spy?' It made sense Sadie thought, but the idea appalled her.

'But I don't want to do that. She hates me, Grandma. You've no idea what it was like to go shopping with her.'

'Your father has fed and clothed you for the last sixteen years. It is your duty to do what he asks. Obey your father until you marry and then obey your husband. That is a woman's obligation. You're going, let that be an end to it. Now leave me to rest.'

The berths on the ship for Sydney were booked for the second of January. Sadie had only a week to think of a reasonable excuse to escape her sentence. She wracked her brains but couldn't think of a way to do it,

74

other than to get Rob to persuade Papa to let her stay. She doubted it would work. Papa had never met Rob. What if he should take a dislike to him? Everything depended on the New Year's Eve party.

Dressing for the party was not the thrill she had anticipated. Her mind was still obsessed with how to get out of moving to Sydney. Grandma walked into her room as she was giving her hair a final comb through, before tying it up in a ribbon matching the pale blue of her dress.

'I approve,' she said, as Sadie turned towards her. 'Did you choose the colour and style or did Caro?'

'Belle Mère had nothing to do with it. The sales assistants helped me choose.'

'I thought as much. Well, you've done well. You won't let your father down.'

The door handle rattled as someone tried to walk in, but Grandma stood squarely in front of the door. Sadie knew it was Caro coming to find fault, even though she would claim any compliments for herself. Her mouth grew dry, and a sick feeling descended on her. Why wouldn't she leave her alone?

'Walk down with me, Sadie.' For once Sadie was glad of her grandmother's support.

Rob arrived with another friend of Stanley's who had borrowed his father's car. Sadie felt Rob's presence before she saw him. Stanley was introducing him to her father. Sadie watched as Papa, a full head shorter, grasped Rob's hand in his. No one doubted Papa's strength of mind or body.

What was Rob saying to him? Was he telling him he was a friend of Stanley's or was he also saying how much he admired his daughter too? No, that would be too fast. Rob barely knew her, although she saw him look up, his eyes searching, casting around until they fell on her and he smiled. It felt as though a pit had opened in her stomach and her heart dropped through. She caught her breath then glanced back at her father. Caro was by his side, cool in a dress of emerald silk. She was looking at Rob, a curl on her lips as she noticed the direction of his eyes. Did nothing pass the woman by?

A voice cut through her thoughts. 'Why Miss Timmins, you're all grown up, and how handsome you look. May I beg a dance off you?'

She turned towards him. 'Mr Tinsdale,' she gave him a distracted smile. 'Yes, indeed, a dance.'

'I will look forward to that.' His smile travelled her body in admiration.

His forwardness made her blush. After dinner, there were to be a few dances; a pianist had been hired for ten o'clock.

'Are you here with your parents?' Sadie asked him. 'Ah yes, I see them now.' Long-standing business acquaintances of her Papa, Mr and Mrs Tinsdale stood chatting with her brother, Joe Junior.

Grandma tutted when she saw how Caro had placed the cards for dinner. Her stepmother's influence on the table plan so obviously designed to discomfort Sadie. All through the first course of dinner, she sat between middle-aged men and tried to make polite conversation, but her mood darkened as the meal wore on. The men turned to more congenial company. How could she feel isolated and lonely in her own home? Could no one protect her from Caro? At least there was the dancing to look forward to. Rob was bound to ask her, but after this evening, would she ever see him again?

Frank Tinsdale insisted on the first dance. She was uncomfortable as he held her too close and her eyes drifted towards Rob.

'I can see I have a rival for your attention, Miss Timmins.' Frank admonished her.

I'm sorry, I...' She flushed with embarrassment. She forced herself to pay attention. He was a good dancer, his hand firm on her waist. His charm began to work on her, and she found herself enjoying herself. His mimicry of some of the older men at the dinner table had her laughing before the dance ended.

With only a handful of young people, Sadie managed to have two dances with Rob.

'I watched you at dinner; you looked sad. Are you going to miss Stanley that much?' His hand gently squeezed hers.

'I'm to leave for Sydney with them. Papa wants me to live there.' Her eyes turned upwards so that he could see the unhappiness in her sapphire eyes.

'Surely you will return?' She caught the concern in his voice.

'Who knows? Papa has contracts in Adelaide. He never stays anywhere for more than a year or two. I don't want to go, but I don't seem to have any choice.'

'I will miss you, but they say Sydney is lively. You'll enjoy it, I'm sure.'

He had no idea, and she did not want to tell him of her troubles. If she did, she would break down in tears.

'May I write to you?'

She tried to disguise the longing in her eyes. 'I will look forward to your letters.' She wanted to say, don't forget me, rescue me, keep me with you, but he was in no position to do so, still at school himself, just eighteen and with no money behind him. She guessed it would be years before he could afford a wife. Meanwhile, Caro would be throwing her step-daughter at anyone who could take her off her hands, maybe someone as old as her Papa. Would she be desperate enough by then, to accept such a means of escape?

In many ways, it was a relief to dance again with Frank whose charm and wit distracted her from thinking too much. His school days were long behind him, but she had no idea what he did, 'a bit of this and a bit of that' was all she drew from him. How lucky to be carefree. The tension dropped temporarily, from her shoulders as he spun her around the room.

She saw Rob looking at her, querying the smile on her face. Was he jealous? The thought made her smile a little wider until she remembered this might be the last time she saw him.

'Miss Timmins, you're making me jealous.' Frank snapped her attention back to him.

His smouldering eyes scanned her face. She apologised once more, and he smiled lazily at her.

'When you are a little older,' he bent his mouth to her ear and whispered, 'I will come back for you.' The music ended, he planted a lingering kiss on her hand, before wandering away.

Sadie stood in shock, a frisson of fear or anticipation swept over her. She didn't know which.

'What a good-looking young man.' Caro stood by her side.

'I'm not sure I like him.' Sadie said.

77

'You're too young for him.' Her mouth curled in amusement. 'He's a bit of a rogue, a likeable one.'

Sadie had a sleepless night, drowsing only as the pink-edged sun broke through the darkness. Arising two hours later, she had one wish on her mind, to saddle up and ride through the valley in the early morning to her mother's grave. She gathered fragrant flowers from the garden to take with her.

Stanley and Bruce offered to go with her, and it felt like old times, the three of them on horseback. Bruce was going to feel lonely without them. It was the end of an era, the end of childhood. There was a significance about this ride which they all felt, but without the need to put into words. Adulthood lay before Stanley and Sadie. She wished she felt a small part of Stanley's excitement, instead of dread.

They stood with heads bent after Sadie placed a vase of white roses and agapanthus on their mother's memorial stone. The space for Papa beneath the mirroring stone on the right was too awful to contemplate. Their father was so important in their lives, their lodestar, their fortunes inextricably wrapped up with his. None of his children questioned his authority. As much as Sadie wanted to stay at Chateau Yering, she knew in her heart, that to go against her father's wishes was unforgivable. She had not even dared to make her feelings known to him.

'Race you to Steel's Creek, 'Stanley broke their reverie.

Wiping away tears from her face, Sadie ran back to her horse, climbing into the saddle, she urged her forward. The black mare needed no encouragement. Galloping a few yards behind her brothers, the summer breeze against her face, she did not see the brown and white, diamond patterned snake slithering from underneath a bush, its mouth spitting in warning, but the horse did. It reared up in alarm. Sadie screamed as she felt herself slip from the saddle, twisting as she fell to avoid landing on her back. The hard, dry ground sucked the breath from her. She heard the bone snap in her leg before losing consciousness.

Sadie was only vaguely aware of her second trip in the Rolls Royce. Her battered and bruised body lay on the back seat, while her father drove gingerly over the rutted earth road after leaving the doctor's surgery in

Yarra Glen. Wooziness clouded Sadie's senses, but she remembered the sharp agony of the doctor's manipulation of the bone until the morphine he administered took effect.

Later, back home in Chateau Yering, Sadie lay on a couch while her sister-in-law made up a bed for her downstairs. Her leg lay in splints, aching, rather than painful. Her father held her hand, concern written on his face.

'I'm sorry Papa, to cause you all this trouble. I've no idea why I fell. I don't remember anything.'

'Anyone would think you didn't want to come to Sydney with us. Is it because of that young man who's so obviously smitten with you?' Her stepmother's voice was light and jokey. A questioning glance crossed her father's face.

'It wasn't deliberate, Papa.'

His hand squeezed hers. 'I know. Caro's teasing. Stanley said he glimpsed an Eastern Brown. But you're not going to be able to travel with us tomorrow, maybe not for several weeks. I hope you're not going to be too lonely. Perhaps it would be better to have another year in school. I'll write to the headmistress.'

Despite the fuzziness from the morphine, relief washed through her. She did not mind school, especially as an alternative to living with Caro. Anything would be better, and it meant she would catch a glimpse of Rob each day.

'The bed's ready; I'll carry you through.' Papa enfolded her in his arms, and Sadie wove her arms around his neck, her cheek against his whiskers. She missed him already.

Chapter Eleven

England
Grimsby, February 1941

Although there had been a few air raids through the autumn and winter, Sadie thanked God that they had experienced nothing like the blitz in London and elsewhere. Despite the news black-out, rumour was rife. She went with Jane and Nibby to the cinema and watched a Pathé news film about a squadron of Spitfires scrambling to fight German bombers. Their manoeuvrings reminded her of the darting swifts on the day France capitulated and the Heinkel dropped its first bombs on the town. The brief film gave only a taste, but it was enough to bring tears to Sadie's eyes. Jane grabbed her hand, words unnecessary. Bombers or fighters, the brave young men of the RAF, deserved every bit of the adulation heaped on them.

Sadie's appointment with her solicitor was for eleven o'clock. After one of the first night-time bombing raids on the town, she had woken with the conviction that she ought to ensure her will was up to date. Everything would go to the boys, of course. Not that there was much apart from the house and an income of a few pounds a week. What worried her most was what would happen if she were blown up by a bomb and left incapacitated. She didn't want to be a burden.

There was no market on a Thursday, but Riby Square, where she got off the trolley bus, was as busy as ever with dock traffic. Turning left into Freeman Street, she scarcely glanced at the taped-up shop windows. Time enough for that on the way back. Long queues snaked outside the butchers and the fishmongers. Sadie regretted forgetting her woollen scarf as the easterly wind bit at her neck. The solicitor's office was on the opposite side of the road, just past Marks and Spencer. The receptionist offered her a cup of tea while she waited. It came, insipid but hot, and for that she was grateful. She had never been able to get used to winter in England. Endless grey skies, mist and drizzle which seeped under all the outer layers of clothing leaving you damp and cold.

'Mrs Tinsdale.' He was a younger man, in his forties with thinning blond hair. He held out his hand. 'I'm Sidney Dewsberry. I believe you saw my father last time. He's retired now.'

Time had moved on. Was it fourteen years since she had altered her will? Not long after she'd arrived in the town.

'What can I do for you today?'

'It's my will; I want to make sure everything's in order. If anything should happen to me, you know.'

He nodded, understanding flooding his face. 'Very prudent of you. I took the liberty of digging out the current one. Has anything changed?'

'Not really, my boys have grown up of course. They no longer need a guardian. I don't want to be a burden should anything occur. You understand?'

'I'm sure you would never be a burden, dear lady.' He meant well, but she bristled at his patronising tone.

'Who knows what will happen. I want to make sure that my income would pay for nursing care. I don't want to end up in an ...' She could not say the word, institution. 'The house could be sold; an apartment would be sufficient. I would want it all managed by a reputable executer along with my eldest son.'

'Ah, I think you need a Power of Attorney set up rather than a new will. Have you discussed this with your sons?'

'No, it's difficult. They have their own concerns.'

'In the army, are they?'

'No, the RAF. Two in bomber command and one in air-defence in Singapore.'

The look in his eyes disconcerted her. His nose twitched as though attempting to hold back emotion. He too, she thought. Maybe a son or a nephew. The moment lay between them, unspoken. A fleeting look of sadness before reverting to cool professionalism.

'I'll draw something up for you, and we'll make an appointment for two weeks time.'

There was nothing much she wanted, but she mooched around Boyes looking at the material. Perhaps Jane would make her a new dress for the summer, but seeing nothing to take her fancy, she wandered back to Marks. Prices appeared to be higher than ever. She fingered one or two cardigans before drifting off to look at the blouses. As she left the store, all she had to show for her morning was a pair of stockings. The truth was that she felt no compunction to spend money on herself anymore. What was the point? The clothes in her wardrobe were serviceable, and with no man, not even her sons to dress up for, shopping had lost its attraction.

She began to retrace her steps to Riby Square, toying with the idea of browsing in Bon Marché before catching the bus home, but her stomach began to rumble. Time for a nice cup of tea and a bowl of soup at home before Woman's Hour, she decided.

Later she could not remember what she heard first. Was it the screams of women and children or the sound of the cannon fire? She was almost at Strand Street when the world split apart. The unmistakable throb of an aeroplane engine and gunfire. How many? People ahead were running for cover; some fell to the ground. Sadie was paralysed with fear until she saw the plane travelling low over Cleethorpes Road. She was close enough to glimpse the pilot's face as he sprayed the area with machine gun fire, his plane low enough to target individuals. She curled into a ball as windows splintered all around her. Had it not been for the tape, she would have been cut to ribbons.

Seconds later deafening explosions rocked the ground as he dropped his bombs near the level crossing. She crawled to find shelter in a doorway before the shopkeeper dragged her inside. She was shaking in terror; gritty dust coated her face and clothes. It seemed like the raid was over in seconds, but Sadie dreaded to think of the devastation it had wrought. The siren was sounding now, too late. That in itself was strange.

She needed to help, but shock still had her in its grip. Taking a handkerchief from her pocket, she wiped her face with shaking fingers, surprised to see the mixture of black dust, tears and a fleck of blood. Was it her own? Her compact mirror showed not. Then whose was it?

That question stirred her into action, and she hurried from the shop towards Riby Square a few yards ahead. Blood spattered the pavement. A woman lay on the ground, dead, no doubt about that; half her head was missing; a young boy too in school uniform, his body all odd angles, blood pooling around him. Sadie screwed her eyes up at the sight. Could she be of any help when she couldn't bear to look at that poor child? She turned the corner and viewed the chaos; trolleybuses hit, shattered glass, cars and lorries askew, the smell of cordite in the air mingling with the normal beery smell of the Lincoln Arms.

'There's nothing you can do here love unless you're a nurse.' A policeman barred her way.

'I'm in the WVS; I can apply a tourniquet.'

'Why don't you offer your services to the landlady. We're taking the walking wounded in there. I'm thinking she could do with a hand.'

Under normal circumstances entering any pub bar on her own would have been out of the question. The Lincoln Arms, the first pub out of the dock gates, had never looked salubrious at the best of times, but Sadie entered without a qualm.

A glance from the doorway was all it took. Half-drunk glasses of beer lay abandoned and littering the bar. The men needed for war work outside. Instead, several women and a few young children sat in the same shock she had experienced moments before. Sadie drew off her gloves and hat and walked to the bar where the landlady was pouring small shots of brandy into glasses.

'They'll need strong, sweet tea and we could do with some warm water and plasters. One or two have cuts.'

'Right you are. Doris, go up to my kitchen and fetch the teapot love, and all the tea you can find. I'm not sure how much sugar we have. It's lucky I have a gas ring here with plenty of hot water on the go for the glasses.' The landlady tossed some keys to her barmaid. Noting her business-like attitude and the strength in her face, she reminded Sadie of Edna at the WVS. 'Fred, pop your head outside and ask someone to nip into Boots for plasters and TCP,' she shouted to a man, who was escorting another couple of people inside.

'I'll do it myself,' he disappeared back out of the door.

Sadie turned back to the women. All she could do at this point was to offer comfort and identify who needed medical attention. Five minutes later, a pharmacist from Boots rushed in with one of his assistants carrying supplies, and he took over that side of things.

Sadie and Dee, the sweet, young lady from Boots, dished out tea and sympathy to all comers for the next hour or so. They wiped the children's tears from shocked faces, comforted their mothers, and listened as they recounted their stories.

A man popped his head around the door every now and again to report the latest news, although his subdued voice conveyed none of the horrors he had witnessed, Sadie saw it in his eyes, heard it in the curses under his breath as he left.

The landlord returned from helping out to let his wife have a break. Sadie decided it was a good time to make her way home.

'Not without something to eat first,' the landlady said. 'It's the least I can do.'

Sadie helped the barmaid carry the teapot and other supplies through the outside yard back up to the landlady's flat. She walked past a couple of bedrooms and a bathroom on the way to the kitchen. All of the windows smashed. The pilot had had a field day.

'She'll need help with cleaning up. Should we make a start do you think?'

'Don't worry; I'll give her hand later. She won't be a minute,' Doris said. 'She's just nipped out.'

Having missed lunch altogether, Sadie's stomach was groaning, and her head was light with hunger. She looked out of the kitchen window. There were still vehicles all over the place, and traffic remained frozen in time, but the injured and dead had been removed. At least she now felt useful, knew that she had something to offer, however minimal.

'Would you like a bacon sandwich, dear?' The landlady asked as she walked into the kitchen. 'Oh, bloody hell. You didn't tell me about this mess, Doris.' She surveyed the damage. Most of the glass was hanging from the tape.

'I couldn't take your rations. Let me help clear up.' Sadie offered.

84

'Never you mind about that. The butcher is often in here for a drink. He left me a little parcel.' She winked as she unwrapped four slices of bacon and Sadie's mouth fell open in surprise. 'We need to give the table and cooker a wipe down first. I don't want you eating glass splinters. Doris, find the dustpan and brush. I'll get a mop.'

All three women set to clearing up the mess before the bacon went in the pan. The smell of it frying, the spit of fat, the sizzling, all of it made Sadie's mouth water, filling her with craving. A bacon sandwich, not a thin piece of streaky, but thick, back bacon. She'd always wondered who got the best meat. Certainly not her. Was it who you knew? She suspected butchers had their favourite customers like this landlady. Who wouldn't swap food and drink if they had the choice?

'Here you are, love. You're always welcome at my pub. I'm Gloria by the way.'

What a glamorous name! Sadie smiled. 'Thank you, Gloria. You're most kind. I'm Sadie. This looks delicious.'

'And this is for afters. It's from the off-licence next door. Thank goodness, the bastard didn't shoot up her stock of whisky.' Gloria produced a Duncan's Walnut Whip from her pocket with a flourish.

Such kindness from this unexpected quarter brought tears to Sadie's eyes.

'You'll have a walk ahead of you, so fill your boots. There'll be no buses up Cleethorpes Road this afternoon. Where are you heading back to?'

'Clee Road.'

'Back to Hainton Square for you then. The number four will take you to Old Clee. At least it's not raining.'

It was dusk by the time she made it home, footsore, tired beyond measure. She sank into her armchair, still in her coat, the fire unlit. Cold seeped into her bones, but she couldn't move. Images of the plane, the bullets and the injured flashed through her mind, like a film on repeat. How could a man do that to innocent civilians? She knew it happened, of course, but to see it with her own eyes. Her head shook in disbelief. This was war, the one her sons faced every day. The war her husband and her brothers had faced last time. Before it was words, written in the newspapers, or images on film. Now it was real, her reality too. Nothing about that scene could she ever forget.

She sat praying for her sons, as she had rarely prayed before. Could they come out of this unscathed either in body or mind? It wasn't possible. But they would never talk about what they did, what they saw, just as she would not talk about what she saw that day. How many had died? It would never make the newspaper. She imagined reading, *In the incident on Thursday a man showed great heroism, or a nurse worked tirelessly and without thought of her own comfort*. Gossip would inform or misinform. She would tell Edna that she had been present and assisted for the WVS records. Beyond that, no questions would be asked, nor answers expected.

Stiff and weary, she decided the best place was bed. Please, don't let the siren go tonight she prayed. I can't bear it in the Anderson shelter, not tonight. She decided to recall the taste of the bacon sandwich instead, a bittersweet memory in more ways than one.

Not that night but three nights hence, the bombers returned. Cold and damp, Sadie sat huddled in blankets, a flask of tea nearby, hoping they were bypassing the town like they normally did. They did not but luckily hit only one house in the town. Most of the bombs fell in fields, she later found out. Mill Road, however, was too close for comfort, just a few streets over from her sister-in-law. Thank God, no one was killed.

Chapter Twelve

Australia –
Yarra Valley, 1913

She lay in bed, all but dead to the world until something roused her. A cry, a shout; alarm. Wanting to shrug it off, she turned over, a bare moment of wakefulness before it came again, louder, sharper more insistent. The sounds of the house awakening; the clattering of boots on wooden floorboards and then on the stairs; of knocking at her door. All thought of sleep fled. Eddie pushed open her door.

'Sis, there's a fire. Get up.'

'Where? Here. Is it the house?'

'No, the dairy. We're all needed to try and save the produce.'

She was already out of bed, throwing on clothes. Rushing out of the house, she saw the flames in the distance. Someone had already saddled her horse.

'Joe took the truck and is gathering neighbours to help.'

Eddie held a lantern to light their way across the fields of dew-laden grass.

She could hear the fire now, crackling, spitting, preparing to roar. Were they already too late? The full force of the heat hit her as she jumped down from her skittering mare, fifty yards from the dairy. The horse reared, nostrils flaring in alarm as she tied her to a fence post. Black shapes ran in front of her, but she could tell from the smell that it was too late. Hundreds of blocks of ripening cheese were toasting in the fuel of melted butter. The stench was sickening. Now she caught another smell, that of barbecued pork.

A line of men formed a chain and passed buckets from the river, but the splashes of water had no effect. Sadie and Eddie ran to join the line as fire licked at the walls. The flames grew higher as explosions began to rip through the building. Papa's pride and joy; the most modern dairy in the valley, full of the latest electrical equipment. It couldn't go. It was the centre and lifeblood of the farm. The produce fed the city from the Elizabeth Street farm shop.

Bruce urged the men to work faster as his older brother attempted to get the hoses into the river.

Sadie watched with horror as the walls of the dairy began toppling in on themselves before her eyes. Putrid black smoke beat them back.

'No!' Her cry was echoed by her brothers as they gazed at the destruction.

The hoses from the river arrived at last, but as the water gushed onto the flames, they knew it was too late. Joe Junior ran back and forth as his man sprayed the fire. His shouts of desperation difficult to witness.

Eddie and Sadie stood helpless, in an agony of impotence, as the dairy crashed to the ground. No other building, trees or long grass stood nearby, so at least there was no chance of the fire spreading. It was small comfort; the jewel in their crown was lost.

Sadie caught sight of Joe Junior's face in the dying flames; the water was beginning to dampen down the fire. Black streaks covered his cheeks, but his eyes were hollow with anguish. She knew what this would do to him. He would blame himself. He was in charge of the farms in the valley and Papa relied on him while he was away contracting.

'It must have been an electrical fault,' Joe Junior explained to a neighbour. The man nodded.

'I hope you're well insured.'

Joe Junior passed a hand over his brow leaving more black marks. His expression was panic-stricken. Oh, Lord. Sadie realised why he was so distracted. Hadn't she heard him say that he needed to update the insurance weeks ago? Did he forget? A sick feeling settled in her stomach, and she turned away to retch into the grass.

'You've got smoke in your lungs, Missy. Go home; there's nothing to be done here.' One of the farm workers patted her hand.

She gave him half a smile. The men must be worried about their jobs. Without the dairy, Papa would have to sell cattle. The significance of this loss overwhelmed her. She saw it in her brothers' eyes. Eddie kicked at the grass by his feet, his eyes catching hers before his head sank back towards the ground. Bruce stood silent, staring at the mess of smoking rubble. Joe, agitated, paced up and down, so unlike his normal calm self. She couldn't bear to look anymore and turned back to her horse, accepting the offer from a workman to hand her into the saddle. Light from the early dawn glimmered sufficiently to pick her way home. Someone needed to organise tea and breakfast for everyone who had come to their aid. She told the man to spread the word.

Papa roared up to the house two days later. Already shouting, he leapt from the car before his driver had chance to switch off the engine, then he rushed into the house, calling for his oldest son. When Joe Junior appeared, his father took him by the arm, shoving him towards the study; the door slammed shut behind him.

'How much?' Papa bellowed. No one could fail to hear him.

A softer voice, Joe Junior's. Then Pa's, bellowing again. 'Dear God! Thirty thousand short.'

As much as that? Sadie's sympathy had been with her brother, but that was a fortune to lose. She caught Olive shrink back as though struck.

'Come, your father will need refreshment after his long journey.' Olive reached for Sadie's arm and led her away, her fingers trembling and clammy as they clutched her. A nervous tic at her eye detracted from the confident beauty she spent ages perfecting.

Fraught and tense, everyone gathered for dinner that evening, their attempt at stilted conversation withering as Papa glowered at them all. He ate sparingly and left the table without dessert to sit in his study with a whisky and cigar, poring over the farm's accounts. The door was ajar, and Sadie could see him crouched at his desk, smoke billowing over his head, his brow furrowed, the cigar clenched between his fingers, ash falling like dirty snow onto the carpet. Silent, she fled back upstairs, wondering what the morning would bring.

The morning brought cataclysmic change.

'The farms, the house and the shop have to go.' Papa announced to his stunned family. I can't manage it all from Sydney.' At no point did he lay any blame. But they had let him down, no doubt about it. Joe Junior and the farm manager should have picked up the insurance problem.

'Even if we had sufficient insurance, they would still go. I don't intend to rebuild, haven't got the time to spend on it. We'll move onto new things. The economy is booming, and I'm confident we can recover. I am inclined to get into horse racing, and that requires a stud farm. Joe Junior, I'll leave that to you to purchase. You'll need a house for you and the children. You can continue to look after the sawmill at Narbethong. I'll send Stanley back to sell Chateau Yering and St Hubert's. Bruce can leave school and get into the contracting business with me. Eddie, as soon as this house is sold, you can move in with me and Caro in either Sydney or Adelaide.' He looked around, seeking no argument, his decision final.

Only Bruce looked pleased. At sixteen, he was itching to leave school like his elder brother. Olive sat tight-lipped while her husband stared at the floor.

'And me Papa?' Sadie ventured.

'You have a choice, live with me or your Grandma.'

Her heart sank. 'Could I not continue to live with Joe and Olive?'

'There won't be room, they'll not need a big house, and one day may have more children, they don't need you.'

Best not to say anything at this point. Sadie needed a plan.

Rob visited most Saturdays. He was at university in Melbourne studying law. He travelled on the train for lunch, and he and Sadie walked in the grounds. Occasionally she persuaded him to take a gentle ride along the river bank, but that afternoon they walked over to see the ruins of the dairy.

'I'll be twenty in a few months,' she began. 'You're twenty-two shortly.'

He knew what she was trying to say. 'It will be years before we can marry. Maybe four or five.'

Marriage had been mentioned before in an indirect way.

'But you do want us to marry?' Sadie looked up, her eyes questioning.

'Of course. There's no one else I want.'

'I don't want to live seven hundred miles away. We'll never see each other. You'll forget about me.'

'Never. But I don't want that either. You can live with your Grandma. It's nearer for me, and we can see each other in the city. We could do the block on Saturdays,' he grinned.

The block. The parade of ladies on Collins Street, showing off their latest dresses, idling at overpriced teashops, gossiping, everything her grandmother despised.

'I'd love it, precisely once, just to irritate her. But then I might love it too much. Shall I become one of those ladies, like my stepmother if she had the chance?'

'No, because I wouldn't love you anymore. I don't want to marry a clothes-horse.'

'Seriously, I can't live with my grandmother without being driven insane with boredom. It may take months to sell Chateau Yering. I need to convince my father to let me live in my house in Carlton.'

'On your own? He'd never allow it.'

'I know, but if he lets me take our housekeeper, Mrs Porter, who's been with us since Mama died, and I employ a maid to chaperone me. And...' she looked up at him. 'Papa likes you. He respects what you are making of yourself. Thinks you'll go far.' Her eyes questioned his. A look of understanding dawned.

'And if we are engaged and I promise to respect you. Do you think he will fall for it?'

'It's my only hope, Rob.' Her smile all but begged him.

He turned away. Had she ruined it? Oh Lord, was she too forward?

He turned back, a box retrieved from his pocket.

'I've been carrying this around for months. It was my grandmother's. I know it's not much but...'

'Oh yes, yes.' Relief and love shone on her face as he slipped the tiny solitaire onto her finger.

'I suppose I should have asked your father first.' He stooped and kissed her on the lips. Her first grown-up kiss. She had not known what to expect. The tingling in her lips spread downwards, and her breath quickened. His arm snaked around her waist, squeezing her, gentle at first and then harder. He let her go suddenly. His face flushed as he said. 'I'm not sure I can wait five years, but I must. I won't live off your money.' He buried his head in her hair, breathing deeply.

'I love you, Rob. I'll wait but will you kiss me again now? I didn't know it could be like that.'

'It will be so much more, but please don't tempt me. A kiss, nothing more.'

Deeper this time, tighter, her arms slid around his neck as he pulled her to him until he groaned and set her aside. She shivered with emotion. Would he be shocked at the desire she felt to go further?

'Let me go and talk to your father.'

They walked back, lost in thought, wrapped in the enormity of what had happened. Sadie locked her arm in Rob's and felt secure and loved for the first time in years. Before they entered the house, Rob bent his mouth to her ear.

'Whatever your father says, I love you, and I'll wait for you.' His lips grazed her ear.

Sadie stood waiting for news by the unlit fire in the sitting room, staring into the gilt mirror above.

'However long you stare, it won't make you any prettier.' Grandma Jane had walked into the room.

Sadie jumped at the sound of her voice but then turned and asked, 'Grandma, how long did you know Grandpa before your married him?'

'Three weeks.'

Sadie gasped. 'Three weeks. It must have been love at first sight.' She had difficulty imagining her grandmother ever being in love.

'What had love to do with it? You think we married for love? He needed a wife, and he liked the look of me. I needed a good provider, someone who would not fritter away his money. Love came later and all the better for that. My parents knew each other for five minutes and married for the same reason.'

Five minutes! How could anyone decide to marry after five minutes?

'In those days, men waited at the harbour when ships arrived with servant girls fresh from Europe. Every one of those girls was snapped up for a bride before they set foot in the town. A man needs a woman to raise his children, and a woman needs a man to be a good provider. That's all that matters, that and respect. There should be respect.'

Sadie wanted to ask more, but at that moment her Papa, followed by Rob entered the room.

'Finally,' he beamed, 'good news. Rob has asked for Sadie's hand, and I believe she has accepted. Let me get you a cigar, boy.'

'Thank you, sir. May I save it for another time?'

'Save it for your first born, or winning your first case, or even,' he paused and slapped Rob across the shoulder, 'When you are elected to a seat in the State of Victoria. What do you think, Mother, shall we have a politician in the family?'

Grandma Jane looked across at Sadie, a rare smile on her face. 'A good provider, well done, girl.'

Sadie lay looking through her window at the stars, dreaming of her future with Rob, a warm glow enveloping her. Everything would be perfect. Once Stanley found a buyer, she would go to her father and beg him to let her live in her own house. Nineteen-fourteen and she'd be living in Melbourne. Perhaps she should open the house sooner, so it could be redecorated and refurbished in readiness. Grandpa Bill had done nothing to it when he moved, happy to accept its old-fashioned state. Had he not hinted once that when the time came, she could make as many changes as she wished? She had forgotten that.

'Grandpa, wherever you are, thank you,' she whispered, before turning over and falling into sleep.

Chapter Thirteen

England
Cleethorpes, January 1941

A letter lay on the mat. Sadie picked it up and turned it over to see the stamp. Straits Settlements – that must mean Singapore. How wonderful! Just the fillip she needed after the Dornier attack. She would steam off the stamp for Stanley's stamp collection, should he ever reappear, although it looked a dull little thing; the King's head beneath a crown surrounded by a curling pattern.

She took the letter into the back room to read with her morning coffee. How Camp coffee could ever be described as coffee, defeated her; mostly chicory with a hint of coffee. Before the war, she wouldn't have touched it with a barge-pole, but now even a suggestion of former glories could be made to suffice. She slipped her paperknife through the envelope to extract the letter. The scrawling handwriting showed a young man in a hurry. She didn't mind; any letter was welcome.

It was nine months since Glen had enlisted and the first letter received since he had arrived in Singapore. He would be nineteen in a few weeks. It made her feel old to think of all her boys would be in their twenties next year.

A vague memory of Singapore resurfaced. The ship from Australia had made a brief stop there. She remembered walking around in dripping heat forcing them to seek shelter in a department store. Better trailing boys around a shop than returning to their steerage cabin. The heavens had opened in the afternoon. She remembered that monsoon rain as a river falling from the sky, filling the drains in minutes.

She spread the letter open and began to read.

Dear Ma,

Well here I am, and it's damnably hot. The temperature never seems to dip below ninety and when it rains it flipping pours. You're wet to the skin within seconds.

Seletar is a tiny base in the north of the island, several miles from the city. Our Catalina flying boats and Vickers Vildebeest aren't as glamorous as the planes Henry and Dale fly, worse luck. But we've been promised Beaufighters next year, and I hope to learn to fly on them. Until then I've been assigned to maintenance, but I like fiddling with engines. Perhaps after the war, I'll do an engineering degree.

The only enemies we have here are the mosquitos and fruit flies which bring up large white blisters on your legs, not to mention a few snakes. I'm not too keen on prickly heat either or the ants which appear from nowhere if you drop so much as a crumb. Apart from that, this is the life.

We have plenty of time for R and R. Some of us like fishing in the Punggol lakes, or we go off to the Singapore Swimming Club which is quite modern, much warmer than the bathing pool back home. I don't think I'll ever be able to enjoy swimming in that freezing water again. Diving from the high board into a warm bath takes the biscuit.

There are quite a few Aussie and Kiwi servicemen over here. You can't avoid them in Happy World; the Chinese version of our Wonderland. It has cabaret, circus and entertainments you've never heard of, like Wayang, a kind of street opera with puppets and dancers. You have to see it to believe it.

The Aussies call me a Pom, even though I say I'm not, but they're good mates. Maybe one day I'll get to Sydney. Anyway, we enjoy a few bevvies; I thought the Brits could drink, but they have nothing on the ANZACs. The food here is something else. If you ever get the chance to eat Chinese, do. Indian food is a bit too spicy for me, but I'm learning.

Don't worry about me, Ma. I'm having the time of my life but feeling guilty that I'm not bombing the hell out of Germany, which is what I signed up to do.

If I could send you one thing, it would be a white, frangipani flower. Some of the Singapore girls wear them in their hair, and they smell delicious. But I shouldn't tell my mother that.

Love to Henry and Dale when you next speak to them. Glen.

Sadie read it through three times, her mood growing lighter each time. 'He's happy and safe, that's all that matters,' she said, hugging the letter to her, before laughing. 'Does he think I've never eaten Chinese, nor seen a Chinese entertainment? Not here perhaps, but in Melbourne.' The memory of her visit to China Town flooded back.

She'd been terrified. The stories in the newspapers were all about opium and gambling dens, but her husband always delighted in shocking her, demanding she accompany him one evening to China Town. She tried refusing, but he never took 'no' for an answer. It was a tiny restaurant just off Lonsdale in Little Bourke Street; everything was coloured red. Red and gold. There were no other white people there, at least she didn't think so at first. She'd held his hand like a vice until she became entranced by the smells emanating from the kitchen. She remembered dressing in a long black skirt, an old cardigan and a veiled hat but still felt conspicuous. As she gained enough confidence to look around, she noticed one or two other white girls with young men.

'See, it's not so strange,' he whispered, winking at her.

How many times had he eaten there, Sadie wondered? He appeared to know his way around the menu, and the old lady greeted him like a long-lost friend. She began to relax and allow herself to be seduced by the strange flavours in a long line of dishes. Most she liked, but she baulked at sea slugs. She tried eating with chopsticks but had smuggled a knife and fork into her reticule. She quickly resorted to them while Frank impressed her with his skill in using chopsticks.

At the end of the meal, they walked out of the restaurant, happy and relaxed. Slipping back into Lonsdale Street, he hailed a taxi to take them home.

'You enjoyed it, didn't you?' Frank asked.

'I did.' She smiled at him and touched his face.

'You should do that more often.' He kissed her cheek, and she found herself wanting him.

'I'll try, Frank.' He nuzzled her ear.

'Frank, remember the driver,' she protested.

'Damn the driver. He's seen it all before.'

By the time they reached home, Frank had been too eager to wait until they were upstairs. He had taken her on the sitting room floor, solicitous enough to pile cushions beneath her that time. Glen was conceived that night, and she found herself almost loving her husband again.

Sadie sat back in her chair, other memories of Frank seeped in where she had spent years suppressing them. There were some good nights, more than some. Sadie sighed. Perhaps she should begin to face her demons. She had married the wrong man, true. Her fault entirely, but she had spent too long harbouring all this blame and guilt. It was time to live again before it was too late.

Chapter Fourteen

Australia
Melbourne, 1914

Nobody expected war, although rumblings were there to read in the papers. Sadie had not long moved into her Carlton house much to her grandmother's disgust.

'What will people think of a young girl living on her own with just a housekeeper?'

'I have my doubts,' her father replied, but I trust young Rob. He will make sure there is no gossip, or he'll have me to answer to. Stanley will be back and forth to Melbourne over the next few months, and he can keep an eye on her. It will be a useful place for him to live as well.'

Stanley was still selling off furniture, plant and other goods and was staying with Sadie when news of war was announced. They sat at breakfast together the morning after, reading the newspaper.

'What does it mean, do you think?'

'Well, the Premier of Victoria has made a statement that we are ready to support the Empire.'

'Will we join the war?'

'I think we already have.'

In fact, later that day, the first shots were fired at a German ship trying to escape through Port Philip Heads before it was forced to return for internment. However, matters lay in limbo while Parliament remained dissolved until planned elections in September.

Sadie sensed the wave of patriotism sweeping the streets of the city. Everywhere one walked or stopped to take coffee, a quiet buzz bubbled in the air. She wondered what Rob thought of it all and looked forward to discussing it when they next took a walk.

He was studying hard for finals in December, and somewhat to her disappointment, spent less time with her than she expected after her move to the city.

'It's because I want to pass with flying colours and get into a good law practice, so we can marry sooner rather than later,' he assured her. There was sense in that. She forced herself to accept it without complaint.

They were both wrapped up against the cold winds; her gloved hand lay on his arm as they sat on a bench in the Fitzroy Gardens, the bare trunks of elms dissecting the clouded sky above. Her chaperone, Mrs Porter, sat to one side, studiously staring off into the distance. Sadie peeked at Rob's face. It appeared grey and tired with burning all that midnight oil. She longed to stroke his cares away. The only chance of gaining a good degree was to put the hours in, how many times had he told her that? She wished he could take some time off for a little fun, but now this war would only add to his worries.

Rob had been quiet and reflective on the tram journey there. That she understood; every man now must be contemplating his duty. It shocked and saddened her to think she might lose him to the war, but part of her glowed with pride for her country and the men who would protect them, fighting to save defenceless Belgium.

She loved the peace and beauty of the gardens, but this day was different. Rousing music from the bandstand encouraged a small crowd of Union Jack flag-waving individuals. Humming along with them, she hardly dared ask the question that was burning on her lips.

'They say it might be over by Christmas,' she attempted to draw him out.

'I think we must all pray that it is. War is a ghastly business.' His face remained inscrutable.

'You think we are right to come to Britain's aid though, don't you?'

'It's very early days. Let's see what happens in the election and what the government intends to do.'

Mrs Porter's presence made conversation difficult, as kindly as she was. Sadie imagined that Rob did not want to burden his fiancée with the thought that he might have to leave her. Her heart beat with a mixture of emotions. When he suggested going for afternoon tea to get warm, she accepted, and they walked towards Collins Street as on any other winter Saturday. Small-talk about family, sport and studies allowed no room for any more serious discussion. If that was what he preferred, she fell in with it, grateful to be with him, longing to steal a kiss somewhere, to feel his arm encircle her waist. Sometimes she felt like an overripe peach, hanging by a whisker from a tree. A small breath from Rob on her cheek would send her tumbling down to burst open on the ground. Overwrought, her grandmother would say, but she did not know what to do with her longings. Perhaps there would be dancing at the Mia Mia tea rooms.

Action came much sooner than she expected. The Australian fleet sailed out to take part of Guinea from the Germans, barely a week later. By the middle of September, news came that they had landed and overcome the enemy, with the loss of two officers and two sailors. Stanley raised a toast to celebrate the victory. He was preparing to leave for Adelaide, his work in Melbourne complete.

'I shall miss the Yarra Valley,' Sadie said.

'Go out to Lilydale and ride once a week, Olive will be happy to see you. Will you be too lonely here, Sis? At least come to Adelaide for the Christmas holidays. Rob will be going to his parents, won't he?'

She already felt lonely. If she saw Rob once a week, she was lucky. Even then she could sense him being elsewhere, lost in a law book, his head full of the most boring case law probably. 'I'd like to see Adelaide, so I think I may join you.'

'Did you know your friend, Lucy, is back in Melbourne? I saw it mentioned in the paper a day or two ago. I forgot to tell you.'

'Is she?' Sadie's heart soared. They had been inseparable until Lucy's father was transferred back to England. 'I wonder where she's living?' At first, they wrote to each other weekly, then monthly, but it must be two years since any letter had arrived.

'Why don't I ask Keith Murdoch? If he doesn't know, someone at the Herald will.'

Sadie sat in the teashop at the Savoy waiting for her friend to appear and then there she was, unmistakeable, elegant, swept-up blonde hair, half-hidden beneath a wide-brimmed hat, freckles disguised under light powder and a maid trailing in her wake. A few years ago, Sadie would have squealed with excitement. Now she half-stood and took her friend's kid-gloved hand with the lightest of touches and smiled, not polite and thin-lipped but the widest one she could muster.

'Sadie, you look stunning, I love that lilac outfit, tell me where you got it and is this a ring I feel under your glove?' Lucy laughed, not a tinkling ladylike laugh, impish, deep-throated.

'I missed you. Why ever did we lose touch?'

Lucy's shoulders rose a fraction. 'You know how it is. I didn't think I would ever see Melbourne again and you were never likely to visit London. Friendships come and go, but now I'm back for the duration.'

'But why?'

'In disgrace. I told my dearest mama and papa that if we were to go to war, I would run away to become a nurse. My brothers are both in the army. Why should they have all the fun? The next thing I knew was that Mama had arranged passage back here for me with a chaperone, out of temptation's way. I'm living with my aunt, who is sweet and good fun. You must meet her.' She paused while the waitress took their order. 'But is that a ring on your finger?'

Sadie smiled and removed her glove. 'I know it's tiny, but Rob says he will buy me a new one when he can. I've grown quite attached to it, though. It was his grandmother's.'

'I might have known. From your letters, I knew Rob was always determined to land you. But don't you find him a little too serious? I like my men more dashing. Perhaps he is more dashing than you described. I can't wait to meet him.' That laugh again, a mixture of mischievous and devil-may-care.

'I love him, have loved him for four years.' Sadie did not need to explain herself.

'I know you do; your letters were always full of him. When is the wedding?'

'Two maybe three years.'

'That long!' Lucy sat back in surprise.

'He's graduating this summer and then needs to find a good job.'

'But how can you bear it? If I can't be a nurse, I aim to find a husband and be married by the time I'm twenty-one.'

Sadie's turn to laugh this time. 'You don't change, Lucy, always looking for fun and adventure, but marriage is a serious business.'

'Of course, it is, my darling. He needs the ability to dance, have superb social contacts and deep pockets. That's what my Mama says. I was presented at court you know. Had this procession of young men calling with all with those attributes, but so boring. There's one thing about men here; I don't find them boring at all.'

'Why not?'

'They lack the pretention and stuffiness of the English upper classes.'

'Their mamas don't.'

'I don't mean to marry their mamas. In any case, a granddaughter of a baronet, and daughter of a senior diplomat is more than a match, don't you think?'

She displayed such confidence. That was new and enviable.

Lucy continued, 'Men here are manlier, more striking, more amusing.'

'How many have you met in the days since you arrived?' Lucy always had a sense of the ridiculous, but she was overdoing it now.

'Oh, lots. I have attended at least five soirées since I arrived. My aunt is well-connected. I'm going to one on Friday. Why don't I wangle an invitation for you and Rob?'

'He's studying for his finals. I can't tear him away from his books at the moment.'

'See, far too serious, what a shame.'

'But Stanley could take me. He's here for another week.' What had possessed her other than a need for some fun? Nor did she want to appear tedious to Lucy. Having her back in her life would fill a hole.

'Now Stanley, I like. All those hours in a saddle and all that land.'

'The land's gone, Lucy. Papa's moving his business to Adelaide. That's where he's based now.' Lucy might baulk at someone solely in trade, for all her fine words about manliness.

'I'll send you an invitation.'

Sadie dropped a note to Rob telling him about the dance. Was she hoping he would agree to take her? He replied that she hoped she would enjoy herself but not too much. She smiled at his words of love and how much he was missing her. After New Year, he wrote, he was going to pay her so much attention that she would get tired of him. Never, that was never going to happen. She kissed the words on the letter with its strong, copperplate lettering. She could see his long fingers, maybe an ink spot or two, caressing the paper with his pen. Dark hairs on his wrists, his cuffs riding above them. Hairs she longed to touch, to stroke.

Stanley drove them to an address in Fitzroy.

'What a grand house! I feel nervous. What if the hostess looks down on us?' Sadie said, clutching Stanley's arm.

'A friend of dear Lucy's, I believe.' The hostess greeted her. 'You attended Stratherne College together, Lucy says?' It was enough of an entrée.

Stanley introduced her to Keith Murdoch.

'I have you to thank for finding Lucy for me,' she said.

'M-my pleasure, Miss Timmins.' A slight stammer hindered his reply. Nearing thirty, he had a rather stern face Sadie thought, along with an aura of authority. Her brother thought him very sound and well regarded by the new Labor Prime Minister, Andrew Fisher.

'He hopes to be appointed war correspondent; he's up against Charles Bean,' Stanley whispered, while Keith Murdoch had turned away to speak to their hostess.

When he turned back, Sadie smiled at him with respect.

'Perhaps, I may have the honour of a dance, Miss Timmins?'

'I should be delighted, Sir.'

After engaging in small talk for a while as they danced, she asked, 'I thought the first soldiers were due to set sail for the front by the end of September. Do you have any news, Mr Murdoch?'

'We must be careful who we talk to about such things, Miss Timmins. There may be spies about.'

She flushed. 'I didn't think. Do you really believe there are men and women here in Australia who would betray our secrets?'

'The government appear to think so.'

'But who?' She stumbled to think.

'Irish Home Rulers, and we have a large German population in South Australia.'

She interrupted, 'but they've been there for years and years.'

'Revolutionaries, Japanese, the list is endless.'

'Are you teasing me, Mr Murdoch?'

'Not at all. Mark my words. People who don't toe the line or talk too much will come under suspicion. We'll see German signage coming down, people changing their names, maybe even interred. It's already beginning to happen in Britain. Fear is one of the most dangerous weapons in war, and fear breeds hatred.'

Sadie was still in two minds about whether he was teasing her when the music stopped. He made it sound plausible, but it seemed un-Australian.

'Too earnest, Sadie dear.' Lucy walked over at the end of their dance. 'You need someone frivolous to cheer you up.'

'I found him quite unsettling. Although he is the one who told me where you lived, so for that I am grateful.'

'Ah, here's someone more like it. What a handsome fellow.'

'Miss Timmins, what a pleasure it is to see you. Rob not with you?'

'No, Mr Tinsdale, Stanley brought me. Do you know Lucy St Vincent?'

'Frank please, don't be so formal, Sadie. We've known each other forever.'

'Well not quite forever. Lucy, Frank's uncle was in partnership with my father. Frank and his family have stayed at Chateau Yering.'

'How nice to meet you, Miss St Vincent, I haven't seen you before; I don't believe.'

'Sadie and I went to school together, but then I returned to England, until recently.'

'Perhaps I could book you both for dances later.'

Lucy and Sadie gave him their dance cards before he left to find himself a drink.

'Do tell, dear. I want to know all about him. Now he exudes manliness.' She drawled on *exudes*, letting the word linger on her tongue.

'He fails your criteria on one important point, Lucy. His pockets are shallow, very shallow indeed. But he is handsome; I'll give you that.'

'Quelle domage! So, he'll just be for fun then.' Sadie could swear she smirked.

Frank was every bit as charming as Sadie remembered from the New Year's Eve Dance, almost four years earlier. Dancing with him was entertaining: he kept his conversation light-hearted, an antidote to Rob's studious solemnity over the last year. He knew of their engagement and gently mocked her for not waiting for him, but she did not take him seriously, only flattered by his attention. Lucy and she joked about it.

'He pays the same attention to all the ladies.' Sadie said.

'Maybe. But I noticed Frank's eyes following you, even when he was dancing with me.'

'Nonsense. He knows I'm engaged.' Sadie shrugged it off.

After a number of such dances and parties over the following month, with Rob still making excuses and Stanley seven hundred miles away, Sadie was surprised one afternoon by a visit from her grandmother. As the door opened, she put down her book, borrowed from the lending library, forcing her mouth into a smile of welcome.

'I thought I'd better see how you were getting on, now that you are living here on your own.'

'I have Mrs Porter living with me and my maid, Grandma.'

'But not a relative, no one to guide you. I hear that Lucy St Vincent is back in town. Have you seen her?'

Sadie knew someone had gossiped to her grandmother. Her name had appeared in the Society columns more than once, and although Grandma did not read the papers, one of her daughters would have read it out to her. She should have known this visit would be the result.

'Yes Grandma, several times.'

'I always thought her wayward, not a good influence.'

'She's very well connected.'

'That's as may be, and if Rob were accompanying you to these parties, I would have nothing to complain about. But there you are, in the papers, unaccompanied.'

'Lucy's aunt is chaperoning me.'

'You have a choice, and your Papa agrees, either I chaperone you in future, although the thought of it makes me shudder, or you go to Adelaide.'

'I am going to Adelaide for the holidays.'

'Not in a month, next week.'

Grandma roamed Sadie's parlour, picking up invitations from the mantlepiece, scanning them as though she could read them, then to the table beside Sadie's chair, picking up her book, replacing it. Only sitting when the maid brought in a tray of tea things.

Sadie's teeth were on edge, but as a trained hostess, she poured tea and offered her grandmother a fresh-baked biscuit.

'What does Rob think of all this gadding about?'

'He's working so hard at his studies that he has only one afternoon free a week. He's given me his blessing. I wouldn't have accepted otherwise.' She tried not to sound as though she were anything other than a grown woman. Why did Granny always make her feel like a naughty schoolgirl?

When the maid closed the door, Grandma leaned forward in her chair. 'Sadie, you remind me of your mother so much, a fine woman, but passionate. Being both passionate and a single woman is a recipe for disaster.'

'But I'm not single, I am betrothed,' Sadie replied in defiance.

'Well act like it. I'm not in favour of long engagements. They can lead to...' Her grandmother paused searching for a word, 'certain feelings, longings. Ladies of a passionate nature can be led astray and thereby lose their good name. Rob can't afford a wife without a good name. You don't want that.'

All Sadie's resolve to outwit the old lady crumbled. She thought of the book she was reading where a daughter had defied her parents and brought herself to the brink of disaster because of an unsuitable young man. That wasn't her. She had no wish other than to marry Rob and be the wife he deserved.

'I'm sorry Grandma. I'll decline those invitations, but please let me stay in Melbourne. I can't bear not to see Rob until February. That's three months away.'

Three weeks later, she stood on the platform at Spencer Street Station to wave goodbye to Rob. Mrs Porter stood a few feet behind, giving them some discreet privacy. His final exams over, he was going home to spend

Christmas and New Year with his family. She intended to board ship for Adelaide the following day.

'I'm sorry I've been such a grouch these last few months. I have a great deal of thinking to do about our future, but we'll talk about that in February, my love.' He put his arm around her and squeezed gently. Then he pecked her on the cheek before lifting his cases to board the train.

'Have a good rest and get plenty of fresh air,' she said, not liking the way his face appeared drained of colour.

He stood at the open window, his expression a mixture of love and weariness raised tears in her own. Two months apart, but why should she complain when other young men were forsaking their sweethearts for months to go to war? That was a situation she could well find herself in at the end of the summer. That they had not talked about the possibility made her sure that that is what he intended. He was going home to tell his parents he was about to enlist. Pride and sorrow mingled in her breast as the train began to move off. Waving madly, she watched his dear face slowly disappear.

Chapter Fifteen

Australia
Adelaide, 1914

Being reunited with her Papa and her brothers was enough of a blessing to distract Sadie from missing Rob. Adelaide itself, once they crossed the River Torrens, looked a gracious and elegant city. Papa had taken the National Mutual building in Victoria Square as his office and a house on East Terrace. He was as busy as ever with a new contract to build Port Adelaide's tramway but smarting from missing out on the contract to finish off the Trans-Australian Railway earlier in the year.

'I don't know how Smith managed it. They say my tender wasn't received, but I know it was. Something fishy went on, I'm sure. Mr Verran, the Labor leader, recommended me, but the minister never got to hear about my offer.'

'Oh Papa, I'm sure other contracts will come up.' Sadie attempted to mollify her father.

'Maybe, but with this war, who knows? Now they are complaining I'm not using local labour, but if they want the work done quickly and at low cost, I need to use experienced men. It's not as though they don't know I will deliver what I promise.' He took a sip of whisky and sighed. 'Ah well, no doubt it will all pan out in the end. Enough of me. How's that young man of yours?'

Sadie told him about their final conversation at the station.

'Well, if he decides to do his duty, good for him.'

'I want to get married before he goes, Papa. I couldn't bear it if we didn't.'

His face softened. 'That's up to you both, my dear. I wouldn't say no. It's good for a soldier to have a wife waiting at home. Might make him think before doing something too risky.'

'Thank you, Papa. I do miss you.' She kissed his cheek.

'And I you. You are so like your Mama, beautiful, loving and caring. Rob is a lucky man.' He blinked, his grey eyes screwed up momentarily against a single hint of moisture.

Eight years and two wives later and he still missed Mama. Sadie's heart contracted.

Caro did her best to ignore Sadie, although outwardly, she was polite. Their relationship had moved from frigidity to indifference, which suited the younger woman. Although Caro appeared to be much taken up with her five-year-old son, Sadie suspected it was an act. The boy's eyes followed her around the room with a mixture of longing and regret. Poor Oliver, she thought, vowing to spend time with her youngest brother. He deserved to be loved as much as Eddie, who at fifteen, sensed the adoration of the little boy and played along with it.

Sadie explored Adelaide over the following days. First Christmas shopping in Rundle Street, then once her packages were delivered and wrapped, she ventured further. The botanical gardens with their exquisite glass palm house became a favourite haunt.

'I wish there were such a building in Fitzroy Gardens,' she wrote to Rob. 'Imagine a perfectly sophisticated building of blue and white glass, two wings with a central atrium catching all the light. I adore it. It may be too hot to sit in at this time of year, but in the winter, it would be sublime.'

On other trips, she took her brother, Oliver, to the beach at Glenelg. He loved the tram and lapped up the dish of ice cream she bought him before the return journey. He seemed a lonely little boy and chattered avidly about starting school after the summer holidays. As he snuck his hand into hers, she began to long for a son of her own son to treat.

One day Stanley invited her to a meeting.

'What kind of meeting?'

'A recruitment meeting. There will be speakers there.'

Stanley was considering enlisting! She wanted to hug him out of fear. He was her closest ally, the one she always turned to, especially since Mama died. People said the war would be over by Christmas, but it was not going to happen. It was only just dawning on everyone that this could be a long and bitter battle. What if both Stanley and Rob were to go? How would she bear it? But should she hold either of them back for selfish reasons? Her heart beat with a mixture of emotions, but she had no idea how she could come to terms with losing her brother or her fiancé to war.

The meeting was in a church hall. Sadie had chosen to wear a sober skirt and blouse, and they sat amongst similarly attired men and women. An air of expectation and tension permeated the hall, bare but for rows of wooden chairs and a table at the back laden with teacups and saucers. The early evening air was stifling, and a few women wafted fans around their faces in a vain attempt to cool down. Although many were chattering, Sadie watched the faces of the women; mothers, sisters, girlfriends she guessed. Some glowed with pride, others furrowed with trepidation. One mother grasped her boy's arm tightly as if to prevent him from leaving her side.

Nearing the half-hour, two men, one in a dog collar, one in uniform, and a well-dressed lady walked up the aisle towards a table at the front, set with a carafe of iced water and three glasses. The man in uniform and the lady sat down, their expressions funereal as they weighed up their audience. Sadie shivered despite the heat.

'Thank you, ladies and gentlemen, for heeding the call to this meeting. We want to talk to you about the progress of the war and how each of you can help. My name is Mr Turner, and I am here to introduce to you Colonel Adams and Lady Fletcher.

Colonel Adams stood and walked in front of the table.

'It's not easy being a soldier,' he began in a modulated voice. 'I should know. I saw service in the Boer War, as did some of your fathers.' He paused to let that sink in. 'They would know that war is dirty, rough, monotonous and dangerous. But when the cause is right, as it most definitely is in this case, it is the duty of young, fit men to fight to save their country, isn't it?' He waited for a murmur of agreement to grow until it became a buzz. Some heads were nodding; a few women mopped at their eyes.

The colonel began again, his voice more urgent. 'Lord Baden Powell said a month ago that when the German army invades Britain, it won't be with a kid glove.' His voice began to rise in outrage. 'See what they've done in Belgium to women and children. Hear their piteous screams as their country is raped, my apologies ladies. Now we hear the Boche are firing on ambulances, full of our wounded men; this could be the fate of our brothers and sisters in the Old Country. You and you and you can help stop it.' His finger jabbed at the young men in the room. More heads nodded, but Sadie heard a woman quietly sobbing at the back.

Before beginning again, he puffed out his chest. 'How many of our men here already know how to fire a gun, how to spend hours in the saddle? How many of you have worked tirelessly in factories and the bush for your families? You men are the cream of the Empire. Remember we are British as well as Australian.' Many men began to whistle and cheer. One young man, full of bravado, stood up, only to be pulled back down by his mother.

The colonel carried on in this vein, cajoling, whipping them up, appealing to the Australian sense of fair play. The audience now hung on every word. Sadie slipped her hand into Stanley's palm, drawing strength from him when she wanted to sob for the plight of those poor slaughtered babies. She could feel the tension and energy in the hall, fizzing and buzzing like an electric light about to blow.

Eventually, the colonel sat down to wild applause, and Lady Fletcher stood up.

'Do not think, ladies, that only men must fight this war. We may not be strong of body, may not be called to give our lives but we too have obligations. Firstly, we must be willing to let our husbands, brothers and sweethearts go. We must show that we have the strength to carry on without them and we should encourage other womenfolk to do the same. Secondly, it is your job to rally our troops, to help encourage enlistment.'

Sadie felt as though the speaker was looking at her directly. My duty to send Rob to war, to make that sacrifice, to bear the separation. She must steel herself to do it, however much it hurt.

The woman continued. 'We should scorn the shirkers, the naysayers, the men who say - not me, let someone else go in my place. Is it your man's job to fight for this country in their place? No, it is not. It is every man's job. Thirdly, we need to raise money for our troops and their families. Yes ladies, there will be bake-sales and sock-knitting and all the things we do best. We women of Australia are homemakers, but we are also determined and strong in our own way. Leave us your names, ladies, so that we can call on you when the time is right.'

After the reverend drew proceedings to a close with a prayer, teacups rattled, and with some men already in line at a recruitment table, Sadie and Stanley walked out of the hall.

'Have you decided?' Sadie asked, half-dreading the answer.

'I reckon so, but I'll discuss it with Pops first.'

'You'll get a commission, of course.' Would being an officer make him safer? She hoped so.

Papa rented a house up in the Adelaide Hills for Christmas and New Year. Sadie wanted to treasure every minute of this last carefree time with all her family around her. Plans were afoot, she knew. Stanley spent hours talking to his father, and she suspected it was not going to be as simple as Stanley joining the Light Horse in Adelaide itself. Sadie could only observe the discussions from a distance and wonder what was going on. Despite her best intentions, she couldn't help feeling anxious. Half of her wanted Papa to put his foot down and refuse Stanley permission. But he was of age. He did not need Papa to sign his consent.

The announcement came the day before they were due to return to the city. Stanley was to leave for London at the end of the month, where he would spend some time visiting engineering works and potential suppliers before joining a light cavalry regiment. Sadie offered her congratulations with a kiss on her brother's cheek.

'Do you know which regiment?'

'No, I will have to see which will offer me a commission when I arrive. It's all so uncertain, but Pops has contacts, especially in Lancashire and Yorkshire.'

Bruce joined them on the veranda. 'I wish I was coming with you. I begged Pops to let me go.'

'You're only eighteen, and Papa needs you here,' Sadie said, attempting to console him.

'He says he'll sign the papers when I'm nineteen, but it may all be over by then.'

'I pray that it will. What's Papa going to do without you both?' Despite the heat, a chilling breeze rustled through the gum trees. Sadie drew a shawl over her shoulders. What had seemed so right in that church hall a fortnight before, now held a hint of foreboding. Could the war go beyond September?

Sadie talked to Papa about what she could do to help.

'You, Sadie? Why your job is to stay at home and wait if Rob goes.'

'But I want to do something. Lady Fletcher said we must heed the call when it comes.'

'Ladies of your class will carry on doing what they always do. Knit socks, by all means, attend fundraising events if you have to, but I will not have my daughter making a show of herself.'

'But in England, girls are volunteering to help nurse.'

'That will not be necessary here. Women of your class do not work in hospitals.'

'I don't understand. We have the vote, but we're not allowed to work. In England, women are denied the vote, but they're allowed to do all sorts of work.'

'And look at the disgraceful way the suffragettes have been behaving.' He started shouting at her. 'I have not inched my way up in society, only to see you bring it crashing down. Do you hear? Things are different here. In my opinion, women were granted the vote because the government thought they would temper their husbands' radical tendencies. It wasn't meant to give them any more rights. Far from it. As much as Australian men like to demand their own rights, they won't tolerate it in their womenfolk.'

Sadie had never heard him so angry with her, and she quailed at his voice as he continued.

'If I hear any hint of unbecoming behaviour, you will return here to Adelaide to live.' He broke off before lowering his voice. 'I speak for your own good, Sadie. Maybe I shouldn't have let you live in Carlton alone. Perhaps Mother was right. I have been too lax.' He patted her hand, as though she were a recalcitrant child, not a woman about to send her fiancé off to war. But she dared not go against him.

'Papa, I promise I will not let you down. I love my Carlton house. Please let me stay there.'

'No more talk of volunteering at hospitals or anywhere else for that matter, understood?'

'Yes, Papa.'

His face softened. 'Very well. I know someone who can take you under her wing. Dame Nellie is planning a few concerts as fundraisers. Go and see her, she may need help.'

'Oh, I will, Papa. That sounds like an excellent idea.'

The first Australian and New Zealand troops arrived in Cairo before Christmas in fine form, the newspapers declared. She wasn't sure why they had been sent there, something about liberating people from the Turks. She had a feeling that Papa, by sending Stanley straight to England, was ensuring Stanley stayed away from Egypt. Why would that be? She knew nothing about politics, but her school had instilled pride in the British Empire, the map in every classroom depicting its lands in red swaddling the globe. The Empire on which the sun never set. Perhaps the Turks threatened it. That had never been mentioned in the church hall. The talk had all been about protecting Belgium.

Sadie helped Stanley shop and pack for his voyage, seeking advice about what one should take for a British winter in Catt's gentlemen's clothing department, although by the time he arrived it would be spring.

'Spring in England, if I may say so, Miss, can be no warmer than the coldest of Adelaide winters,' the salesman confided.

'Dear me,' said Sadie. 'We'd best double up on vests then.'

Papa arranged a farewell dinner for his son, men only, at the Prince Alfred Hotel. It must have been a fine evening because she gave up waiting for him and retired knowing that he would need to be up early the next morning. Tomorrow was the day she dreaded, waving off her brother from Port Adelaide. What danger lay ahead of him? And after, was she to do the same for Rob? Her stomach clenched with fear and anxiety.

Chapter Sixteen

'What do you mean you're not joining up? Almost everyone in your class at school has enlisted. It's your duty.'

'I don't believe it is, no. We can't denude our country of a generation of its men. If Australia is to progress it needs young men to build it.'

Sadie stared at Rob, stunned. 'Stanley is on his way there already, and Bruce will go too. Would you tell them they are wrong to their face?'

He shook his head, his expression inscrutable, his words too considered. He should feel shame. Anger simmered inside her. He had delayed his return to Melbourne until the end of February, and she assumed it was to spend more time with his parents before enlisting. Why had she spent another month alone if not for that? Resentment for his absence lay beneath her words.

'Look, Sadie; I have an offer from one of the best law firms in Melbourne. They want me to start next week. It's everything I worked for, what we planned for, surely you must see that.'

She hardly listened. 'Your family hail from Scotland, as did my grandfather. Dame Nellie Melba says we must show our support. Father says it's a chance for Australia to make its mark.'

'And that's a good enough reason to bear arms against another man? To show support!'

'What about Belgium? The stories are horrendous. Dame Nellie has begun a series of benefit concerts in their aid.'

'Much of it propaganda no doubt. You shouldn't listen to Dame Nellie.'

Sadie flinched at his disrespect. 'She was very kind in offering me tea last week at her house in Lilydale. I said I would drum up support for her concerts. Write letters, you know, that sort of thing.'

'I am quite happy for you to do that, a laudable pastime no doubt.' His tone annoyed her, belittled her, reminding her of her father.

She tried another tack. 'I thought you were leaving it until your final exams, that you deserved the summer break after all your hard work. I didn't think you would be a shirker.' Now he looked as though she had slapped him; flecks of anger lit his eyes. His brows drew together in a frown.

'I do not consider myself a shirker. It's not our war, what argument do we have with the Turks for God's sake?'

'Don't blaspheme, Rob. And why did you not return earlier? You left me stewing here, wondering what was going on?'

Spots of colour rose on his cheeks. 'I was trying to talk my brothers out of enlisting, but I failed. Sadie, there's nothing you can say which will change my mind. I have been backwards and forwards over these arguments for weeks, but my mind is made up.' He paused and attempted to take her hand, but she shrugged it away. 'Sadie, darling, don't let us fall out over this. I'm no coward whatever you think. Our future depends on our young men and Turkey is not going to be a walkover, whatever they may say. You may not want to hear this, but I believe it's going to be a long and brutal fight. I hope I'm wrong.'

Sadie's face drained of colour. His brothers were going in his place, and he wasn't ashamed. How could he be so callow? Fighting tears, she countered, 'You admit that you could be wrong. The army needs everyone to do their bit, which includes you.' She sounded shrill, even to her own ears. Take a deep breath she thought, feeling her pulse race.

'Sadie, it sounds as though you have swallowed the recruiting posters.' He pushed a lock of dark brown hair from his face in exasperation. 'I think we should calm down and take a walk outside. It's a bright blue sky and not too cold.'

What drove her to it? Over the following weeks, she had ample time to review this conversation and her actions, but a tight fist of anger in her stomach drove her.

'I can't marry someone who won't fight for his country,' she said, removing the solitaire band from her finger.' The shock on his face as she handed him the ring remained with her long after.

He stared coldly at her. 'I think you need time to reflect, Sadie. I will not take career advice from you. It's apparent to me that we do not agree, but I expect you to change your mind. If you do not, then you are not the woman I thought you to be. Take a few weeks, and then we will discuss it.'

He did not try to talk her round. If he had, would she have given in, taken back her ring, forgiven him as she longed to do? No, he stared long and hard at her, as though she were the one being judged. Then he shrugged his shoulders; his lips sealed themselves shut in a tight line, biting back any words he may have wanted to utter, turned on his heel and left the house. What were those words he thought about saying? Were they more words of anger or love? That they might have been love, tortured her. Once she heard the door close, she threw herself on the couch and sobbed.

As the solitary female in her close family, she had no one to advise her. For days after, she expected him to write to her, took up a pen herself several times, but crumpled up her half-written letters every time. Nothing sounded right. She would not apologise. She did not know how to say sorry and dismissed his reasoning. Was it her fault or his? She swung back and forth, her mind in a turmoil of love and regret. She had convinced herself he would enlist, to the point that not enlisting, appeared to be a betrayal of her as well as his country. Was it also at the back of her mind that if he enlisted, they could marry before he left? To wait another three years was agony.

Sadie didn't even know if he considered them still engaged. She decided not to tell her Papa, hoping it would all be resolved. At tea with Grandma Jane the previous Sunday, she had been telling her how much she was looking forward to Rob's return.

'I am sorry I won't see him, especially if he enlists, although I would think he would be a fool to go. I am taking an extended trip to New South Wales to see my daughter.'

Sadie did not take any notice of her grandmother's views on many topics, but now she wished she had asked her why he would be foolish to go.

She wrote to Lucy, feeling guilty that they had not talked since her grandmother's visit in late November, after which she had excused herself from parties and dances, saying she needed to prepare for her trip to Adelaide. Their friendship had drifted apart once more.

They met in a coffee house off Bourke Street. Sadie sat in a darkened corner because she knew she would resort to tears in the recounting of her heartbreak.

'What did I tell you?' Lucy said. 'He's not dashing enough to be a soldier. Too much of a pen pusher, although I never did get to meet him, did I? Darling, you need some distraction, and there are many delightful young men enlisting in their droves. Two a penny, in fact. Why not have some fun, you deserve it. Rob will still be around if you change your mind and you might. Time enough to beg forgiveness then, don't you think? Why not come to a fundraising dance next week?'

'I'd love to, but I can't have my name in the newspapers.' She explained about her grandmother's visit months before.

'I shall prime my aunt to say you are a visitor from Adelaide. What shall we call you?'

'Miss Smith.' Sadie giggled. 'I hope no one guesses.' She got up to leave. 'Thank you, Lucy, I knew you would raise my spirits.'

Walking back up Collins Street, she passed a brave woman handing out white feathers to every young man, not in uniform.

The dance was a small, select affair. No reporters graced the invitation list, much to Sadie's relief. Half of the men were in uniform, the other half, including Frank she noted, were not.

'Where's Rob?' He asked as he booked her for a dance, looking down at her ringless finger.

She coloured. This was a mistake; I shouldn't have come she thought. How can I explain?

'They argued about enlisting.' Lucy cut in to save her. 'Why are you not in uniform, Frank?'

118

That took the wind from his sails.

Throughout the dance, Frank made Sadie laugh again; he seemed to know how to lift her spirits. Where Rob was serious, Frank was light-hearted, teasing. Sadie found that refreshing. It was what she needed to take away her anguish.

'Do you think I should enlist, Miss Timmins?' Frank quizzed her as he escorted her to the buffet.

Sadie blushed again. She began to say that she wasn't sure and then remembered the woman handing out white feathers. 'Yes,' she said. It's every young man's duty.' She stared at him with resolve. 'Stanley's gone, Bruce will go. Why not you, Frank?'

'If I do, will you write to me? Shall I be your Billy Boy?'

She looked up at his teasing face, tapped his hand with her fan and said, 'Frank, when will you ever learn to be serious?'

A fortnight later, Frank and his mother visited Sadie. He stood there, resplendent in his lieutenant's uniform, passing his officer's hat from one hand to another.

'I'm proud of my son, Sadie dear. He says it was you who convinced him to enlist.'

'I doubt that, Mrs Tinsdale,' Sadie said, dumbfounded.

'Oh, but you did, Miss Timmins,' Frank said, his eyes twinkling. 'If I remember correctly, you were quite impassioned.'

'Well, I have come to invite you to a small celebratory soirée before Frank leaves for training in Tasmania next week. Do say you will attend.'

'Of course, I would be delighted.'

After they left, she sat in confusion. She didn't believe for one minute that Frank had enlisted because of her. He must have already been thinking about it. Secretly, she was pleased that he gave her the credit. If Frank can think of going, why not Rob, who has so much more to offer.

Her maid, Bridie, accompanied her to Mrs Tinsdale's house in Box Hill, but then went to sit with the servants. It was quite a crush. Mrs Tinsdale had invited all of Frank's friends and her acquaintances, who brought their unattached daughters. The house was not large enough for such a throng. The late March air was balmy, and the older ladies quickly began to gravitate towards the wide veranda, leaving enough room for the younger ones to dance. A pianist and violinist began to play, and Frank immediately asked Sadie to dance.

When Frank confessed that he had loved her for years, only biding his time until Rob let her down. He actually said that – let her down – she laughed at him.

'Don't be silly, Frank. You're more like a cousin to me.'

'Never a cousin! Rob can't have loved you enough if he was willing to give you up so easily,' Frank dripped doubt into her ear.

'He hasn't given me up. We are considering our future,' Sadie told him, firmly.

But perhaps Rob had not loved her enough. That doubt would fester in her mind.

Sadie danced with several other young men, but Frank kept returning to her side, begging her to dance again.

It was no hardship to waltz with Frank. Tall with glistening, dark hair and liquid dark brown, almost black eyes, he was by far the most good looking of his circle, not that Rob wasn't handsome too, but in a more understated way. Frank's smile lit his face and began to draw her to him like a moth to the flame. As he moved his hand up her back, his fingers caressed her through the silk dress and sent delicious shivers down her spine. Someone once told her that he had Indian blood, she could believe it. A touch of the exotic laced with the experience of an older man began to have an unsettling effect on her. Why had she never noticed him before? Was he too familiar? But it was no good. He had no fortune and few prospects. And she still loved Rob.

'I'm leaving on Monday, Sadie.'

'Yes, Frank, I know.'

'Will you miss me?'

Part of her would.

'Kiss me goodbye.'

'No, Frank.'

He scurried her through the door onto the veranda, now abandoned as the night had cooled. He took her protesting body in his arms, kissing her passionately. She tried to squirm away, but his tongue forced his way into her mouth, his fingers stroking her neck. She shivered before breaking away, her hand poised to slap him but, at that moment, his mother came to find them.

'I'm sorry, I couldn't resist you any longer. You have me bewitched,' Frank whispered in her ear.

'No, Frank. What you did was wrong,' she whispered back. 'I'm sorry, Mrs Tinsdale, I have to go. Dame Nellie is expecting me early in Lilydale.' A small but expedient lie.

'Thank you so much for coming. I do hope we see you again. Frank thinks the world of you.'

Sadie smiled in confusion. Had his mother seen the kiss? She hoped not. It would not do to raise hopes in that department. Thanking his mother for her hospitality, Sadie collected her maid and bid farewell.

Her dreams that night featured both Frank and Rob, and she awoke in a state of longing and shame, her maid commented on the crumpled sheets.

'Not sleeping, Miss? It can't be the heat; it's been quite chilly at night this week.'

Was it possible to desire two men at the same time, she wondered as she took her morning bath? Frank's kiss, despite its shamefulness, had been more exciting than she was willing to admit. The trouble was they were like chalk and cheese. That sudden frisson she felt with Frank, how could it be set against the safe, quiet calm she felt with Rob? She was relieved that Frank was leaving. No good would come of him staying, but at least he was committed to the war. Was it true that he joined up because of her, or that he loved her?

Chapter Seventeen

Australia
Melbourne, 1915

Dame Nellie was planning a large concert at the Melbourne Town Hall at the end of April, and Sadie threw herself into a frenzy of activity selling tickets, appealing for flags to sell at the concert, anything which the great singer asked of her. Sadie travelled over to Lilydale to see her and to spend the night with Joe Junior at least once a week, leaving her little time for other pursuits. Dances and other parties only brought confusion she decided. She had told Joe about Rob, who advised her to write to him and try and sort out their differences.

'I will,' she said, 'as soon as this concert is over.'

The newspapers were full of somewhere called Gallipoli and the Dardanelles. In the days before the concert, they reported large forces landing and digging in under heavy fire. Sadie prayed the men would stay safe. There were bound to be friends of Stanley there, maybe even of Bruce. She pictured the young men in their uniforms marching through Adelaide to Waltzing Matilda before she left. They had looked so proud and determined.

Joe Junior escorted her to the concert. It was a glittering affair.

'Oh, Joe, isn't she wonderful?' Sadie said, as Dame Nellie finished singing *Les Anges Pleurent*. Tears smarted in her eyes as she looked around the hall. Everyone appeared entranced with Dame Nellie's voice. 'She's going to raise such a lot of money for the poor Belgians.'

'We're lucky to have her as a neighbour,' said her brother. 'She's a true patriot.'

Yes she is, thought Sadie. A patriot.

The concert finished with *There's No Place Like Home*. Sadie's eyes watered. Glancing around, she noticed both men and women dabbing at their eyes with handkerchieves.

On the Monday following the concert, Sadie picked up the Argus to see if there was a report about it. She was intrigued to find out how much money was raised, considering her small part in the affair. But all thought of the concert fled when she saw the photographs of the first casualties from landings in Gallipoli. She read through them, here a lieutenant from Scotch College, there another from Essendon, another from Ballarat, the list went on. Oh, one, a sergeant employed as an office worker in Collins Street had been married the day before sailing. She grieved for his poor wife, married for a single day. Sadie wept for all their families while praying for Stanley's safe return. These men had sacrificed their lives for Rob to stay safe. It wasn't right. It was time to write to her Papa and tell him that she thought she could not marry Rob.

His reply bid her not be hasty.

I'm too busy at the moment, but I will come over to Melbourne, and we can talk it through. Joe says you have been a great help to Dame Nellie. Spend as much time as you can in Lilydale, and don't worry. The course of true love is rarely smooth, as they say. Rob is a good catch. One day he may be a government minister. Think how beneficial that would be for the family. Don't be too harsh on him.

How could she not be harsh when the casualty lists kept on growing? Frank wrote to her from his training camp. He told her how he missed her, begging forgiveness for his presumption. That kiss had disturbed her more than she liked to admit. If she closed her eyes, she could feel his fingers stroking her, taste his lips against hers. She left it a week before replying, then wrote politely, but in a noncommittal tone of trivial matters while accepting his apology. She did not wish to encourage him. He replied telling her how wonderful it was to receive a letter from her and that he missed her. She left it two weeks before her next note. His letters disturbed her, but it was impolite to ignore them when he was giving so much up for his country.

Dame Nellie had a new project; to hold a concert given by a wounded Belgian pianist in Lilydale.

'Such a brave man, my dear. We must support him.'

'Do you think it wrong, Dame Nellie, to refuse to serve your country, if you are fit and able?'

'Without a doubt, Sadie. Thank goodness we have a large number of men volunteering to aid the Empire, but I think we should have conscription. That would be fairer, don't you think? Leave the decision to the authorities on who should go. Too many men are ignoring the call. Why I hear there are whole areas like Richmond, where hardly any men are enlisting. That can't be right.'

Conscription – Sadie thought about it, but somehow it didn't sit right with her. Who would choose? Would rich men be able to bribe the authorities to leave their sons off the list?

Her mind was all over the place, one minute convinced that Rob should have gone, the next reminding herself of her father's words. It was not just that he was *a good catch*, she missed him hugely and the fun they had together, before the war soured everything.

She decided to write to Rob. Asking him for more time would at least require a response. It had been nearly three months since she broke up with him. Why hadn't he tried to mend things with her? She thought he would have made an effort considering how long they had been together. His stubbornness more than matched hers.

He wrote back within hours.

My dear Sadie,

I was beginning to give up hope, but your letter gives me reason to think that not all is lost. I have thrown myself into my work to distract myself from daydreaming about you. I will continue to wait but not for too much longer. If I haven't heard from you by the end of July, I will assume the worst, but I'm sure by then you will have understood my reasoning for not enlisting. My place is here, working for a better future for our country. Look beyond the reports of glory in the newspapers and understand the desperate situation of the men in Gallipoli. Would you really wish me there? Rob

A few weeks grace he had given her, and his words were not of love, nor of apology. He was expecting her to change her mind, the husband's right to expect support from his wife. There was to be no meeting half-way, no attempt to cajole her into accepting his point of view. She threw the note down in irritation.

When she read the letters from the front in the newspapers, she didn't see the desperation. She read of the boys' unfailing sense of a job well done; of humour in the face of a barrage of bullets and shrapnel; of pride in their fallen comrades and the muted heroism of others. Billy Khaki, the editors, called them, these letter writers who wrote 'come quickly or you'll miss all the fun.' She read of women who were paying their own passage to Egypt to volunteer as nurses with no idea they would be accepted. Had their fathers given permission or had they defied them? She admired their bravery.

Lucy wrote her a note in early July.

Shall we have some fun, Sadie? It might help you to make up your mind between worthy and boring or dashing and heroic – you know who I mean.

There's a meeting of the Women's Peace Army on the 8th. I'm all agog, but totally opposed, of course; my brothers are soldiers after all. Let's go incognito to hear what it's all about. I hear Adela Pankhurst is to grace the meeting.

Trust Lucy to stir things up, but Sadie was intrigued to hear the other side of the argument. Like her friend, Sadie's loyalty would always be to her brothers.

'Did you ever go to a suffragette meeting in England?' Sadie asked Lucy as they took their seats in the crowded hall.

'Not for want of trying. I saw them marching with their banners, but Mama would have chained me to the bedpost if ever I dreamed of sneaking out to a meeting.' Both Sadie and Lucy wore veiled hats, hoping no reporter would recognise them. 'What do you know of Vida Goldstein?'

125

'I've never met her. I think Dame Nellie knew her when she was a child. I'm sure they would have disliked each other. I'm excited to hear Miss Goldstein talk. She's famous for fighting for women's equality and even stood for parliament. I think it's outrageous that you can't vote in England. Whatever are they scared of?'

Lucy shrugged. 'The British establishment is full of men of little imagination and tinier brains, my father says.'

'He must support women's suffrage then.' Sadie ventured.

'Absolutely not! The thought fills him with terror. Men are strange creatures, don't you think?'

The hall was filled to capacity as the speakers filed to the front. It was the first time that Sadie had set eyes on Miss Goldstein, a handsome if severe-looking woman in her mid-forties.

'Look, there's Adela Pankhurst,' Lucy pointed to a younger woman. I've seen her with her sisters.' Several heads turned to watch her walk towards the front.

'Papa told me that Australian men wouldn't stand for women speaking up, but it's not true, is it? Look at all these ladies!'

'It helps to be unmarried, of a certain age and with a face like a trout.' Lucy giggled as a woman in front turned to glare at her.

The atmosphere was different from the recruitment meeting in Adelaide. It was more excitable than tense, more lively than nervous. As the speeches progressed, Sadie found herself agreeing that wars should be opposed. What woman wanted to send her sons to war? But it didn't answer the question about what to do in the face of evil? The Belgians hadn't asked to be invaded.

'What did you think?' Lucy asked as they got up to leave.

'I won't be joining their peace army. They're very worthy and principled, but they won't achieve anything. Men hold all the power, don't they? If men want wars, they will have them.'

'I mean, has it helped you make up your mind about Rob?'

'Possibly. I can understand his opposition to the war better, I think.'

The first casualties from Gallipoli arrived home later that month. Sadie took the tram to Port Melbourne, meeting Lucy there along with many other women to cheer them home. Lucy's carefree attitude had been tempered by news of the death of one of her cousins at Gallipoli. Her mother now wanted her home, but the threat of German torpedoes put an end to that idea.

'Frank is back in Melbourne, ready to embark in a couple of weeks. He was asking after you at Lady Lennox's fundraiser last night. I told him you'd become a grouch and refused all invitations.'

'That's because he took advantage of me on the evening of his leaving party.'

'Did he? How ungentlemanly. Be careful, Sadie. I have a feeling about him.'

'No, he's harmless enough. I like him most of the time.'

'Really! He's a trained killer, don't you know.' Lucy burst into laughter. 'Seriously, he said he was going to call on you. I told him he should not, with your housekeeper being away at her daughter's. He'll probably write you a note.'

The sight of the first men to leave the ship profoundly shocked them both. Men without legs or arms, bandages across eyes, cripples in wheelchairs or with sticks, their livelihoods likely lost forever. The cheers of the crowd dissipated to groans and cries until the effect they were having on the men dawned on the women, and they began to cheer again. Nurses accompanied some of the men, and Lucy turned to Sadie.

'I should be there in uniform, not dressed for parties and dances. Damn Mother and her propriety. I have a good mind to go back to England on the first ship and volunteer, without her permission. I'm twenty-one after all. Did you read Dame Nellie's letter to your countrywomen about sacrifice? It was so moving. This brings it home doesn't it?' Her eyes glistened with tears.

'It does. I wish I could do more. Dame Nellie is leaving soon, and I need to make a decision. Either I take Rob back or return to Adelaide. Father has given me an ultimatum.'

Lucy held her hand. 'Do what makes you happy, Sadie. Life's too short not to be happy.'

Sadie spent the early afternoon penning a letter to Rob. The sight of those injured men had affected her. She was beginning the think the price too high for a far-off war. Australia was certain to be the poorer for the loss

127

of all these young men. This was only the start of repatriations. How many more would return incapacitated?

Sadie wrote that she needed to talk to Rob and asked him to call on her that evening. As soon as she saw him, she would know if her feelings were still the same. If they were, she would apologise and beg him to take her back. If not, then she would wish him well and say goodbye. The tension in her body was becoming unbearable. She didn't doubt he would come. Rob's sense of propriety would leave him no choice.

All evening she sat waiting, but he didn't make an appearance. Perhaps he's out of town, she thought, but a seed of doubt settled in her gut. Had he fallen out of love with her? No letter arrived in the morning from him. Her nerves grew taut with disquiet.

She cancelled her plans to go to Lilydale, hoping he would call during the day. As Sadie ate a lunch of cold cuts which had been left for her, a knock sounded at the front door. She stood, a sense of relief swept through her, knowing that she must love Rob to be this excited to see him. After wiping her hands on her serviette, she walked as calmly as she could down her hallway.

She opened the heavy wooden door and was disheartened to see Frank standing there alone, even more handsome than the last time she saw him. Hard work and army rations had honed his body and chiselled his face. It suited him, but he did not make her heart flutter. He wasn't Rob.

'My housekeeper's not here, Frank. I'm sorry, but you can't come in,' she said, attempting to disguise the disappointment in her voice.

'I have to see you, Sadie. It can't wait a moment longer. I hoped you would be at Lady Lennox's.' He took her hand and pulled her into the house.

'Frank, my maid is not here either. I sent her out on some errands. You must go. Think of my reputation.'

Something calculating flickered in his eyes as he pushed the door to with his foot.

Sadie protested, but before she had a chance to open the door for Frank to leave, he fell on his knees, right there in the hall and asked her to marry him. She almost laughed, her nerves jangling. This wasn't right; it was not supposed to be this way, not with this man. From his pocket, he produced a special licence and a ring with a huge opal surrounded by diamonds. He grabbed her hand and forced the ring on to her finger as she attempted to draw back.

'Once we've beaten the Turks and the Boche, we'll have a wonderful life together. I've got big plans you know. People will be desperate for fun once this war is over and I aim to provide it. You and me, we'll be great together.'

'But I have given you no cause to think we could be married, Frank. This is preposterous. I'm expecting to make up with Rob.'

'You wrote to me in Tasmania. No girl does that unless she has feelings for a man. I told my fellow officers you were my sweetheart.'

'You did?' Sadie's confusion grew. Was it her fault that this was happening? 'No Frank, I'm sorry if I gave you any hope.'

'I told Mother what I intended, and she insisted you have her ring. She's so delighted that she's sent a telegram to Uncle George in Adelaide.'

'Then my father will know,' she stammered.

'Probably. He'll know soon enough in any case. My mother is putting an announcement in the evening paper as soon as she hears.'

'Before you'd even asked me? She can't do that.'

'Why ever not?' A look of anger swept his face.

'It's too soon. I haven't agreed?' What if Rob were to arrive now? How would she explain herself? She began to shake with distress.

'A war's on for God's sake. People will understand.' He grasped her wrist and drew her to him then hungrily sought her mouth. 'You don't know how long I have wanted to do that,' he whispered before kissing her again.'

'No, Frank. This isn't right. I want you to leave.' She struggled, but he held her fast.

'Sadie, my love, do you know how I have longed for you, how I've dreamt of you? You can't send me to war without marrying me first. I enlisted for you.'

Guilt stopped her struggles. Was she to blame for this situation? As his mouth covered hers once more, confusion reigned in her head. Her mind went numb as she shrank into herself.

'Rob never kissed you like this, did he? He never did this to you, or this.' Frank played her; his fingers were everywhere as he picked her up and carried her limp body to the couch in the parlour.

'No, not like this Frank, please.' She began to struggle once more, kicking at his shins with her heels, but he was not to be deterred. He pinned her down, his chest heavy across hers while snatching at her clothes with the other.

She did not have the strength to resist him. Somewhere at the back of her mind, she knew that this was not his first time, nor even his second. It was no use willing her maid to return. As his fingers crept under her bloomers and began to massage the skin of her belly, she gave in. Marriage to Frank had become inevitable. No other man would want her now. She was sullied, and while shame flamed her cheeks, her mind sought rescue from this nightmare.

If she were to marry this man, their first time must not be rape. That would destroy her. No marriage should begin on that basis. Opening her eyes wide to engage his, she took a deep breath before saying, 'Frank, yes, I will marry you, but do not force me. Can we not wait for our wedding night?'

His face was flushed with desire, his pupils large enough to drown in, his breathing fast and urgent but he stayed his hand momentarily.

'No Sadie, I can't wait,' he groaned. 'We have so few days left to us before I embark. What difference do ten days make, my darling? Everything changes in wartime.'

Now that she had stopped fighting him, he began to make love to her. She allowed his expert hands to caress her skin. Closing her eyes, she surrendered to his touch, allowed herself to take pleasure from his fingers. It was as though she was looking down from above on two strangers engaged in intercourse. Perversely it gave her back control. Bitter though this was, Frank was going to be her husband, and she had to learn how to love him. The physical attraction was a point she could build from. She began to lose herself in his lovemaking; the animal cries were not hers, the shudders of satisfaction must belong to someone else. She glimpsed the triumph on his face as her body arched and she moaned, then adeptly, he entered her and rammed his body into hers until he spasmed and cried out.

130

Later, after he left to announce the wedding, she sat shaking in her chair. Confused and upset, anger raged through her mind. The whole experience lasted barely twenty minutes, but Frank had used that time to wreck her life. She looked down at her dress, seeing it stained and torn. No one must find me like this, she thought. Hurriedly, she tidied the room then stumbled into the bathroom to wash and change her clothes, surprised to see a smear of blood on her silk bloomers. Grasping the sink, she stared at her reflection in the mirror. Her face was flushed, mussed dark tendrils of hair clung to her cheeks, an angry bruise marked her breast where he had pinched it. She lifted her hand to touch it and smelt him on her skin. She turned to the bath and ran the hot tap on full. As steam filled the air, the mirror clouded, and her image began to disappear. She imagined herself being rubbed out, then scored her hands over the smooth surface. 'You are going to get through this,' she told herself. 'You are strong; you will get through this.'

She soaked in the bath, stroking herself, still feeling the sensation his hands left on her skin. Was she wicked to give herself to him? If she had continued to fight, she knew the outcome would have been the same. Had she the stomach to forgive him? The cooling water began to calm her. As she began to drift off, she wondered what it would be like to be married to Frank? Would it be fun, as he promised? Her hand stroked the skin around her nipples. She was going to have to get used to his touch, even welcome it. She would learn to do it. What other option was there? Salty tears fell into the water as she saw all her plans dissolve and reform into something intangible, unfathomable.

The maid tapped on the door. 'Miss, your grandmother is in the sitting room and wants to talk to you.'

What! Oh no, the last person she wanted to see. The news was spreading obviously. She climbed out of the cold water, astonished that she had slept for so long, and rubbed herself vigorously, as though her grandmother might see the guilty evidence beneath her clothes.

Five minutes later, Sadie tentatively opened the door to her sitting room. Her grandmother was seated, staring at the door, waiting to pounce, a telegram in her hand.

'Your father has cabled me. He demands to know what's going on. Is it true? You've broken your engagement to Rob Fraser and are to be married to Frank Tinsdale. Are you out of your mind, girl?'

'Rob and I haven't seen each other for five months. My father knows that. Frank is about to embark for the front and he...' What could she say, when she was only just coming to terms with what had happened?

'Rob's worth ten of Frank Tinsdale. He's going places, and you girl will go with him. Don't be so foolish as to give him up because he won't enlist. We don't owe the Old Country anything.'

'It's too late.'

'There's no too late about it, at least until you say the wedding vows. Your father is disappointed with you, but he'll catch a train over to help you sort it out with Rob.'

'No, it really is too late.'

Her grandmother stared at her hard. 'You stupid girl, he's had you, hasn't he?' Seeing no denial on Sadie's face, only shame, she paused then said in resignation. 'Well you've made your bed, so you must lie in it.'

Sadie cast her eyes down to the floor, her grandmother's withering gaze breaking her composure. 'I did not say yes to his proposal; he assumed and ...' She could not finish.

'He took you?'

Sadie nodded.

'Your father must never know. No one needs to know. It's a secret between you and me, do you hear?' Sadie nodded. Her grandmother didn't need to tell her that. Her shame would go with her to the grave.

'Well, you know what you're marrying, a blackguard, a well-known womaniser, and a fortune hunter. Don't expect him to be faithful. Where is Mrs Porter, why didn't she put a stop to this?'

'She needed to visit family; her daughter is having a baby.'

Grandma sucked in her cheeks in disapproval. 'Rob is honourable, wouldn't take advantage, unlike the man you are going to marry. Can't you see that? This is not the action of an honourable man. What about Rob, does he know about Frank?'

'I sent him a letter yesterday afternoon, thinking we could try again, but he didn't reply. It's too late now.' Tears clouded her eyes.

Her grandmother sighed, shaking her head at Sadie's foolishness. 'I can see I will have to pray for the only thing that will improve this situation.'

'What's that?'

'That the Turks make an honest widow of you. If Frank returns, you can kiss goodbye to your fortune. I will go home to pack; it's obvious I need to stay here until the wedding to ensure he does not presume again.'

Rob arrived with a copy of the newspaper that evening; the announcement ringed in black pen. The maid let him in and wanted to stay until Sadie dismissed her. His faced looked thunderous.

'You never thought to tell me you were seeing someone else. How could you? I thought we had an understanding.'

'I hoped you would call last night.'

'I made other plans.'

'But I needed you. If only you had come last night.'

'What difference would that have made?'

How could she tell him? Maybe she would not have opened the door to Frank if it had been settled between her and Rob. She may have been wearing his diamond solitaire, not been forced to wear Frank's ugly opal. Why didn't you fight harder for me, she thought? If only you had fought for me.

'It was very sudden.' She explained, as her heart broke. 'I'm sorry. Frank sprang it on me before I had a chance to tell you in person.'

'But you have developed an understanding with another man before informing me. You are not the woman I thought you were, Sadie. When I received your letter yesterday afternoon, I was full of hope. This,' he shook the newspaper at her, 'has shaken the wool from my eyes. I'm only too pleased to discover my mistake.'

'I apologise that you found out in that way.' She tried to keep the anger from her voice. You didn't fight for me – it was like a loop running through her brain. I loved you, still love you, but it's too late for us because you didn't fight for me.

'You have left me a laughing stock.'

'You deserve better.'

'I do.'

Despite the coldness in his voice, she could see the strain in his eyes. She wanted to drown in them but instead offered her hand for him to take his leave. He barely touched her fingers before turning on his heel.

Too late Rob, you were a day too late.

She heard the door slam then rushed to throw herself on her bed, weeping for the loss of the man who retained her heart.

Frank knocked at the door with his mother the following day and was dismissed after five minutes in the curt manner which Grannie had perfected over a lifetime. She informed Mrs Tinsdale that all the details would be organised by the bride's family. Frank's mother left, first kissing Sadie on the cheek and squeezing her hand.

'I couldn't be happier, dear. You'll be the making of Frank. Let's hope this war doesn't last too long, so I can hold my first grandchild before I go. Such a shame his father is no longer with us.'

Sadie kissed her cheek. She liked Mrs Tinsdale. With a mother like her, Frank could not be as bad as her Grandmother painted. He must love her to have asked her to marry him, not knowing if he would be returning. The way he had smiled at her today and then kissed her chastely on the hand while stroking the underside of her wrist with his finger, did not stir her blood, nor did it sicken her. She could do this.

Days later she stood outside the Collins Street Baptist Church. It was not the wedding she imagined. Grandmother had baulked at white but the oyster, glazed cotton dress suited her dark colouring, and the pink hat was charming. The saleswoman had clapped her hands in delight.

You look perfect, Miss,' she had said, and in the mirror this morning, Sadie agreed. The dress showed off her slim waist and ankles. Grandma had objected to the length at first, but the saleswoman assured her that all the ladies were wearing dresses a little shorter.

Sadie had applied a touch of rouge to her pale cheeks and painted her lips in a bow, a shade darker than the colour of her hat. It gave her a confidence she did not feel. All week she had been beset with doubts even toying with the idea of running away or settling for life as a spinster.

'Are you ready?' Uncle Jonnie asked. She looked up at him, set her lips firm and nodded. All choice removed when she woke that morning with the conviction that she was with child. Strange to say, she welcomed the idea. It offered her hope.

Her sole bridesmaid, orphaned Cousin Mary, followed them up the steps between the fluted columns of the elegant stone church and through the door. They processed slowly down the left-hand aisle to the sound of the Wedding March, past the smattering of guests, conjured at so little notice. Lucy sat with her aunt. She wished she had been able to talk to her before the wedding. Lucy's bemused expression spoke volumes.

It was the men in uniform who stood out. She knew several of them by sight, Frank's friends, all willing to heed the call, despite the dangers. They calmed her nerves. If they could go to war, she could get through this and marry a man willing to die for her, a man she was steeling herself to love. Her eyes settled on Frank who was beaming at her, and her heart thawed a fraction. She gave him her hand willingly when she arrived at the altar. He smiled at her with his dark eyes, mouthing to her, 'You look beautiful, my darling.' The tightness in her shoulders eased. Maybe all would be well.

After the wedding breakfast at the nearby Vienna Café, they set off by train for a honeymoon in Sydney, at the house her father had given her as a wedding present.

Frank delighted in the spacious, grand old property, but after she waved him farewell on his way to Egypt and then on to Gallipoli, she took little pleasure in it. The view of the harbour was striking enough when the winter mist cleared, but she knew no one. Beyond the house, lay an unfamiliar city. Shopped out after three days, and with nowhere to wear her new clothes beyond cafés, she grew lonely. The cold, damp weather did not encourage her to explore the Botanic Gardens or take a ferry to Manly. Instead, she pined, partly for Frank, surprisingly. She missed his lovemaking, the feel of his fingers on her skin, the way her body melted in his hands. In the dark nights she could forget this was the wrong man. She could not deny that he had been sweet to her. Apart from that one incident, two nights before his embarkation.

How he'd found the place was a mystery.

'It's discreet,' he told her as he led her down a back street from the furthest reaches of William Street in an area called King Cross.

'It doesn't feel safe here, Frank. How do you know about it?'

He tapped a finger to his nose and grinned. 'You have to be in the know.'

'I'm not sure, Frank.' She hesitated as he opened a nondescript door which led to a staircase lit by a gloomy lamp. He caught her hand, encouraging her forwards. Once upstairs, she found a large room with a tiny stage, in front of which was a dance-floor. At the back lay a narrow bar with tables and chairs crammed between. Soldiers were cheering a female singer who stood on the stage. She bowed and began another song. Sadie could not place it.

'She's American,' whispered Frank. She looked brash to Sadie, and her voice had a strident quality. They found some spare seats near the front.

Frank kept filling up her glass with cheap wine and encouraged her to drink it, even though she told him it tasted sour and harsh. After the singer left the stage, Sadie excused herself to visit the powder room. It can't have been more than five minutes, but when she returned, Frank was not at their table, and she assumed he had taken the opportunity to visit the men's room. She sat down to wait for him, but he did not reappear. A trio of musicians stood on the stage playing slow waltzes, and several couples were dancing, touching each other intimately, sometimes kissing.

Sadie's cheeks grew hot. Her eyes scoured the gloomy room for Frank. She felt uncomfortable sitting on her own, surrounded by people her family would not approve of and where they sold illegal liquor. At last, she caught sight of him at the bar. His arm lay loosely around a woman, his mouth pressed against her ear until she threw back her head and laughed. Turning his face, Frank looked back towards Sadie and raised his hand to wave, withdrew his arm from his companion's shoulders and bid her farewell, pointing to his wife. Even in the darkened room, Sadie saw the woman's painted face and low-cut gown.

'Who's that?' Sadie asked when he rejoined her, having lit a cigarette on his way back to the table.

'Just an escort girl.' He shrugged his shoulders breathing out a ring of smoke. So nonchalant, as though talking to an unaccompanied floozie was the most natural thing in the world. Seeing her expression, he laughed. 'Don't get prissy on me, Sadie. She's just a girl down on her luck. Not born with your silver spoon, hey! Come on let's have one last dance; then I'm going to take you home and make love to you until the sun comes up. You're not going to spoil my last twenty-four hours, are you?'

Maybe it didn't mean anything. That was Frank, always charming, always friendly, but it hurt her that he could make light of her sensibilities. Sadie shook her head as she stood to dance.

'Not like that, Frank.' She pointed to a man whose hand clutched his partner's buttock. They were kissing as they danced.

'I know what you're thinking; Rob would never have brought you somewhere like this.' His voice harsh, as he ground out his cigarette in the ashtray.

She looked at him in confusion, as if he had slapped her. 'I wasn't,' she faltered. Tears pricked her eyes.

'You're a married woman, no longer innocent. Grow up, Sadie.' He paused, and his mood changed abruptly. 'Let's go now, sweetheart. I'm sorry, I shouldn't have said that. I must be getting nervous at the thought of leaving you. You know you mean the world to me.'

They took a taxi back to the house. Solicitous and apologetic, Frank coaxed Sadie back to good humour. They ran into the house in a shower of rain, and by the time they reached the bedroom Frank had torn off his shirt and shoes and clasped his arms around her, nuzzling her neck as he fiddled with her skirt buttons. Arguments it seemed, added extra spice to his passion.

No, her honeymoon had been bearable, short as it was. She had begun to miss Frank. Her tears caught her by surprise as she stood along with other more agonised wives and sweethearts as they watched their men steam from the harbour, bound for Egypt.

But now that her husband was gone, Sadie wanted to go home to be comforted by her father. No one else would do. That her grandmother knew her secret, disinclined her to return to Melbourne. It was also where Lucy would pump her for the reason for her marriage. Worst of all, there was always the chance of bumping into Rob. That left Adelaide. It was time to face her father. She would cable Mrs Porter to close up her Melbourne House. Goodness knows when she would see it again.

Chapter Eighteen

Australia   -
Adelaide, April 1916

Sadie lay deep in the soothing water, relaxed at last. Her hand caressed the gentle swell of her stomach with her expensive frangipani scented soap. At last. She had been longing for this in the maternity home. They recommended she stay there ten days, and despite attempting to wheedle her father into taking her home after four, she remained in hospital. The matron stood tight-lipped at the door as Papa settled Sadie and her baby in the Buick, but gratefully accepted a large donation to hospital funds, offering a momentary wave as they drew away.

'How are you feeling, sweetheart?'

'Exhausted. You can't get a wink of sleep in there.'

'I've received a telegram from Frank. He's delighted of course. Can't wait to see little Henry.'

Frank wrote that he wanted his son named after his father. As a postscript, he added 'Hilda, if a girl'. Well, he had got what he wanted.

'The nursemaid will be waiting, so you can go straight to bed and have a long sleep.'

'What I want most is a good, long bath.'

She got her wish. She moved slightly and winced as her stitches pulled. She had not enjoyed childbirth but what woman would. 'Like shelling peas' Granny had said when she heard the news of her pregnancy. 'More like torture,' Caro protested in a rare moment of empathy with her stepdaughter. Somewhere in between, maybe. She would gladly go through it again to gain such a wonderful result.

The Turks declined to grant her grandmother's wish. Frank was now in France, and Sadie felt guilty to think of his living conditions while she wanted for nothing. Comfort and luxury knew no bounds in this Adelaide house. At first, she had dreaded her father's reaction when she arrived, not long after Franks departure. She couldn't help but see the disappointment in Papa's eyes. However, he showed her the letter her grandma had dictated to Joe Junior. 'Don't be too harsh on the girl,' it had said. 'Frank bowled her over, and they are in love.' Sadie was grateful for the lie.

Once she told Papa about the baby, he directed her to stay with him and Caro. Any displeasure with her forgotten in that instant. Would he realise that Henry, far from being prematurely born, was spot on time? Papa had shown no sign of it so far.

Was any baby as beautiful as Henry? She could study his features for hours. While she saw Frank in his wisps of dark hair, the dark, fringed violet of his eyes swept through her like an electric shock of recognition. His face square and strong, but not like his father's. The tiny milk blister on his lips, the frown as his eyes closed in sleep, the way he sometimes stared at her, looking into the depth of her soul, his dimpled cheek as it lay soft against hers, the sighs, the yawns, all leading to a rush of love which took her breath away.

At first, she was worried about living in the same house as Caro, but she continued to treat her with indifference, which suited Sadie. The less they had to do with each other, the better. At mealtimes, they were studiously polite, and the property was big enough to provide her with a suite of rooms to herself on the top floor. Her father spent less and less time down in his office on Victoria Square now that the tram system was complete.

'This war means there's no money and no men to build new railways or bridges.' He grumbled. 'I have a mind to buy a sheep station.'

Sadie suspected he was growing bored. Boredom and her father did not sit well together. To compensate, he and Caro spent a lot of time at the races, dashing back and forth between Melbourne and Adelaide. He began to replace his passion for work with horseflesh, winning races the only thing that counted. For Caro, it was the dressing up. She was already planning her outfit for the Adelaide Cup in May.

The water was cooling, and milk throbbed in Sadie's breasts. Time to seek out little Henry for a feed. She loved the feeling of his tiny gums as they latched on to her breast.

Caro had been horrified. 'You don't mean to feed him yourself. Just think how saggy you'll become.'

That was enough to make up Sadie's mind, and she did not regret it.

A letter arrived from Stanley towards the end of the month.
Dear Pa,

Last Friday, I arrived with my company in a town called Cleethorpes. I'm staying in the officer's quarters. It's a very pleasant, square three-storey house, reminding me of houses in Carlton. It has wrought iron verandas on the second floor with a pleasant view of the estuary.

There was an unfortunate incident, but that resulted in me meeting the woman I want to marry if God spares me. Her name is Jane Phillips, and she's a volunteer nurse with the VAD. She's twenty-five and the sweetest girl I have ever met. I can't wait for you to meet her. Her father is the manager of the brickworks, a humble man but honest. You would like him, Pa.

We'll be here for a while. I'm on a recruitment drive, so I'm going to be based in a pub called the Dolphin, further down the seafront. You can write to me at Yarra House, Yarra Road, Cleethorpes, Lincolnshire. Can you believe that name? A good omen, I thought.

My love to Sadie, Eddie and everyone,
Stanley

'Do you suppose they are engaged already?' Sadie said. 'It seems awfully fast.'

'I fell in love with your mother at first sight.' Pa said, not noticing the look Caro shot at him. She hated any mention of his former wives, all rivals in her tiny mind, thought Sadie.

'But he doesn't say if he's asked her?'

'He'll let us know when he's good and ready, Sadie. I wonder what the incident was?'

'I hope it wasn't anything too serious. Do you think it might have been a bomb?' Sadie asked.

'At least Australia will never be bombed. It won't, will it?' Caro's eyes narrowed with nerves.

'No dear, that will never happen.' Papa reassured his wife.

'What about that Afghan attack?' Sadie asked, innocently enough. She enjoyed unsettling her stepmother.

'That was a one-off, and they were dealt with.' Papa glared at his daughter.

The attack on the New Year's Day Broken Hill train outing, the year before, had shocked everyone. No doubt it led to the enlistment of many young men before the Gallipoli landings. Sadie felt admonished. It was in bad taste to mention it when people had been killed and wounded.

'I'm sorry Papa. I didn't think.'

He nodded, acknowledging her apology, before changing the subject. 'I'm going up to Broken Hill next week. There are a few properties to see. I'm taking Eddie with me.' At seventeen, Eddie had been working with his father for a year. There was no talk of him joining up. Two sons at the front were enough.

'You will be back for Cup Day, won't you, Joe?'

'Need you ask? I should be back the week before.'

Papa's mood after the Adelaide Cup that year was as black as the days after the fire at St Hubert's.

'Not a single winner.' He stormed around the house. 'After all that money spent on trainers and horses.'

Caro didn't enjoy her day either. She was forced to watch other wives lapping up success in the winner's enclosure. Her mother-in-law's presence further depressed her mood. Grandma Jane, always prepared to celebrate her son's successes, this time mentally calculated his losses at the turf.

'I never knew a rich gambler,' she told her son.

'I don't gamble,' he retorted. 'I'm only in it to win the stakes and for the stud fees.'

Grandma pursed her lips into a dubious frown. Sadie refrained from speaking at all. She had stayed at home with Henry and thought it best to stay out of the argument.

'Next year, that cup's going to be mine even if I have to spend a fortune doing it.'

Grandma's face was a picture. 'Son, there's a war on. There's no work. You'll be throwing money away.'

'What I do with my money is my business. I'm going to scour the country for the best horses and trainers. Kidman's good, but I'll need more trainers if I'm to buy winners. Once the war's over, work will come flooding back.'

This sounded reckless even for Papa.

'And why is Charlie Kidman working for you as a trainer and not running his own business like his brother, Sydney, the cattle king?' Grandma emphasised the last phrase. 'I'll tell you why; because he frittered away his money on the highlife and horses that didn't win. Sydney Kidman buys land.' Only his mother dared talk to Papa like that.

'I'm buying a sheep station, so my money will be safe. I've seen details of a likely place. I just need to negotiate a good price.'

'Where?' Caro asked.

'North of Wilcannia. It's on the Darling. You can get all the way by paddle steamer from Morgan.'

'How many acres?' Grandma asked.

'With what I can lease on a walk-in walk-out basis - a million.'

'Good on you, son.' Grandma was mollified. Land she understood.

Chapter Nineteen

England
Grimsby, March 1941

The timeless normality of Chamber's grocery shop always acted like balm on Sadie's fraught nerves. But of course, it was wartime, and there was a different normal. In the first year of the war, Sadie liked to convince herself that she could still catch a whiff of that wonderful aroma of roasting coffee beans from the machine in the window. It used to permeate the marketplace, drawing her in like a spider to its web. Inside the hams and cheeses reminded her of her father's farm shop in Elizabeth Street. She always chose Chamber's for that reason. Her sister-in-law preferred the Guy and Smith's café, but Sadie would never desert this shop. Memories, romance, call it what you will, scents of her childhood and courting days with Rob, mingled in pre-war Chamber's.

Sadie took a table by the balcony in the upstairs Tudor café. She enjoyed looking down on the counters, despite their paucity of wartime fare. The two violinists were playing *Bizet's Habenera*; their repertoire reduced now that Strauss and Brahms were out of favour. The musicians reminded her of the voyage on board ship to England. Even from steerage, she could hear the strains of violins as first-class passengers danced their evenings away.

'Aren't you pleased that I suggested we have a morning out?' She asked Jane.

'It's ages since I've been to Grimsby. I make do with St Peter's Avenue and Freeman Street. You can't beat Boyes for material.'

'But just to come in here is a treat. Don't you think it's worth the bus journey? I miss the Melbourne coffee palaces, don't you?'

An elderly waitress stooped beside their table to take their order, dressed in black with a white band on her head, she was another timeless relic.

'I confess I miss little about Australia.' Jane said as the waitress shuffled away.

Sadie hoped Jane wasn't going to spoil her mood. 'You know I love you, but as soon as I set eyes on you at Nelyambo, I knew you weren't comfortable. Like a fish out of water.'

'Nelyambo!' Jane shuddered in distaste. 'When I think of that place I imagine being trapped in a hot bath, the air slowly being sucked out of my body. My energy draining away, unable to lift a finger because of the exhaustion and constant terror of guarding my babies from snakes and spiders. Little did I think, they would be the least of its problems.'

'Why did you marry my brother, Jane?'

Jane sighed before answering. 'Ever since we met, Stanley was determined to marry, but now he's abandoned me.' She pursed her lips. 'I don't know. He didn't sweep me off my feet, but there were few choices back then. I didn't believe his tales of riches at first. It all seemed far-fetched. Rolls Royces, racehorses, chateaux. Madness more like, I told him.'

Sadie laughed, 'Those were the days. I'm not surprised you thought him mad, looking at what we have now.'

'Somehow, despite all that, I was drawn to him. And at twenty-five, I began to see that I would end up like my sister, a skivvy to my mother. Was that all life had to offer me? When he left for France, I began to miss him but, honestly, I never thought I would see him again.'

The waitress arrived with their order of tea and a toasted teacake with real butter melting into it. Jane and Sadie both took a bite and smiled at each other in delight.

'Oh my, this is a treat,' Jane conceded.

Sadie lifted the teapot and poured the tea into china cups.

'I can't stand what passes for coffee these days, and at least this is fresh tea. I try to eke mine out four or five times these days.'

Jane nodded, 'You should hear Mother on the subject.'

'And when Stanley came back a few weeks later?' Sadie asked as she poured milk into Jane's cup. Her sister-in-law took a long sip of tea before answering.

'I've had years to think about it, but I know when I made my decision. I have a vivid memory of Nibby and I watching all those fine young men who enlisted in the Grimsby Chums, marching four abreast down Isaac's Hill. We were all cheering them, so smart, so young. Nibby's sweetheart, Fred, was there with several old schoolfriends amongst them. They left for the front in January, a year after they joined up.

There was a film about them, only a few minutes long and we all went to the cinema to see it. I'll never forget the date, July 4th, 1916. We scoured the film for men we knew, and there Fred was, digging a trench in France, the broadest smile on his face. My sister was ecstatic to see him. She couldn't stop talking about him all the way home. How fit he looked, how cheerful.' Jane paused, her face clouded with the memory. 'We didn't know he had died three days earlier. The Chums were in the first wave of the Somme attack, trapped in the crater at Loch Nagar.' Jane grimaced. 'When we got the news, I decided if Stanley came back, he was my last chance, no matter if his tales of home were true or not. I took a gamble.'

The music stopped for a moment to polite applause. Chamber's paid no lip service to modernity. Frank would be itching to pluck the violins from the women's fingers and replace them with jazz saxophones. Sadie could imagine the scandalised looks on people's faces; no music allowed here to set a foot tapping. Sadie found it soothing.

She smiled at her sister-in-law, so trim and ladylike. Perfectly groomed, tinted blonde hair and looking nothing like her fifty years, 'But you married him, and I'm pleased you did.'

'I'm not saying there hasn't been joy with the birth of our children, but there have been more than enough tribulations.' Jane took a final bite of her teacake, delicately mopping her mouth with a linen serviette. 'When I saw him with his head half-bandaged, I convinced myself that I loved him. Enough to defy my mother who was horrified by my leaving. She thought she would never see me again, but Stanley promised he would bring me back for a holiday, every three years and he did. I just never expected him to abandon me here.'

'Back in the same old place, in the same house with your mother and sister. Things don't turn out how we expect.'

'We both chose badly, Sadie.'

Sadie bristled a little. Her brother wasn't bad, disappointed maybe. He had begged Jane to return with him after Papa died, but she had refused. As for herself, yes, she had chosen unwisely, but the choice was subjective. In the end what choice did she have?

'I was unfair earlier. I did like Melbourne and Adelaide. They're beautiful cities. I enjoyed the horse racing, the opera, the social events. I was like Cinderella at the ball, and he made me feel special, you know.' Jane's smile was wistful.

Sadie put her hand over Jane's. 'He will return someday. He loves you.'

'But when? And will I forgive him?'

'Let's go and browse in Guy and Smith's?' Sadie wiped her buttery fingers on her serviette and drew on her leather gloves. She stood, her mind still on the conversation. She hoped her brother would not delay too long before he returned. It was difficult to keep making excuses for him. If he made a success of logging in Borneo, would Jane agree to live there? She suspected not. The heat and humidity alone would put her off.

Jane pushed her chair back and hit something or someone, judging by the muted cry of pain. 'Oh, I do apologise. I wasn't thinking.' Concern creased her brow.

Sadie watched as a man with greying-blonde hair rubbed his leg where the chair had caught his shin. He looked up: his grimace a mixture of pain and acceptance.

'No real damage.'

A slight accent, Sadie tried to place it and then forgot. What was it about him that puzzled her? An ordinary man in a business suit. His eyes crinkled in a smile and she found herself returning the smile.

Jane said, 'Shall we go?' Sadie took one last look at him before agreeing. He was staring at her, a query on his face but she didn't think she knew him. She gave him a non-committal nod before following Jane to the stairs.

Chapter Twenty

Australia   -
Adelaide, 1916 /1917

Papa wanted to spend Christmas in Melbourne, but Sadie decided to stay in Adelaide. The thought of shopping with Caro in Bourke Street was enough to freeze her blood, and there was a remote possibility of bumping into Rob at a party or the races. Instead, she planned to journey up to the new sheep station Papa had bought in New South Wales.

She had envied Eddie and Papa when they made their preparations for the journey, poring over maps and lists as they planned their route. Papa had ruled out taking the long river journey to Wentworth where the Darling met the Murray. At that time of year, the Darling would be too low and closed to paddle steamers. A train to Broken Hill and a wagon onwards was the only viable way.

'Why have they never put in a train line from Broken Hill to Menindee?' Papa growled. 'One hundred and thirty miles is all they need. Those fellows in Sydney want their heads examining. It's thirty years of missed opportunity. Perhaps I'll offer to do it for free if we make enough money at sheep farming.'

'They can't see the profit in it, Papa. The ore will still go to Adelaide or Melbourne.'

'I know that, Eddie. But it would open other opportunities. And if they locked the Darling, there could be year-round river traffic. It's like the outback doesn't exist for them in Sydney, but that's where the wealth is, in sheep, now that the gold's run its course.'

If it weren't for the baby, Sadie would have loved to have gone with them. Papa's eyes lit with excitement as he talked of a wagon journey across the desert and sleeping under the stars. Before she was born Papa,

148

Mama and Stanley, then a babe in arms, had crossed from east to west in a wagon. He was on his way to make his fortune in West Australia. Gold had been discovered, and the State needed railways. Now it would be Eddie's turn to experience a fraction of that trip, before living the life of an outback sheep farmer. He was growing into a man before her eyes, and Sadie envied him.

Her Christmas plans to visit Nelyambo fell apart. The Murray floods in November proved so bad that all paddle steamers were forced to stay put because the bridges were impassable, and Sadie faced a quiet Christmas with Henry. She did not mind because it was a joy to chase after him as he crawled around and began to try and stand up. Every day was a discovery.

Papa returned with Caro in late January, overjoyed with his win at the Caulfield Races with Cherubini.

'We're on the up. Just you wait for the Adelaide Cup. It's going to be my year; I can feel it in my water.' He tickled Henry under the chin making him burst into giggles. 'It was Stanley's wife's first time at the races, imagine that. Stanley put on a bet for her, and you should have seen her face when he counted out the winnings in her hand. That's more than my father earns in a year, she said, a trifle disapprovingly I thought.'

'What's she like?' Sadie asked.

'Blondish hair, petite, shy.'

'I took her shopping,' Caro butted in. 'You should have seen the clothes she brought with her. Shapeless black skirts, a drab woollen coat and a few blouses. She told me that is normal dress in England. Well not here and certainly not in society, I told her.'

Sadie winced for her sister-in-law. She could imagine the scene. Caro would have turned up her nose, dragged her into town and supervised her shopping, probably blind and deaf to Jane's wishes.

'She refused to buy much, says she makes her own clothes.' Caro's face was a picture of distaste. 'But then it turns out she's expecting, and her new clothes will be out of fashion next year.' Caro tutted while Sadie beamed at the news.

'Oh, that's wonderful.'

'I don't know why you bothered spending any of my money,' grumbled Papa. 'There's no society to speak of in Nelyambo. Nobody cares what anyone wears in the outback as long as it's white to keep cool, and decent. I'm pleased she's not a spendthrift. He's got himself a sensible wife.'

'Joe, you don't mean it. You like to display your wealth, and what better way than to have a wife who does you proud.' Caro tapped her husband on the wrist in admonishment.

'Are they on the way there?' Sadie asked.

'They are; the river levels have fallen.'

'How do you think she'll cope with the heat and everything?'

'I've told your father that there is no way I will live in the back of beyond,' Caro butted in. 'No other white woman within a day's ride, no doctor, no shop.' Caro shuddered her distaste.

'The girl is from a humble background. She'll learn to make do.'

Sadie wondered if she would. I could she thought, but I grew up here. What must it be like for someone like Jane? She hoped she was hardy.

Papa decided to take his friend Sidney Kidman's advice.

'Buy up adjoining land; then if there's a drought or floods, you can move stock elsewhere.' Kidman had been doing this for a while. It made sense. In February, Papa bought a nearby station on the Darling closer to White Cliffs. The stations didn't join, but his plan was in its infancy. Better sheep than railways or bridges for the duration of the war, he said. Now that Stanley was installed at Nelyambo, Eddie could move to Momba Station, closer to Broken Hill.

Apart from his sheep station acquisitions, it was preparations for the Adelaide Cup in May which took all of Papa's time. Eddie arrived two days before the race, but Jane was nearing her time, and could not contemplate the arduous journey. Stanley refused to leave her.

Leading up to Cup Day, rain dampened everyone's spirits. The continuing news of casualties led women to choose sober outfits, out of respect, although Caro grumbled. She wanted to look her best and most vibrant for the photographs.

'Grey doesn't suit me,' she complained.

Sadie smiled to herself, what difference would it make in a photograph?

The day dawned bright for a change, and the crowds descended on the racetrack at Victoria Park. Despite it not being a public holiday, people thronged the course.

Everything was riding on Green Cap, Papa's bay gelding. Sadie had not seen him before, but she had to agree, he was an impressive horse, deservedly the favourite. The Cup was the third race, and Papa's horse, Miss Maderick, was running first in the Maiden Handicap. This day was a few leagues up from the Point-to-Point, and Sadie's excitement mounted as the horses lined up. The sight of her father's racing silks of purple with a white sash made her heart sing. They were off, flying past, Miss Maderick and Hotfoot quickly rode into the lead; it was neck and neck as the two horses fought it out over the mile. Sadie, Caro, Eddie screaming out for Miss Maderick as she crossed the line, half a head in front. Papa beamed as he was presented with his cup, but this was not the one he craved.

Sadie's mouth was dry, despite the champagne she had quaffed following the first win. If Papa could only win this race, it would be the crown of his racing career. They stood waiting for the off; within three minutes Papa would be either standing dejected or proudly accepting handshakes and cheers. Sadie prayed for a win. The gun sounded, horses surged ahead, and she kept her eyes on the purple shirt. Was it third or fourth? Gold Cuffs, the second favourite was in second place. No, it was slipping to fourth, Green Cap had overtaken but lay behind the leaders, the same placing as they rounded the turn.

'Don't worry,' Eddie shouted in her ear. 'He's biding his time, you'll see in a moment. There! There he goes! Come on Green Cap!'

'Look at him go; he's flying!' Sadie screamed as the horse streaked ahead, running his heart out to win by two lengths. She turned towards her father who displayed the broadest smile on his face with a cigar clamped between his teeth. Men were already surrounding him, clapping him on the shoulder. Sadie's heart was fit to burst. He'd done it; achieved his ambition. It had cost him a fortune, but it was worth it. He was the best Papa in the world. Oh, if only her mother were here to see it. Caro, of course, was basking in the glow of Papa's success, already simpering for the camera.

Later that evening, with Papa still celebrating three wins in all, Eddie sought out Sadie in her sitting room. She offered him a glass of whisky knowing that something was bothering him.

'Spit it out, Eddie dear. It can't be that bad.'

'It's delicate. I'm not sure I should say anything to my sister and a lady.'

'Let's have less of that. Do you know how I long to spend the day in the saddle like you? Sometimes I wish I could have been a boy too. You get all these interesting things to do. I'm bored with being a lady. Not with being a mother, that I love, but why was I educated if not to work at something?'

'I meant it's something delicate about Pops.'

Sadie was taken aback. She couldn't imagine what was coming.

'Promise you won't say anything? It's been eating me up. I didn't get chance to speak to Stanley before I left Nelyambo.'

'Of course, I won't say anything. Papa's not ill, is he?' The hairs on Sadie's arms stood up as the heat drained from her body.

'No, not that. It was when we were in Broken Hill. It took a couple of days to buy the wagon and bullocks and the stores we needed. One afternoon around five, Pops said he needed to see someone. While he was out, I took a stroll around and found a hotel bar. Then I noticed Pops and I thought he was with Joe Junior. Pops had his back to me, but I recognised the clothes he was wearing. I realised it wasn't Joe Junior; he was about the right age, maybe a little older but shabbier than our brother and with less hair. You know how Joe always likes to look smart, or at least Olive makes him look smart. I stayed watching. They appeared to be on friendly terms.'

'Who was it, Eddie?' Sadie said, her mind on tenterhooks.

'I asked the barman if he knew the younger man and he said; 'Oh that's Joe Timmins.' I replied, 'No, the younger man.' He got irritated with me and said; 'I've just told you, Joe Timmins. He's in most days after his shift in the zinc mine.' I asked him if he'd ever seen the older man before; 'Maybe two or three years back, it's Joe's father, isn't it?' After I caught my breath, I drank as quick as a cricket and scarpered.'

'What does it mean, Eddie?' Sadie floundered. She couldn't get her head around what Eddie was telling her.

'That man was so like Pops, he could have been a younger version. If there was a cousin in town, do you think Pops wouldn't have mentioned it? I asked him the next day if he had met the man he wanted to see, and he said that he had, that it was just some old-timer he'd worked with on the railways. He lied.'

Sadie let out a deep breath of disbelief before Eddie continued.

'I said to him that I knew Grandma used to live in the town and asked if we had any relatives here still; 'No,' he said, very brusque he was too.'

'Just let me try to understand. You think Papa had another son before Joe Junior? How can that be?'

'I don't know, but when I try and get my head around it, it's the only thing that makes sense.'

'Oh, my Lord. You can't say anything to him. What if it isn't true?'

'You can see why I have been getting het up about it. I'm going back to Broken Hill tomorrow. Should I try and find this other Joe Timmins, before I return to Momba?'

'No, leave it alone. If it's true, Papa will surely have some arrangement with him. He wouldn't see him short.'

'Do you think so? He looked none too prosperous.'

'How do you dress when you're working? I bet you don't care what you look like. Do you even comb your hair?'

'You're probably right. I'm glad we talked. Best leave it be for now.'

'Don't mention it to Joe Junior either. It would upset him to think he might have a brother with the same name.'

Once in bed, Sadie could not sleep for thinking about Eddie's revelation. Her relationship with her Papa was simple. She idolised him, believed he could do no wrong, other than marrying Caro. But having a son with another woman before he'd married Agnes, Joe Junior's mother, and then abandoning him, could it be possible? Why hadn't he married the mother? She hated to think that her father might be less honest, less upright, less reputable than she thought. Tomorrow, would she look at him differently? Perish the thought. He was guilty of making a mistake. She had made hers; she would not judge Papa on this.

As they waved Eddie off the following morning, Papa's ebullience defied Sadie's concern that she would judge him in a less favourable light. She loved to see the pleasure on his face as he told Eddie he would be up to see him soon. What did it matter that he had another son as long as he stayed in contact with him?

It was only the continuing dreadful news from the front and lack of contracts which acted like a leaking tap on Papa's confidence. When America entered the war in April, everyone's hopes were raised, but page after page of casualties and rising prices in the shops ate at the public enthusiasm for the war. At social events, in the shops and restaurants, Sadie heard mutterings of discontent. The stalemate could go on for years. As fewer and fewer young men volunteered, she thanked God that conscription had been voted down and there was no talk of Eddie going to war.

'More horses,' Papa said. 'Kidman's giving them two hundred for the war effort. 'They'll have to buy mine, but I won't volunteer horses as I did at the start of the war. Poor beggars. Apparently, they've got through a million or more already. Perhaps I should send them camels.' He threw the newspaper down in disgust.

As the winter wore on, the mood worsened. Emboldened by the February Revolution in Russia and angry about soaring prices, groups of workers began to strike. The newspapers and the government screamed treason. In August new productivity cards were forced on the rail and tram workers who promptly rejected them and downed tools. Within days, other workers joined in the stoppage bringing the eastern states to a standstill.

Papa's view of the war was changing. Giving up on a sensible conversation with Caro, he sounded off at Sadie. As a businessman, he supported the management, but he had begun as a labourer; he shared an amicable relationship with his workers and supported the Labor Government.

One day - 'Yes, there were disputes, but we sorted them out. If you're too hard on them, they'll dig their heels in. You can push only so far.'

The next – 'We mustn't let the militants win. Why are the seamen and the dockers joining in?'

A day later – 'The unions have sold the workers out; they're scared of the government. Some of those Sydney men are profiteering; I'll wager. Have they sent their sons to war? Not if they can help it.'
Sadie did her best to keep up with his changing mood. His main frustration was the lack of work. For God's sake, let this war be over soon, she prayed.

Sometimes Sadie thought her life was in limbo. She ached to set up her own home with her husband and son. Yes, she could return to her house in Melbourne, maybe she should, but whenever she broached the idea with her father he sought to dissuade her. I like having you and Henry around, he would say, and she gave in.

Letters from Frank were scored through with the censor's black line. Only the blandest of sentences got through; 'I am well, looking forward to some leave in Blighty. Send me socks.' She had been knitting socks for the war effort for months; what did they do with them? It was always socks. Her marriage seemed like a distant dream and her husband merely an actor in it. How would they get on when he eventually returned? She scarcely knew him, and his letters were worse than useless. She tried to think of him with love, but it was the desire which coloured her nights. The only love she had known was Rob's, and she screwed that into a box deep in the further reaches of her mind. Could a marriage based on desire turn into love?

She longed to ask Stanley what the front was really like, wishing they had a telephone up there in the outback, especially when the cable announcing his daughter's birth, arrived from Dubbo.

As soon as the Murray reopens for steamer traffic, I will visit, she decided.

Chapter Twenty-One

Australia
Nelyambo, 1917 (Darling River)

Papa drove them to the station not long after dawn. 'Have a wonderful trip,' he said, as he saw her on to the early train for Morgan. 'Bridget, hold Henry's hand at all times, do you hear? I don't want him falling into the river.'

'Don't worry, Papa, we'll have reins on him. We're not about to let him wander about on his own.' Sadie reassured him.

He grunted then raised himself on tiptoe to kiss Henry and finally his daughter. 'I'll miss you.'

'You'll be enjoying yourself at the races in Caulfield, no doubt.'

'Time your husband came home to keep you in check, Missy.'

Sadie laughed. 'Yes, I think so too, Papa. But I'm looking forward to seeing Stanley and his wife and little Nancy.' She kissed Papa goodbye again, seconds before the whistle blew. Waving with one hand, the other on her hat, she watched her father disappear as the train picked up speed.

'Move away from the door please, Ma'am.,' a passing guard advised before he pushed up the window.

Sadie was pleased to stretch her legs after the four-hour journey and allowed Henry to toddle around the quayside with Bridget holding tight onto his hand. Signs of the recent Murray River flood remained in sandbag strewn embankments and puddles of water.

The paddle steamer sat squat and ungainly in the water. Three decks of uneven sizes containing cabins and lounges like some strange rickety house, perched above This untidy craft was to be their home for the journey up to Wentworth.

Once on board, Sadie was shown to her cabin by a porter. It was narrow and spartan with bunk beds on a wire frame. The walls were boarded and painted white. A tiny window with a thin curtain on a wire above afforded the only light. A jug and basin lay on a bracket in the opposite corner. There was hardly room for the makeshift canvas cot for Henry who would sleep with her.

To spend days in the company of strangers would prove a new experience which she meant to enjoy, rather than holding herself apart. She was the daughter of an outback sheep station owner, not a railway magnate, nor did she intend to be a society lady. Caro would be horrified at the contents of her trunk; simple cotton dresses, even a pair of Eddie's trousers which she had cut down and remade to fit her, together with a pair of old scuffed riding boots from the days of the Yarra Valley rides. They were the first items she had packed in the trunk.

Sadie stepped outside to watch the greasy gangplank removed as the clock struck two, feeling the vibration of paddle-wheels begin to churn the grey water after it cast off and sallied forth into the river. She almost felt like clapping her hands in glee. Taking Henry from the nursemaid, she began to point things out to him.

'Look Henry, a black swan, over there, can you see it?'

'Birdie,' he lisped, almost jumping in her arms.

'Now, Henry, you must hold on tight to Mama's or Bridget's hand, all the time, do you hear?' He looked gravely up at her.

'Hold tight. Henry hold tight,'

'You clever boy!' She smothered his face in kisses.

'A late lunch, Ma'am,' a young steward boy said. 'It's served in the saloon aft.' He pointed to the rear of the boat.

'Come, Henry, let's see what food they have for you. Are you hungry, sweetheart? I know I'm starving.' The sandwiches cook had prepared for the train journey were only a distant memory.

Everyone sat together for meals. A good chance for Sadie to survey her fellow voyagers. Two women, apart from themselves, and six men, all but one man in working attire. Of the women, one was married to the only man dressed in business clothes, the other a lone female, a teacher making her way to Wilcannia to take up a post as schoolmistress. Sadie guessed her age as mid-twenties, maybe two or three years older than herself. The conversation at the table was varied and interesting with Sadie content to let it flow over her, answering only when questioned as to the purpose of her journey by the bank manager's wife.

'My husband's in the army, and I'm joining my brother for Christmas.'

'Your husband's In France?'

'Yes.'

'As are two of our boys.'

Sadie caught the shifting glance of the woman, trying her best to forget her constant fear.

'My brother was injured on the Somme, but he's recovering.' Did she seek to allay the woman's anxiety with her own relief? How ridiculous. She now knew how the mother felt because of her son. God forbid that Henry would ever have to fight in any war.

The woman smiled and patted her hand. 'That's good news, dear.' Her smile did not quite reach her eyes. She turned away to talk to her husband, and Sadie saw her put a handkerchief to her eyes.

The heavily bearded old man sitting opposite sported a sun-lined, weather-beaten face. His right eye cloudy but his left less so, an old-timer, with plenty of stories to tell, but so used to his own company that they no doubt remained untold. In some ways, he reminded her of her grandpa, although dressed in clothes which had seen better days twenty-years ago. Papa always said that you could tell a true outback person by the age of the clothes they wore; 'there's a fierce pride and lack of pretention. What care have they for fashion? An honest day's toil for both boss and men is all that counts,' he would say. Looking at the bushman opposite, Sadie could see the truth of that in his face.

Mrs Taylor, the bank manager's wife turned back towards her, 'Do you play whist, my dear? Would you care to make up a foursome after supper?'

'Yes, that would be delightful.' Sadie turned towards Henry who was sitting on Bridget's lap and beginning to grizzle. 'Excuse me, my son is due a nap. I need to settle him down.'

The afternoon passed pleasantly. Sadie sat on the upper deck underneath a solid awning, gazing at the scenery and wildlife. The river remained high. In some places the orange sandy cliffs were no more than gentle banks, in others, the river appeared as wide as the eye could see, the trunks of river gums, the only visible sign of the river bank. There was much to show Henry as ducks, swans and even the odd pelican vied with paddle-steamers and barges sailing in the opposite direction.

The skinny schoolmistress made up the four for whist on the first evening. She partnered Sadie, and after the game ended, the two young women sat together for a final cup of tea before bed.

'You have a beautiful son, Mrs Tinsdale,' Envy showed in the schoolmistress's eyes.

'Thank you, Miss Watson. His father has never seen him. We married days before he embarked.'

'I wish we had married. My fiancé was killed at Lone Pine.'

'I am so sorry, Miss Watson. I noticed your badge. You must miss him terribly.'

'I do; we were childhood friends. I would give my right arm to have him back, and I would love to have his son or daughter. At first, I didn't know how to live without him. My parents are dead, so the little money they left me, I used to train as a teacher. I heard that there are very few women in the outback.' The wistful look on her face spoke of desperation as she fingered the 'sweetheart badge' on her collar, demonstrating her sacrifice for the war.

That night, as Sadie tried to sleep to the background of paddles slicing through the water, she thought about Frank. Would she give her right arm for his return or not know how to live without him? The truth was, she managed very well alone. There had been no photographer at their wedding, an oversight, Grandma claimed. But it wasn't just his face she found difficult to remember, it was her feelings too. She looked forward to his homecoming, so that they could become a family, but was that mostly for Henry's sake? What she most wanted was another child. Her son should not have to grow up alone. For the first time in months, tears moistened her eyes.

She turned her face into the pillow trying hard not to sob. With walls as thin as these someone was bound to hear. For the remainder of this trip, she must try not to dwell on Frank but concentrate on the happy Christmas celebrations ahead.

The lazy days and evenings passed peacefully, but not without entertainment. A piano in the main saloon offered the schoolmistress practice, and there was dancing or jigging on occasions, accompanied by piano and the steward's harmonica. Sadie did not claim a singing voice, but she joined in choruses of popular songs. A variety of books sat in the lounge, newspapers too, replenished each time the boat stopped at one of the river ports.

As goods were loaded and unloaded, the passengers stretched their legs on shore, taking in the sights of the small towns or the opportunity to have a bath in one of the hotels straddling the wharves. A timely whistle always brought them scurrying back.

The steamer slowly ate up the miles, and as the river turned eastwards towards its junction with the Darling, the heat became dryer. Cloudless blue skies and a relentless sun by day, but it was the cool, star-strewn nights which captivated Sadie. Just before bed, the male passengers in their black felted hats would sit with their legs up on the railings, smoking pipes and yarning to each other. Echoes of their voices comforted her to sleep, reminiscent of her brothers chatter in the childhood bedroom next door at Chateau Yering.

When at last they arrived at Wentworth and the transfer to a Darling River paddle-steamer, Sadie said goodbye to the Taylors who were journeying on into Victoria. The smaller Darling steamer had fewer cabins, requiring her nursemaid to bunk with the schoolteacher, but Sadie retained sole use of her cabin.

The yellow waters of the swollen Darling passed through a new landscape, flatter, but still inundated. The old-timer named for her the mulga trees and salt bushes, which appeared to float in the water. Some afternoons, the male passengers took pot shots at the ducks, swimming ahead, but rarely scored a hit. At sundown, kangaroos took advantage of the lower temperatures to feed, and as night fell, only the occasional bark of a fox or a wild dog disturbed the peace that shrouded the boat. With a bright lamp at the front of the boat and a watchman careful to avoid snags and floating hazards, they continued upriver at night, but the view the following morning rarely changed.

Riverports became further apart, but the captain drew in at sheep stations to unload goods, sometimes marked only by a stake or a fleece thrown over a branch to signpost a property. Only experience told him where to look. As the river began to subside, they arrived at Wilcannia, the last port before Nelyambo. The pepper trees offered welcome shade as Sadie inspected the shops and amenities of her sister-in-law's local town. Nelyambo lay fifty miles further north by bullock cart and more by meandering river. Sadie guessed Jane would be unused to such distances and wondered how far Cleethorpes was to its neighbouring town.

Stanley was at the landing stage to meet her. He'd been listening out for the whistle. Sadie waved, waiting impatiently for his ordered goods to be unloaded. She did not wish to subject Henry to the force of the midday sun until necessary. When all was loaded into the wagon, Stanley bounded onto the deck to greet her with a hug.

'It's jolly good to see you, Sis. So, this is Henry. Hello little fella.'

'Say hello to Uncle Stanley, Henry. You have to watch him like a hawk, Stanley, or he'll be off. I think he's looking forward to running about after the confines of the boat.' They began to walk towards the gangplank, where her luggage was waiting.

'Let's get him out of this heat. Climb up into the wagon. It's only a minute or two to the house, just up there on the rise. You can see it.'

As soon as they were all aboard, Stanley swished his whip and the bullocks moved off towards the bluff. Minutes later, they were standing on the veranda of the homestead built on the only high ground around, a large, square building, newly painted white with a surrounding wide veranda. Beyond it was a similar, smaller building, the offices and station manager's quarters.

'It looks quite new, Stanley,' Sadie complimented him.

'Yes, it's only a few years old. The station was quite run down, and we've spent a lot of time fencing. Got a real nice horse for you to ride, so I can take you for a look-see tomorrow, if you're up for it?'

'You bet. It's a shame little Henry is too young for a horse.'

'In a couple of years, he'll be jackarooing with the best of us. Pops will make sure of that.'

Jane greeted them at the door, wearing a simple cotton dress. Petite, with the curves of a nursing mother, greyish blue eyes and light-brown hair underneath a white cap, it was the sweet shyness of her smile that made Sadie fall in love with her.

'I've been looking forward to your visit for so long,' Jane said, in her soft English accent.

'She misses her sisters,' Stanley said, by way of explanation.

'I hope that you will consider me a sister from now on. I always longed for a sister. Look, Henry, this is your Aunt Jane and your cousin, Nancy.' She picked him up, so that he could see the five-month-old girl jiggling with delight in her mother's arms.

'Let me show you around, and then we'll have dinner.'

There was a large sitting room with a view of the river to the east and a morning breakfast room to catch the early morning light. Four bedrooms and a good-sized bathroom lay to the north while the kitchen faced south, shaded by the other house. The furnishings looked new and modern helped by bright, new cushions. Sadie's bedroom was plain apart from a beautiful patchwork quilt.

'Have you made this quilt?' Sadie asked.

Jane nodded, 'I hope you like it. Stanley thinks me silly to save up all the scraps of material, but they can make nice furnishings. You don't need to spend lots of money to make a comfortable home.' Sadie couldn't help thinking how outraged Caro would be to hear that and chuckled.

'It's gorgeous; I'd like one if you ever run out of things to do.'

'To be honest, I have too much time on my hands, so expect one next time we meet. Come and have dinner.'

The station-cook provided meals for the family and some of the hands.

'We've been eating altogether. I hope you don't mind.' Stanley said.

'And I like the company,' Jane said, quietly.

'Not at all. It was the same on the steamer, and it was fun.'

'You may get fed up with the fare, but he cooks well. It's mutton most days unless we shoot enough rabbits, then it's underground mutton.' He laughed, a wry smile on his face. 'I did once catch a Murray cod in the

162

river. That was a nice change – they're big. The one I caught must have been thirty pounds or more. Do you want to try your hand at fishing?'

'Like old times, Stanley. I wish Mama were here,' Sadie sighed. 'Wouldn't she have loved seeing us with our children?'

After dinner, Jane retired early. Stanley and Sadie sat out on the veranda.

'It's so peaceful and look at those stars.

'Too peaceful for Jane, I'm afraid. When I asked her to marry me, I thought we would be living in Melbourne or Adelaide. It was a shock for her when we ended up out here, miles from anywhere.'

'It will take a bit of getting used to, but she'll come to love it, I'm sure.'

'Do you think?'

'I don't know. I was trying to reassure you.'

'I promised her the earth, but what she has is a big house and no one to talk to, until Nancy begins to speak. I worry it won't be enough.'

'Is this what you want, Stanley? If Nelyambo and managing a sheep station is what you want, maybe she'll come to accept it.'

'Strewth, I don't know. I'm happy for the moment. After the trenches, this seems like heaven, and I was there for only a fortnight. I don't know how Frank is coping with it. I never had him down as someone who would enjoy roughing it. Why ever did you marry him, Sadie?'

She shrugged, lost for words that Stanley should be critical of her without being able to speak up in her own defence.

'Rob wrote to me afterwards. He was sick to think of you with Frank. You know Rob is going places. I wouldn't be surprised to see him in parliament, one of these days.'

'I was stupid, but Frank isn't bad. He joined up and is fighting for King and country. I'm sure he'll be a good husband when he gets the chance.'

'Sis, he has a bit of a reputation. Let's hope marriage makes a difference. When he returns, if he doesn't treat you right, you can count on me, on all of us.' His eyes slid from hers in embarrassment at her expression of disquiet. 'Let's get to bed. If you're coming out with me for a ride tomorrow, you need to be up at four.'

His words chilled Sadie. All her doubts flooded back, and she lay awake tossing and turning until midnight.

On the veranda next morning, she drew her cashmere shawl against the chill of an acacia scented dawn. To the east, strips of violet, blood red orange and yellow vied with the remains of a sequinned, indigo sky. Standing breathless in awe of the sunrise, she waited as the shrill of the crickets faded, and the kookaburra woke, laughing with him as rose-winged galahs began to flit among the rustling river gums. Somewhere close, nickering horses trampled the ground. Stanley joined her on the veranda, dressed and ready for the day.

'We don't have a side-saddle for you.'

'Don't worry about that.' She drew in a breath as a sliver of sun rose and the day broke, the sky pink, laced with silvery clouds. 'I would never tire of seeing that.'

'It's a beaut, isn't it? Time to get a move on though. There's coffee in the kitchen.'

Suitably admonished, she returned to her bedroom and threw on her clothes. Henry was still asleep and with luck would remain so for a couple of hours. He normally slept through until seven. They would be back by ten.

Stanley laughed when he noticed her trousers. 'Are those Eddie's? Glad to see you're putting them to good use.' He handed her a slouch hat. 'You'll need this.' He wore a white pith helmet.

As they cantered away from the homestead, the sky settled into cool blue, highlighting scrubby green shrubs and tall grasses puncturing the rusty earth. It felt good to be in the saddle again. She had missed the early morning rides with her brothers, but this was no lush Yarra Valley. It owned a beauty of its own; a harsh beauty. Treacherous if you became lost. In a few hours, the sun would begin to burn up the land, the temperature rising to over a hundred degrees and with no shade, a body would quickly dehydrate.

Three miles from the house, Stanley showed her the empty shearing sheds, used only for two months of the year.

'Why so far from the homestead?' She asked.

'I wondered about that, but an old-timer remembered the flood of 1890. He distinctly remembers the boat coming all the way to the sheds to pick up the wool.'

Sadie gawped at the thought. It must have flooded the house too.'

'I think they rebuilt it after.'

'Did you have a go at shearing?' She asked him.

'Yes, they dared me to. But those men are fast, the black shearers too, and they work like billy-o. Just wait another year or so for the stock numbers to go up. Then we'll see some profit. I reckon we'll have to double the size of that shed.'

'Black shearers?'

'They're some of the best drovers too, even black women drovers.'

'I'd no idea.'

'There's a mob or two on our land. One of the women comes in to do the cleaning. Watch out for her; she's called Pearl.'

As they rode on, Sadie asked Stanley how many paddocks they owned.

'Once we've fenced them all, we'll have fifty.'

'That doesn't sound too many.'

'Each one is a hundred square miles or sixty-four thousand acres. This land will only take one sheep to ten acres, so that's three hundred thousand sheep if we don't have a drought. It will take time to build up.'

'So, you see yourself as a sheep farmer?'

'It's a good life for a man, but it's lonely for single men. Many of the boundary riders we have working here don't see anyone from one month to the next. We'll drop in on one of them and you can see for yourself.'

Sadie commented on the silence. 'Where are the birds? I can only see crows.

'Blasted rabbits eat their favourite food. Some get poisoned too when we put it down to kill the rabbits.'

They rode on in silence until Sadie caught sight of a coolibah tree. Next to it sat a humpy made of flattened oil-drums and branches with a canvas door. Outside a man appeared to be damping down the remains of a fire. Once they got close enough, Sadie saw a man anywhere between forty and sixty, but judging by the lack of grey in his beard, nearer to forty. Despite his slouch hat pulled well down, the wrinkles around his eyes and sunburnt face pointed to a life spent outside.

'This is my sister, Dennis. We've brought some tucker, flour, tea, more jam.' Stanley handed him a saddlebag after Dennis touched his hat to Sadie.

'Would you like some damper, Miss? I've now got jam to go on it, thanks to you.'

'Just a little, please.' It would be impolite to refuse. She dismounted and found a handy rock to sit on. 'How long have you lived out here?' She asked as he passed her some flatbread still warm from the fire.

'Six months or so. Time to be moving on soon, I reckon.'

'Any problems?' Stanley asked.

'Too many bloody rabbits in the east section. I shot a load, but I think we'll have to put more poison down. I needed to repair the water tank after that blow last week. The lambs are fattening up nicely.'

On the ride back to the homestead, Stanley told her that the boundary men often moved on after a few months. They rarely saw anyone from week to week, and the loneliness eventually proved too much.

'We pay them by cheque and, by all accounts, they make their way to the nearest hotel, hand the cheque over to the landlady, drink themselves stupid for a few days, and move on to the next place.'

'Why do they choose to live like that?'

'It's what they're used to; they couldn't live in a town. I suppose it's like going walkabout for the blacks.'

Arriving back at the homestead, Sadie's first thought was Henry. She was relieved to find him playing happily with Bridget.

'He woke at seven thirty, Ma'am. I gave him breakfast and a cup of milk. He's been very good.'

Jane was up. She sat at a table, her hand sewing-machine whizzing through a seam.

'Did you enjoy the ride?' She asked.

'I did, although I'll feel it tomorrow, I think. It's ages since I was in the saddle. Do you ride, Jane?'

'No. I've only been on a donkey at Cleethorpes beach, and I didn't like that much. It bit me after I patted him.'

'That's a shame. You really should give it a go. I love the freedom of being in the saddle. To be out in the dawn was just magical. Stanley will find you a gentle nag, I'm sure.'

Jane looked doubtful. Sadie decided not to press the point. 'I'll go and have a bath and then join you.'

Sadie sat in her bath, feeling sore but exhilarated. How many years was it since she had ridden, two, three? She aimed to make the most of these months at Nelyambo. What a shame that Jane had looked utterly horrified at the thought of riding. Could she persuade her to try?

She thought again about Stanley's warning about Frank and managed to dismiss it. She needed to believe that he would be so delighted to be home after the war that he would easily settle into the family. His poor mother had died without seeing her grandson, so Sadie and her brothers were his only family. It would be strange, and they might take time to readjust, but Frank was charm personified. He may have been a little wild in his youth, but they would have knocked that out of him in the army.

After a quick breakfast of coffee and warm rolls oozing with butter and jam, Sadie sat with Jane as she hand-sewed on a button.

'What are you making?'

'A dress for New Year's Eve.'

'Don't you have dresses that you bought with Caro?'

'Yes, but I doubt I could get into any of them at the moment.' Jane blushed. 'Stanley has invited people over from other stations. I still can't get my head around people driving fifty miles for a party.'

'That will be fun.'

'Yes, I'm looking forward to it. I'm pleased you're here, Sadie. You don't know how much I have been looking forward to your visit.'

Her forlorn expression cut Sadie's heart. 'I can stay until March, but I daren't stay longer in case the river drops.' Jane nodded in understanding. 'Tell me how you met my brother. I want to know everything.' Jane's expression turned from forlorn to anguished, and Sadie was shocked. 'Surely it can't have been that bad? You did marry him.' She joked, in an attempt to lighten the conversation.

'It was the most awful day of my life, and I think of Stanley's.'

'What! How?' Sadie stumbled for words. 'Surely that can't be true?'

Jane put down her sewing and reached for a handkerchief. 'A zeppelin bombed the Baptist Chapel on the seafront. It was the middle of the night, so no one should have been in there.'

'But there was?' Sadie was puzzled.

'Yes, the Manchesters had arrived the day before. The poor men were billeted there.'

'Oh, my word! He wrote about an incident, but I had no idea it was anything as bad as that!'

'I was a volunteer nurse. They gave us a little training, mostly about how to make up beds with hospital corners. But nothing can prepare you for what happened that day. It was very early, still dark when Sally knocked on the door. My mother didn't want me to go, but I told her it was my duty. My friend and I rushed towards Alexandra Road. We'd been told to go to Yarra House.'

'Stanley mentioned that in his letter. It was his quarters if I remember.'

'Yes. But on that day, it was a makeshift mortuary and hospital.'

Sadie's mouth opened in horror. 'Stanley's men died?'

'Yes.'

'How many?' Sadie's eyes watered in dismay.

'Over thirty dead, many injured. Sally and I stood frozen in the doorway at the sight. I probably would have turned and run, but an officer said; 'Please help them, nurse.' Tears were running down his face, and I remember there were splashes of blood coating his uniform. We gritted our teeth and set to work, helping clean them up. Doctors and real nurses told us what to do of course. We did the best we could. It wasn't enough.' Jane's shoulders slumped.

Sadie stroked Jane's back, her mind in turmoil. How easily it could have been her brother who had died. 'How awful, but at least you did something. I wasn't allowed to volunteer for anything.'

'I was sitting holding the hand of a soldier, singing him a lullaby. He was dreadfully injured. Some were burnt, others cut to pieces by shrapnel.' Jane shuddered at the memory. 'Another man was staring at me; it was your brother. As much as I tried to ignore him, concentrate on the poor man who was dying, his eyes never left me. Stanley said that he fell for me then. I'm not sure I believe in love at first sight.'

'Don't you? I think I do.' It was Rob's image that flickered in Sadie's mind. She banished it with a guilty shrug and turned her mind back to Jane's story.

'I suppose at first, I felt sorry for Stanley when he asked me out. He was in agony at losing his men. He told me how writing letters to their mothers and wives was the hardest thing he would ever do. One woman lost two sons. Poor woman! Stanley still thinks about her. I wanted to comfort him, you know.'

'So you two fell in love.'

Jane didn't answer. She looked pensive; leaving that question unanswered. That troubled Sadie.

The cars arrived before dusk in a cloud of dust seen for miles. Stanley had strung coloured lanterns around the veranda, and Jane decorated the tables with her best-embroidered napkins and dinner service. Sadie gathered rose buds and sprigs of myrtle for vases from the dusty garden. The wind-up gramophone Stanely brought back from England, was prepped with a pile of dance records by its side.

Sadie looked on as Jane greeted the guests in turn. Most Jane had met before on a shopping trip to Wilcannia, or an irregular visit to a neighbouring station. A party stretching over two days was the social event of the year, and as Sadie showed the ladies to their rooms in the adjoining house, words tumbled from their mouths as though they had not spoken in weeks or months, other than to their taciturn husbands or the chucks.

They served dinner on the veranda. No mutton that night, but roast pork with all the trimmings followed by a syllabub and fresh fruit. As the light fled, so did the warmth, and the diners moved inside. They pushed back the furniture to leave room for dancing. It took Sadie back to the party on New Year's Eve at Chateau Yering, but dancing with her brother and gruff sheep station owners made her want more; a husband's arms to caress her and love her. Despite that moment of wistfulness, she enjoyed the evening, and she could tell Jane did too.

While Stanley called for everyone to toast the King at midnight, his next plea was an end to the war. Everyone raised their glasses to that, none more so than Sadie. She caught the eye of a woman, whose sons were in France, a tear rolling down her cheek and Sadie felt her eyes water. Come home soon, Frank, she prayed. You've been away far too long. Your son needs you; I need you.

Chapter Twenty-Two

England -
Cleethorpes, April 1941

There had been no further raids in Cleethorpes since the ones in February, but other cities and dock areas were under heavy attack. The newspapers were reticent, but the bombers overhead on their way to Yorkshire cities told their own story. The WVS ladies were called in one day for training.

'I wonder what it is this time?' Sadie asked one of the newer ladies, Vera, a little younger than her, who carried a decided air of mischief.

The door opened. Edna walked in with the man Jane had bumped into in the Tudor Café, a few weeks before. Sadie blinked in surprise.

'This is Captain Peters from the Home Guard who is going to train us to use the stirrup pump.'

'Good morning ladies. Edna has been nagging me to visit. But now I'm here, I can tell we 're going to have a delightful morning, but I warn you, you may get wet.'

The ladies turned to each other and laughed. They didn't mind being a little wet.

'As you may know, the damage done by incendiary bombs has been enormous throughout the country, but we can counteract them with very simple measures. We need volunteers for fire watching, and hopefully, after I have shown you how easy this is to use, some of you may step forward or encourage other ladies or gentlemen you know.'

'He's got an accent a bit like yours dear,' Vera whispered. 'Handsome as well.' She tipped her a wink.

People always confused Australians and New Zealanders. To Sadie, it was as plain as day, by the way he said encindiary instead of incendiary. Interesting! What was he doing in the Home Guard in Cleethorpes?

A fun-filled hour followed. They trooped outside to learn how to pump water from a bucket at sixty-five pumps per minute, spraying water at the spent incendiary bombs. Everyone got to pump and hose while Captain Peters watched and encouraged.

'Don't I know you from somewhere?' Captain Peters asked Sadie, as he was packing up to leave.

'My sister-in-law bumped into you a few weeks ago at the Tudor Café.'

His eyebrows shot up, 'Australian, what are you doing in this neck of the woods?'

'I might ask the same.'

He glanced at the ring on her left hand.

'Divorced,' she said, astounded that she had volunteered such information to a man so recently met. He would think her forward.

'Widowed, he said. 'I know this is presumptuous, but may I take you to lunch after I have stowed this equipment in my car?'

'I don't normally...' She didn't know how to finish.

'Accept offers to lunch from strangers,' he finished for her. She nodded, temporarily unable to speak. 'But this is wartime, and we are close neighbours in a strange land.'

'Not too strange, I've been here for fifteen years.' She found her voice. 'But yes, thank you. I will accept your offer.' She had never been so instantly attracted to a man, not since Rob, anyway. What was it about him? Not just his accent. Certainly not men in uniforms. That lesson was learnt. Other than his height, his features did not resemble the smouldering good looks of her husband.

'And I've been here for over twenty years, since the last war, in fact.'

'Yet we still retain our accents,' she mused.

'Shall we walk to the Criterion?'

'Why not?' She preferred not to be seen getting into his car. Walking along Alexandra Road, both in uniform, no one would gossip about that. 'I'll get my coat while you put all your bombs away.'

She had to hold onto her hat as they turned left onto the seafront. The sea was a dirty brown colour beneath the overcast, threatening sky, disappointing for mid-April.

'Don't you still long for bright blue skies and hot sunshine?' His voice was light and jokey, muffled by the strong easterly wind.

'Sometimes. You wouldn't know those days, being from New Zealand.' The jokiness of her voice matched his.

He turned to look down at her, blue eyes searching her face and then twinkling with silent laughter. It was the easiness of his manner that was attractive. Not serious like Rob, nor devilishly debonair like Frank, somewhere in between. He's comfortable in his own skin, no need for pretence, she thought.

They arrived early at the Criterion, before the rush. Walking past the chip fryers, the gloominess of the café at the back suited Sadie. She was less likely to be noticed by prying eyes.

'Have you been here before?'

'Many times,' she said, thinking of her boys, warm and sandy from the beach. They loved this little café with its neat gingham cloths and rack of soda bottles with their screw tops, always taking an age to choose which flavour they wanted.

Sadie and the captain studied the limited menu before agreeing on their choice.

'Haddock and chips twice. Pot of tea for two, please.'

Would you like bread and marge?' Sadie shook her head at bread and marge, while Captain Peters nodded. The pretty, dark-haired waitress did not need to write down their order.

'What would we do without fish and chips? Once upon a time, my stepmother would have been horrified by its vulgarity, but at least it's not rationed. I haven't introduced myself, Sadie Tinsdale.' She proffered her hand still in its leather glove.

He took it, 'Alex Peters, late Auckland Light Infantry, now a member of His Majesty's Home Guard, for my sins.

'Gallipoli?'

'Briefly, and then the Somme. I was lucky. I got shot early on in Sniper's Alley, was invalided out to Cairo and then sent to the Western Front. Why they didn't send me back to that hell hole, I'll never know.'

172

'My brothers were shot on the Somme.'

'Did they survive?'

'Yes, but one was gassed later. He was never the same and died very young. Why did you stay here?'

'I met a girl, simple as that. I was looking up family here. My grandfather emigrated from Laceby back in the 1880s. We have a sheep farm, but my older brother inherited it, and I had no interest in farming, so I opted to stay. I trained as a surveyor before the war and there was plenty of work here. My wife never wanted to leave her family. And you? Why are you here?'

'My brother, Stanley, married a girl from Cleethorpes. After the Somme, she went back with him to Australia, but it didn't work out, and they returned to England. When my marriage broke up, I joined them here, although my brother left again in 1930. My move seemed sensible at the time, but now I'm wondering. It rather feels like opting for the fire rather than the frying pan.'

'Children?'

'Three sons all in the RAF. That's why it feels like the fire. Would they have all joined up if we had stayed at home?'

'Young men and war, it's a big adventure until you learn otherwise. I'm sure they would have joined up, maybe not the air force.'

'Do you have sons?'

'No, one daughter. My wife died young, so her granny and I brought up Marion.'

'I'm sorry,' Sadie put a consoling hand on his, as his eyelids flickered with regret.

'It's so long ago; sometimes I find it hard to picture her. We didn't even have a photograph of our wedding. My daughter takes after me, tall, blonde and blue eyes. Margaret was dark-haired with brown eyes and petite, like a doll, but strong until the cancer got her. Then she faded away to nothing; it was like she was being rubbed out, every day a little more erased until all that was left was pain.'

Sadie gripped his hand, withdrawing it as though scalded when the young waitress arrived with their order. She removed her gloves, placing them in her handbag. The fish in its crisp golden batter lay on a bed of steaming chips. Alex liberally covered his with salt and vinegar, Sadie with just a little salt. She moved the mushy peas to one side, unable to bear the taste or texture, and pushed the plate of triangular cut bread and margarine towards Alex.

'This looks good. I can't remember the last time I went out for lunch. I've taken a liking to haddock.' Sadie found she was gabbling. The touch of his hand had unnerved her.

'Me too, haddock, I mean. It was always trevally back home or John Dory.'

Sadie cut into the batter; the white flakes beneath never more inviting. For a few moments conversation ceased as they ate with concentration.

'Is your daughter married?' Sadie ventured, as they paused to digest.

'No, she's a WAAF at RAF Leconfield, near Beverley.'

'Even daughters are in danger and here's me envying you.'

'Everyone has to do their bit. Look at you and me.'

'What I'm wondering, is why a Captain in the Home Guard came to demonstrate the stirrup pump, why not a fireman or an ARP warden?'

'Because ever since I moved next door to Edna last Christmas, she's been asking me to come in and do some training. I now realise she's been trying to engineer a meeting between us. The crafty old bird, but I'm not sorry.' He put his hand on hers. 'Are you?'

Sadie felt a blush rising in her cheeks. Oh, my word! I feel like a schoolgirl, she thought, before shaking her head slightly to clear her mind. 'I haven't looked at another man since my husband.'

'And I not a woman since my wife. But there's something between us, can you feel it? As soon as I saw you in the Tudor Café, I knew.' His hand still held hers.

'Are you sure it's not because we have so much in common?'

'What, just because we are both from twelve thousand miles away?'

'No, both children of sheep farmers, our children in the air force, both mislaid our partners for whatever reason, have brought up children alone, and I had a New Zealand stepmother for all of nine months.' She giggled slightly to release the tension in her body.

'Not at all. I fell in love with my wife within seconds of meeting her. I have never forgotten that moment of instant connection, and now I have it again. I'm not going to let it go.' He raised her hand to his lips and kissed her fingertips.

Sadie's insides melted as his lips caressed her fingers. She didn't care what the other few diners thought. She wanted him. Her need so powerful that her hand shook as she lifted her teacup to distract herself. He placed her other trembling hand back on the table. Caution – she needed caution. And yet? A turmoil of longing and wariness were at war inside her head. Had he asked for the bill and led her outside, would she have taken him back home and surrendered? The craving she felt was indescribable, ridiculous. Was Alex different or would she live to regret this?

'You haven't said anything?'

'I can't. I...' Sadie's eyes stared into his, a shade lighter than her own, searching for reassurance that her mind wasn't playing tricks.

'You feel it too?'

She nodded.

'Look, I have to get back to my office, and this evening, I have a Home Guard meeting. Tomorrow, I have an appointment in Lincoln and will return late. Perhaps on Thursday we could go out for a meal, or I could take you to the cinema.'

She nodded again. Her voice appeared to have deserted her. Picking up her handbag, she delved inside and tore a page out of the notebook she kept there.

'My address and phone number.' She scribbled them on the paper, her hands shaking as she wrote them down and handed it to him. Sudden circumspection crept into her voice. 'Am I being mad? My husband was bad news. I don't want to go down that route again.'

He took her hand in his and looked at her. 'I am not like your husband, whatever he was like. I promise. Trust me. I would never let you down. I have this feeling about you – it's like meeting a soul-mate. Don't you feel it too?'

She nodded. 'God help me, I do.' Her voice no more than a whisper.

He took the bill to the cashier's desk. Sadie thought she knew the girl, tall with blond hair and a cheeky grin on her face; ah, yes, a friend of Glen's. The girl gave her the second wink she had received in one day.

Sadie would normally have shuddered in embarrassment, but today she simply smiled.

As she walked the short distance home, Sadie reviewed her surreal morning. After they left the Criterion, they had turned into the Market Place before she ducked into the greengrocers. Alex gave her a soft kiss of farewell on the cheek in front of everyone. Rather than flinch away, it left her wanting more.

She thought she was done with men; always refusing any invitations that came her way. Why was Alex Peter's different? There was no denying the instant attraction between them. She detected it, not in the café, but as soon as he walked in the door with Edna that morning. When Edna asked her to stay behind to help clear up, she noticed him glance at her, a tiny smile on his lips. But even clever old Edna could not have known what she was unleashing when she invited Alex to the meeting.

Sadie's mistrust of men as lovers was ingrained; how had this man shattered that into a thousand pieces with a single touch? The drizzling rain fell soft on her face; the cold wind cooled her feverish brow, a passing car splattered her with muddy water, and she laughed. Nothing could shake her joyful mood.

That night, after saying a prayer for each of her sons, her thoughts were of Alex. She dissected their meeting minute by minute, wondering what it all meant. Had she been carried away, was her brain playing tricks? That electric touch of his hand on hers, the way she felt compelled to kiss him, would have begged for a kiss on the lips when he brushed her cheek before parting. Was she ridiculous? A forty-six-year-old woman with the yearnings of a twenty-year-old. She had not sensed anything like this yearning since Rob, rarely with Frank, if she were honest. But now her hand crept to the inside of her thighs as she imagined his touch.

Chapter Twenty-Three

England
Cleethorpes, 1941

True to his word, Alex telephoned, and they arranged to meet at the Savoy Café above the picture house in Grimsby. It was convenient for him. More importantly, she deemed it unlikely that she would bump into anyone she knew. The encounter with her sister-in-law the day after her lunch with Alex still fresh in her mind.

'Hello, Sadie.' Jane was crossing the road from Woolworth's as Sadie came out of Humphrey's. 'You look as though you've been shopping for a few things.'

'Just thought I needed new underwear. It's been ages since I last bought any, but the prices have shot up. It's a good job I don't have three hungry lads to feed these days.' Why had she said that? It wasn't true. She would give anything to have them safe at home.

'Well, at least clothing isn't rationed. By the way, I've just met Muriel Brown, and she told me that yesterday a man in uniform kissed you outside the greengrocers'. I told her it must have been one of your sons, but she said he was too old.' Jane cast an enquiring glance at Sadie.

Damn and blast. Sadie was not prepared to share Alex with anyone yet. It was too new, too unnerving. What if it was a huge mistake and she was about to make a fool of herself?

'Oh, that!' She stumbled, racking her mind for some excuse. There was no man of her acquaintance Jane didn't know. A milder version of the truth would have to do. 'He's in the Home Guard and gave us a demonstration yesterday. We were both in the Criterion afterwards, so we shared a table.' Sadie was sure her ears were glowing, she tugged her hat down to disguise them.

'Well, it seems quite forward, giving you a kiss in public.'

'A peck on the cheek, no more, and he's a New Zealander, they're friendly types.'

Jane looked doubtful while Sadie cursed the nosy Mrs Brown, one of the most judgemental Chapel ladies. She could see her look of disapproval, her lips like withered prunes.

'Look, would you excuse me, Jane. I need to get home and change; I'm on duty this afternoon.' And she was longing to try on her new purchases and inspect her body. This last year of rationing meant that she had lost a few pounds, not that she had ever been anything other than slim. But her saggy stomach muscles were beginning to recover their tone. What was she thinking? The blood was rising in her cheeks as she wished Jane good day and set off down the hill to home.

The first evening with Alex sped by as they chatted about their children, nothing too serious, almost as though they were backpedalling from their emotionally charged lunch. In the cinema, they sat watching a romantic comedy like any other middle-aged couple. Their intermingling laughter calmed her nerves. She had not known what to expect from the evening and was grateful for this respite.

'Have you enjoyed yourself?' Alex asked on the bus home.

'I have. It's been delightful.'

'Good.' He smiled and tucked her hand into his. The chasteness of his gesture belied the feelings churning in her stomach. He was determined to be a gentleman. Once again, a brief peck on her cheek, before he lifted his hat at her door and saw her into the house. She wished she could wave at him from the window, but the black-out put paid to that.

After three such evenings out, the peck turned into a kiss but still he left to walk home, and she did not invite him in. It was early May, a fortnight since the cinema. Something was about to change. Was it up to her to push for it? Had they skirted around their attraction enough? She spent her evenings at home safe in the knowledge that he would not take advantage of her, but her body held its own opinion. How do I let him know, without seeming unladylike, she wondered?

'Are you sure?' Alex said to her invitation to come in for a nightcap, after their next evening out. His hand crept to her face as he stroked away a strand of hair in the bright moonlight. 'You have such silky skin, my love.' His breath ruffled her eyelashes.

'Yes,' her voice husky.

As soon as the door shut, she wanted to fall into his arms, but an all too familiar wail rent the air.

'Not now, damn it,' she heard him say.

'It's probably a false alarm, but we'd better get to the shelter.' She led the way through the house to the back door. By the time they were outside, they could hear the drone of the engines and scrambled the last few yards.

'I hate it on my own in here,' she said. 'I know they're on their way home and some other poor blighters have been hit. I try to tell myself I'm lucky, that they use the dock tower as a guide to Hull and Leeds, but one day, will it be our turn?'

He put his arm around her and pulled her close. That kiss held all the promise of her future; she drank him in.

'Sadie, I've been longing to do that for three weeks. Is that long enough to wait?'

'It is. I'm sure.' They kissed again.

The planes were overhead, the roar of the engines shaking the ground as they crouched on a strip of old lino. Let them pass, she prayed. Alex held her tight and she could hear his heart beating as he cradled her. Dogs began barking all around. The noise of the engines beat through her body, so close, too close. A loud whistling in the air outside, then an enormous explosion. Alex's arms tightened. It was too dark to see his face. Was it as terrified as hers?

Shock-waves travelled from the ground through her body. It felt like an earthquake, the earth shifting beneath her, crashing noises, children screaming, dogs howling. It felt like her breath was being forced from her lungs.

'Oh, God! Is it my house do you think?' She sobbed when her breath returned.

'Somewhere nearby, but not yours. Otherwise, the rubble would be falling on top of the shelter.'

Dust seeped beneath the makeshift door. It began to coat her face and clothes before a new terror arrived, the smell of burning. Was that the sound of adults screaming, bricks falling, maybe even whole walls? God forbid that any of her neighbours were trapped or suffocating. No children, please God, let no children die tonight. She was rocking back and forth in agitation as Alex tried to calm her.

'Sadie love, it was one bomb only. The engines are fading. It's going to be alright. They're on the way home.'

'You think so?' She couldn't see him in the dusty gloom. They'd never got around to lighting the lantern. Could she tell him what was on her mind? She opened her mouth to say it, to tell him that she wanted him, needed him, longed for him to stay with her, but the all-clear began to sound and the moment vanished.

They clambered out of the shelter and looked first at her house. It was still standing, the reflection of fire from behind in the remaining shards of glass in her back-bedroom window. Turning, they saw a bomb had hit houses in Bursar Street. The level of destruction rendered her speechless.

'I must see if I can do anything.' Alex said.

'So must I.'

'No, you stay put. It's too dangerous.' He ran up the garden path to the alley dividing the houses, but then turned back as a wall crashed to the ground, showering bricks into the passageway.

The sound of the fire engine bell, of men's voices shouting instructions, indistinct amidst the roar of the fire, spurred Alex into renewed action.

'I'll go around the other way. Stay here, and I'll call later this morning.'

She watched him go, then calmly walked into the house to pick up the phone.

'Edna, are you alright? Good. We'll need a mobile canteen in Bursar Street. There's a great deal of damage. I'm going there now to see what else we can do. You'll arrange it? Thank you.'

Grabbing her WVS armband, she stopped at the front door. Grim laughter as she saw she was still wearing one of her best coats and hats. She slipped on some comfortable shoes, tied a scarf around her hair and picked up the shabbiest of her coats. Whatever she was wearing would smell of smoke and brick dust on her return.

The ARP wardens had beaten her to it by the time she arrived. Straggles of women and children stood outside the school on the opposite side of the street, looking shocked and scared. Some of the younger children stood crying and clinging on to their mothers. At least four houses were gone; gable-ends standing but rooms exposed to the air, strips of curtains flapping at non-existent windows. How could that be?

'I'm with the WVS,' she introduced herself, but they looked through her, their thoughts elsewhere.

A man shouted, 'Get away! These walls are about to collapse.' Sadie looked up. Where was Alex, was he alright? She snapped back to her responsibilities.

'Let's get the children somewhere safe and in the warm. There's a rest centre I can take you to, and I bet you could do with a nice warm drink.' Maybe it was the warm drink that did it, but she got their attention. 'Move away from here, ladies.' She ushered them further away from the school.

'Everything's gone. What are we going to do?' A young woman nearing her time stood wringing her hands. 'I got everything ready for the baby. The cot, the pram, the baby bath it's all gone, even the terry nappies. My sister-in-law will be that narked at me for losing her pram.'

'We'll help you find replacements, don't worry dear.' Sadie patted the young woman on the arm.

'Come and stay with me, Elsie.' A middle-aged lady in curlers and hairnet offered.

'Where's that?' Sadie asked.

'My house is over there.' She pointed to one beyond the school. 'I've a spare room since my lad joined the navy.'

'Thank you. I'll call around tomorrow, so we can sort out what needs to be done.' Mothers, can you gather your children together, then I can see how many homes we are likely to need. Ah, four, no five families, good. What about your husbands, ladies, do they need accommodation?'

'Mine's at sea.'

'So's mine.'

'Mine's in the RAF at Binbrook, but my brother's still in there. God, please let them dig him out. I'm not leaving 'til they do.'

'Do you have children, dear?' Sadie asked the young woman whose hands were twisting in distress.

'No thank God. Who would want to bring children into this world?'

Another woman butted in, 'My hubby's over there, talking to the fireman. Here, Ernie, the lady wants you,' she shouted.

Ernie walked over. 'It's all gone Marge. 'There'll be nothing to salvage.' He looked crestfallen. 'All that work I did on the kiddies' bedrooms.'

'At least you're safe. That's what counts. Let's go and find you somewhere to stay.' Sadie reassured them.

'There's three unaccounted for,' Ernie whispered to Sadie. 'I'm not going anywhere. Don't tell the wife; her friend is missing.'

'Good job we were in the Anderson,' Marge said, oblivious. 'I never really bothered until they dropped one on the library up top town in February. I says to Ernie, if they can hit the library instead of the docks, they can drop one on us by mistake too.'

'I don't think they care where they drop them.' Sadie replied, thinking of the Dornier which had gunned down innocent women and children.

One of the little girls grabbed Sadie's hand. 'She thinks you're her granny,' said her mother.

'I'm flattered,' Sadie said, as they walked towards Isaac's Hill, passing the mobile tea-station van on its way to the scene. They'll be there a while, she thought. It looked like a long night for the rescue services.

'Duke! Duke!' a man called. 'Have you seen my dog, Missus? He scarpered when the sirens sounded. He's a goodun, saved the life of a drowning child a year or two back.'

'There's a dog back there,' Marge said. She laid her hand on the man's arm. 'Shrapnel got him, by the looks of him. Sorry love.'

'Ah, God love him.' Sadie caught tears glistening in his eyes in the light of the fire behind. 'I'd best find him, take him home.' He wandered off towards the fire.

'Cut in two he was,' Marge whispered. 'Poor beggar; bloody krauts.'

Another WVS lady arrived. 'If you take these families to the Rest Centre, I'll take this family home with me.' Sadie pointed to the child holding her hand. 'She's done in, poor mite.'

Sadie told the women she or someone else would call first thing in the morning to take down their names, arrange for next of kin to be informed, check if they needed ration books, etcetera. Mentally she was ticking off a checklist of things to do, as she guided the family down the hill towards her home.

'I'll go and make up some beds for you, Mrs Jones. Will the children sleep in the same bed?'

'Anything, Mrs Tinsdale. We're very grateful. Tomorrow, I'll take them to my mam in Healing. Lucky for us, I didn't put the children in their pyjamas, isn't it?'

'You're very sensible, Mrs Jones. The WVS will find you some extras; you can't go with just the clothes on your backs. Come with me tomorrow, and we'll sort you some out.'

'Jeannie here's wiped out. Look at her face; it's black with soot and smoke.'

'I'm afraid we all are,' Sadie said looking at her coat, once navy but now smudged grey and black. 'We'll see what five inches of water can do for us tomorrow.' Another luxury gone, hot deep baths with fine soap and a maid to lay out her freshly laundered silk underwear. What wouldn't she give for that now?

'I don't suppose you have any dripping? That's what they love on their toast for breakfast.'

Sadie surveyed the fraction of margarine left in the dish. 'I'm afraid not.'

The only dripping Sadie could tolerate was chicken dripping laced with a liberal amount of salt, but when would she next roast a chicken? She walked into the pantry, glancing at the empty shelves where stocks of tins and jars used to line up like rows of soldiers, constantly reinforced by new supplies as her sons grazed their way through them. A single jar of Tickler's jam remained since it became rationed in March. She'd been

183

keeping it for one of her boy's visits home but picked it up and carried it to the table.

'Look what I do have, bramble jam! I've been saving it for an occasion but what better one than this? It's lovely to have children in the house again.'

It was worth it to see their faces as she spooned out a globule of the dark red fruit onto their plates. 'What big eyes you have, my dears.' They laughed, a tinkling joy to her ears.

'They'll love that. It's cheese that I'm going to miss. I could have wept when they put it on the ration list last week,' said their mother.

A knock sounded at the front door. 'Excuse me, help yourself to more tea from the pot, Mrs Jones.' Sadie closed the door to the back room and walked down the hall. Opening the door, she found Alex standing there. Her mind flooded with relief.

'I was worried about you. How long did you stay to help?' She asked.

'Not long. There were more than enough firemen and ARP. I came back here. Banged on your door, but no answer.'

'I know. I'm sorry, Alex. I have a family here. I put them up overnight. They'll need new clothes, and I've a broken window to sort out, so I'll be busy for the rest of the day.'

'You went there when I told you to stay safely here?' His hand gripped her wrist and she shook it off. Someone else had done that. Suddenly she was unsure.

'Yes, I too had a job to do.' Her voice edged cold with annoyance.

'Damn it, Sadie, we need to talk. I can't wait another day for you. Who knows how long we'll have if the war carries on like this.'

Her expression softened. 'Can you meet me tonight?' Her sudden need to kiss him overwhelmed her.

'I'll book a table at the *Kingsway*.'

She walked back to her family of strays after he left. The *Kingsway*. Why there? Why not her house. A secret smile lit her face as she walked into the room.

Chapter Twenty-Four

England
Cleethorpes, May 1941

Sadie scoured her wardrobe for a suitable suit. Nothing was less than four years old. She wanted to look her best for the *Kingsway*. The navy suit looked too severe and the mustard too old fashioned, it must be seven years old at least. At last, she picked out a damson shaded skirt and fitted bouclé top with a white v-neck collar, a lacy, black blouse underneath completed the look. Smart, understated and it fitted her like a glove. Precious silk stockings and black shoes completed the ensemble. Dare she wear her sable wrap? She took it out and laid her face on it, stroking the soft fur. It needed airing; she wrinkled her nose at the odour of mothballs. No, she would wear her serviceable black, woollen coat.

She had managed to book a late appointment to have her hair cut and washed, the silvery strands amongst the black curls of her gentle perm were still far too few to be remarkable. After her bath she put on her recently acquired black brassiere and rayon panties, regretting that French knickers were unavailable in Humphrey's. She rejected the restriction of a corset, so a suspender belt held up her stockings. Next a sheer black underskirt. Now for the suit. Finally, she applied moisturiser to her face, pleased that her skin felt firm and silky, a little dab of powder and some lipstick. She stood back to view herself in the mirror, not bad, turned around, no slip showing; no unsightly bumps, seams on her hoarded stockings straight. Et voilà, she chuckled. When did I last dress as carefully, she mused? All she needed was a hat; her little black felt one would do, oh and a final dab of *Coty L'aimant* perfume.

Promptly at seven, a heavy knock sounded on the door. Sadie sauntered towards it, not wanting to appear too eager. She opened the door to a fine evening. Alex's mouth opened when he saw her and then he whistled in appreciation.

'Let me help you with your coat, my lady, although perhaps we should forget dinner.' His teasing tone lightened the suggestiveness of his words, but her insides tingled nonetheless.

She grabbed her handbag, gloves and gas mask and followed him outside, before locking the door. He tucked her arm in his as they walked to the bus stop.

There was more than a touch of spring in the air as they left the bus to cross the road to the best hotel on the seafront. Sadie had never visited the *Kingsway* before. From the front, it looked no more than a row of ordinary brick houses with bow windows. A larger oblong window sat to the right of the entrance, making it look more like a hotel. As soon as they entered she knew what set it apart from all the others in town. The air of calming comfort and good service developed over the years, pervaded the space. A waitress took their coats and led them to a bar where they were offered menus.

'Someone will be over to take your orders, Sir. May I get you both drinks, a dry sherry for you, Madam?'

Sadie nodded as Alex chose an ale. She opened the menu expecting to see a limited choice, but wartime did not seem to have affected it too much. 'Roast sirloin of beef. Oh, my word, do you think that is real sirloin? My mouth is watering already.'

'My mouth is watering just looking at you,' Alex replied, taking her hand. 'I've been dreaming of you.'

His hand felt electric in hers. They had sat side by side on the bus, his thigh touching hers. She almost agreed with forgetting dinner, but Sadie was hungry, starving in fact. She'd had no appetite for weeks, not since they met. Tonight, it returned, with a vengeance.

'And I of you. I feel like a giddy schoolgirl.'

'Well, you don't look like one. You look beautiful, sophisticated, glowing. How could any man have given you up?'

'Quite easily it seems. I don't want to think about him. Tell me about New Zealand.'

'No, you tell me about Australia. I want to listen to your voice.'

When it arrived, they attacked their meal with the gusto it deserved. Two slices of perfectly cooked pink sirloin, roast potatoes, crisp on the outside, fluffy in the middle, vegetables, not boiled to death, and rich meat gravy over a crisp Yorkshire pudding.

'I think I have died and gone to heaven,' said Sadie, placing her cutlery on her empty plate. She dabbed at her mouth with a linen serviette, hoping no fragment of gravy clung to her chin.

'I like a woman who enjoys her food.'

'Tell me one woman who wouldn't have enjoyed that.' She laughed. 'Thank goodness the siren didn't go off before I had time to finish it.'

'The beef was delicious wasn't it?'

'I can never buy it at the butchers, all I ever get offered is scrag end of lamb. All the best meat must come here.'

'Would you like dessert and coffee?'

'Don't tell me they have real coffee?'

'I think that would be difficult even for the *Kingsway*.'

She looked at him, fine lines around his eyes crinkling with laughter, drawing her in. His mouth, full and kissable, short hair, no need for Brylcreem, a few freckles across his nose, pointing to a sun-filled childhood. Oh, God, she wanted to feel his hands caressing her.

'Would Madam like a dessert? We have apple crumble or bread and butter pudding.' The waitress's interruption made her draw breath.

'Apple crumble,' she said, looking towards Alex. He nodded.

'Make that two please and whatever passes for coffee.'

He took her hand once the waitress had left. 'You know that I can't get you out of my mind. I want you tonight.' She swallowed hard as his thumb stroked her palm. 'There is nothing to stop us; we're both free.'

She nodded, unable to speak. Her insides turned to jelly. She didn't remember ever feeling like this, her nerves at exploding point. The apple crumble, when it was served, offered a feeble but welcome distraction.

'You haven't said anything.' Alex looked at her directly as she lifted the spoon towards her mouth.

She laid the spoon back in her bowl, her hand trembling. 'I thought all that part of me had died years ago, but I can't express these feelings.' Her eyes lifted to his. 'I want you too.' She looked around to see if anyone was within earshot. 'The longing I have is driving me insane.'

'Oh, my darling.' He grabbed her hand again, his smile promised much. 'I hope you won't think me presumptuous, but I have booked a room here.'

She burst into laughter, as fellow diners turned their heads to stare. 'Alex, thank the Lord for that.' Doubt left her. She quivered in anticipation.

They left the hotel separately after breakfast served in their room. Sadie gave Alex a deep kiss, his stubble scratching her face before he paused at the door and gave her that look again. Her stomach took a dive. She ached with desire for him. After he'd gone, she made full use of her five-inches of water to soak and play scenes of their lovemaking through her mind. Her skin shivered in the hot water; she missed his touch already. Her body sang like a finely-tuned instrument. The decadence of a night of passion in a hotel when his and her home were within walking distance, showed him in a thoughtful light. He had honoured her by it. Time enough later to consider the gossipy implications, if they were seen leaving each other's houses at breakfast time.

With a nonchalance she did not feel, she crossed the road outside the hotel to walk towards Brighton Slipway. A soft breeze bathed her face with no hint of cold north-easterly wind. The tide was in, covering the sand with more than a tinge of blue. Once on the promenade she made for the first bench and sat, breathing, almost gulping in the morning air. Her legs trembled. She closed her eyes and replayed the moments after the bedroom door closed. How they had fallen on each other like parched nomads discovering an oasis. No hint of shyness as he divested her of her jacket. The moment his fingers found the curve of her breast beneath her blouse, a pause as his eyes caressed her face. That look of wonder and his words; 'You are beautiful, do you know that?' That sharp intake of breath as she discovered that no man had ever looked at her in that way, never, not even Rob. Two or three seconds undid all those years when she had backed away from longing to be loved, to be touched, to be wanted.

188

She opened her eyes and looked about her. People passed by oblivious to the tumultuous emotions trampling through her mind. Her overwhelming hunger for this new man in her life, this joyful submission, no not submission, never submission with Alex. Everything about him was different. He had worshipped her body. She closed her eyes again in remembrance of her body glowing as his eyes kissed every inch of her before his mouth even touched her skin.

Frank had always been hungry, never tender, always demanding, rarely giving, always holding something back from her. A man judging his performance and finding it perfect, the light of triumph lighting his eyes when she came. When did Frank ever look at her with anything beyond hunger, then sardonic amusement, later impatience, followed by indifference and finally cruelty?

Her fault was that she continued to try to hold on to her marriage long after she should have walked away. She always made too many excuses for Frank, had been too ready to accept blame when he criticised her. Was it only now that she understood how easily Frank controlled her?

Sadie stood up and walked purposefully over to the railings above the flat, sandy beach; raised her hands and flung away all memories of Frank. She pleaded silently with the seagulls to swallow him up, fly him out to sea and spit him out to sink and drown. His power gone, she renounced him, as she renounced the devil in chapel. Could Alex's love sustain and bless her now? Although she hoped so, a deep part of her told her to be wary. She had been let down before. Maybe this man would be the one, but - there was always that *but*.

Turning away, a smile lighting her face, she decided to walk back through the station to Prince's Road. She had no wish to meet prying eyes who would question why she was dolled up to the nines in the morning. Alex was her secret for now, and she wanted him to remain that way. A secret, but not guilty, pleasure, a wondrous, glorious one.

Chapter Twenty-Five

England
Cleethorpes, 1941

Sadie revelled in her secret love affair. No air raids disturbed their nights together. The Germans had gone quiet for some reason, and the tension began to evaporate. Alex arrived at her house after dusk, which got later and later as the summer advanced, and he left with the dawn chorus. He never used the front door, always the passage which led from Bursar Street.

Every night he said, 'Marry me, then we wouldn't have to pretend.'

Every night she prevaricated, saying, 'Yes, but only when we have our children home. I want Henry to give me away, and I want to tell them about us, in person. I don't want to write to them. It would seem too cold, too uncaring.'

He disagreed, 'A letter would prepare them.' He wrote to his daughter after their first night together, telling her he had met an amazing woman and he longed for them to meet. Her response was 'How wonderful, Dad. Tell her I can't wait.'

In the end, Alex lost patience. 'It's not enough to spend three nights a week with you. I want to spend my Sundays with you too. I want to meet your sister-in-law and walk around the boating lake like other couples, have afternoon tea in the *Birds Nest Café*, take you dancing and most of all I want you to wear my ring.'

He had bought her an engagement ring of sapphire and diamonds the week before, 'to match your eyes', he'd said, as he placed it on her finger. She always wore it when she was with him, but he knew she removed it during the day. He had dropped into the WVS, and there she was, no ring on her finger, nor congratulations proffered by Edna or the other ladies.

'I'm fed up with this subterfuge, Sadie.' That night, he left angrily without taking her to bed. The door slammed behind him.

She could not bear to argue with him, but her feelings remained complicated. Because she had buried all thoughts of love and marriage the day she left Adelaide, this illicit reawakening thrilled her; even more that it was private, unshared. She lost her concerns about scandal the evening he first made love to her in her own bed. Nights were spent in delicious lovemaking, not talking about themselves. They knew little more about each other than they had disclosed over the fish and chip lunch or at the cinema.

But now, his words made her understand how unfair she was being. She forced herself to consider the reason she was keeping their romance secret. For hours she thought about it until the answer came in the early hours. By taking pleasure from their lovemaking but not committing herself, she retained control, allowing him her body, but not herself. While no one else knew of their affair, she could walk away without disappointing anyone but Alex. The damage Frank had inflicted on her went deeper than she realised. She needed to learn to trust once more. But trust was the hardest thing to give. Could she learn to offer it unreservedly?

The following day, she wrote to each of her sons, pleading with Henry and Dale to wangle a weekend pass home soon. To Glen in Singapore, it was easier to write that she had met a man she wanted to marry. His memory of his father was negligible, he never mentioned him. Maybe Henry had told him not to. Her oldest son knew some of what had gone on, being almost ten when they boarded ship for England.

Next, she donned a jacket and walked around to Jane's house.

'Come to tea on Sunday; there's someone I want you to meet.'

Jane pumped her for more information, but Sadie refused to be drawn. Her ringless hand did not give the game away. After Sunday, she intended to wear her ring for anyone to see.

Before leaving for her afternoon shift at the WVS, she scribbled a note to Alex for Edna to drop into his letterbox. Edna would enjoy knowing that her subterfuge had worked. Although she would ask no questions.

My darling Alex, I have been selfish keeping you to myself, I know. I have invited Jane to meet you for tea on Sunday, and I have written to my

191

boys asking them to wangle a leave. Don't go home on Saturday after Home Guard, come to me, bring a change of clothes and we'll spend Sunday together.

I do love you; please be patient with me. There's a lot to tell you.
Sadie

Sadie bathed on Saturday night. She found a bottle of *Eau de Paris*, a forgotten Christmas present from one of her boys, at the back of the bathroom cabinet, and put several drops into the water. After drying herself, she slipped on a peach, silk negligée, an unworn relic from Adelaide, bought in more optimistic times. The silk glided over her body, her fingers stroking it, loving the sensual feel of it over her hips. Why she had packed it, she did not remember, but was grateful that she had.

Her wardrobe sported several new outfits which would be impossible to buy now. Clothes rationing, announced at the beginning of June, shocked everyone. Maybe it was just as well because she could not continue spending money. As her desire for Alex had grown, so had her appetite for new clothes. She enjoyed seeing the appreciation in his eyes as they scanned her body and then he slowly undressed her. None of her new clothes had seen the light of day. On Sunday that would change too.

He arrived at ten o' clock, the last remnant of light leaving the sky. Sadie bundled him inside before revelling in his kiss. His hands urgently swept her body, the thin silk rippling over her skin, taunting her.

'Sadie, Sadie, Sadie.' His breath devoured her.

'Come.' Her hand reached for his, and she led him through to the back room, intending to take him upstairs. They got no further. He pulled a cushion from her fireside armchair, throwing it onto the floor and pulled her down. The illicit feel of this affair was exciting, but would it change once they were married? Would it be a marriage of equals this time?

Alex is different, Alex is a good man, he won't hurt me. She knew she was drowning, aching for the feel of him inside her, for the look of adoration in his eyes as he matched her pleasure. Was this love, rather than passion? If so, she had not known it could feel this way. When she was in his arms, she was content to abandon everything she knew about herself. Could she stop holding herself back from giving all of herself?

They lay there, on the carpet, his arm draped over her breast until she shivered.

'Come to bed,' she said. 'Tomorrow we'll talk. I'll tell you about my marriage and why I hesitate to remarry.'

Chapter Twenty-Six

Australia   -
Nelyambo, 1918

The telegram arrived in late January. *Come home, Frank arriving Adelaide any day, Papa.* Sadie stared at it, at first uncomprehending. A multitude of questions flitted through her mind. She passed the cable to Stanley. There had been no telegram saying he was boarding ship before she left, no notification of injury requiring passage home.

'You have to leave, of course.'

Sadie caught Jane's frown as Stanley spoke.

'You must be excited about having your husband home,' Jane said, overcoming her disappointment. 'I'll miss you.'

Sadie wasn't sure what she felt. She needed time to digest the news.

'It could take me weeks to get home.' Half of her craved those weeks.

'Not if you go overland. I can take you in the truck to Wilcannia; then you can get a coach to Broken Hill. It will be a hard, overnight slog. They only to stop to change horses and eat.'

'What about Henry? He's only a baby, not two until March.'

'I crossed the Nullarbor as a baby. But if you're worried, let Bridget take him home by river.'

Sadie tossed the idea around. Could she bear to be parted from Henry for that amount of time? What would Frank think if she did not arrive back with his son? On the other hand, without Henry, it would give them time to reacquaint themselves, to learn how to live with each other.

'What do you think, Jane?'

'We brought Nancy back from Dubbo when she was days old, but that was winter.'

'You're right. I'll take Henry back with me.' Never let it be said that she was less able to cope with hardship than her sister-in-law.

Bridget looked horrified at the idea. 'All that time in a coach, Ma'am? It will be awful for the little lad.'

Sadie glared at Bridget. 'Bridget, you can go back by river. Maybe it's time we found a governess rather than a nursemaid. Or perhaps Mrs Timmins needs a nursemaid?' Sadie would not be dictated to by a servant, but then felt guilty as tears formed in Bridget's eyes. What is wrong with me? I'm all at sixes and sevens, she thought. 'Bridget, it will be alright. He can cope with a couple of days of hardship.'

'It's this heat, Mrs Tinsdale. Little Henry will be that crabby with it. He'll be screaming and squirming and upsetting all the other passengers.'

That was true. Why put the boy through hours in a coach when the temperature could reach a hundred? Her mind was in turmoil. She decided to see how Henry coped with the truck journey.

They set off at dawn. Sadie hugged her sister-in-law and begged her to visit them in Adelaide before too long. Jane waved them goodbye, little Nancy in her arms. The forlorn expression on Jane's face tugged at Sadie's heart. Poor love, she was not meant to live a life without female companionship.

They squeezed together in the cab like sardines. Henry sat on Bridget's lap, at first content to stare out of the window, still sleepy from his early morning wake-up. The motion of the truck along the ruts had him dozing again, and Sadie sighed with relief. Bridget's dire predictions may prove to be groundless.

The sun worked its way higher, infusing the bush with an orange glow. Sadie's thoughts slowed as she let the beauty of dawn take over. Puffs of clouds shaded the saltbush and grass-strewn earth, like an ever-changing tableau of crimson and green. Sheep bleated as the river gums stirred in the slight breeze and Henry stirred with them.

By the time they got half-way to Wilcannia, a decision had been made. Henry would travel back by steamer with Bridget. His cries of frustration at being held on Bridget's lap when all he wanted to do was get down and run around, wore down their nerves. Sadie tried holding him and pointing things out, but there was a limit on how interested he was in the flat, scrub-covered land. He grizzled in the heat and grizzling turned to cries and cries turned to screams. To pacify him, Stanley halted the truck, while Sadie let Henry get down and run around for a few minutes, keeping a close watch out for mulga snakes.

'How on earth did our parents cope with you on the trip to Perth from Sydney?' Sadie asked Stanley.

'I think I was younger, probably not walking. But if I was anything like Henry, I'm surprised I survived without them throttling me.'

They reached Wilcannia by midday and made for the nearest hotel. Sadie booked them in while Stanley parked the truck. Bridget took Henry to see the riverboats while Sadie soaked in a bath to soothe her shaken body. When Stanley arrived back at the hotel, he came with news.

'We are in luck. A steamer's departing tomorrow for Wentworth, and a mail coach is leaving for Broken Hill early tomorrow with one free seat inside. Travelling through the night, it will take less than two days to get there. Do you think you can manage that?

'Yes, and that will let you get back to Jane tomorrow.'

I'd rather not leave her too long. Otherwise, she gets lonely. I called at the post office to send a telegram, and they gave me this for you.' He handed her another telegram, which she ripped open.

'Frank home, foot injury, recovering well.' She read out, noticing Stanley's frown. 'What is it, Stanley?'

'Nothing probably.'

'No, tell me.'

'It's winter in Europe. Not much fighting going on. How has he injured his foot?'

Sadie shrugged, she had no idea what he was getting at.

'Let's just say, shooting yourself in the foot is a way of getting yourself sent home.'

'You don't have a high opinion of Frank, do you?'

'I spent all of two weeks in France. He's been through Gallipoli and two years in the trenches, so I can't criticise. Sometimes men have had enough; they can't cope with another winter in freezing mud, the constant barrage of whizz-bangs. I've heard of men going mad in the trenches.'

196

'I haven't heard you talk much about the war.'

'No man who loves his family will talk about it. We want to forget, don't want our families to know the worst. Forget I said anything, Sadie. It's best you don't bring it up.'

Sadie stooped over Henry's cot in the early hours of the following morning and stroked his face.

'Bye-bye, my little love. Mama will see you in three or four weeks.' She stood and grasped Bridget's hand. 'You will look after him, won't you?'

'Never you mind, Ma'am. I have his reins. He'll be happier on the boat.'

'I know. Let me know which train you catch from Morgan, so I can send a car to meet you.'

'I will. Have a good trip yourself, Mrs Tinsdale. You must be relieved that your husband is home safe.'

Sadie nodded. She wiped a tear from her eye as she bent down to kiss Henry goodbye.

Stanley accompanied her to the coach.

'I'll see Bridget and Henry on to the steamer with your trunk. It was grand to have you for Christmas.'

'Jane is such a darling; I loved staying with you. Try and bring her down to Adelaide some time.'

'I will,' Stanley said, as he handed her into the coach. 'Look after my sister for me, coachman.'

'We will sir; the little lady will be safe with us.'

Seconds later the coach and horses set off. Sadie waved at her brother and settled back in her seat, taking note of the other passengers, all male, all smiling at her in that courteous manner of the outback, where women are rare and treasured beings. She smiled back, before looking out of the already dusty window. Her thoughts turned to her husband.

Now that Frank was back, where would they live? What would he do? Would Papa buy another sheep station for them to run? Would Frank be any good on a sheep station? Unless he had changed dramatically, she thought not. What would he be like? Still his charming, debonair self or someone different, changed by the effects of war?

As they crossed the bridge over the Darling in the early morning light, she sensed she was saying goodbye to her carefree youth and entering the world of her grown-up self.

Sadie slept little on the coach. Every few hours the coachman blew his post horn, signalling their imminent arrival at a hostel to change horses and take some refreshment. Otherwise, the journey was a relentless slog through the flat bushland. Occasional camels grazed the land amongst the sheep, the first Sadie had seen. They stared back at the coach, their mouths slowly chewing clumps of salt bush, looking for all the world like mythical beasts from a child's picture book.

'You're staring at the camels, Ma'am. Is this the first time you've seen them?' One of the passengers asked.

'It is. I was wondering if they were the descendants of those used by the Burke and Wills expedition?

'Ah, you're a romantic,' he chuckled. 'Probably not, they're most likely descended from those that were brought over back in 1882 when the Darling ran dry.'

'Dry! Does that happen very often?' Sadie asked in some apprehension.

'Every ten years or so. Camel trains are vital for carrying provisions when that happens.'

Ten years! Sadie wondered when the Darling had last run dry. If it were so often, the station owners must have ways of dealing with it.

The conversation of her male companions swirled above her head as she tried to sleep, but it wasn't that which made sleep difficult, nor the jolting of the coach, but apprehension. Frank, her husband, waited at the end of this journey. For two and a half years, she had been able to ignore her marriage. She never wished him ill, but there was always the possibility he would not return, and that she could continue to ignore it. Her mind now tried to grasp details of how he looked, how he smiled, how he talked, how he danced with her in his arms and the feel of his hand around her waist. The memories were shrouded in a mist of her unresolved feelings. It was time to face up to them, to concentrate on their future together.

As they entered the streets of Broken Hill at noon the following day, she smelt the greasy smoke from the tall chimneys; it caught in the back of her throat. Her fellow passengers began fidgeting with their belongings, gathering newspapers, pipes and other small items together. They all knew she was returning to Adelaide to meet her husband, home from the war, and each wished her a joyful reunion. Sadie had asked advice about hotels. She intended to stay in one overnight and freshen up before the fifteen-hour rail journey back to Adelaide.

When they came to a halt, the coachman hopped off his perch, men atop the coach began handing down luggage as the coachman opened the door. Sadie stepped down onto a wooden box; her eyes cast down to make sure she did not miss the makeshift step and was grabbed from the side, lifted into the air and kissed soundly on the mouth. Her shocked eyes met those of Frank, inches from her own. When at last he released her, she felt her heart pounding in her chest. She couldn't speak and was grateful to her fellow passengers each shaking Frank by the hand in turn.

'Now, look after the little lady, mate,' one said.

'Don't worry; I intend to, mate.' Frank replied, smiling, his free arm encircling her waist.

She was proud of him, standing there in uniform. How could she have forgotten him? Thinner, yes, fine lines around his eyes, his olive skin a shade lighter than she remembered, but so handsome that her heart began to flutter. She released her doubts into the hot, dusty air. Her husband, returned from a long and gruelling war, deserved her respect and love.

'Come,' he said after everyone had shaken his hand and wished the couple well. 'I have booked us a room in the Imperial Hotel. You look tired, and I am sure you could do with a nice, hot bath.'

She noticed him limping slightly as they walked the short distance towards one of her grandmother's old hotels.

'How are you, Frank?'

'Better now that I have you back. What have you done with our son, by the way? I assume you didn't lose him along the way.'

'No, he's travelling back by steamboat with his nursemaid. I couldn't bear to let him travel by coach.'

'I hope she's trustworthy.' She detected a slight chill in his tone.

'Of course. Bridget has been with him since he was a few days old. He adores her, and they should arrive back in Adelaide in three weeks or so. I know you must be longing to meet him. How did you know I would be arriving here today? Did Stanley send a telegram?' He nodded.

They arrived at the hotel, brick built with a green and gold veranda wrapping around it. Frank checked them both in.

'The best room in the house, please.' He winked at Sadie. Her insides trembled. Could it be that she desired him?

He guided her up the stairs, the key to a large room with its own bathroom next door, in his hand. A maid arrived soon after to draw the water for her, while she unpacked her few belongings.

'I didn't bring much with me, only a single change of clothes.'

'Don't worry, my love,' he whispered in her ear. 'For the next three days, you won't need any clothes. I don't intend sharing you with anyone.'

He wooed her and charmed her until she began to fall under his spell. While he slept, she traced the marks of war on his body, puckered lines of cuts where shrapnel or barbed wire had pierced the skin, but no bullet wounds. He told her that a piece of shrapnel had cut a tendon in his foot at the raid on Cambrai, putting an end to his marching days. She stroked the furrowed skin of his foot, thanking it for returning her husband to her. Her doubts about this marriage began to be assuaged. The care, the love and the passion he professed, reworked their magic on her. On the second night, she woke to feel him shuddering beside her. She laid a hand upon his chest, and he screamed as though in terror.

'Frank, wake up, you're safe.'

His eyes opened wide, staring at something, but not seeing.

She kissed him on his cheeks, murmuring endearments until he calmed, and her heart softened with love for him as it did for her son when in pain.

The few times they left the hotel for an evening walk, she noticed the glances he received and glowed with pride to be on his arm. It did not stop her from looking at men's faces as they passed, remembering one could be a half-brother. She kept silent on that front; the secret belonged to Eddie and herself.

On the final evening, when she was regretting her second honeymoon was about to end, Frank said, 'We need to find our own house in Adelaide. I don't want to live with your father and stepmother.'

'Yes, we must. We'll start looking as soon as we get home.'

'I haven't sorted out my mother's estate yet. We'll need to go to Melbourne to do that.'

'Have you any idea about what you want to do for a job?'

'I told you before I left, I want to open a nightclub once the war is over and the men are home. It may take a couple of years, but there will be a lot of planning. I'll take something to tide us over until then.'

Sadie had a vague memory of him saying that, but it didn't seem like a proper job to her. 'I thought Papa might offer you something.'

'He's got no contracts, and I'm not going to be stuck out in the bush on some sheep station.' He stopped and turned to face her. 'Sadie, I'm a city person, never expect me to be anything else. Men will want to forget about the war, and I will provide somewhere they can. With you by my side, we will have entry to all the best families. It's going to attract people with money, not be some sleazy affair like that place I took you to in Sydney.' He laughed. 'I'll never forget your face. You were shocked, admit it.'

'I was a bit,' she agreed. 'But won't it cost an awful lot of money to open such a place?'

'Leave that to me; I'm not having you bother your pretty head with money.'

He took her in his arms and kissed her deeply, right there in the middle of the street. She struggled a little, conscious of disapproving stares, but it only made him hold her tighter until he groaned and said, 'We might as well make the most of our last night here.' He took her arm and marched her back to the hotel. His limp barely visible.

She walked willingly, her eyes focussed on him alone, scarcely believing how much she wanted him, it was as though he only had to lift a finger and she would run to him. All doubts about their marriage dispersing as her body began to rule her brain.

Chapter Twenty-Seven

Australia
Adelaide, 1918

Frank found a small house in South Terrace for them to rent. They were packing up to move on the day the steamer docked at Morgan. Over the past weeks, Frank had showered Sadie with such attention and affection that she began to believe she was falling in love with her husband. Even Papa had been charmed.

Sadie was on tenterhooks, waiting for the moment her son met Frank. I should have asked Bridget to prepare Henry, she thought. I wonder if he is excited to see his father? She kept looking out of the window, waiting for Papa's Buick to draw up outside, while Frank read the situations vacant in the newspaper. As yet, no suitable work had turned up, and Sadie could sense his frustration. He was due to be discharged from the army any day.

The gruff throb of a car engine drifted through the open window. Sadie glanced down.

'They're here!' She began to race across the room to the door. 'Come on Frank, let's go downstairs to meet them.'

'My foot's aching. They'll be here soon enough. Sit down, Sadie.'

She stopped at the door, surprised and disappointed. How could he be so calm, when her heart was pounding? She opened the door, hearing murmurs of the maid greeting Bridget and Henry two storeys below.

'Sit down. It's best we meet him here. I don't want the nanny gawking. Take Henry from her when she reaches our landing.' Frank sounded irritated with her.

'I suppose not.' But the sound of her father greeting Henry reached her from below. Henry was giggling in delight. He loved his grandpa's whiskers tickling his face. In the end, she could not bear to wait and ran down the stairs to Henry, calling to him.

'Mama, Mama, I been on a boat,' he lisped, from his Grandpa's arms. He held his arms out to her, and she ran to pluck him from her Papa and covered his face with kisses, thankful he had not forgotten her.

'Have you, Henry? Did you like the boat?' He nodded his head to her. 'Come, there's a very special person for you to meet upstairs.'

'Is it my papa? Bidgy said my papa come home.'

'He has, my darling. Let's go upstairs to find him, shall we?'

Sadie carried him back up the stairs with Bridget trailing behind. She put him down on the first landing, finding him almost too heavy to carry. How he'd seemed to have grown in the last few weeks, and his language was improving. Frank would be proud.

'Let me take him,' Bridget said.

They walked to the next landing, and Sadie opened the door to find Frank still sitting with his newspaper.

He looked up. 'I asked you to stay here, Sadie.'

'Oh, but I couldn't wait, Frank. Here he is, Look, Henry, here's your papa.'

Bridget walked in with Henry still in her arms. Sadie expected him to clamour to be set down on the carpet and to run to his father.

Frank remained seated, 'Hello, Henry. I am your Papa. Come and say, hello.'

What was it, his stern tone of voice, his lack of smile, the strangeness of his face? Henry stared and then burst into tears and clung to Bridget, who looked embarrassed.

'Henry, stop your tears and come here.' Frank's command reinforced Henry's fear and his cries turned to sobs.

Sadie took her son from Bridget and crooned to him. 'There's no need to be afraid, darling. Here is your dearest Papa who loves you and who has come a long way away to meet you.' His cries continued louder. He clutched at his mother's hair, burying his face in hers and kicked his legs against her skirt. She heard Frank throw his newspaper down. He stood and grasped their son then put him on the floor.

'Stand up Henry,' he commanded, repeating it louder when he failed to comply. Slowly the boy looked at him, his thumb lodged in his mouth.

'Stand up this minute, boy.'

'Frank, he's still a baby,' Sadie protested. 'It's all too much for him. Be gentle, and he'll come to you in good time. Maybe he's tired. I'll take him for a nap.'

Frank stood glaring at Henry, still cowering below him, and stalked out of the room to their bedroom, his face thunderous.

Sadie began to shake, unbelieving. What had come over Frank? Bridget ran to pick up Henry who burst into renewed sobbing.

'I'll settle him and get him to sleep, Ma'am.' She scurried off with him, not looking at Sadie, whose face was white.

What should she do? Should she go to Frank or wait for him to calm down? How could he have reacted like that to their son? Poor Henry, he'd been terrified. Walking to a chair, she crumpled into it, her legs turned to jelly, her palms sweating. Did her husband have no idea how to treat a child? She left it a minute or two before deciding to go and confront Frank.

She walked into their bedroom to find him donning his outside coat.

'Where are you going, Frank?'

'It's really none of your business, Sadie. Why didn't you do as I asked and stay upstairs? I didn't want to meet him with a servant looking on. Do you realise how bad you have made me look?'

She stepped backwards in surprise, not expecting his accusation. 'Calm down, my love. Why get so upset? Henry will come around after he's had a nap. Tiredness can make a child crotchety.' Sadie walked over to him and attempted to put her arms around him, but he shook her off.

'I can't stand the sound of cries and screams! It brings it all back. I need peace in my home.'

'I'm sorry my love. I didn't think. He won't cry when he's used to you.'

He made for the door without another word. Sadie could hear him stomping down the stairs, his limp more pronounced, leaving her feeling upset and guilty. Had she been thoughtless? Was it her fault?

Frank did not appear at dinnertime. Her father asked after him, a frown in his eyes. Sadie did her best to cover for him, saying he had gone out in search of work. It was late in the evening when he returned. Sadie had contemplated going to bed, but she stayed up worrying. As she heard his steps on the stairs, she felt relieved. They had never argued since Sydney, and her heart raced with relief at his return.

'What are you doing up?' His words slurred as he stumbled towards her.

'Where have you been? I have been going out of my mind.'

'Where do you think?'

'But they stop selling alcohol after six.'

'There's always somewhere willing to break the rules. Come here, Sadie. Kiss me.'

She sat still and dismayed as he swayed over her. He grabbed hold of her, pulling her up before planting a whisky laden breath on her lips. She struggled to free herself, but his grip tightened.

'You know what I want, Sadie dear.' His voice thickened with lust.

'You're drunk.' She tried once more to get away, but he pushed her onto the floor and dropped to his knees, fiddling with his buttons.

'No, Frank, don't. Not like this.'

'Yes, Sadie, Like this. You know you love it, you always love it. That's what I like about you.' He covered her mouth with his, while he pulled at her undergarments.

Was that true? This didn't feel like the first time he forced her. He didn't try to woo her, to make her want him, his mouth bruised hers as he tore her drawers. She felt him ram into her and all she felt was pain. Once more she tried to struggle, but it only made him more determined, so she forced herself to lay still. Tears came unbidden to her eyes. Over the last few weeks, she had convinced herself that she loved this man, but this was his second betrayal of that love. His body pinned her to the carpet, burning her cheeks as he continued to force his way between her legs. At last, he came, shuddering, his mouth widened in a rictus of release and pleasure. He flopped off her without noticing her, without caring for her feelings and within seconds was snoring.

She moved away, trying not to wake him. Her torn bloomers lay beside him like a white flag of surrender. She picked them up between her forefingers in distaste; her legs wobbled as she forced them to walk her to the bedroom. After stripping off her clothes and wiping herself with a cloth, she lay on her bed, covered only by a sheet, shaking and weeping until the clock struck midnight. She couldn't leave Frank there for the maid to find, but neither did she want him beside her in bed.

Deciding that the maid discovering him in disarray was the worst of two evils, she forced herself to rise, put on her nightgown and returned to the sitting room. Frank lay on the floor, still snoring, oblivious. She knelt down and shook him for several minutes until he roused himself sufficiently for her to pull him up and encourage him into bed, where he lay comatose for the rest of the night.

They were moving the following day. Sadie busied herself packing as a distraction from her hurt and rage. Bridget had taken Henry out of the way. There was no sign of Frank resurfacing until mid-morning. When he did show his face, Sadie did not know what to expect. Would he be apologetic? She hoped so or how else could she continue to live with him? Should she even move from her father's house? What she did not expect was that he treated her as normal, with no sign of remorse for what had occurred.

Sending the maid away to fetch breakfast for the master, she considered what to say.

'Where's the little fella?' Frank asked in all innocence. 'I haven't had a chance to meet him yet.'

'He's gone out for a walk with Bridget. Frank, about yesterday…'

'What about yesterday?' His look, was it guilt free or daring her to mention it? 'I was in pain yesterday. I took some pills my doctor gave me, and for the life of me, I can't remember anything after lunch time. I hope I didn't disgrace myself,' he laughed. 'Today is a new day, let's forget yesterday.'

Could it be true? 'You don't remember going out and coming home drunk?'

'Did I?' He shrugged his shoulders. 'Oh good, here comes breakfast. I could eat a horse. You don't know what I would have given for bacon and eggs in the trenches.' He beamed at the maid as she set it out for him.

When Henry appeared at the sitting room door a few minutes later, Frank smiled at him. Henry looked uncertain.

'Come and give your Pa a hug, little fella. Frank's voice was warm and gentle. He smiled encouragement as Henry took a step forward, looking from Frank to his mother.

Sadie walked towards him and took him by the hand. 'Your Papa's been longing to meet you, sweetheart.'

Henry climbed on to Frank's lap where he was offered a slice of toast with butter. Sadie saw him relax as he began to chew. Henry's fingers explored his papa's face, and Frank encouraged him, before tickling him under his arm and making him giggle.

Sadie let out a breath. Whatever those pills were, she needed to get rid of them and replace them with something less strong. She couldn't risk another day like yesterday.

However much she searched over the coming days, she found no pills. If she asked Frank about them, would he think her prying? Best to leave it for now. Their move went to plan. Frank mostly left her and the servants to it, as he stayed out searching for work. He reported one or two leads, and she kissed him each morning, wishing him luck.

She had her own concerns. No more than a taste but a taste she recognised from before her wedding, like chewing a piece of rusty iron. It was only to be expected, of course, the number of times they had made love, but she retained the awful suspicion that it had happened when he forced her. Did pregnancy occur more when…? She couldn't use the word rape and had no one to ask. What did she feel about it? Her longing for another son or daughter versus the way begotten. Silly me, I won't care once it's in my arms, but it niggled somewhere in the back of her mind.

Five weeks after they moved, she found Bridget in tears.

'Whatever's the matter?'

Bridget looked at her with some suspicion. 'You don't know?'

'Know what? Is there something the matter with Henry?' Sadie's voice rose in alarm.

'No, Ma'am, nothing like that. Oh, I will miss the darling boy.'

'What, why? Where are you going?'

'The master gave me my marching orders this morning. Says he don't want no live-in servants. I'm to leave by the end of the week. Where will

I go, Ma'am? I've only my brother in Port Adelaide, and he's no space with his brood.'

'It must be a mistake. Let me talk to the Master.'

'No mistake, Ma'am. He said,' and she sniffed, 'he didn't like me singing Fenian songs to Henry, but it was only an Irish lullaby.'

'But that's nonsense.' No nanny! What was he playing at? Anger simmered in Sadie's brain. He was worried about money, but she had enough. Plenty! Papa would be horrified to think of her without a nanny. What about the cook, had he dismissed her? She was Irish, only hired when they moved into the house. Sadie marched off to find out.

'Is everything alright, Mrs Sykes? How are you settling in?'

'It's all good, Mrs Tinsdale.' A jovial smile lit her thin face while her knobbly hands attacked dishes in the hot, sudsy water. Grey straggly hair tumbled from her cap in the steam.

'Has my husband spoken with you this morning?'

'He did so. He knows I have a daughter looking for a job and he asked her to come to the house tomorrow. Begging your leave, Mrs Tinsdale. Is that alright?'

'Remind me, what job is that?' Sadie felt both embarrassed and confused. What was going on?

'Day nanny. He says that Bridget is leaving. My daughter's a good lass, so she is. Mary will be perfect for little Henry. She loves babies.' Mrs Sykes looked at her strangely, doubt in her washed-out eyes. Even she could tell something was not right.

Sadie fought for some reasonable explanation. How could Frank put her in this position? It was her job to deal with servants. Poor Mrs Sykes, she had been that grateful for the job with her husband unable to work after an accident. Her cooking was wholesome enough, and she had received some training in a good kitchen before her marriage. But her daughter looking after Henry? That was another matter entirely.

'Thank you. I'll come back to speak with you later.' She turned and left the kitchen with as much composure as she could muster, her hands clenching and unclenching.

She heard the door slam around five, his footsteps heavy along the hallway. She stood to greet him, but he met her with a scowl. Her prepared and practised harsh words died in her throat as he threw his hat on the chair.

'It seems the shirkers have all the best jobs. Just what was the point, eh? My service for the Empire counts for precisely nothing.' He glared at her, daring her to say something.

She moved to pick up his hat, and he grasped her by the wrist, whisky breath again.

'Shall I call for tea, dear?' She attempted to deflect his anger.

'No, a whisky.'

'Don't you think you've drunk enough?'

His grip tightened. 'Not by a long mile. Never tell me when or what to drink, do you hear?'

'I'm sorry, Frank. Shall I run you a bath and bring you a whisky to sip before dinner?' Anything to calm him down.

His released his grip He smiled but without humour. 'Playing the good wifey now, are we? Yes, why don't you, then you can join me.'

'Frank, I can't. Henry needs his tea.'

'Let Bridget give it to him. That's what we pay her to do.'

'About Bridget.' Was this a good time? He had brought her into the conversation. 'She tells me you've given her notice. I don't want to lose her; Henry loves her; he'll be heartbroken.'

'We can't afford her.'

'Of course, we can. My money can stretch to that.'

'Your money, your money!' He spat out the words and gripped her wrist tighter, this time so tight she tried to wriggle away, but he only increased the pressure. 'It should be me that pays the bills, and I have no money. The lawyer in Melbourne wrote that my father left nothing but the house, and that will go for less with this war on.'

'I didn't realise. When did you hear?' Tears threatened as his fingernails dug into her flesh.

'Yesterday. Bridget had no business blabbing to you. I don't like her. Her brother's a shirker, did you know that? Don't want her in the house. I'm sure she set Henry against me, that first day.'

So, he did remember! 'Bridget's brother has four children to support.'

'Yes, but those damn Irish Australians didn't exactly flock to enlist, even before 1916. They mostly support those dogs who rose up in Dublin, don't they? Sixty thousand in Melbourne turned out to cheer on the 'brave' on St Paddy's Day last week. Not men like me who fought in Gallipoli and France, but those traitors upholding the 'glory of Ireland' for God's sake!'

Sadie remembered reading that Dr Mannix had raised his berretta to the martyrs of Dublin but replaced it during the National Anthem. She found that shocking and sympathised with Frank's view, but still thought he was treating Bridget shabbily. 'Cook's Irish and her daughter too, Frank.'

'Her husband's English, a good Protestant and so's the daughter.' He began to shout to make his point. 'I'll not have Fenians in this house, do you hear.'

She nodded, her body began to quiver in alarm. 'Let me run you that bath, Frank.' His grip slackened.

'Yes, do that and bring me an extremely large whisky.' He patted her bottom as though nothing had happened.

She turned away, her eyes smarting, but they threatened to spill over with tears as soon as she left the room. Sadie stumbled through the door and up the stairs towards the bathroom. What was wrong with him? Was it all to do with his lack of money and a job? It must be that. She should be more sensitive to how he felt. Of course, he wanted to be the man of the house, the provider. All men wanted that, didn't they? She had never lacked money, never wanted for anything, but maybe she was selfish and unthinking. If that was how he felt, then her job was to support him which meant Bridget had to go. 'Oh dear, marriage is much harder than I ever thought.'

Mary started work a week later. Sadie gave Bridget three months wages sealed in an envelope together with an excellent reference. She could not see her cast on to the streets. Frank did not know, of course, he had no access to her bank account. Bridget told Henry that she needed to visit her sick brother, but his sobs as she left, tore at Sadie's heart. He wasn't used to sleeping alone, and his cries woke Sadie more than once in the night. The first night she rose from her bed to comfort him. The second, Frank stopped her.

'He has to learn. You're not helping him. Leave him, Sadie.'

'But,'

'But nothing. Do as I tell you, woman.' His voice softened, 'Come here, I want you.' He covered her mouth with his, rode his fingers beneath her nightdress and up her thigh.

She struggled, unable to bear her son's heartbreaking cries. Her attempts to get away only inflamed Frank further. His tongue forced its way between her teeth and his body pinned her back on the bed. She tried to feign pleasure as his fingers opened her up, steeling herself to fake it, but Frank was nothing if not an accomplished lover. Guilt washed over her as she came, and still Henry sobbed.

'Let me go, please,' she begged.

'It's my turn now, and I'm going to draw out my pleasure.'

He did. Several times she thought he was about to climax, but then he slowed. Only when Henry quietened, did he give a shuddering gasp and flop onto her belly.

'There, you see. All quiet. You just needed some distraction, and it worked, didn't it?' He stroked her face, wiping her tears. 'You need to stick it out, be firm. For his own good, my love.'

Only when he was snoring did Sadie rise and go to Henry. He lay sideways in his cot, one arm reaching out, his other thumb in his mouth. He'd never sucked his thumb at night before. Even in the dim light, she saw his salt-encrusted cheeks. She sat beside him, crooning, hoping he could hear her, her hand reaching through the bars to hold his. Before she left, she tucked him in, her feet heavy on the carpet as she trudged back to bed.

Henry began to cry before they retired the following evening. Frank sat engrossed in his newspaper. Sadie stood and moved quietly towards the door, hoping not to disturb him. Maybe he had not heard. His hand stopped her as she passed.

'Leave him be.'

'Just let me sing him a lullaby. My mother always sang a lullaby to Eddie to pacify him. It worked without fail.'

'You're too soft, my darling. Boys need to learn to toughen up. You've spoiled him.'

'Frank, please let me go to him. I promise I'll only stay for a minute or two.'

'No.'

Frank, darling, I think I'm with child again, and this is upsetting me.'

He rose from his seat and took her into his arms. 'Oh Sadie, that's wonderful news. Now it's very important that you don't get flustered. I'll go instead.'

She heard his voice through the door. No words of comfort for Henry, only an instruction to be quiet and a threat if he wasn't. Poor love, he was only two. How could he understand? Surely, he was more likely to howl in fear than comply. Was that the way Frank's father treated him? Was that why his mother had always fussed around him, trying to make up for her husband's harsh ways? Papa had trusted Mama to do the best for her children, and that's what Sadie wanted. Could she change Frank? It would take patience and understanding, but she determined to try because her children being brought up in a house being seen and not heard, was an unbearable thought.

During the day, Sadie attempted to make it up to Henry by showering him with attention. Mary, while pleasant enough, lacked gumption and training. Left in her company, Henry soon became bored. Perhaps the best way to encourage Henry to sleep through the night was to tire him out. She suspected that Mary's walks with Henry consisted of her pushing him around in his pram rather than lots of exercise.

Although the weather was cooler, Sadie took him on endless trips on the tram to the seaside, the zoo or Lake Torrens. She let him run on the grass opposite East Terrace, threw balls to catch and read him stories from a book of fairy tales. Mary accompanied them, Sadie constantly encouraging her to join in, to entertain her charge. While Frank admonished her for overdoing it, he never offered to accompany them, nor understood that Mary was less than half the worth of Bridget as a nanny. It worked. By the time Henry went to bed, he was exhausted and did not wake until after Mary arrived at six each morning.

'That didn't take long to sort out. He soon learned not to wake. You have to trust me, Sadie.' Frank's self-satisfied smile irked, but she said nothing.

On a visit to her Papa, he observed her for a few moments before speaking. 'You're looking tired.'

'I'm expecting again.' A shy smile on her face.

'Oh, Sadie love. That's wonderful, but you need to get plenty of rest.'

'I know. I've given up fundraising for the League of Loyal Women to spend more time with Henry. He's so much fun, Papa. I adore him.'

'Of course, you do.'

'You enjoy having young children around, don't you?'

'I only wish I'd had more time with you all when you were younger. I'm looking forward to lots of grandchildren. How's Frank? Found work yet?'

Sadie shook her head. 'He's getting downhearted. Could you put in a word with any of your friends?'

'He told me he didn't want an office job, that he preferred a sales job where he could get out and about.'

'Yes, but I think he needs any job at the moment.'

'I'll see what I can do, sweetheart.' He kissed her cheek. 'You take care of yourself and grandchild number five please. I'm going to meet little Nancy next month. I think we'll have a good crop of sheep and wool to sell. Your Papa may have a treat in store when the cheque's in the bank. How about a sable wrap for my favourite daughter?'

'I'm pleased for you, Papa and yes, I'd love a sable wrap. That was a good move buying sheep stations, though I'm not sure Jane's cut out for living there.'

'Well, if he will marry an English rose who doesn't know one end of a sheep from another. Another piece of news, Bruce is back in Sydney. He's staying in the Manly house, resting after the sea voyage.'

'Is he alright?'

'I don't know. It's going to take time by all accounts. Poison gas, what an evil weapon. Those Huns deserve everything that's coming to them.'

'It's wonderful that we got our men back, Papa. I'm thankful that Bruce only served for a few weeks in Gallipoli, and you stopped Stanley from going. What did you know?'

'I may not have had much education, but one thing I knew from stories about the Crusades in school was that the Turks would fight. They've had

213

an empire longer than we have. I didn't want my boys becoming prisoners of the Turks.'

'Frank said the Turks fought hard, but they were also honourable.'

'I'm glad to hear it. What I didn't expect was that it should have been such an ill-planned expedition. We've been let down by London.'

'Let's hope it's all over soon and all our young men return.'

'Amen to that. And I need to get back to what I do best, building railways.'

Peace reigned by early July as Frank began work in the offices of a bank in Adelaide. Sadie silently thanked her Papa for his contacts, although she breathed not a word to Frank about her part in the job offer.

'It's not what I want to be doing long-term,' he said over dinner after his first day, 'but it's a good way to make contacts. Mr Duke wants me to meet potential clients and charm them into switching over their accounts.'

'You'll be good at that, Frank.' Sadie smiled at him. 'When you want to, you can charm the birds from the trees.' He did not pick up the undertone of irony in her words. She was not above charm herself.

Things are on the up, she told herself. Papa telegrammed he had sold a record number of lambs – a-hundred-thousand in all. At fifty shillings average, that was two hundred and fifty thousand pounds for the sheep and more with wool prices at a record. In one season he had recovered his fortune.

Frank beamed when she read out the cable. 'I knew he could do it. Your Papa has a gift with money, I believe. All Adelaide will be at his feet now that he's teamed up with Sydney Kidman.'

'Where did you hear that?'

Frank tapped his nose. 'I'm not at liberty to say, dear one. My lips are sealed.'

Chapter Twenty-Eight

England   -
Cleethorpes, June 1941

'Have you heard the news?' Jane said as Sadie opened the door.

'No, I've been out walking around the boating lake with Alex.'

'Alex, who's Alex?'

'The person I invited you to meet, Jane. Do come into the front room and meet him.' Sadie rarely showed irritation, but she had steeled herself for this meeting, and now Jane appeared to have forgotten the purpose of this invitation.

Alex and she had begun talking at breakfast and never stopped. She missed chapel to walk with him along the prom all the way to the boating lake and the wooden café, where they drank tea. The summer season was underway, so he paid for a boat and rowed her around the tiny island as they shared memories of their children. Over the years they must have been here at the same time, their children running freely around the grass, across the ornamental bridge, along the shore, and yet they had never met. Wartime regulations restricted them to the inward path, away from the battery, but there were plenty of families out enjoying the sun. Sadie discovered how much she enjoyed walking with Alex, smiling at other people, sharing the sunshine – simple pleasures he called them. And she agreed.

She told him about life with her husband and their break-up. He held her hand, his lips tight against his anger. I'd like to murder the bastard, he'd said.

'As would I sometimes,' she replied. 'He fooled me for so long.' Too long. 'We'd best go back. I need to prepare some tea for Jane. I'm longing for her to meet you now.'

On the long stroll back, arm in arm, she saw one or two faces she knew but avoided their inquisitive eyes. Jane should be the first to know.

Sadie hung up Jane's summer jacket on the peg and opened the door to where Alex was waiting.

'Jane, this is Alex Peters, my fiancée. Alex this is Jane, soon to be your sister-in-law too.'

Jane shot her a look of astonishment.

'I've heard such a lot about you, Mrs Timmins. I'm delighted to meet you.'

'While I have heard nothing about you, Mr Peters. But I too am delighted to make your acquaintance. How long have you known each other?'

'Since April. Alex is a captain in the Home Guard, and he came to give a talk at the WVS.'

'That sounds very respectable, but I'm surprised we haven't bumped into each other before. Where have you been hiding him, Sadie?'

'You did bump into him once, Jane, at the Tudor Café. You shoved your chair into his shin.' A neat deflection, Sadie hoped.

'I overheard you say there's news.' Alex cut in to save Sadie from more questions.

Jane drew her thoughts back to what she had been bursting to tell Sadie.

'Germany,' she paused for dramatic effect, 'has invaded Russia!'

'No, what?'

'Oh, that's good news indeed.'

'Why is it, Alex?' Sadie asked.

'Because they've given up on invading us. Don't you see, Sadie? Hitler will throw everything he has at Stalin. There'll be no threat to us while they are fighting Russia. That's why the air raids have all but stopped.'

'We're safe?'

Yes, my darling, for the moment.'

Sadie jumped up and down and caught both their hands in happiness.

'I think this may be his first big mistake. Invading Russia defeated Napoleon.' Alex said.

'This is the best news. What do you think it will mean for my sons?'

'I'm not sure if anything will change for them, my love. Germany's nowhere near defeated and the air force will still be bombing them. It may give our fighter boys a bit of a break, though.'

Sadie's heart sank a little. She'd hoped for a respite for her boys too.

'What do they think of your news, Sadie?'

'They don't know yet. I wrote to Glen in Singapore and will tell Henry and Dale when they come home on leave.'

Jane looked at her in puzzlement, 'Why would you wait? They will be overjoyed for you.'

'Which is what I keep telling her. Jane, I can tell you are a woman of good sense. Make her understand. God knows I've tried.'

'Alright, alright. I'll drop them a line tomorrow.'

As they washed dishes after a tea of potato salad with lettuce and dressed crab, tinned gooseberries and what passed for shortbread biscuits, Jane gave Sadie her opinion.

'He's lovely. You deserve some happiness, and I truly believe he will make you happy.'

'I can't believe my luck.'

'Have you set a date?'

'Possibly late September. I want Henry and Dale to be there at least.'

'Too bad we have clothes rationing now. Whatever are you going to do for a dress?'

'I bought a suitable one in May. When Alex's not here, I'll show you. It's perfectly divine.'

'Sadie, you are such a dark horse.' Despite her wet hands, Jane hugged her. 'Something to look forward to at last.'

'I'm meeting his daughter next weekend. It's already making me nervous. What if she hates me?'

'She won't, just as your sons won't hate Alex. You are perfect for each other, even if he is Australian.'

'Not you too, Jane. He's a Kiwi, can't you tell?'

Jane flicked the tea towel at her. 'Joking, Sadie. Can't you tell?'

'That wasn't so bad was it?' Alex said after the front door closed on Jane.

She leaned into him, and he stroked her back. 'Will you stay tonight?'

217

'I can't; I need to be early, another trip to Lincoln unless you'd like to come along for the ride? It's official business, so I can go by car.'

'Another time and I would love that, but I'm on duty tomorrow morning.'

'And you have letters to write.'

'I promise. Jane's right. It should be the boys I tell first before all the gossip mongers in chapel get to work.'

'I'll put a notice in the Evening Telegraph for next weekend. We've never discussed where we'll marry, register office, chapel or church. Come to the service in Old Clee next Sunday; it's a lovely old church.'

'I'd like that, but I'm divorced.'

'There's no record of that in this country. Tell a white lie. Then we have to decide where to live.'

'Steady on, one thing at a time.' Could she lie to a vicar? But then, did she even know if her husband was still alive? Alex, it seemed, had fewer scruples than she thought.

Things were moving fast now that she had agreed to announce their engagement. After he'd gone, she turned on the radio and sank into her armchair in the back room to listen to some cheerful music. Having lived in this house for all the years of her boys' childhood, could she bear to leave it? What would they think?

The phone rang on Wednesday afternoon.

'Mother, it's Henry. I've wangled a pass for Friday, just one night, I'm afraid. Will I be able to meet Alex? I must check out the man who's managed to snare my Ma. You've kept this very quiet.'

Sadie listened for clues, did he sound simply surprised or concerned? 'Oh, that's wonderful, Henry. I can't wait for you to meet him and I'm sure you'll like him.'

'I hope so. If I don't, I'll see him off sharpish. Jesting, Ma! But I worry about you.'

'Thank you for worrying, but there's no need.'

'Must go, we have a briefing.'

'Take care, my love.' The phone died. Sadie sighed, another worrying night for her. But Alex needed to book a table for four for dinner on Friday night. Wouldn't it be wonderful if Dale could make it too? He was now based at Topcliffe near Thirsk, not as close as Driffield.

'I can't, Ma. We have a lot going on at present.' Dale sounded tired when he phoned an hour after Henry.

'I understand, love, but you haven't had any leave in ages. Will you be able to make the wedding, do you think?'

'I spent my last leave in York. I should have told you.'

'No, no. You have to live your life. I understand.'

'Let me see what I can do. This tour should finish around then.'

'Love you, look after yourself.' A wry chuckle from Dale as he said goodbye.

Her heart beat faster, and a low sick feeling settled in her stomach. Talking to her boys on the phone always did that to her, certain that their war was worse than she could imagine. How much longer was this damn war going to go on? At least Glen was safe. 'Thank God, for small mercies,' she whispered.

They all met at the Dolphin. Alex walked in having collected his daughter from the station. There was no mistaking father and daughter; they shared the same colouring. Marion stood maybe two inches shorter, but it was her open, sunny face which immediately endeared her to Sadie. I'm going to love having her as a step-daughter, she thought. Henry stood to greet them both. Why he's the same height as Alex, she realised. She watched the easy interaction between them and relaxed.

'I've been looking forward to meeting you, Mrs Tinsdale.'

'Sadie, please. So, you're Marion. Come, sit beside me, I want to know everything about you.'

She loved listening to the young people chatting about the escapades they got up to on their stations. Her house had always been full of young voices, and she missed that. Now here they were, her handsome son and this beautiful young woman, family to be, and her heart overflowed with happiness. She caught Alex's expression and knew he was feeling the same.

'You have Polish fighter pilots at Leconfield, your father told me.'

'We do, they're a spirited bunch, a great sense of humour and dedicated airmen. One day they disobeyed orders to fight the Germans while they were still in training and were heroic. We were all so proud. The whole base lined up to cheer them back when they landed.'

'Any romance there?' Alex asked, teasing.

'No, and there won't be. I have my own announcement to make,' Marion replied. 'I have been transferred to Hibaldstow near Brigg.'

Was that a smile from Henry? They'd only known each other an hour, but was there a spark of interest? Wouldn't that be something!

'That's wonderful darling, but won't you be bored. It's a tiny airfield.'

'It's a promotion, Daddy. From Monday, I'm Corporal Peters.'

'I approve, Mother,' Henry wandered into the kitchen while she made a cup of tea for them all.

'I'm so glad.' She hugged him. His arms slid around her, and she breathed in his smell, a mixture of cigarettes and engine oil from his motorcycle ride that day. 'Will you give me away?'

'I would consider it an honour.'

'It will only be a small wedding. Aunt Jane and Nibby, a few of Alex's business friends and a couple of ladies I know from the WVS. You can bring a lady friend if you have one.'

'I don't, yet.' That grin again.

'She's fun, isn't she? Marion, I mean.'

He pecked her on the cheek. 'No meddling, Mother.' He picked up the tray to carry it through.

As she opened the door to the front room, she wondered if the same conversation had been happening there in reverse. It made her smile.

Chapter Twenty-Nine

Australia   -
Melbourne, December 1919

A long journey lay ahead. Sadie settled herself in the carriage having waved goodbye to Frank, worrying about how they would cope without her. At least she had managed to track down Mrs Porter to keep house while she was away. Henry cried in her arms, begging her to be back for Christmas and she promised him she would. Three and a half-year's old! It hardly seemed believable. Which was worse, her guilt at leaving them or not being beside her father's bedside? The telegram sounded stark. *'Papa in hospital. Condition serious. Come soonest.'* For once Frank set aside his wishes and encouraged her to make the train reservation. It was his disappointment at how things turned out at the end of the war which made him so volatile. She understood that; really, she did.

All those celebrations at armistice had dissipated by the New Year. But then Dale was born, and it lifted Frank's mood again. Sadie's hopes were high that Dale would show him what a father needed to be. He'd missed Henry's baby years. 'Look, Frank,' she'd said, 'Dale's so helpless and gorgeous. He needs his daddy.' She'd offered him Dale to cradle, flattering her husband with how well they looked together. When the little mite began to cry, Frank sought to hand him back. Sadie didn't take him, showing Frank how to stroke him back to comfort. It worked for a moment. Perhaps he was softer with Dale, or was that wishful thinking? His judgmental, authoritative attitude with Henry hadn't lessened with time.

'I have to deal with my mother's estate soon,' Frank had said soon after. 'Let's move back to Melbourne. We can sell her house, and I have contacts there, someone will offer me a job.'

She knew he was right. Adelaide offered them no future. There was a sense of hopelessness in the air as soldiers arrived back in their hundreds to no work, high prices and shortages of food and power.

Things were better in Melbourne. For one thing, they had coal and timber; the lights weren't being switched off as they were in Adelaide and Perth. By June in Adelaide, there had been rationing of power to shops and houses. Imagine, she thought, only having power to cook breakfast and supper – and in the middle of winter. Yes, moving was the right decision. Frank's instincts had saved them from a miserable winter. He found a sales job within days and was happier to be out of the house and bringing home a wage.

At least she had a live-in nanny again. Frank hated his nights being disturbed and demanded she cease breastfeeding after they moved back to her house in Carlton.

Stanley arrived back in Melbourne with Jane around the same time. He was to take charge of his father's racing stables until they were sold, while Jane waited for the birth of their second child. Like his father, Stanley began to look for something else to interest him and decided to invest in a failing opera company.

Sadie's thoughts turned back to her Papa. What would she find when she arrived at the hospital? Would she be too late? Why hadn't Caro been more expansive in the telegram? It was hell not knowing what was wrong. She regretted never having installed a telephone in the Carlton house. Could his illness be from the effects of the bushfire back in February?

She'd visited Papa at his house in the Yarra Valley once they returned from Adelaide. Her taxi from Lilydale Station took her through the valley towards the house in Healesville. Blackened tree trunks and branches darkened the mountains towards Alexandra. As she got out of the car, the pungent smell of burnt eucalyptus lingered in the air. She stood looking at Yambacoona for a moment before entering the house, a smaller house in comparison to Chateau Yering or St Hubert's, but Papa greeted her at the door looking almost his usual self, and she relaxed.

'Joe Junior said you weren't in any danger, but I needed to see for myself.'

'Let me hold him.' Papa stretched out his arms.

She handed him the latest addition to the family. He swept him up with a delighted smile on his face.

'He has a look of Eddie.'

'Do you think? He has his father's eyes though. Frank was pleased about that.'

'Hello, little Joseph.'

Sadie floundered a little. 'Actually, we call him by his second name, Dale. I named him after you, of course, but Dale seems to have stuck.'

Her father smiled amid a flicker of memory in his eyes. Sadie squirmed to think she knew the reason.

'Too many Joes in the family as it is, and Sadie rather than Sylvia stuck with you.' He coughed then, a deep hacking cough.

Sadie took Dale back, her face full of concern as the cough continued. He put a handkerchief to his mouth and spat into it. She couldn't help but notice the flecks of black sputum.

'Oh, Papa!'

'It's alright. The doctor says I'll have a cough for a few weeks, but there's no lasting damage.' He coughed again, his shoulders shaking with the effort.

'You shouldn't have put yourself in danger like that, Papa.'

His face became stern. 'You can't leave people to burn, Sadie. I had a truck and men to help. When the telephone kept ringing with people pleading for the lives, what would you expect me to do? Ignore them? I couldn't have lived with myself.'

She'd read the report in the Argus. 'Time and again, Mr Timmins and his men braved the flames and the suffocating smoke to rescue people from their holiday villas further up the mountain.' It was only by chance that he had been visiting the saw-mill that day.

'You should get a medal.'

'Pah! I care nothing for medals. I just wish they'd let me build a railway line from Healesville to Narbethong to bring the timber down. But now the timber needs time to recover.'

A guard's head popped around the sleeper door, interrupting her thoughts. 'First sitting for dinner, Ma'am.'

223

'Thank you; I'll be there shortly.' Sadie pulled herself back from her reveries and stood ready to leave the carriage for the dining car.

The waiter showed her to a table for two. A woman sat there already. Sadie sat down and nodded at the woman. I should have insisted on my own table, she thought, her mood too low for chatter.

'Why it's Mrs Tinsdale, isn't it? What a surprise!'

Sadie recognised the voice but was unable to place the woman at first.

'We met two years ago, on the Murray.'

'Oh! Mrs Taylor, isn't it? Yes, I remember. I'm sorry, my mind is miles away.'

'How's your lovely son, Henry, if my memory serves me well.'

'Yes, he's just as adorable. I have another son now, Dale.'

'So, your husband came home.' The expression on the woman's face was one of relief.

Didn't Mrs Taylor have two sons at the front? It was always difficult to ask directly.

'My sons came home too. One's married, and I have been visiting them in Melbourne. They have a new baby daughter.'

Sadie nodded, 'I'm very pleased for you. And how is your dear husband?'

Her dinner companion's eyes clouded. 'The influenza took him.'

The air sucked out of Sadie's lungs. 'I'm sorry for your loss.' She managed to say in a dull voice, her mind pulled back to her father in his hospital bed. She looked away, attempting to stop tears from forming.

'All those years worrying for my boys and it was Sam who went.' Mrs Taylor dabbed at her eyes. 'I took him for granted, thinking he would always be there, that we'd enjoy our retirement. He worked too hard, I told him. Now he'll never get to enjoy the home in Mount Gambier that we'd bought in readiness.' She sighed. 'That Spanish flu has a lot to answer for.'

'It does.' She caught Mrs Taylor looking at her, waiting for some other expression of sympathy. 'I was terrified for my boys, and on top of that, there was a measles outbreak in Melbourne. We had to stay inside for weeks for fear of contagion.' Sadie glanced back to the window for several seconds, helpless in the face of another's grief when Papa could by dying. Her comment did nothing to lift the widow's mood, who looked

224

at her askance, but Sadie had been out of her mind with worry back in March when both epidemics were at their height.

'I've lost my appetite, dear. I think I'll go back to my carriage.' Mrs Taylor stood up.

Sadie flinched back to the present, realising how unsympathetic she had been to Mrs Taylor. 'I'm sorry, I truly am.'

'Not your fault, dear. I'm poor company these days.' She turned and walked up the aisle. The waiter stopped her, but she shook him off.

She thinks me uncaring, Sadie realised. I wasn't thinking of her. Too wrapped up in my own family's problems.

The waiter arrived with her starter, and Sadie asked if it were possible to deliver some food to Mrs Taylor in her compartment. 'She isn't feeling up to company. Recently bereaved, I'm afraid.'

'I'll see what I can do, Ma'am.'

Sadie began to eat her melon. Influenza, yes it brought disaster upon her family. She reflected on that evening in April, when they thought the danger had passed.

She'd managed to get her pre-baby figure back before shopping in the best Melbourne stores for the perfect dress for the opera. It was such a relief to be planning for a night out after the panic and dire forecasts about influenza.

She hadn't even managed to visit Jane because of the fear of passing on any germs until the week before.

Jane was still recovering from the long journey back from Nelyambo.

'If we'd left it any later, I don't think we would have made it. The river was that low. The heat and drought have been relentless this summer. I know Stanley and Roy are very concerned about the state of the sheep.'

'I'm pleased you're here. We'll pray for rain. Things have to start getting better soon, surely. Let's look forward to our night out. Have you managed to buy a suitable dress?' Sadie pressed Jane for details of her outfit.

When Frank came into the bedroom as she was dressing, he whistled his approval. The iridescent peacock-blue dress matched her eyes. Cut in a low V-neck, both front and back, it had a taffeta underskirt below the silk layered top dress, all finishing mid-calf.

'You'll knock them dead. Turn around.'

She twirled as he whistled again.

'I have the perfect necklace. My solicitor gave me my mother's jewellery box yesterday. It's mostly worthless, but I have saved a piece for you.' He fastened it around her neck and then escorted her to her dressing table mirror.

'Oh Frank, it's lovely.' The gold filigree chain was set with freshwater pearls which gleamed against her skin.

'I'll get your wrap.' He placed the silvery-blue cashmere around her shoulders. 'You look a million dollars. I will have the best-looking wife in the Princess Theatre.' He said, guiding her to the waiting taxi.

Stanley stood in the foyer of the vast theatre on Spring Street, with Jane by his side. He greeted people as they entered, pumping the hands of the men and kissing the hands of the ladies. Sadie smiled at her brother.

'You're quite the impresario, brother dear.' She caught Jane's eye, and they giggled.

'He's here every night,' Jane whispered. Her red silk, layered dress disguising the curve in her stomach.

'I have to protect my investment.' Stanley looked affronted at their amusement.

'It's a success then?' Frank asked.

'Well, better now. People are still wary about venturing out, but we're getting good reviews. After Melbourne, we open in Sydney for ten weeks, then Newcastle, Brisbane and back here for the winter season. Mr Rigo, the director, is a genius.'

'It's a bit of a gamble though.' Frank looked sceptical. 'It takes a lot to fill a theatre of this size every night.'

'The Gonzales Opera Company made twenty thousand pounds profit after their season here.' Stanley snapped back.

'Where is Mr Rigo?' Sadie changed the subject, embarrassed at the sudden tension between her brother and husband.

'Preparing for the opening. I must let you go. Mr Dyer and his wife have just arrived.'

Frank led her away, a proprietorial arm around her shoulders. Her annoyance with Frank turned to concern as they sat in the stalls waiting for the curtain to rise. There were a lot of empty seats, especially the more expensive seats. The opera, Faust, was a creditable performance, with Miss Johnson not quite reaching Dame Nellie's standard, but an enjoyable entertainment, none the less. The audience was appreciative, with several men standing to applaud.

'He has the right idea; I just don't believe it's the right time.' Frank said as the curtain was about to drop after the clapping subsided. 'The performance was good; it should be attracting more of the right kind of people.'

Sadie silently agreed as Stanley came on stage to thank everyone for coming. She was proud of her brother. It took guts to take a risk and then stand up in front of hundreds of people to encourage them to return, but nothing could disguise the fact that the theatre was only half-full.

Sadie finished her meal bound up in those memories. Frank had been right. Stanley was forced to close his season a week early because of poor ticket sales, hoping for better from Sydney. They had been due to open at the Grand Opera House in early May, but it remained closed because of the influenza. There was only so long the company could be retained on full pay before Stanley was forced to call it quits. Goodness knows how much money he'd lost in his month-long gamble.

Tiredness overwhelmed her. She blamed her lack of sleep on the shock of receiving the telegram the day before. Would she sleep against the sound and motion of the train? She needed to try. She would need all her strength for tomorrow.

Chapter Thirty

Australia
Adelaide, December 1919

'Papa? Papa, can you talk to me?' Sadie grasped his hand, his fingers as white as the cotton sheets they lay on. 'Oh, Eddie, he looks so poorly. What does the doctor say?'

'It's not looking too good, Sis.'

Sadie sank onto the wooden chair beside her father's bed. She'd come straight from the station and was exhausted after two near-sleepless nights.

'Do they know what's wrong?'

'They're going to do more tests and x-rays tomorrow, but they figure it's something to do with his kidneys.'

Kidneys, then there may be no hope. 'What will we do without him, Eddie?' Her brother did not answer, mute despair written on his face.

'The last few months have been awful. To think only a year ago, we were celebrating the end of the war. How can hope disappear so fast?'

'I hear Frank has a job he likes.'

'A sales job, nothing special but he likes it. He never did like being stuck in an office.'

'Perhaps the bank did him a favour.'

Sadie didn't respond. It hadn't felt like it at the time. His anger at being dismissed reverberated on her, his verbal punch-bag. The excuse given to Frank was that his job belonged to an Adelaide veteran, now returned from the war. She made the mistake of saying; 'If they promised him before he enlisted...' The fury in his eyes had frightened her, and she had paid for it over the following weeks. But things were better now. Melbourne had improved his mood.

Her father stirred. Her fingers closed tighter around his hand. 'Papa, can you hear me? It's me, Sadie.'

His eyelids fluttered open, a half attempt at a smile before they closed again.

'Why is he so sleepy?'

'They're keeping him sedated.'

'Do you think they know what they're doing?'

'It's the best private hospital around. Look, I can see you're bushed, Sis. Let me take you home to rest. We'll come back tomorrow.'

'Nothing's going to happen soon, is it?'

'No.'

'I wish Stanley weren't back in England; he should be here.' She replaced her father's hand on the sheet, stood and bent to kiss his bristly cheek, wiping away the tear which slid from her eyes onto his pale brow. 'Stay safe, Papa, I'll return soon.'

Eddie picked up her suitcase. She had dashed straight from the train to the hospital by taxi, unable to restrain her concern for a moment longer. Eddie opened the door to escort her out, but she lingered at the bedside for another second or two, willing her father to recover, praying that she would see him standing strong and unbowed once more.

'Come, Sadie,' Eddie spoke softly. She turned and followed him.

Her father had bought another grand house, Sunnyside, in the foothills between Glen Osmond and Burnside. Caro was sitting in the garden which looked out over the Adelaide Plains down to the gulf beyond. She stood as Sadie and Eddie arrived, a more welcoming smile on her face than usual.

'Thank goodness you made it in time.'

So, she also thought Papa was going to die. Was she foreseeing her future as a young, rich widow with equanimity? All the old resentments flooded back. Before she had time to reply, another figure joined Caro.

'Sadie, you're looking very well.'

'Bruce, oh my word.' In the four years since her brother left for Egypt, he had aged at least ten years. She swallowed hard before hugging him tightly, his body slighter against hers than she remembered. What had they done to the boy they waved off, the one who stood strong, proud and trim in his new uniform? Her hand on his back felt the rasping, shallow breaths and the gentle wheeze of air forced into his injured lungs.

The maid arrived with afternoon tea, offering Sadie a moment to recover herself.

'How long are you staying, Sadie?' Caro asked.

'I promised to be back in time for Christmas. Henry's looking forward to it.'

'Do you like being back in Melbourne?'

'It's good to be back in my own house. How long are you staying, Eddie?'

'I need to get back to Nelyambo before Christmas too, or Daisy won't forgive me.'

Eddie marrying at eighteen had been a shock at the time, but with Stanley and Bruce away at war, Papa depended on him, and he'd grown up fast.

'Do you mind if I refresh myself before dinner?'

'Do, Sadie. Dinner will be at six, so I can visit your father at seven.'

'I won't be late, Caro.'

Eddie and Sadie sat up late into the evening, long after Bruce and Caro retired. Papa was still sedated, and Caro had no further news to report.

'Do you think his illness has anything to do with the smoke in his lungs?'

'No, I asked about that.'

'He's not a young man to put himself in that much danger.'

'I think it's more to do with the worry and stress this year has brought.'

'Jane told me about the drought at Nelyambo last summer.

'It's looking just as bad for this summer if we don't get rain soon. We're expecting losses of two-thirds of the stock. No profit, only losses for the foreseeable future.'

'No wonder Papa's been selling everything off. I couldn't believe him getting rid of all his racehorses.'

'The trouble is the price of land has fallen through the floor. No one wants it. He was lucky to sell off most of Momba Station before the end of the war when wool prices were still high. The profit he made last year may have to keep us going for a good while.'

230

She shivered although the evening was balmy. A memory from the past fluttered in her mind. Something her mother once said about owning land. Her grandmother too. They had always believed that owning land was a source of security, but what if it were also a millstone, dragging them down?

'I'm wondering if I should inform that Joseph Timmins in Broken Hill about his illness. After all, he may be his son.'

'No, Eddie. Don't. If Papa dies, you can. That would be kind. But it would raise too many difficult discussions while he's ill. Imagine Papa's humiliation if that man came to visit.'

She couldn't sleep again with all the trials of the year preying on her mind. The bedroom was stifling. Sadie climbed out of bed and walked over to the window to open it further, fanning herself in the cooler night air. Everyone had welcomed the soldiers home last winter, thousands upon thousands of young men returning to the safety of their families. But there was no work and no money. All that economic confidence in 1914 had descended into the bottomless pit of war. And now Bruce. Her darling brother, Bruce, was suffering. She had resisted thinking about him, but the health of two of the men she loved best in the world, lay in peril. What could she do but pray? She walked back to her bed and knelt down on the floor, something she had not done since she was a child, praying to God to spare her father and brother.

It helped her drift into a fitful sleep.

She slept in late and came down for breakfast long after Caro left for the hospital to meet with the doctor. Bruce was finishing his cup of coffee as she entered the room.

'Stay and talk to me,' she said, as she rang the bell for the maid to bring her scrambled eggs and toast. 'I want to know how you are and what your doctors say.'

'The short answer is, not good. I'll never be able to do any physical work again.'

'Oh, Bruce. I'm so sorry. We thought you were being invalided out after you were shot. If only you had been discharged. Why didn't they let you go?'

'My choice. I refused.'

'What? Why would you do that?'

'Unless you had been there, you couldn't understand. I couldn't leave my men, simple as that.' He gasped and coughed, a deep, hacking cough which made Sadie rise from the table in alarm. He held up his arm to stay her. Eventually, he caught his breath and carried on. 'If there's one good thing to come out of war, it's the bond that keeps men together, like a vice only death can remove. In the end, you don't fight for King or Empire; you fight for each other. Only each other. Frank would know.'

Would he? He'd never mentioned that. She'd only ever heard complaints about the biting cold, the constant wet clothing, the rats, the poor rations. He looked at her sometimes as though she were to blame, and she shrank away, knowing her encouragement had played a part.

The maid entered with a tray for her and stood while she spooned out the eggs on to a plate and took up her fork.

'But now I'm home, and I want to get on with what life I have left.' Bruce said.

Saying it like that with such brutal honesty, sliced at Sadie like a knife. She swallowed hard before saying, 'If you take it easy...'

'Be an invalid, no. I need to live. There's a girl in Sydney I aim to marry.'

'Do you think you should?' Sadie wished she could have taken it back as soon as she said it. Bitterness darkened his eyes. 'I mean, of course, you should, if that's what you both want.'

'Alice knows the risks. It's her father I need to persuade. If anything happens to me,' another pause. 'When something happens to me, I want you all to promise to look after her and any family we may have.'

'Need you ask? No question that we would if it happens.'

His expression was impatient. 'Sadie, listen to me. Don't give me platitudes just because it's something you don't want to hear. I need that promise.'

She put down her fork, stood and walked around the table to sit beside him. 'I promise that I will help look after your family. None of us will let you down, Bruce. I have that spare house in Sydney, if necessary. This family sticks together; we always have, you know that.'

He took her hand. 'I do. We're strong together, aren't we?' His kiss on her cheek sealed the deal.

'Like a vice, unbroken by death,' she vowed before turning away to disguise the tears in her eyes.

Good news greeted them at the hospital. 'They think they can operate,' Caro reported. 'Not yet, when he's stronger. Maybe in the New Year. He'll stay in hospital until then.'

'Do they know what it is?' Eddie asked.

'Yes, as they thought, it's his kidney. One isn't working and needs to come out. But he can survive with one. Isn't that marvellous news?'

She does care for him, thought Sadie, catching the relief on Caro's face.

'Yes, it's bloody wonderful news,' Eddie said.

'Don't let father hear you swear in a lady's presence.' Sadie warned.

'I wish he would hear. Bloody, bloody wonderful.' He pulled out a handkerchief to mop his eyes.

Sadie sank onto a hard wooden, chair in relief. 'Thank God for that.' Her shoulders began to shake.

'You children, where are your manners?' Caro burst into a nervous laugh, and for the first time, Sadie considered her one of the family, not the outsider she'd been for ten years. Have I forgiven her, she wondered?

'Is he awake?' Eddie asked.

'They're going to reduce the sedation; maybe when you come tomorrow, you'll be able to talk with him. Go and sit with him for now. They say he may know you're there. I'll go home and return this evening.'

On the afternoon before her return to Melbourne, Sadie sat on her own with Papa. He'd woken two days before, but either Eddie or Bruce was with her, and they'd kept the conversation light, not wanting to tire him. But Sadie was determined to speak her mind before leaving. Otherwise, she would never forgive herself. Her conversation on the train with the distraught Mrs Taylor uppermost in her mind.

'Papa, you've given us all such a fright. When you're better, after this operation, I beg you to retire. You've worked too hard all your life. It's time to rest, spend time with your family.' He began to speak, but she shushed him. 'We're all so proud of you, Papa. What you've achieved from nothing is amazing. Everyone looks up to you, your men, your fellow businessmen. They will understand. Let Uncle Charles take over the firm. You know he's itching to do it.'

There, she'd said it. She looked beseechingly at her father. He was their rock, their anchor. They could not afford to lose him. Uncle Charles was younger by twenty years and had worked with Papa ever since they moved from West Australia. Stanley thought him solid and reliable.

'Sadie, my love.' He took her hand, stroking her palm, a lifetime of hard graft in his hands. Never afraid to wield a pick or a spade in his early days, he enjoyed returning to it on his farms. My relaxation, he called it. 'It's not that I don't want to rest, but now is not the time. We need to get our young men back to work. They've done their duty to the country, served in a war far more gruesome than we ever imagined. They need to be given back their pride by working for an honest day's labour and a fair wage.'

'But why you, Papa? There are others who can give them that.'

'Look around you. South Australia is struggling to cope. Our politicians are running scared. We have to force them into action. I'm not sure Charles is the man to do that. With my contacts, I can make a difference.'

'Papa, no. You're too tired. Let others take over, please.'

'There are no others. Henry Smith is finishing the Western Railway and tied up with that. Sidney Kidman and I tried our utmost to get the politicians to agree to the North-South railway in August. We would have built it for them at no cost, on the promise of government bonds. You'd think they would jump at the chance to link Adelaide with Darwin, but no, they declined, laughed at us. They used to have vision, but they've lost it. The people need men like us who won't give up. We'll browbeat the State into it eventually.'

'Are you sure,' she hesitated to say it, 'that it's not just because you like to win?'

He chuckled. 'Perhaps you know me too well, sweetheart. I can't bear losing, but the stakes are high. The country is bankrupt. Either we invest, or we face years of depression. People need food and goods, and our shipping isn't coping. Railways have to be the answer.'

'What if they won't build it? Will you agree to give up, say in a year's time?'

'No, Sadie. I need to work for the family too. One big contract will set you all up for the future. I don't want to leave this earth knowing I haven't achieved that.'

'But you have, Papa. There's enough money now, isn't there?

'Oliver's still a child, Bruce isn't well, and to be honest, I'm not sure about your husband, Frank. He's charming, but that doesn't always put money on the table.'

Sadie's eyes flooded with tears. 'Have I let you down?' She dreaded the answer.

'I can see why you thought Rob let you down. Sometimes we rush into things without thinking it through. I've done that in my youth.' His voice was gentle. 'But no, you could never let me down, only yourself. Promise me, Sadie, don't let Frank hurt you. I'd rather you separate than cling to a marriage which brings you unhappiness.'

'I'm not a quitter, Papa.'

'Maybe you're more like me than I thought. I should have given you a better stepmother to guide you. Don't think too badly of Caro; she can't help the way she is. I've indulged her too much.'

Sadie sat in the carriage on the way home from Adelaide. As much as she was looking forward to seeing the children, she hated saying goodbye to the family. She vowed to visit again after her father's operation. The doctors told Caro that he would require six months to recuperate and he had promised to take it easy. Maybe he would enjoy the rest so much he would change his mind about continuing at his frenetic pace. Stanley would be back from England by then. She would write to him and tell him to return. He was needed. If anyone could make Papa sees sense, it was Stanley.

She begged Eddie to write and keep her informed about Nelyambo. He seemed too pessimistic about the station. Surely things couldn't be as bad as he suggested. Rain would come. It always did, eventually.

Chapter Thirty-One

Australia   -
Nelyambo, 1919/1920

Eddie wrote to Sadie in February that he hadn't been able to visit Papa after his operation because things were too grim at Nelyambo. A little rain fell in the middle of January, but nowhere near enough.

Sadie was optimistic. She had written to Caro asking if she should return to Adelaide but was reassured that everything had gone well, and her father was out of danger.

Eddie wrote again in May.

Things go from bad to worse. It rained a couple of weeks ago, and we decided to take the sheep down to the river to see what water they could find. It's normally safe there, but the mud was much stickier than we realised, and they ended up trapped. It was pitiful to listen to the sheep bleating while we tried to get them out, but as they struggled they just got wedged in further. In the end, we were forced to abandon them.

I could blame myself, but there is no water, all the tanks are empty, the government ones too. We haven't washed for weeks. Everything has to be brought in by camel train, even hay for the horses. If my letters are delayed, it's because they're being sent by camel train. There's no water for the mail coach horses. I'm worried there'll be no water left for us to drink soon.

Papa has given up a block of land for ex-soldiers to settle on the land, but the government chose the wrong time. This is no place for the unwary and inexperienced. All that will happen is that the poor blokes will be saddled with debt. If Pops can't make a go of it with his resources, those fellas have no chance.

Pray for rain, Sadie. It's our only hope.

Eddie

His words in June shocked her further.

Well, we have shot the horses and cattle; the skins may give us a few pounds, but there was no forage left for them. You know how Pops loves his horses, it broke his heart to instruct me to do it. He wants to get up here, but it's no rest cure, and in any case, the road is impassable from Broken Hill to Wilcannia, there's no water even for bullocks. We can't get in or out even if we wanted to.

Old-timers say the river has never been so low. Low, that makes me laugh. It's bone dry. We even had to remove the dead fish out of the river and burn them, the smell was unbelievable, some of them weighed over a hundred pounds, we reckon.

We won't be lambing this season. There are no lambs. We're reduced to picking the wool off dead sheep.

Poor Eddie, he sounded defeated. Her brother was not prone to exaggeration, and the newspaper reports were as dire as he suggested. Surely it couldn't get much worse. His July letter offered no respite. The conditions were deteriorating further.

We've had some rain, but too late I fear. There's another problem - feral dogs. Men are abandoning their stations but leaving their dogs to roam. I think they've teamed up with dingoes and bred with them. I have seen it with my own eyes – dogs rounding up sheep and leading them off to feed their pups. I shot a whole litter last week, but there's too many of them. You can hear them howling at night. I would be scared to let children out of my sight; the dogs are getting that bold. At least there aren't so many rabbits. Better rabbits than wild dogs. Sadie. I bet that's something you'd never thought I'd say. I don't know if we can hold out much longer.

Even if it rains, we can't afford to restock, not with dogs preying on the sheep. I'm afraid you are going to see the price of meat rising. It seems

Sidney Kidman is taking advantage of the land price crash and buying up stations for rock bottom prices. I think Pops will do anything to avoid that humiliation.

Sadie had hoped that being in partnership with Sidney Kidman would help her father, but this situation on top of the downturn in the economy caused her many sleepless nights. The fortune accumulated over the years seemed to be slipping from her father's grasp.

What she wanted to do was discuss the implications with Frank, but she kept this letter to herself. For one thing, Frank liked to boast about his father-in-law's association with the Kidmans. 'Sydney Kidman has the touch of Midas,' he delighted in saying. 'My father-in-law is in business with him.' A statement designed and bound to impress any audience, especially potential investors in his nightclub idea. For another thing, she was wary about upsetting his mood. Keeping Frank happy had become the way she avoided upset or worse in the household.

As for food prices, they were going up and up already, especially meat. If Sadie were to depend on Frank's wage, then they wouldn't be eating much lamb or beef. It was no good pointing that out to Frank. He expected to see a juicy steak or two lamb chops on his plate, whatever the situation.

She read in the newspapers of the desolation of the Darling lands, of homesteads abandoned to the blacks. One station owner who owned hundred and thirty thousand sheep was now reduced to thirteen hundred, so Eddie wasn't exaggerating. Shifting hills of red sand had replaced the pastureland, devouring the mulga and belah trees. Her heart bled for Eddie and his wife who were living with the destruction. Papa too. How did he feel about this new calamity? She daren't ask.

The rains came in September and Sadie began to hope that disaster could still be averted. Stanley had returned from England earlier in the year and was left twiddling his thumbs in Sydney until he and Jane could travel to Nelyambo to relieve Eddie. Sadie received word that they were on their way. It was bound to be a tough journey with two young children, but at least the temperature was on the low side. Sadie was grateful that Jane had agreed to give it a second go.

A letter arrived from Jane towards the end of October.

Dear Sadie,

We've arrived after a journey of sheer hell. I never want to repeat it.

On the train up to Bourke, we could see the bleached carcasses of animals around the water holes at Nyngan. I imagined the poor beasts desperately waiting for the holes to fill up and slowly dying of thirst. It was too heartbreaking. I had to shield Nancy's eyes from the sight. Last time I remember the chain of muddy water holes stretching for miles, now they are little more than puddles.

We saw no cattle or sheep grazing although the grass is growing. Stanley says it will take time for graziers to raise enough funds to start again. Our journey was spent looking out on mile after mile of red box and budda trees until we hit the scrubby lands I have come to dread.

After Girilambone, Stanley got talking to a man about the conditions at Cobar where the mine has closed, throwing hundreds out of work. Apparently, the mine is now on fire and has been burning for months. He said the town is in dire straits and is begging for help from the government. I remember Cobar when we travelled from Dubbo by horse and wagon to Wilcannia. It had a very fine hotel and appeared prosperous. We couldn't make that journey now for lack of water for the horses.

When we arrived in Bourke, we found that the Darling was not navigable, and we would have to buy a wagon and horses for the six-day journey. I'm sure Stanley suspected that because he came prepared with enough money. Although the price he paid for horses was ridiculous.

Fully stocked up, we crossed the river and turned south. I had hoped for a pleasant trek with welcoming homesteads where we could expect a soft bed, a hot meal and good company. On our first night out, the homestead where we planned to stay we found abandoned. Everything was shuttered up, and there were no animals to be seen. We wandered around searching for clues, and then we came across the bones of a herd of cows, all picked clean by the crows. I turned away with Nancy, feeling sick. Stanley said they were shot and left maybe two or three months ago. We'll have to sleep in the barn, he said, there'll be straw there. But when we got to the barn, it was almost empty, save for a pile of sacking. Let's

239

check for snakes and redbacks he told me. 'Don't worry. It will be alright.'
I can't tell you how we argued about that. I told him we should turn back,
that he was putting the lives of our children at risk. But he was not having
it. All I got was 'if my father and mother could travel all the way across
the Nullarbor in a wagon, then we can do this. Trust me; I know what I'm
doing.' What other option did I have but to go along with it?

All I can say is that it was a little better than being outside in the
drizzling rain. All night I dreamt about the children being bitten by spiders.

We ran out of fresh milk the next day. Thank goodness I had packed
milk powder for little Brian.

Sadie paused to picture the scene. She could imagine Jane's
consternation at being faced with hardships she had never encountered,
while her brother would think little of it. It was more of an adventure to
him. She had sympathy for both. Chuckling, she turned back to the letter.

I was so relieved to find a homestead where we could stay on the second
night and forgave Stanley. The owner had only just arrived back having
fled four months before. I didn't realise that would be the last occupied
homestead and we'd be sleeping in empty barns from then on.

The grass after the recent rains is quite high, and there was plenty for
the horses to eat, and enough water in the river for them to drink. Stanley
thought he would be able to shoot some wildlife if we got stuck, but as
we got travelled onwards, normal signs of life disappeared. It was quite
eerie. No bleating sheep, no cattle lowing, just the cawing of crows. Even
the kangaroos and wallabies seem to have gone elsewhere. What we
would have given even for a rabbit to cook! The children got more and
more cranky, and I began to worry about their health. I knew we wouldn't
starve with all the tins and packets of food we were carrying in the wagon,
but they needed fresh milk and eggs, not cold beans and crackers.

They told us in Bourke us to look out for feral dogs. I don't think I slept
the last two nights of the trek because their warnings were true. On our
last night, we thought we could stay with some of our old neighbours, but
they'd given up too. As we bedded down in their barn, we could hear the
howling start and then scratching outside. The horses began to whinny in
fear, so Stanley went to check on them. A pack of dogs were beginning to

snap at their feet. If they hadn't been hobbled, I doubt we would have seen them again and would have been stuck there until Stanley walked to Nelyambo for help, still twenty miles down-river. Luckily, he had his gun and began to shoot, and the dogs off, still snarling. One turned back; its fangs flecked with blood. The horses stayed in the barn with us that night. One had been bitten near its tail. I did my best to clean it up, praying the dogs weren't rabid, although I know Australia doesn't have rabies. By then, I was being irrational, so my dear husband told me.

How many times, I have asked myself, why I agreed to return? I don't know how you Timmins put up with this kind of life; drought, floods, deadly animals. Farming with this constant fear and hardship is madness. This land is treacherous – it's like battling with the plagues of Egypt.

Now that we're at Nelyambo, things aren't much better. Eddie's young wife has been struggling to cope with the lack of water and food. I thank my lucky stars we weren't here through the worst of the shortages. But rain has fallen, and the tanks are filling again. Eddie says the sheep losses are very high, maybe seventy percent. Stanley seems convinced that if we have enough rain over the next few months, we can recover, though it will take time to restock. The biggest problem is the dogs. They're going to have to try poisoning them. Stanley won't let me take the children out of the house without a man to guard them.

I hope to have better news when I write again,
Jane

Was Stanley putting on a brave front for Jane? How could he possibly feel optimistic in the face of such calamity? Sadie wished she knew, but Stanley was not a letter writer. He left that to his wife. The only thing Sadie did know was that Stanley would try his hardest to make things work. Would it be enough? She hoped so for all their sakes. How much money was left in her father's coffers, she wondered? Even Frank was beginning to be concerned, although reports of rain had allayed their fears a little.

As the months wore on, Jane's letters became no more positive. Drought still held the land in sway. Two years without appreciable rain. No one without the land resources of someone like Sidney Kidman could withstand that pressure. But even Sadie did not foresee the end.

She picked up the Argus in early November, and a brief report on an inside page caught her eye.

'Oh Frank, did you read this?' She pointed it out to him.

'Great bushfires, pastoral areas swept,' he read. 'Dear God, it's near Nelyambo, isn't it?'

Sadie nodded, her heart hammered in her chest. 'What if they can't get away?'

'They'll take to the river. Don't worry, Jane and the children will be safe.'

'But my brothers, they'll try and fight it, won't they?' She could tell by Frank's grim expression that she was right. Maybe it was already too late. The report in the paper spoke of fires over the last few days. 'I thought when the drought broke in May that everything would be alright.'

'Until we have real news, try not to worry. They may escape the fires.' He put his arm around his wife and comforted her. In some ways, that was worse because it was unusual for Frank to be aware of her needs.

'Can we go back to Adelaide? I need to be with my family.'

'We'll go for Christmas,' he promised her.

Jane and Stanley arrived back in Adelaide with their children only a day before Sadie arrived for Christmas. The long journey would give them a chance to recuperate, Sadie thought, until she saw them. Her brother may have survived the war, but the backcountry had beaten him or was it Jane's utter determination to return to England at the earliest opportunity and stay there.

'We can't give up, not yet,' he told her. 'We have to try and recoup our losses somehow,' his shoulders slumping.

'What happened, Stanley? Is it all gone?' Sadie asked.

'Yes,' said Stanley. 'Nearly every blade of grass and fencepost for scores of miles. There were lightning strikes, and with the grass so high, once it caught, nothing could stop it. We thought we'd die trying. At least we saved the house.'

'Is Eddie still there?' Sadie asked.

'Yes, he'll stay until we can sell what remains. It's all going to be in his name.'

'Why?' Sadie didn't understand.

'He'll have to declare himself bankrupt. Pops can't go bankrupt.'

Sadie put her arms around Stanley as his body heaved. Jane looked at a loss. She didn't understand the apocalyptic nature of that statement. Sadie's world felt about to collapse around her.

Her Papa refused to be downhearted, however. It was the first time Sadie had seen him in two years, and he looked even stronger than before.

'We're not giving up,' he berated Stanley. 'We have the Tod River Reservoir works on the go, and there's a couple of railway contracts I'm determined to win. Now that Henry Smith is dead, Kidman and I have a good chance of beating the opposition.'

So, the partnership was still intact. Sadie's worst fears subsided.

Chapter Thirty-Two

England
Cleethorpes, September 1941

Old Clee Church was booked for September 27th. Sadie had fallen in love with it as soon as she walked past the clipped yew hedge towards the ancient stone porch. Inside it was such an intimate space with its carved and pillared archways and the rich wood of the pews. No other church in Cleethorpes dated from Saxon times. The very stones seemed to speak to her of the history binding generations to the land. The neat cottages beyond the churchyard with their Dutch gable-ends and small-paned windows said the same. It was like a tiny village in a past century, where war scarcely ever penetrated. Death came naturally from a lifetime of toil on the land.

Why had she never bothered to explore the tiny church and its surroundings before? It was just a few steps from the bus stop, but tucked down a narrow lane, remaining a hidden gem, and she had always been keen to get home.

Now it would forever be part of her history, the place that she and Alex would swear their vows to each other. The vicar appeared content that she would attend church there rather than chapel, her faith as fickle as the wind. What did it matter? He was the same God. Her divorce was never mentioned. Had Alex told his white lie?

She had persuaded Alex to live in Clee Road where there was room for the boys to stay on leave. His house, although sweet with its small cosy rooms and period detail, had only two bedrooms. He decided to keep it to rent out. Maybe one day, Marion would live in it.

In the week leading up to the wedding, she took her dress and jacket from the wardrobe to lay on the bed and show Jane.

'I love it, the blue of the dress matches your eyes. Try it on.'

The tight waist and A-line skirt added height to Sadie's slim frame. She smoothed the crisp linen over her hips.

'I have to say that ivory jacket looks very chic against the blue. Are you going to wear your mother's pearls?'

Sadie retrieved them from her jewellery box and tried them against the V neck of the dress. They had been restrung into a more modern setting years before, and now they gleamed against her skin.

'Perfect. What about a hat?'

'I blew my ration on it.' Sadie took the small blue hat with its ivory rim from its box and set it at an angle on her head, the rim low over her forehead.

Jane wiped a tear from her eye. 'Your father would be proud of you.'

'I like to think that he would say I have chosen well this time. Made up for my early mistake.'

'This time you have found a diamond.'

'Or gold rather than cheap brass,' Sadie quipped back.

They burst into a fit of giggles.

Two days before the wedding, Sadie heard a sharp rap at the front door from the back room where she was writing to Glen. She walked towards the door, the blackout curtain drawn across the glass. It's probably a good luck telegram she told herself when she saw the telegraph boy there, but his young face bore a look too sombre for wedding congratulations. Panic began to rise in her chest. He forced the telegram into her reluctant hand, barely able to look at her before beating a retreat through the gate.

Sadie stood with the door wide open, her hand on that scrappy bit of paper, unable to move. She knew the world was about to crash in on her and had no idea what to do. People walked past and looked at her. Slamming the door, she retreated to the stairs and sank onto the second step, her shoulders heaving but no tears.

Which son? How was she going to bear it? Better not to know. Better never to know. She wanted to screw up the telegram and throw it onto the fire.

I have three sons, will always have three sons, she vowed. Tears came. They ripped from her like a storm, a torrent of weeping, uncontrollable, animal-like howling and still she did not know.

She crawled to the telephone and dialled Alex's number. He answered, and she couldn't speak.

'Sadie! Is that you?' Alex asked as she attempted to utter his name. 'I'm on my way, love.'

Alex arrived half an hour later, letting himself in with his key, to find her huddled up on the floor next to the telephone. He crouched next to her, taking her into his arms he rocked her, kissing her hair as she sobbed anew. He took the telegram from her.

'You haven't opened it?' She shook her head. 'But it may be something entirely different.'

'I know something's happened. The way the boy handed it to me, his expression, it was too sympathetic, too apologetic.'

'He may be injured, not dead.' A glimmer of hope flickered in her eyes. 'The only way we will find out is to open it.'

'I can't.'

'Let me.' A barely perceptible nod. He ripped it open and read it while she stared at his face for reassurance. 'Missing in action. Not dead. No one knows that he's dead my darling.'

'Who?'

'Henry.' A tide of grief rose up and devoured her.

She lay in bed on the day of her wedding, unable to move.

Jane had sat with her through the last two nights. 'Sadie love. Henry wouldn't want this. Dale has arrived. You must get up.'

'Send him up to me.'

'No, I won't. Not when you're like this. You must get up. I've run you a bath, and you will get in. It's not fair for Dale to see you destroyed. Think of his feelings. He's still got a job to do.'

She was right. As hard as it was, Dale was a pilot too and needed his mother to be able to handle this. She dragged herself from her bed. Jane handed her a dressing gown and helped her to the bathroom.

'I'll sort you out some fresh clothes. Dale is eating breakfast, and I'll make you some too. Be downstairs in twenty minutes.' Jane never gave instructions, yet it was what Sadie needed, someone taking charge.

After her bath, Sadie stared at the clothes on her bed, remembering what had lain there two days ago, replaced now with a dismal navy skirt and twin set. A ridiculous thought occurred that she should be wearing black, but she owned nothing in black other than her new underwear. A sound half-way between a sob and a laugh bubbled up in her throat. Music from the radio drifted upstairs. Life goes on. Her duty was now to Dale. He must be hurting as much as she. She scrambled into her clothes and headed downstairs, took a deep breath before opening the door to the back room.

Dale looked up. Apart from his father's brown eyes, he looked so much like her brother Eddie; it was like another punch to the stomach. She attempted a smile. He jumped up and hugged her long and hard. His wiry frame was all muscle.

'Do you still do cross-country running in your spare time?'

'Every chance I get. It's great for stress.' He released her. 'A letter has arrived from Scampton.' His voice gentle but insistent.

'You read it, please.'

'Come and sit down then. Let me pour you a cup of tea.'

As she sipped the tea, he tore open the letter, scanned it and looked up. 'There is hope. No one saw his plane go down. There was lots of flack over Holland on the way back, and he was in contact until then. If he got out, there's a chance he will be picked up by local people and hidden. I shouldn't tell you this, but there are smuggling routes for downed pilots. A few have made it back.'

'I will clutch at any straw you offer me. Thank you, my darling.' Her mind had been tortured by images of burning planes plummeting from the sky, her son helpless, trapped, calling for her. Could she now picture a parachute drifting gently in the night air? Friendly faces assisting him when he landed.

'The other possibility is that he's been captured by the Jerries. The Red Cross will inform us if that's the case.'

Jane rattled away in the kitchen. 'I'm making toast,' she shouted. 'Nearly ready.'

'I had to show her how to light the gas. My toast was an interesting colour.'

They smelled burning. 'Oh, I'd better go and help.' Sadie jumped up to go to her sister-in-law's aid.

Not long after breakfast, there was a knock at the door. Jane went to answer it and showed in Alex and Marion. Sadie saw from Marion's stricken face how things lay. It was her turn to offer comfort.

'We'd seen each other six or seven times. He often used to come up on his motorbike and take me for a spin or to the Red Lion in Redbourne. I can't believe it, Sadie.'

'We have to hope, Marion, until someone tells us otherwise. Show her the letter from Scampton, Dale. I'm so glad he found happiness in his life before ...'

'We were happy, we are happy.' Marion struggled to smile. 'I'm sorry you have had to postpone the wedding.'

'Thank you. Has everyone been informed, Alex?' She looked up at him. His face tired and greyer than she'd ever seen it. This must be dreadful for him, coping with a heartbroken daughter as well as his fiancée. She held out her hand, and he took it.

'Everyone who needs to be told. I thought we might go to church tomorrow to pray for Henry. The vicar is going to mention him.'

'Thank you. I'd like that. Dale, how long can you stay?'

'My tour's over Mother. I have to report as a flying instructor sometime in the next fortnight. I'm not sure where yet.'

'That's the best news you could have given me. It will give you time to get to know Alex too.'

'Perhaps we can rearrange the wedding before your next tour begins,' Alex said.

'It's too early to think about that yet,' Sadie said, sharper than she intended, then watched Alex's face cloud over. 'I'm sorry, my love. I'm just too raw.'

'I know but Henry gave me strict instructions to look after you, and I promised him I would. He wanted this marriage for you. Told me you deserved to be happy. Don't leave it too long.'

'That's right, Mother. He wrote to me too, saying the same.'

'He did?' Around this time, she should have been getting ready to marry the man she loved. It was impossible now, but she still longed for that. 'Give me a little time please, Alex. We'll talk about it soon.'

After everyone but Dale had left, Sadie sat in her armchair and came to a decision. Until her dying breath, unless she was given proof otherwise, Henry was alive. She would never give up on him. It was the only way she knew how to carry on living. Her sons were everything to her, more important than herself or Alex, and while there was hope, there was life. If anything happened to Dale or Glen, hope and prayer would sustain her - that and work. With the demands of the new WVS Restaurant at the Constitutional Club and the Make Do and Mend programme, there was more than enough to keep her busy.

She went upstairs to Henry's room where she had slept the last two nights, curled up in his bed clutching an old shirt of his, breathing in what little remained of his scent. She opened his wardrobe, but the smell of mothballs hit her nose. Back to the tallboy, she hunted for one of his jumpers, worn but left unwashed. Nothing, everything smelled fresh. Her desperation to bring him back to life left her scrambling around the drawers, lifting out handkerchiefs, socks, pants, all washed. Her hand closed around a tin. She stared at it, unbelieving, remembering with a shock the last time she had seen it. She sank on to the bed, clutching it in her hands, rocking backwards and forwards. She'd thrown it out in disgust, but Henry must have rescued it. Misplaced pride in a father who cared not a jot for him, who had abandoned him. Had the boy carried around some unspoken love for his father all these years? What if she were to write to Frank to tell him about his son? If he were alive, would he reply, would he even care?

Dale entered the room and sat beside his mother.

'You've got father's medals.'

'Have you seen them before?'

'Yes, Henry would get them out and show them to us. He was proud of them, proud of Dad's service in the Great War.'

'Do you ever think about him?'

Dale considered his answer. 'My memories are hazy. Most of the time he didn't pay us much attention, but sometimes he was great fun to be with. I also remember being scared of him, especially when he came home from work in a bad mood.'

'That just about sums him up. He was mercurial, on a good day there was no one you would rather be with, but those days got fewer and fewer. He craved fun and excitement and adoration. In the end, I didn't offer him that.'

'You did the right thing, Mother. He was his own worst enemy.'

'Do you think so? I'm pleased you don't blame me.'

'Never. We couldn't have had a better mother.'

Sadie's eyes filled with tears. 'Thank you, darling. I appreciate that. Here, you have them.' She placed the medals in his hand.

'Are you sure?'

'Yes. Give them back to Henry when you next see him.'

'I will.' She saw something else was on his mind.

'Spit it out, Dale. Whatever it is.'

'It's not the best time.'

'Go on. Nothing can be worse than Henry going missing.'

'After the war, there'll be a move to air travel. The progress they're making now with planes is incredible. I want to be in on that, but I want to be based in Australia.' He looked at her to gauge her reaction.

'I think it's wonderful you are making plans. There was always a chance that any or all of you would want to go back someday. I knew that when I ran away.'

'You don't mind?'

'No, Perhaps Henry and Glen will join you.'

They sat with their arms around each other, clinging on to hope.

Chapter Thirty-Three

Australia
Adelaide, December 1924

'Hurry up, Mummy, the taxi's waiting. Daddy said you mustn't be late.'

'Henry, you should be fast asleep in bed. Where's Dolly?'

'I'm here, Ma'am. I'm sorry, but he's over excited.'

Sadie finished putting on her lipstick and patted her chignon a final time. 'Pass me my shawl, Dolly please.'

'Oh, Ma'am. You look so glamorous! I love the colour. What's it called?'

'Thank you. It's fuschia. It makes a change from mourning black, that's for sure. Come here, sweetheart. You may kiss mummy on her cheek and then off to bed with you. I'll tell you all about it tomorrow.'

Her beaded-silk dress rustled as she entered the taxi. She smoothed it carefully around her ankles. All Frank's hard work was paying off at last. Perhaps she'd misjudged him. She had been happy to return to Adelaide two years before. Less happy that he wanted her to sell her house in Carlton to pay for his big idea. It was his contribution to the partnership, he'd told her, along with the money from his parents' house. His partners reminded her of gangsters, thin moustaches, eyes that didn't quite look at you, sweaty palms. Papa said you should never trust anyone with sweaty palms. Frank laughed at her when she told him.

But she had to admit the Floating Palais de Dance did look amazing. It appeared to be the talk of the city and tickets for the opening night sold out within days. All the younger members of her family in Adelaide were going, apart from Alice, of course. It was too soon after Bruce's death. Poor Bruce, in and out of hospital these last few years, but he had achieved his family, although the children were too young to be left without a father and Alice too young to be a widow. Sadie dug in her evening bag for her lace handkerchief to dab the moisture from her eyes before it did any damage.

Papa wasn't attending the opening, although she thought Caro would have liked to come. He was far too busy with his new project, and up at the crack of dawn every morning to oversee the work, the biggest house building project in Australia. He'd beaten off all the competition to get the thousand homes contract that would save the family fortune. All his children were proud of him despite worrying about his health.

It had been touch and go whether the Palais would be ready on time. Some city official ordered The Torrens dredged, leaving the barge squat and lopsided amongst the mud. Frank had been beside himself with rage. It took much persuasion, maybe of the monetary kind, to refloat it in time for the grand opening. The name of Lady Moulden, who was opening the event in aid of the hospital, did the trick.

The taxi joined a long queue disgorging their passengers into the breezy summer air. Sadie was late; Frank would be angry. She was supposed to stand with him and greet everyone. Sweeping her shawl from the seat, she paid the driver and walked towards the gangway, but there was a crush to board. Surely there were more people than had bought tickets. It was supposed to be only seven hundred unless - Frank did like to bend the rules.

Sadie breathed deeply to still her twitchy nerves. She looked around. Plenty of smaller boats surrounded the barge, a flotilla of winking lights demanding to play their part in the opening. The electric lighting lit the Palais, showing off its exotic Moorish domes. As she waited, the orchestra began to play. There would be hell to pay when she arrived or when they got home more likely. She listened to the excited chatter around her as the crowd moved slowly forward.

'How much do you think it cost?' A voice asked nearby.

'Thousands,' the reply. Ten thousand, Sadie knew the answer. The cajoling, the insistence which turned to demands and veiled threats, wore her down until she sold a chunk of her investments to help fund Franks dream.

At last, she was on board, and there was Frank. He caught sight of her, glowered momentarily, and then beckoned her over. He was at his most charming by the time she arrived at his side.

'I didn't expect everyone to arrive so early,' her whispered apology.

'This is the biggest event of the year. People are dying to be here, apart from you it seems,' he muttered, before switching off his anger to greet the next couple. 'Dancing is downstairs and refreshments upstairs on the promenade deck. We're offering the first drink from the soda fountain free for tonight only. Just show your ticket to be stamped. Yes, I know, I wish we could serve champagne too. These blasted six o'clock licensing laws will be the death of honest businesses like ours. Speak to your local representative.'

As people continued to stream onto the boat, Sir Frank Moulden called for three cheers for the businessmen who had invested their money in the enterprise, reminding them of their generosity in donating the first night's takings to charity.

Thousands of people lined the shore watching; some danced to the muffled strains of the orchestra. It was like a fairground with hawkers selling food. Sadie was astounded. Frank had been right. People were clamouring for music and entertainment even amidst the continuing recession. Many of the people out there would never be able to afford tickets, but their determination to enjoy themselves at the spectacle remained undimmed.

The night passed in a whirl of music, dancing and congratulations. Sadie danced her feet off with a succession of men, young, old, paunchy, handsome; it didn't matter as long as they had money to spend, Frank instructed. She laughed at their jokes, encouraged them to buy a soda, flattered their wives. Her husband should be proud. She caught his approving glance several times and hoped she had made up for her earlier mistake. This was not her life; it was his. After this evening, she would attend only for special occasions. He would be here several nights a week. How exhausting she thought, to be putting on this constant act.

He arrived home long after she got to bed and stayed in bed until lunchtime.

'You must be overjoyed with how it went,' she said, as he served himself a double helping of devilled kidneys. 'How many people came?'

'Eighteen hundred, I'm told.'

'But that's more than twice the number of tickets you were allowed to sell.'

'What the Town Clerk doesn't know about won't hurt him.'

'Do be careful Frank. He has already threatened you with legal action because of that top deck.'

'For Christ's sake Sadie, stop your nagging. Leave me to run my business as I see fit. Do you interfere in your father's business? No! So, stop it. Limit yourself to bringing up our sons.'

Sadie busied herself cutting up some meat and vegetables for Glen who was sitting on her lap, playing with his spoon.

'Why is he in here? Dolly should be giving him his lunch in the nursery. That's what I pay her for.'

'She's taken Henry and Dale to the beach. It's such a glorious day. I thought they could do with some fresh air.'

Frank glared at her but had no answer to that. He opened the newspaper instead and ignored her for the rest of the meal.

She did not mean to annoy him, but over the last few months, his temper frayed at the slightest upset. He had been so busy with this project, but now it was finished and open for business, she hoped they could get back to happier times. Christmas was around the corner, she would plan for some family outings where they could all relax and enjoy themselves. A holiday too, a week away from everything in the Adelaide Hills, not too far so that he couldn't get back if there were an emergency. Her brain ran away with ideas.

Over the weeks which followed, Sadie became worried about the hours Frank was working. He rarely arrived home before three in the morning, slept until lunchtime and then departed for his office. He reappeared for an early dinner then set off for the Palais. The boys never saw him other than on Sunday.

'I thought the Palais closed at eleven on week-nights,' she said one lunchtime. 'You're working yourself to a frazzle.'

'I have to supervise the clearing up, work out what's needed to replace stock.'

'Surely someone else can do that.'

His eyes slid away from her face. He didn't bite back as he normally did. What wasn't he telling her?

'We're not in financial trouble, are we?'

'See, there you go again, worrying unnecessarily. It's a roaring success. Your husband has created something to be proud of, and all you can do is carp, carp, carp. I'm sick of it.' He stood and threw down his napkin. 'Don't expect me back before four tonight! We have a big Christmas party onboard.' He slammed the door on the way out.

His outburst did nothing to assuage Sadie's concerns. Something was wrong.

Sadie saw little of him in the week before Christmas. Adelaide was determined to party. It will get better once the holiday season is out of the way, she told herself. I should have expected this.

At least Christmas Day was a family occasion. The house burst with laughter from Papa's grandchildren. Only Stanley's two were not present, Jane's second promised trip back to England had begun the previous month. Sadie was troubled by the number of trunks Jane took with her. Would she ever see her again?

It was a bittersweet day, the first Christmas without Bruce, but his children were too young to remember him.

'Even Kenneth has stopped asking,' Alice said.

'That's so sad. We must try to keep his memory alive.' Sadie said, watching the three-year-old play with his cousins.

'I'll be happier when we have a headstone for him.' Papa had aged since his son died; his energy dimmed by disappointment and grief. Bruce was buried near his mother at Yarra Glen. It was as he requested, but Sadie regretted not being able to attend his funeral and that none of them lived close enough to visit the grave.

'I hear your friend Mr McNamara died suddenly,' Sadie said, changing the subject.

'Yes, poor chap.' Papa looked subdued. 'He was a true friend. Helped me out no end of times.' Eddie's son, Jeff, tugged on Papa's trouser leg, begging to be picked up. 'Hello little fella, what do you want?'

'Play with me, Grandpa?'

'What's the matter with all your cousins? Let's see what they're up to, shall we?' He wandered off into the dining room, where the older cousins were playing cards after all the dishes had been cleared away.

'He looks tired Eddie.'

'Well, he's sixty-five. The time most men hang up their boots.'

Frank stood talking to Joe Junior who had taken the plunge into the wireless industry. He was now the director of the South Australian Radio Company.

'Frank has suggested we could do a broadcast from the Palais after we open in February. An evening of dance music from Adelaide's premier nightclub – sounds good, doesn't it?'

'It does. Frank is full of good ideas, and wireless sounds exciting Joe. The boys would love to own a set. Will you have childrens' programmes?' She smiled at her husband, and for once he smiled back. Maybe tonight they would make love, it had been more than three weeks, and she missed his embraces. He'd not been near her since the opening night of the Palais. That must be why he was in such a bad mood.

In mid-January Frank decided to go on a fishing trip for a few days.

'I need a few days to relax.'

'I agree. But can't you at least take Henry? He would love to go fishing, and school doesn't start for another week.' Sadie suggested.

'No, I want time on my own, away from everyone. Can't you let me have four days to myself without complaining? All the hours I've put into making a success of the Palais; it's been harder than you know.'

Sadie acquiesced. Once Frank had made his mind up there was no changing it. She packed his bags and waved him goodbye; wounded for her oldest son, who stood with her on the doorstep. It broke Sadie's heart to see the expression of longing on his face, but his father barely acknowledged him. The eight-year-old boy needed to spend time with his father and didn't understand why he showed such a lack of interest. An occasional game of football wouldn't go amiss. Sadie didn't understand it either and tried to make up for it.

'I'll take you riding instead,' she said before placing a comforting arm around her eldest boy.

On the third day of Frank's break, the maid entered the sitting room.

'There's a Miss Matthews to see you.'

Sadie knew the name. It was Frank's secretary. She hoped nothing was wrong at the Palais. 'Show her in, please.'

'Good morning, Miss Matthews, is there anything wrong? Do sit down; you look upset.'

All blonde curls, cornflower eyes and bright lipstick, she looked nothing like her father's secretary, plain, efficient Mrs Brown. Sadie wondered how proficient this young woman was at her job, perhaps there's been a minor hiccup and she was panicking.

The secretary sat down, picking at her handkerchief, her left foot and neat ankle jiggling up and down.

Sadie waited for her to speak. The girl tried, opened her mouth and closed it again, cleared her throat, gave a little cough.

'I don't have all day Miss Matthews. I'm taking my sons to have their hair cut for school next week.' She looked at her watch. 'In fifteen minutes.'

The girl opened her mouth once more, her hands working overtime at that poor handkerchief. 'It's about Mr Tinsdale,' she said. 'You see, I'm in a certain condition.'

Sadie opened her mouth to ask what on earth she was talking about before realisation struck. Cold anger swept through her body. 'You have been having an affair with my husband?'

The girl nodded, emboldened. 'He wants to marry me, but he hasn't told you, and you need to know.'

'How long has this been going on?'

'Six months and lately he's been staying with me after the Palais closes. But he always leaves before dawn and I don't think he should have to. He's tiring himself out.'

'No doubt!' Sadie's voice was icy. Was the girl totally without decorum? She picked up the bell on the table beside her and rang it sharply. The maid popped her head around the door. 'Miss Matthews is leaving, please show her out and ask Dolly to come and see me.'

The girl stood. 'He always said you were a cold fish.' She placed a hand across her stomach, gloating as she saw Sadie's eyes drawn to its gentle swell beneath the pink linen coat. That colour didn't suit her.

Sadie sat and watched as the girl sashayed from the room, her hips swaying in triumph. Confidence oozed from her now that she had accomplished what she set out to do. All Sadie saw was a pathetic dupe. She did not pity her; the girl deserved everything she got. Frank would drop her like a hot potato.

Dolly arrived a minute later. 'Please take the boys for their haircut, Dolly dear. I seem to have developed a headache and need to lie down.' If only she could get to her bedroom without letting rip to the anger and humiliation consuming her.

Should she have known or at least suspected? What a fool she was. Grandma Jane had been right all along. Her mind was in turmoil. Once in her room, she threw herself down on the bed, buried her face in the pillow and howled – a mixture of fury and loathing. Loathing for herself at being taken for a fool, fury at Frank. He'd used criticism to control her, always putting her on the back foot, making her doubt herself. Well no more. The veil had shifted; he wasn't going to get away with this. She had a day to decide what to do before his return.

Chapter Thirty-Four

England
Cleethorpes, December 1941

There had been no further news of Henry. She was sure she would have been informed by now if he had been taken prisoner. She clung to the hope that somewhere in Europe he was being sheltered, looked after by people who would see him through the war or onward to safety. Her belief became so fixed that she pictured him hidden, maybe underground or deep in a forest. images of a young woman bringing him food and drink, or of an elderly man in working clothes with a sympathetic smile discussing escape plans, popped into her mind several times a day. When they did, she repeated a mantra – 'Stay strong, Henry, believe in yourself, you will come home to us.'

Her relationship with Alex remained sound, but there were nights when he could only hold her against the terror which gripped her. Nights when she fell asleep as he stroked her hair and lay troubled in his arms. Their lovemaking, once so urgent, so demanding had faded into comfort. Solace not passion ruled her, and it was beginning to drive them apart.

At the beginning of the month, he said. 'That's it. You need a change of scene. I'm taking you away next weekend.'

'But it's winter.'

'Bring a pair of thick trousers, some stout walking shoes and a waterproof coat.'

She laughed. 'Very romantic.'

'See, the thought is doing you good already.'

'Where are we going?'

'Louth.'

'Which one?' She raised an eyebrow.

It was his turn to look surprised. 'What do you mean?'

'Louth, Lincolnshire or the one in New South Wales, near Nelyambo.'

He grabbed hold of her and lifted her into the air, swinging her feet off the ground. 'Oh, Sadie, I love you. Come back to me. I've missed you.' He kissed her long and hard, and she opened her mouth, feeling his hunger for her.

'I'm sorry, Alex. A weekend away would be lovely. Will we drive?'

'No, we'll catch the train. My petrol rations won't stretch that far.'

He stayed on Friday night, and they left early on Saturday morning to walk to the station.

'Going somewhere nice, dear?' Her neighbour, Mrs Brain, asked, passing them at the gate.

'Just to Louth. We'll be back tomorrow.'

'Oh, I always like Louth.' She gave Sadie a quick peck on the cheek. 'Look after her, Captain Peters.'

'She winked,' he said, laughing, as they walked down Princes Road.

'I have her blessing for my wicked ways. She told me to grab every minute with you and all will come right in the end.'

'I like her attitude.'

The train was standing at the platform, already belching out a mixture of steam and smoke. They managed to find a compartment on their own, and Alex stowed their battered suitcases in the luggage rack. One case should have been enough for them both, but Alex insisted on bringing one of his own.

'Do you know, I have hardly left the town since I arrived? The odd shopping trip to Hull, a Methodist bus outing to Hubbard's Hills or Mablethorpe, I can count them on my fingers. My world has shrunk to scores of square miles, less than the size of my father's sheep station. It's ironic really.' She sat on the scratchy, plush seat. 'Does every compartment have a photograph of the Forth Railway Bridge? I seem to see it every time I get on one of these trains.'

'When this war's over, I'm going to show you the world,' he said. He sat beside Sadie and kissed her.

The door to their compartment opened, and a lady in an old-fashioned black coat sat primly opposite them, her lips pursed and disapproving. Thank goodness it was only two stops to Grimsby Town where they would change trains.

He had booked a room in the King's Head, an old coaching inn in the centre of town. The room was generous, a large bay window looked out over Mercer Row. The street unusually narrow to her eyes, more a laneway than a main street. It had a quaint feel to it. How she had imagined England in her youth. She caught a glimpse of a church steeple soaring above the rooftops to her left. Alex put his arms around her and nuzzled her ear. Despite the December greyness, romance pervaded the room and she shivered deliciously.

'I'm almost minded to forget food, but I have other plans. Go and get yourself ready for lunch, love.' His voice was husky with promise.

She had felt no shame, checking in as Mr and Mrs Peters, only fate had intervened to stop her claiming that title. Frank's ring rather than Alex's still encircled her finger. Sitting at the dressing table repairing her make-up for lunch, she felt an overwhelming desire to put that right.

After a light meal, he told her to don trousers and presented her with a pair of his daughter's riding boots. 'These are old ones; I hope your size. It's a good thing they weren't chucked out when I moved.'

'But it's years since I rode.'

'You won't have forgotten.' He tucked a woollen scarf around her neck and gave her a pair of old, leather gloves, slightly too large for her. 'Wear these over your other gloves. I don't want you getting cold. I have called a taxi to take us to the livery.'

When he assisted her into the saddle, and she felt the horse between her legs and her hands on the reins, it was as if all the cares of the world had drifted away. As they trotted away from the yard, drizzle began to fall, but she didn't care. A hot bath back at the hotel would warm her up.

'We'll only have a couple of hours before the light goes, and we get thoroughly cold. I'm sorry about the rain.'

'People may think us mad for going out in this, but it feels amazing to be in the saddle again. I never thought anything about riding in the rain when I was younger, although it was rarely this cold.'

They entered the valley of Hubbard's Hills, rode past the small, shuttered café and along the track of the stream as far as the stepping stones. She reined in her horse to stare, remembering the Methodist summer picnic. The boys had played in the stream for hours while she sat on the bank watching, laughing at the fun they were having.

'What is it, darling?'

'Lovely memories.' Her eyes sparkled through her rain-splattered lashes. 'Thank you, Alex, for reminding me of such a wonderful day.'

He grinned. 'Are you ready to trek up through the woods to the top? Take care; it might be slippery underfoot.' The drizzle had given way to rain.

He found a dry rug to put around her when they got back to the stables, deliciously tired, wet through, full of enthusiasm when he booked another ride for the morning.

Once they got back to the hotel and divested themselves of their wet clothes, she told him she was going to run a bath, but he pulled her to him. He ran his hand over her wet skin and taking a clean towel from the bed, he wrapped her in it, rubbing her dry. She did the same for him until they cast them aside and fell under the covers. He pulled the blankets over their heads to stop her shivering, and she relished the dark nest, hiding them from anything but their private world, where everything but love lay forgotten.

The morning lay clean, crisp and bright after the heavy rain of the evening before. They checked out of the hotel after breakfast, wearing their riding clothes the hotel staff had dried for them overnight, and headed back to the stables. Sadie's muscles groaned, her knees felt twisted out of shape, but she was determined to ride through the pain.

This time they cantered across farm tracks and galloped towards Market Rasen, stopping at Ludford Magna Church, before hacking back to Louth.

'Can we do this again?' She asked as she fell into his arms, her body screaming its mixture of joy and agony. 'I can hardly walk, but I have missed that exhilaration of riding in the countryside.'

'You like it that much?'

'You have no idea. I think my poor old bones don't, but maybe they could get used to it again.'

'If we moved out to Laceby, you could go riding every day.'

Surprise and delight lit her face. 'Now there's an idea. I might take you up on it. Do you think I will be too old at fifty to ride?'

'Nah, maybe at seventy, lots of old blokes and sheilas ride in Australia, I hear.'

'That is true,' she laughed. 'God, I'm so hungry I could eat the crotch out of a low flying duck as my brother Eddie would say.'

'You'll be lucky. I hear there's Spam pie for lunch.'

Her face dropped. 'There are some things I will never eat again after the war; Spam pie is one of them.'

They arrived home in the late afternoon. The hotel allowed them to change their clothes in one of the bathrooms before lunch. Sadie had been delighted to see a pork chop on the menu. It may have been small, but it made a welcome change.

'Are you staying tonight, Alex? There's something I want to discuss.'

'Not the whole night. I need to go to Scunthorpe tomorrow. A possible new client, so I need to be in my best bib and tucker. This war isn't helping me pay my bills.'

'That's good news about the client.'

'Yes, they are few and far between these days. He's in the home guard too, so I'm hoping for a bit of favouritism, I guess.'

He helped her make tea by slicing a loaf and spreading the bread thinly with margarine.

'I managed to get some potted meat on Friday.' She fetched it from the larder to show him. 'Let's splash out and have it all.'

'I knew the weekend would do you good. I can't quite believe how much good.'

She smiled. 'Thank you. I feel it's given me a whole new lease of life. It's still difficult, but I've turned a corner, hopefully.'

They sat at the table in the bay window of the back room, the gas fire glowing orange, curtains and black-out drawn.

'I think it's time to reset the date. That's if you still want me, Alex.'

'There's no doubt in my mind, never has been. It's what I have been longing to hear. When?'

'The spring, I'd like a few daffodils in the churchyard. It will be nearly six months since...' she swallowed, 'Henry went missing. Time enough to wait. I want to let Dale know.'

'I wish I could open a bottle of champagne.'

'Let's celebrate in a different way,' she said softly.

She was up early, having slept soundly. Alex had left at eleven 'clock the night before, and her heart was lighter than it had been for weeks. I've done the right thing, she told herself. Henry will understand. Humming softly, while making her morning tea and toast, she turned on the radio to keep her company. Total shock swept through her body as she listened to the news. A Japanese attack on somewhere called Pearl Harbour, the Japanese navy steaming towards Thailand. All of the South Seas at risk of attack.

Banging sounded on the door, was it Jane? No, it was Alex.

'When I heard the news, I cancelled my trip to Scunthorpe.'

'What does it mean? I'm going out of my mind. Is Glen at risk?'

'Darling everyone says Singapore is impregnable.'

'Didn't they think that about Pearl Harbour?' She put her hand against her mouth, her body heaving in anguish. 'Not my Glen, he's too young; barely nineteen. I thought he was safe.'

'Darling, the Japs are going to have the British, the United States and Australia after them, some of the very best fighting troops. Don't despair. We'll see them off. One thing to celebrate, at least, the Americans will be in the war. Roosevelt will persuade them.'

Singapore fell on Jane's son-in-law's birthday in February. Nancy's Jimmy was still in North Africa, but where was her son now? Had he escaped to Australia? Had he been torpedoed on one of those ships sunk by the Japanese or was he surrounded by troops, a prisoner? Anything was possible. What Sadie could not deny was the feeling of dread in the pit of her soul. It was more than dread. She recognised the feeling from years before when she was a child at Chateau Yering. Superstitious nonsense or death foretold. She couldn't shake the feeling, and it terrified her.

Alex telephoned. 'I'm coming over now.'

'No, I'll walk over to you. The only place I want to be is in church. I'll make the morning service.'

'Try not to worry, Sadie.'

Try not to worry; it was the stupidest thing he had ever said to her. If someone dug under her skin all they would find was worry; blood, bone, sinew, muscle all turned to beads of worry. She imagined them as little spiders crawling under her skin.

He met her at the door, his face full of concern. He had aged with her over the last two months, streaks of grey lined her hair, worry lined her mouth and eyes, and she saw those lines mirrored in his face. It was unfair on him. All she had brought him was anxiety. Back to square one after that single weekend in December when she had felt alive once again.

She lost herself in prayer through the service. It brought her the only comfort she could accept. The vicar prayed for those left in Singapore and mentioned her son by name; her tear-soaked eyes thanked him.

After the service, she sat with Alex in his sitting room.

'I suppose the wedding is off again,' he said, searching her face.

She nodded. 'I can't do this anymore.'

'Do what?' His voice pressed in on her.

'Us. I don't have the strength to continue with us.'

'No, Sadie. We'll get good news eventually. Until then I'll be here giving you strength. You need me.'

'That's the trouble. All I do is need you. I'm sucking you up, but I have nothing left to give you in return. I love you too much to allow that to continue. I've made up my mind. It's over.' She handed him back her engagement ring.

His head shook in disbelief. 'You're not thinking straight.'

She placed a finger against his lips. 'You are the best thing that has ever happened to me, but I can't bear your pain for me as well as my own. I have to live with this on my own. You care for your daughter, and I will continue to live for my sons. That's all we can do.'

'Sadie give it time. You can't do this now. It's too sudden.'

She shook her head. 'I can. You don't deserve this, and I couldn't live with myself if I dragged you down too. If none of my sons return, you will have saddled yourself with a sad, embittered woman, with nothing left to give you. I won't do that to you.

'You're not doing anything to me. What you are doing is throwing away something precious, maybe our last chance. I can't believe you would do that.' Anger had crept into his voice.

'Try to understand.'

'Understand what? We could all die tomorrow. What's the point of love, hey? You don't get it, do you? When we love someone, we stick by them, in bad times and in good. You're so selfish. Don't pretend you are sacrificing yourself for me. You're not. You're giving in, telling yourself you don't deserve me. That bastard husband really did a job of work on you didn't he?'

'Alex, that's not fair. I'm only thinking of you.'

'No, you're not. If you were thinking of me, you wouldn't be giving in. You would fight. What are you going to do if the Germans invade, Sadie? Roll over, let them walk all over you. I'll be fighting, will probably die fighting. We may have only days, weeks, months left to us.'

He was shouting now. Sadie put her hands over her ears, and he forced them back by her side. She shook them off, but he took her face in his hands and kissed her, bruising her lips. Her body grew rigid, and he released her.

'I'm not your brute of a husband. Don't make me out to be like him.'

She hadn't meant to. It was her normal reaction to force of any kind. But she couldn't apologise. She needed all of her resolve to do this. Picking up her handbag, she made for the door.

'I think it's best we don't see each other again. I'm sorry if I have disappointed you.'

'Disappointed me!' Don't you see, you're making the same huge mistake you made last time when you threw away your first love. How did that turn out Sadie? See a pattern there, do you? There must be something very wrong with you.'

She glared at him. If he couldn't understand her pain, then it was never going to work between them. She needed all her energy for her sons.

As she closed the door, she heard him slam something into it behind her. His rage somehow made it easier to walk away without telling him the real reason they could not marry. Twice they had set the date and twice she had lost a son. She would not risk Dale. What if there were some vengeful being who was determined to make her pay for the sin of loving a man? It wasn't worth the risk. She wanted the terror in her body to go away. This was the only way she could think to assuage the evil spirit that continued to haunt her since the death of her mother.

Four days later, Darwin was bombed. She and Jane sat together, holding hands.

'I've been thinking a lot about Australia these last few months. All of my nieces and nephews, are they caught up in this war? They must be. We worried about the Japs in the last war, but this is going to be as bad if not worse for the family, and I don't know about any of them.'

'And where is Stanley? Did he get out of Borneo? My wayward husband wouldn't be so stupid as to stay, would he?

Sadie had no answer to that. 'Do you think I was right to let Alex go? Am I mad to think the relationship jinxed?'

'Has that awful feeling disappeared?'

'It has. It was like I couldn't breathe on the day I gave Alex up. But it's gone now. Strangely, I felt at peace that night. I'm still terrified for Glen.'

'We've lived without men for so long. Has Alex tried to contact you?'

'I've taken the phone off the hook. He came over last night, but I didn't answer the door.'

'It's only our children who matter.'

'Is Brian out of Burma?'

'No, Sadie, I don't think he is. He's with General Slim, and I'm worried sick.'

'We can only pray for our sons; waiting and weeping will see us into an early grave. Let's go to chapel and then find ways to keep ourselves busy. So busy we don't have time to think.'

Chapter Thirty-Five

England   -
Cleethorpes, June 1943

Staying busy proved not to be a problem. It was the only way to save her sanity. There was still no news of Henry, but Glen was now a prisoner of the Japanese somewhere in Asia. She looked into the faces of other women and saw the same stress. It was a mystery how any of them coped. But they did, with humour and little complaint. Mothers, wives, sisters, all struggling to put food on the table, clothe their children while praying that their loved ones survived whatever the war threw at them.

Sadie enjoyed her shifts at the National Restaurant. She enjoyed working with Vera who lived not far away in Garnett Street and who was lucky enough to have four daughters and no sons. Her husband was an ARP warden and had plenty of tales to tell. Vera didn't have a serious bone in her body and lifted Sadie's spirits with her inconsequential chatter. Her husband was also a fish merchant, and Vera often slipped Sadie a piece of plaice or a fillet of haddock, wrapped in brown paper. It saved her queueing at the fishmongers.

'We don't go short,' Vera whispered out of earshot. 'Harry swaps fish for meat. You should come over for some of my steak and kidney pie sometime.'

A summer evening jaunt to Vera's always lifted Sadie's spirits. As Vera said, 'Card games, laughter and a sly tipple, what could be better?'

Sadie had also heeded the call for volunteers to make refreshments for the young women and American airmen who thronged the *Café Dansant* on Saturday nights. The men were bussed in from their station at Goxhill, which they called Goat Hill. All brashness and swagger, they completely bowled over the eager Cleethorpes girls. They brought ciggies for the men and stockings for the women and a great deal of laughter and envy. Her shifts brought back memories of other dances in her youth, before she and Frank married. She hoped some of these girls didn't make her mistake.

It seemed Frank was making the most of the Americans in Sydney too. Eddie enclosed a newspaper cutting about Frank's scandalous cabaret bar in Kings Cross which had been closed down at the request of the American authorities. That he was reduced to running a disorderly house did not surprise Sadie. That he was doing it on the back of her Papa's money horrified and sickened her.

Eddie did not mention Stanley. Where was Jane's husband?

The Americans changed Cleethorpes. It was not uncommon to see groups of confident young men with their arms around girls, strolling in the sunshine and taking liberties which shocked the chapel ladies. But she could not begrudge those boys. They came over here to die, strapping young men who would see no wives or children, but most likely crash and burn in their steel coffins. Vera's husband begged his second daughter not to bring any of those delightful young men home anymore. He couldn't bear meeting them only to lose them to war a week later.

When the next telegram came, she had been expecting it. Everyone knew Lancaster crews had a fifty percent chance of survival. Why not her son too? Her life was cursed. Nothing else made sense.

She took it round to her sister-in-law. Jane's son, Brian, had been reported killed in another foray into Burma a few weeks before. They sat quietly, reflecting on their losses, words too painful, while dear Nibby clucked around them offering tea and sympathy.

'I've made a decision,' Sadie said. 'I can't sit around and wait for news that Dale's found or confirmed dead. I'm going to go to his airbase to speak to the commanding officer this time.'

'But he'll write to you, Sadie.'

'I want to hear it from the horse's mouth.'

The journey to Grantham shouldn't have taken so long. She calculated two hours at a push. But delays and unexplained halts saw her later into Grantham than intended. In her eagerness to beard the lion in his den, she caught a taxi straight to Bottesford, a few miles west. They had talked over Dale's reasoning to transfer to the Royal Australian Airforce, but it was still a shock to be greeted by so many voices from her youth. It seemed, however, that nationality failed to discriminate over who lived and who died.

'Dale said you hail from Melbourne, my home city, Mrs Tinsdale.'

'Yes, Wing Commander Ashcroft, although I was born in West Australia.'

'Well, Dale's a good bloke, despite his pommy accent.'

'You said is. You don't believe he's dead?' Her heart beat painfully as she clutched at straws.

'Parachutes were seen. Maybe two, maybe three. I can't promise anything, but only one plane was reported missing in that area.'

'Which area, Squadron Leader?'

'Germany, Mrs Tinsdale. I can't be more specific; it's not allowed.'

'Then he could be a prisoner.'

'If he made it out, and it's a big if, we should find out soon enough. The Jerries are pretty efficient at informing the Red Cross.'

'Thank you. You have no idea what that means to me.'

'Dale told us about his brothers. Bloody hard luck; excuse my language, but Dale fitted right in here.'

'I know, he told me how at home you made him feel.'

'One of us. Strewth, a better bloke you could not find. I hope you get good news of Glen too. My brother was in Singapore. It was touch and go, but he made it out.'

She hitched a lift back to Grantham in a jeep, thanking God she had taken that journey to the camp. It had given her the hope she craved. The jeep dropped her at the station, along with a handful of young men hitting the town for a night out. A train was due in five minutes, but she took the time to shake each young man by the hand and wished them well, their accents giving her a moment of homesickness. They knew who she was and said they were keeping their fingers crossed for Dale. She smiled her thanks.

As she walked towards the platform, a guard stopped her.

'Where are you going, Madam?'

'Cleethorpes.'

'Not tonight, you're not. There aren't any trains beyond Newark. A signalling problem, so they say. Best you stay in Newark tonight and travel in the morning.'

At least it's light, she thought. Tramping around looking for somewhere to stay in the dark would have been awful. She sighed and settled down for the short journey. It was teatime by the time she got to Newark, so she set off looking for any respectable hotel that offered accommodation. It seemed everyone had beaten her to it.

At the Newark Arms, they said, 'No dear, try the White Hart.'

'Nothing here, Madam, try the Clinton Arms.'

'Sorry. Try the Olde Market.'

Running out of hotels, she screwed up her nerve and entered the Boar's Head, tired and dispirited, her earlier euphoria competing to keep her positive. A woman stood at the bar. 'Do you have a room for the night, please. I'm at my wit's end. I've been searching everywhere.'

She shook her head in sympathy. 'I'm sorry, me duck. It's been a heck of a day.'

Sadie's shoulders slumped. 'Can I get a cup of tea here? I stupidly didn't pack my thermos, and I'm parched.'

'I'll see what I can do. Would you like a sandwich?'

'Do you know, I would. That's very kind.' She suddenly realised she was starving.

A man came out of an office behind the bar. He looked at her with a sympathetic smile. 'You're looking for somewhere to stay?'

She nodded. 'Can you suggest anywhere else? I've been all around the market area.'

'We have a snug. It's a small room, mainly used by ladies. I could get some cushions and blankets for you if that wouldn't be too uncomfortable.'

She grasped his hand in thanks, tears in her eyes at his small kindness. He nodded and patted her hand.

After she had drunk her tea and consumed a better sandwich than she'd eaten in a long time, a thin slice of beef with mustard on a thick slice of bread, she made her way to the empty snug.

271

'Oh, it's cosy, thank you. I'll curl up here with a newspaper and be very comfortable, thank you,' Sadie said to the woman.

'There's a ladies' cloakroom, right there.' She pointed to the door. 'I'll bring you a towel.'

Sadie sat down on a chair and kicked off her shoes; how these wooden soles made her feet ache. She longed for the bygone days of soft leather and picked up her foot to massage life back into her toes.

As she settled down to read the paper, daylight filtered through the taped windows. No need yet for the blackout. Her mind drifted back to Dale. The certainty that he was a German prisoner struck her like a bolt of lightning. Three sons, at least two prisoners. Could it be? Could she hope? She was still terrified for Glen. The stories of Japanese brutality in China and from rescued Empire troops unnerved her. She couldn't help thinking of him starving in some hell hole. Whereas Dale – maybe he had only to sit out the rest of the war in discomfort. She would get him back, please God; enough hope for now.

She slept surprisingly well on her bundle of cushions. The landlady woke her with tea and toast around eight o'clock.

'I need to sweep up in here, soon.'

'I'll be out of your way in no time, thank you.'

She freshened up and made her way to the desk to pay. The landlord who had offered her the snug was writing in a ledger. He looked up and smiled.

'I can't thank you enough for letting me stay. If you don't mind me asking, why did you do that?' Sadie asked. 'No one else in this town was willing to take pity on me.'

'It was that fine airman standing behind you. He was nodding at me, and I couldn't let him down. Your son, is he? We're so grateful for all they do. The bravest of the brave.'

Sadie stood in shock, unable to speak. She shook as she handed him some coins from her purse.

'Dear lady, you've gone as white as a sheet. What have I said?' He gripped her hand.

'I don't know; I don't know. My son...' she couldn't continue. 'I'm sorry, I must go.' She turned blindly and stumbled to the door. What did it mean? She didn't believe in ghosts. All she knew was that one of her sons had helped her when she needed him most. They were all with her, looking after her and she loved them.

How she made it through the door to the street, she didn't know. She couldn't remember the route back to the station but walked aimlessly in a direction she hoped was north. Passing an ancient church, she turned, retraced her steps and entered. She stepped towards the altar, found a pew and sat there, staring up at the image of Jesus, without taking it in. The cool, quiet space offered her time to reflect. She wondered how many mothers had sat here over hundreds of years worrying about their sons in battle. An invisible thread bound them to her, and she felt them reaching out to her with their prayers. Warmth began to flow through her blood, bringing her the peace she craved.

A priest approached her to ask her if she needed help. Smiling, she thanked him but shook her head. It was not God she needed, but sisterhood, the company of strong women to sustain her. Jane and her friends in the WVS were the answer. Hard work, don't think, work together, stay strong. It would be her new mantra.

The sirens sounded early on the following Monday morning. Sadie turned over in bed and groaned. Not another bloody false alarm. There had been so many over the years. She peered at the clock in the light of her torch, one thirty in the morning. No way was she getting out of bed. The last real attack had been two years ago. She sank back and closed her eyes. The siren went on and on, and she began to pick out a low droning noise. She shot out of bed, donned her dressing gown then ran downstairs. She grabbed her gas mask, stuck her feet into boots left on purpose by the back door and ran out to the shelter. The flares of incendiary bombs already lit the sky above. She sat huddled in the gloom feeling the reverberations from large bombs hitting the ground. This time there were lots of small explosions too. The dogs around howled their heads off.

The clang of fire engine bells followed the all-clear. Sadie couldn't see anything from her back door, so walked down the hall to the front and stepped outside. Smoke, the smell already strong in the air, gave the game away even without the glow of fire towards the docks. Poor blighters.

I must check my ceilings, she thought and ran back inside, no evidence of smoke in the house, but she inspected each bedroom. It was getting light. Sensing a long day ahead, she made her way back to bed, ready to be woken by a ringing telephone.

Small, distant explosions punctuated her walk to the WVS that morning. A policeman stopped her in St Peter's Avenue.

'Don't pick up anything strange. Those bastards have dropped anti-personnel mines all over town. Kiddies have ...' he wiped his hand across his face. Another explosion sounded in Bentley Street and he ran off towards it.

'We've got to help get the message out, ladies.' Edna handed them a mimeographed drawing, still smelling of the duplicating spirit. 'They're going to get some leaflets printed, but in the meantime, we have to try and let everyone know while we're manning canteens.'

'My Harry's that shook up,' Vera said. 'They were on duty first thing. His friend, Len, saw one, walked towards it and kicked it. Next thing Harry knew, Len was on the ground, no legs. No one knows if he'll live.'

Sadie stared at the drawing. It looked innocuous, like an overlarge child's yo-yo in one picture and a metal butterfly in another. 'How many came down, do you think?'

'They say thousands. They've called in bomb disposal. It's going to be a huge job. We'll be providing canteens for army personnel, but I want some of you ladies out there helping get the message across. No one should pick one up, nor go anywhere near. They must report any sightings. Some exploded on impact, but others have delayed detonation. These winged ones floated down and may be caught in trees, power-lines or anywhere.' Edna wiped a hand across her brow.

An image of little boys finding one and thinking it was a toy or even spent shrapnel, made Sadie shudder. How sickening to think that anyone could target innocent children like this.

'The police are visiting schools to warn the teachers and pupils, but four boys that I know of in Park View have already been maimed. There are probably more. I hear there have been many deaths and injuries in

Grimsby. Oh, and you'll be sad to hear that the Tivoli Theatre and Bon Marché got hit too. Thank God, it was night-time.'

Sadie sensed the unease in the town; people were afraid to go outside for fear a bomb would explode nearby. They were small enough to have rolled into bushes or be caught in the branches of trees, now in full leaf. The police had closed all parks until they had been scoured. What about the beach, she wondered? What if one fell deep into sand only to explode when a child first built a sandcastle after the war?

Over the next days, US airmen were drafted in to help clear the deadly butterfly bombs with the main roads inspected first, then the side roads, and every garden. The heavy undergrowth was left to the POWs from the camp in Weelsby Woods.

Sadie welcomed her garden's turn. She had not set foot in it after the attack.

'No more tea, Ma'am, please. What is it with you English ladies, always a cup of tea.' The polite young man stood grinning at her back door, itching to do his job and get on to the next garden.

'I'm sorry. It's what we do. We're conditioned to offer tea, perhaps a biscuit?'

'Now, I never say no to a cookie.'

'I'm sorry they're not very appetising.'

'That's the other thing you do, always apologising.'

Sadie laughed.

'You look happy, Ma'am.'

She felt herself tear up. 'I am. A telegram has just arrived, you see. I'm over the moon. My son's been taken prisoner in Germany. He's alive, Airman.' She choked back a sob. 'Would you please give me a hug.' She wanted to tell the world.

To do him credit, the airman obliged as she sobbed into his tunic, his arms tentative at first, then fierce. He was no older than Glen, poor thing. She let him go and smiled up at him. 'Stay safe, young man.'

He saluted and left, whistling Colonel Bogie as he marched back up the garden and on to her neighbour's.

She wiped her eyes and wished him a silent farewell. She wished she could write to his mother to give her thanks for sending him over here.

Lingering in the garden, she continued to listen to his whistling as it competed with the clucking of her neighbour's hens and the occasional snort of a pig in the distance.

A fortnight later Sadie was asked to join a team cooking for a weekend invasion exercise involving the Home Guard. She joined the other volunteers at five-thirty in the morning and was faced with a mountain of fish and chips to cook, but they worked cheerfully together and served two hundred men at the appointed hour.

Alex appeared as she was finishing the clearing up. 'Can I give you a lift home?'

She knew he would have been in the building, but it was still a shock to see him. All those feelings she had buried, resurfaced. Was he still angry? He looked weary but concerned. She passed a hand across her face. She must look a sight, greasy, dirty, smelling of fish, a turban perched on her head. Tiredness gripped her, and she accepted rather than walk home.

'Edna told me about Glen and Dale,' he said. 'I'm pleased they're safe.'

'Dale is, but I worry about Glen.'

He slipped his hand from the steering wheel and gave her's a momentary squeeze.

'How are you? How's Marion?'

'She's fine. I think she will find life too quiet once this is all over. She's still at Hibaldstow and has a lot of fun, I gather.'

'Give her my love. And you, how are you?'

'There's no one else, Sadie.'

Her heart went out to him, but she couldn't offer him any hope. Not yet, maybe never.

'You know Dale wants to return to Australia when all this is over. He told me that he feels more Australian than British, wants to give it a fair go.'

'Will you go with him?' His eyes appeared crestfallen.

'I need to stay for Glen, but...' She couldn't finish. If only one son remained to her, a difficult choice lay ahead.

'Let's see how it all pans out, shall we?' They stopped outside her house. He turned to her and held her hands. 'I'll be here. I haven't given up on you. Although you've put me through hell and I'll never understand why.' He leaned over and kissed her on her cheek. 'Oh, the aroma of wet fish,' he chuckled. 'Nothing like it to kill a man's ardour.'

It was her turn to laugh. 'I miss you Alex.' She turned and got out of the car, then waved him off. 'I love you.' He couldn't hear, and she didn't want him to.

This man, the love of her life with the patience of a saint. She longed for him to be back in her life. 'If I get my sons back, then I know I will have been forgiven,' she mouthed at the disappearing car.

There were no more butterfly bombs, but the biggest raid on the town came two weeks later This time incendiaries, then phosphorus bombs to force the rescue services out fire-fighting, followed by the largest bombs. Sadie sat shaking in her shelter worried for Alex. This sounded like the biggest raid on the town so far. She was past caring for herself, but the thought of those bombs raining down on women with children and the men out so gallantly trying to do their job was more than she could bear. The days ahead were going to be difficult for everyone.

Chapter Thirty-Six

Australia
Adelaide, February 1925

She had his bags packed in the bedroom. Despite her determination to remain calm, her heart beat wildly as the hour of Frank's return approached. The older boys had been sent to stay at Joe Junior's for the night. Her brother appeared reluctant at first when she telephoned him.

'It's a bit awkward at the moment, Sadie. There's a lot going on.'

'I can't have them in the house this evening, Joe. Please, you have to help me.' The desperation in her voice must have swayed him; strangely he didn't ask her to elaborate. 'I will collect them first thing in the morning, I promise.'

She instructed the servants they were not to be disturbed. They knew something was afoot, of course, you can't hide packed suitcases without the rumour-mill going into overdrive.

His key turned in the lock. Footsteps sounded across the hall, the door opening, her not rising to greet him, nor offering a cheek to kiss.

He stood, frowning. 'This is not much of a welcome home.'

One suspicion of hers was allayed. Sadie thought maybe he knew of his paramour's visit, had even engineered it while he was away. That would have been a coward's way. Frank was not a coward, a bully, yes.

'Your secretary visited me yesterday.' She let it sink in, studying his face, expecting to see shock, penitence, anger at the girl's impudence. Instead, his lips curled up into a smirk, and he shrugged.

'So now you know. I suppose you're going to say, 'Oh, how could you Frank, think of our boys, please dismiss her and promise you'll never see her again.' His voice had risen to a simpering tone, a mockery of her voice.

The need to hit out at him was overwhelming, but she knew what he was capable of if she tried. She forced herself to sit tight in her seat, talk in an even voice, not let him under her skin.

'No, I'm going to say, your bags are packed. Go, be with your tart. Leave us alone. I want a divorce.'

'And why should I leave my house?'

'It is not your house. I bought it with my money. You may remember, my father insisted. My name alone is on the deeds. I may not have much left of my inheritance, but I do own this.'

That rattled him. Sadie continued, 'Go and live with your secretary in her paltry rooms, I hear you've spent enough time there already. But you'll drop her now that she's become an embarrassment. I'll be speaking with a lawyer on Monday.'

'You've grown some backbone, at last, my darling,' he sneered. 'You may think you have the upper hand, but it's not going to last. I'll be speaking to my own lawyers. Be careful what you wish for, Sadie because you will be begging me for help very soon.' He laughed. 'I'll call a taxi; I have an idea where I can get a much warmer welcome than here, someone very warm, very young, very pretty, willing to do anything for me, to me. Whatever I ask.' His sneer grew wider, his face sickened her. To think she had once cared for this man.

He turned his back on her to leave the room. She heard him pick up the telephone. Crazy thoughts sped through her mind, thoughts about running after him with something heavy to crack open his skull. She longed to be rid of him, felt sick to think he had ever touched her.

He returned to the room. 'The taxi will be here shortly.' He sat in an armchair, his long legs crossed, a hand tapping on the antimacassar.

'Did you ever love me, Frank?' Why had she asked that? Stupid, she knew the answer.

'I thought I was marrying into the new squattocracy, a family going up in the world. My mistake. I needed a cash-cow after my father gambled his way through my mother's money. It turns out your father has gambled away his money too.'

His grin unnerved her. He was talking nonsense. She listened for the taxi, praying it would arrive soon, unable to bear his presence or his contempt any longer. A car drew up, and a door opened followed by a rap at the door.

Frank unwound himself slowly from the chair. 'I will speak to you soon, Sadie. Prepare to pay for me to leave you alone, or I will take the boys.'

Her heart somersaulted. What on earth did he mean?

He blew her a kiss of farewell from the door. It wasn't until the front door slammed behind him that she dared to breathe. It came in painful gulps of air as his parting threat squeezed her heart. Bile rose in her throat, and she ran to the bathroom before retching into the toilet. What did he mean? How could he take her boys from her? He was at fault, not her. No judge would let her boys go to an adulterer, would they?

She knew judges were hard on wives with stains on their character, but her conduct had been exemplary. A whole weekend with this hanging over her would drive her mad. If only she had consulted a lawyer this morning, but this was unknown territory to her. Divorce on the grounds of her husband's adultery sounded simple, uncomplicated. Proof lay in his mistress's pregnancy. Had she been naïve? She needed Papa's advice.

He sat in his study; a newspaper laid out on his desk.

'I wish you wouldn't disturb him, Sadie.' Caro pleaded. 'It's not a good time.'

Sadie barged her way past. 'Papa, I need your help.'

He looked up from the newspaper, 'Sadie.' His voice sounded tired and old. 'Come and sit here. I need a friendly face.'

'Whatever's the matter, Papa?' Her troubles fled into the shadows of the evening light.

'I fear the wolves are gathering.' He placed his head in his hands. 'This time, I fear I have undercut too much.' He pushed the newspaper towards her.

She read a letter from a builder criticising the Colonel Light Gardens contractor for the cost of each house rising to seven hundred pounds. 'He's just jealous that he didn't get the contract, Papa.'

'If only it were that simple.' He sighed.

'But that delegation from the government inspected the site last week. They congratulated you on the completion of the first homes. I read in the newspaper that they were very impressed with the standard.'

'True, but I can't afford to carry on with the build unless the bank or government help me out. The foundations have cost me a great deal more than I quoted for.'

'That's why you were upset when Mr McNamara died.'

'Yes, he gave me some leeway, but this new man is obdurate. I should never have signed the contract without some room for negotiation for contingencies, but I was desperate, and I thought I could build them at six hundred and thirty-six.'

'Is there no hope?'

'Only if I can get the government to lend me money against my brickyard.'

She took his hand and held it. He wiped away a tear, and her heart broke for him. Her beloved father, admired and celebrated for all that he had achieved, now looked bowed and shorn of all pride.

'Did you want some help with something, Sadie?'

'No Papa, it's nothing that matters. Let me sit with you.' How could she add to his troubles?

She sat in her lawyer's office a month later while he perused the letter from Frank's lawyer.

'It's not good news, Mrs Tinsdale.'

She stared at him in confusion. 'I don't understand. He admitted adultery to me, and she is expecting.'

'Not any more. If she ever were; she lost it. There is no evidence of adultery. They both deny it, and it's your word against theirs.'

'But is he not living with her?'

'No, he sleeps in his office, an anteroom, I believe.'

'Well, I'm not taking him back.'

'I don't think you understand, Mrs Tinsdale. He is countersuing you for divorce.'

She sat back in her seat, staring at him, the colour draining from her face. 'On what possible grounds?'

'That your son Henry is not his son.'

'What?' Her voice strangled in her throat. 'Of course, he's his son.'

'Born only eight and a half months after your wedding?' The lawyer's expression was judgemental.

'Yes, but...' How could she tell this insufferable man the truth? 'Frank had relations with me on the day of our engagement. He forced me.' Her face coloured and her eyes slunk to her lap.

'You were engaged previously, this letter says.'

'Yes, but I broke it off months before.'

'And yet, this man visited you on the evening of your engagement?'

'For a few minutes only. He came,' the unhappy meeting flashed through her mind, 'to congratulate me.' How did Frank know about the visit? Had he been spying on her? Was he guessing?

'Your housekeeper witnessed this, perhaps.'

'No, she was away visiting her daughter who had just had a happy event.'

'Your maid?'

'Yes, she let him in and saw him out a few minutes later.'

'Good, her name and address please.'

'It was nearly ten years ago, and she left my employ when I married. All I can remember is her first name, Bridie, I think.'

'Most unfortunate. Mr Tinsdale says that this child bears no resemblance to him, dark blue eyes, mid-brown hair, dimples in his cheeks.'

'He resembles my mother; she had dimples and dark blue eyes. His hair got fairer by the time Frank first saw him; he was quite dark at birth. My father has brown hair. But this is all nonsense. I have never had relations with any man but my husband.' She blushed profusely; there was blood when he...'

He smiled at her. 'I am sorry Mrs Tinsdale. I needed to test you. This letter is scurrilous, but a judge may view it differently. Is it possible to ask your ex-fiancé to be a witness? If he were a man of integrity, his word could go a long way.'

The thought horrified her. 'I couldn't drag him into this. He's a lawyer, hoping for a career in State politics. It would ruin him.'

'The perfect witness then.'

'No, absolutely not. You may not drag his name into this sordid little affair. My husband married me for my name and my money. As I said, he forced me into marriage. He must not be allowed to get away with this. You must fight him, Sir.'

'It is best that it does not come to a fight, Mrs Tinsdale. We need to bargain, I think. Leave it to me, my dear lady.'

She left the lawyer's office in tatters. Her mind couldn't grasp Frank's treachery. How could he possibly think Henry was Rob's child? Was that why he had ignored him all these years? No, He did not care about any of his children, until the last few weeks when he had rung to say he would like to take them out on Sundays. What was that about? The boys, of course, were happy to see their father, a little shy at first but they returned laughing and in high spirits. What was he trying to do? She stopped dead in the street. Oh God, did he think he would get custody? No, no, no! I will do anything to stop that, she thought. I can't have my sons brought up by that man and his trollop.

So far, all she had told her family was that she and Frank were undergoing a trial separation. She had to tell them that, worried that the boys would say something about Frank not living at home, anymore. They commiserated and acted surprised but were too bound up in their own worries to offer any support. She wished Stanley and Jane weren't in England. Jane was the one person who she could talk to.

Two weeks later, yet another meeting with the lawyer.

'He's keen to get this settled, Mrs Tinsdale,'

'He's not getting custody of any of them.'

Let's hope it doesn't come to that.'

'He's bluffing if he asks for it. He doesn't want the boys, never has until now.'

'And yet, I understand he's been taking them out every Sunday, lately.'

'Yes, but he doesn't want them. They're pawns in his dirty game.'

'You may well be right. But your husband's visits will hold sway with a judge.'

'One look at his floozy, and the judge will discount her testimony. You only have to see her to know that.'

He sighed. 'Mrs Tinsdale, a competent lawyer would see she wore an appropriately modest suit, a veiled hat, maybe even spectacles to court. Appearances can be deceptive.'

'Tell me what I should do? I'm begging you. I can't lose my boys.' She had kept her tears in check, but now hot splashes spilt onto her cheeks.

The lawyer looked at the letter in his hands in embarrassment. He waited a moment until she wiped her eyes before clearing his throat. 'Your husband's lawyer writes that your father's business is in trouble. He speaks of wrongdoing, backhanders, that sort of thing.'

'No!' Sadie could not contain her revulsion. 'Frank is a liar. My father is the most honest man there is. Everyone knows it. He must not be allowed to say such things. Surely that's libel.'

'Tainted gossip, but gossip can wound, especially at such a delicate time. I too have heard rumours about Mr Timmins's business. Not about wrongdoing, of course. But such rumours can be enough to bring a man's business to its knees.'

'What does Frank want? I won't give him my sons but is there something else that would satisfy him?'

'He's asked for the house in Sydney. Give him that, and he will walk away. Offer no contest, sign anything you want.'

'But it's worth thousands. It was a wedding present to me, not to us.'

'I strongly advise you to consider it, Mrs Tinsdale. This could turn very ugly for you, your boys and your dear father, whom I greatly admire.'

'Will I get maintenance for the boys?'

'I will try, but his lawyer shows a great hole in Mr Tinsdale's finances. It seems he took out a loan which he's struggling to pay back. I have documentary proof.'

'Could I not sell the Sydney house and pay him half?'

'He needs it as collateral for the loan. I fear a sale may take too long and the threat to your father is imminent.'

'That's blackmail.'

'It is. You can take the risk, Mrs Tinsdale. If your husband's business fails, he is unlikely to achieve custody, but things could take a nasty turn. I fear your husband is a vindictive man. Think of your reputation, dear lady.'

'I need to consult my father. I can't give up the house without talking to him.'

'He wants an answer immediately. He says he will go to the newspapers this afternoon unless I telephone his lawyers with your answer.'

He'd won. Frank had won. Sadie knew it. He would have no qualms in carrying out his threat.

'Draw up the transfer for the house, but I want maintenance in return, at least until Glen's sixteen. He owes the boys that.'

'A pragmatic decision, dear lady.'

Joe Junior turned up at her house ten days later and a few days after signing away her house. She was still seething, but mostly ashamed. She had brought disaster upon herself and daren't admit it to her family. The boys were out with Dolly, disappointed when their father failed to turn up to take them out.

'There's a nip in the air today, make sure they don't get cold, please, Dolly.' Bells pealed from Adelaide's many churches as she closed the door. She was going to have to talk to her sons about their father when they returned. She hated the thought that he could let them down so easily. He'd promised them a day's fishing, and for all she knew he had gone fishing, but on his own.

But here was her brother. She couldn't remember the last time he visited. 'Come in, Joe. You look dreadful.'

Joe Junior was still the most handsome of her brothers. His hair, thick and dark where the others had thinning, brown hair like their father's. At forty, he had matured into a respected, honest businessman, maybe lacking the flair and vim of his father, but well-liked. Yet she scarcely recognised the shell of the man on her doorstep, with his haggard, greying, unshaven face and haunted eyes above a crumpled, stale shirt. He stepped into the hall. His gait was stumbling and weary.

'Come and sit down. It's Papa, isn't it?' She led him into the parlour and sat him in Frank's chair.

'He's tried everyone he knows, called in favours, but we're at the end of the line. No one has any spare money to invest. Times are too hard.'

'What about Sir Sydney Kidman?'

'They're not on speaking terms since their partnership broke down last year.'

'Then it's over.'

'The bank foreclosed on Friday, Sadie. Work will cease on site tomorrow. I've been up all night with father. I daren't go home.'

Sadie slumped in her chair, guilty that she had been so wrapped up in her separation from Frank. 'I knew things were serious, but not that serious. I don't understand how everything can go that wrong so quickly. Oh, Joe, what is he going to do?'

'Sell everything. But it won't be enough. There's nothing left.' They sat, mute, staring into space until Sadie rose to put her arms around Joe. He broke into sobs.

'Olive's beside herself. The children will have to leave their private schools tomorrow. I haven't paid their fees, and I don't know how to tell them. They've always had the best of everything, and now I can't afford even to buy them shoes.'

'But your job, Joe, your directorship.'

'Father will have to sell his shares in the company. A new owner will want his own director. We're all going to have to look for work, even Father. You know how tough that's going to be. He may get taken on as an engineer. But me, what can I do?' He stood up, a lost soul.

'Something will turn up. You have contacts.' She buried herself in his shoulder, arms holding him tight.

He broke apart. 'And what about you, Sadie? Has Frank returned?'

'No.' She looked away, fighting tears. 'We're getting divorced because of an affair with his secretary. He got her pregnant for God's sake, and she had the effrontery to come and tell me herself.'

'Why didn't you say?' Joe shook his head at her. 'Oh, Sadie love, we would have helped. I am sorry you dealt with this on your own.'

'You know why. I didn't want to add to Papa's troubles. Now, you can't go home looking like that. Let me run a bath for you and order you some food.' She rang for the maid, unwilling to discuss the end of her marriage any further. She was afraid that if she began to cry she would never stop.

Chapter Thirty-Seven

Australia -
Adelaide, April 1925

Packing cases sat in every bedroom, and Sadie attacked the cupboards and drawers ruthlessly, discarding clothes, books and toys into piles. Glen had grown out of this, let it go to Alice's youngest. Old rattles, cloth picture books – there would be no more children – why keep any of it? She had no idea where she was going to live, but she wanted to leave this house. There were too many dark memories, and she needed the money.

They would have to make do with somewhere smaller, three bedrooms only, no room for a servant. Glen could manage now without a nursemaid. She bought the house for two thousand pounds. It would sell for around the same money, maybe a little more with housing being scarce. She had a few investments and shares. With Frank's maintenance, it would leave her poor but not destitute. That left a few hundred in her bank account. At least she was spared having to look for work like her brothers.

She moved on to Frank's room. When they had moved into this property, he decided he needed his own room for when he came home late at night. He had taken what he wanted a few weeks before. Everything else could go. His furniture might bring in a few extra pounds; it was all good quality mahogany. She walked to the wardrobe, empty now, save for a couple of old shirts with fraying cuffs. His cupboard drawers were mostly empty. She pulled out some old handkerchiefs and a pair of socks with holes in the heel, underneath lay a tin box.

She remembered it. On the day he received the Victory and George V Medals he had tossed them into the box, dropped it into a drawer and forgot about it. Every move since, she had religiously packed it, unpacked it and given it to him. Each time, he tossed it back into another drawer, uncared for, discarded like it meant nothing. At the ceremony, she remembered burning with pride for his service to Country and Empire. While to him, it amounted to two and half years of sacrifice and the hardship of battle symbolised by discs of heavy scrap-metal. She took a brightly coloured medal from the box, its ribbon of rainbow coloured silk, slightly fraying and crumpled. 'The Great War for Civilisation 1914-1919' surrounded by laurel leaves, on the edge she could just about make out his engraved name and service number.

She had no idea where he acquired the Queen Mary tin, perhaps he swapped some cigarettes for it at the beginning of his service, when he still retained some pride. By the end of the war, his feelings were only of anger and resentment. Would he have joined up but for her? She suspected so, however much he deceived himself, if only for the adventure.

Did she want Henry to have the medals? She sat on the bed thinking of the moment she told the boys about their father leaving, trying to be gentle, non-judgemental. Glen was too young to understand, but he took his cue from his brothers, and all three wept. She had held them in her arms and promised to love them forever, but it didn't make up for their loss.

Why should any of her boys honour a father who cared so little for them? She picked up the box and threw it on the floor amongst the shirts and cast-off socks. Let it go in the waste sack.

Papa was her big concern now. She went to visit the day after the announcement in the papers. He scarcely had time to speak to her. Demands from reporters for interviews, his bookkeeper, his secretary, creditors, his foreman all lining up begging for attention. She stood on the sidelines, unsure what was going on. Eddie attempted to keep her informed, but the situation appeared to change daily, and now there was talk of an official enquiry. Recriminations flew around the newspapers, and even the boys were upset by the gossip in school. Henry and Dale adored their Grandpa. It was too much for them to bear. Sadie longed to flee with them back to Melbourne. Perhaps she would. A little house at Saint Kilda or Brighton might offer some peace.

Her father came to visit on a Wednesday towards the end of the month.

She sat him down and ordered tea.

'You're moving too?' He looked around the room, noticing gaps where ornaments and small tables stood. Scarcely a question, more a statement of the inevitable, his voiced drained of emotion.

'I am, although I'm not sure where. I'd rather be close to family.'

The maid arrived with a tray of tea and cake. Sadie poured and offered her father the plate. He shook his head.

'You look as though you're running on…' She wanted to say thin air. His face was like a death mask. 'You must sleep, Papa. Try to put your health first.'

He hadn't the energy to summon up a hollow laugh. 'How can I put myself first when the children are starving? Sadie, you are my only hope.'

'Whatever I can do, Papa.' What did he mean the children were starving? Whose children?

'The Sydney house, will you sell it and lend the money to your brothers. Otherwise, all is lost.'

He knocked the breath out of her body. She grasped the tablecloth almost pulling over the teapot.

'What is it, Sadie?'

'I can't; I can't help you.' Her hand quivered as he took it in his.

'Sadie, I'm begging you.'

'Papa, I'm sorry. I don't own it anymore.'

His mouth dropped open, and his hand tightened around hers. 'When?'

'Six weeks ago. I had to let it go. Frank threatened to take the boys and to lie about you to the newspapers.'

'Why didn't you tell me? I'd have seen him off. What possessed you, Sadie?' The disappointment in his voice was unbearable.

'My lawyer advised it.'

'Your lawyer is a fool and a blackguard.' Anger suffused his face. 'Are you sure he wasn't in Frank's pocket?'

Sadie's mouth gawped like a fish. Her whole body shook. It wasn't possible, was it? 'I got his name from the telephone directory. He seemed genuine. Oh, God, Papa, what have I done?' She collapsed in her seat.

He stood and held her like a drowning man. 'Give me his address, and I'll look into it. It's probably too late.' She could feel the tremor in his arms as he let her go.

She scribbled down the address, the biggest fool that ever lived. She had let the whole family down, broken her vow to Bruce and destroyed Papa's trust in her. She wanted to sink through the floor and disappear.

He took the blotched paper. 'Come to the house on Sunday morning. Don't bring the children. We'll know by then.' Defeat threaded his voice. He left, head bowed, unable to look at her streaming face.

Joe Junior let her in. Where was the maid? She entered the drawing room; everyone was there, even the children, the younger ones sitting subdued at their mother's feet. The women looked at her briefly, but then cast their eyes down to their children. Eddie stood and walked over to hug her, but his eyes appeared dead.

Papa came into the room and asked her to go into his study. There was only one word to describe him, broken. Sadie shuddered with dread. Why was she here?

'Sit down, Sadie.' He sat at his desk. 'I asked around and went to visit this lawyer of yours. He's not crooked, just lazy and useless. If he had been crooked, I might have stood a chance of suing for retribution. As it is, we have to kiss goodbye to the Sydney House.'

'Papa, I'm so sorry...'

He cut her off. 'No, it's not your fault. I've been too distracted to look after your interests. You came to me for help back in January, didn't you? I couldn't see your need, too scared about my impending bankruptcy.'

She nodded, unable to speak, her mouth choking back tears.

'I never mentioned the Sydney house to your brothers, for all they know it's been swallowed up like everything else I own. Don't tell them. That is the least I can do for you.' He caught her hands and kissed them.

'What's happening, Papa? Why is everyone here? You told me not to bring my children.'

'You don't have to stay. You're the only one of my children, apart from Stanley, who can escape what's going to happen this morning. Be thankful for that small mercy. I've let your Mama down.' He took a moment to control himself as his shoulders shook and he rammed his fist into his mouth.

Sadie began to panic. 'Please, Papa, tell me.'

He looked at her, his grey eyes smoky with tears. 'You have to say goodbye to the children. We've found homes for them, not orphanages. They're going to family.'

'What?' Sadie screamed. 'No, say it isn't true, Papa.'

'There's no money for food. The houses are being repossessed tomorrow. We have to let the children go.'

'It's my fault, Papa. If I still owned the Sydney house, I could have saved them.'

'No, Sadie, a temporary reprieve, perhaps.'

'But it would have been enough.'

He didn't reply. He slumped to the desk. 'I always did the best I knew how. It was the war, you know. It ruined everything. Blame the war, Sadie. Try not to blame me.'

She moved beside him and knelt at his feet putting her head in his lap. He stroked her hair while she wept, her heart breaking for her family.

A knock at the front door. Papa stood and pulled her up. 'Dry your eyes.' His voice sounded gruff, and he pulled a handkerchief from his pocket and mopped her face and then his. 'Put a smile on your face and wish them farewell.' He caught her hand in a firm grip and pulled her into the hall.

Olive's sister stood at the door. Her face a mask of haughty displeasure.

Sadie's heart withered as the children, accompanied by Olive filed into the hall. Why had she not noticed the bags lined up when she arrived. The oldest girl looked sullenly at her father.

'I can't believe you're doing this.'

'We have no choice, my darling.'

'Come, I haven't got all day,' Olive's sister looked at the children with distaste.

'Please look after them well.' Sadie watched her proud sister-in-law reduced to begging her sister.

'They'll have to earn their keep.' Her cold words cut at Olive and her children shrank back. Joe's fists balled but he dared say nothing. His children's well-being depended on her.

Sadie moved towards the children and stood between them and their new guardian. 'Goodbye my loves, stay strong, look after each other.' She kissed each of them in turn, feeling their bodies quake beneath her touch. She walked back into the drawing room to let the parents have some privacy but was faced with a new horror. Alice sat with her youngest on her lap. She rocked back and forth, her face tormented. Bruce Junior was only a year old, four-year-old, Kenneth, sitting at her feet, looked up at his mother in concern.

Sadie sat with Alice and picked up Noelle to cuddle, burying her face in the girl's dark curls.

'Who's taking them?' Sadie asked, softly.

'An aunt of mine,' she whispered, 'but I wouldn't trust her with a dog. She's promised to take them to my mother in Sydney but refused to pay for my train ticket, so I can't go with them.' Her eyes glistened darkly with tears.

The door opened, and Joe Junior beckoned to Alice. A fierce, well-padded woman stood there glowering, and Sadie's heart broke into pieces. Putting Noelle back on the floor, she stumbled past her brother and the woman, ignored her father, who stood with his arm against the wall sobbing. She ran from the house. Her mind refused to contemplate her family being torn further apart. If she stayed, she thought she would smash into pieces like Alice. As it was, she could never forgive herself for breaking her promise to Bruce. Blindly stumbling down through streets, unaware of where she was going, Sadie blundered onwards. She ought to go home, gather her boys into her arms and never let them go but dared not. They must not see broken, raw with grief and shame.

She paced the jetty, unaware that her wild eyes and tear-streaked cheeks were drawing looks. Her beloved Papa's face. Would she ever forget how his eyes streamed with tears to watch his grandchildren's terror, knowing all hope was lost? His life's work in ruins, his reputation sullied, his children thrown onto the scrapheap.

A woman stepped towards her, a gloved hand outstretched, almost touching her arm. Her kindly eyes showed alarm; she looked motherly, concerned. Sadie's heart screamed in silence. Was the horror of the morning written so plainly on her face? She attempted a smile to reassure the woman, nodded as the woman withdrew her arm, eyes flickering in relief.

Sadie slowed her pacing, drawing her collar around her face to hide her anguish from the curious. Stay calm, think it through. Her hand strayed to her hair; the dark bob beneath her cloche hat felt strange - a recent act of independence. No, she would never give in, never let the bleakness in her heart take over. She must learn to be a lioness when it came to her boys. They needed her, only her and she would do anything to protect them. At the end of the jetty, Sadie stared at the ocean as though its inky depths would answer her lurking questions.

Far out on the horizon, a band of sunshine highlighted the cumulus clouds, a kingdom of snowy peaks, dark hills, even a crenellated castle. Another land; mysterious, unobtainable. The light drew her in, calming her. Her pounding heart began to quieten; she counted the wheeling gulls, anything to still her nerves. The guilt weighed in on her. All she could think to do was to run, run far away from the memories.

Looking out on the Gulf of Saint Vincent, leaving for the Old Country felt like the ultimate betrayal. This iconic jetty, a testament to the first settlers who built Adelaide, should be rooting her to Australia. As the ocean whipped the waves into foam, she tried to capture the men and women's joy at reaching the safety of land after the seasick, endless days, weeks, months of their voyage. What courage they must have had. She admired their pluck, their endeavour, but did not feel equal to it. She imagined their feelings as they left the ship and set foot on the strange land, nervous, exhilarated, purposeful, frightened maybe. Had they knelt on the shore, thanking God for their safe delivery? Her flight would throw their hope and perseverance back in their faces, but she saw no choice.

While they faced an uncertain future building a home and a life in this hostile environment, she was contemplating abandoning their endeavour. And this city, this beautiful, elegant city, less than ninety years old, her heart cried out at the thought of leaving it behind, probably forever.

But how could she stay? She could never forget the pain and horror witnessed that morning. The imagined screams of the children torn from their mothers pierced her soul. Shame and guilt that her children had escaped their fate prevented her from remaining here. There was no hope of saving her nieces and nephews when her marriage was in ruins and her fortune lost. Her resources only stretched to saving the boys from their father.

'I have to face the future by abandoning the past. It's the only way.' Sadie turned back from the sea; her mind made up. 'Our future lies in England where living costs are cheaper. Stanley and Jane are making the right choice for their family, and I must do the same. At least I will have one of my brothers close by.'

Although the decision was made, it left her with a feeling of dread. Exchanging the life she knew for a small seaside town in northern England, would have sounded mad a year ago. But she deserved no more. Her inheritance could have cushioned this blow. Now she had barely enough to keep body and soul together.

'Mama, Papa, forgive me. I've let everyone down.' She stared into the sea until she began to shiver with cold, then turned. Time to go home and plan for her escape, after sending money for Alice's ticket back to Sydney. It was the least she could do.

Chapter Thirty-Eight

England
Cleethorpes, May 1946

Sadie opened the door. Marion stood there looking trim in her short-skirted suit and nifty hat.

'Do come in, dear. It's lovely to see you.' Sadie took her through to the back room. 'I'll put the kettle on.'

'How are you, Sadie?'

Sadie turned to her, seeing what might have been and was not. 'As well as can be expected.' That was a bit unfair. 'No, I'm fine. It's been tough, but I'm getting better each day. Our family's been lucky. My niece's husband, Jimmy, is returning shortly with a Military Cross to his name. My nephew, Brian was unexpectedly found alive in Burma. The only one we don't know about is my brother, Stanley. We can only hope to hear eventually.' In her heart, she believed the worst. She sighed in resignation. 'I'll go and make tea; then you can tell me your news.'

She bustled out to the kitchen and brought in three cups and a plate of scones. 'Pour yourself one while I take this through to Glen.'

A minute later she returned and poured her tea.

'I came to tell you I'm moving to America.'

Sadie's heart twisted, but she managed to smile. 'A GI bride?'

'Yes, his name's Artie. He's from Colorado. It's wild west country, I understand. His family own a ranch.'

'It sounds exciting, dear.' Sadie smiled. 'You'll be able to go riding every day. That's wonderful.'

'I met him at Hibaldstow. One night all these American planes couldn't land at their airfield and used ours. We ran around finding food and beds for them when we scarcely had enough for our boys. They even had to share knives and forks. I met him then.' She looked happy. 'But I didn't dare hope, not after Henry.' Her expression turned sad.

'At least Artie returned,' Sadie said, gently.

Marion nodded, her eyes full of sympathy. 'Yes, he did. He's a nice guy, Sadie. I'm sure he'll make me happy, and Father likes him.' She paused. 'Did you ever find out what happened to Henry?'

'Only recently. A Dutch farmer found him and looked after him, but he was too badly injured. I'm unbelievably thankful to have been told. The hardest part is not knowing. So many men are missing, so many mothers not knowing where their sons lie. I am luckier than most.' Henry had died on the day she broke up with Alex. The curse of a death foretold was for her first-born, not Glen or Dale. What she had put Alex through was unnecessary, but she wasn't to know that.

'Dale is in Australia, Father says.'

'Yes, he got repatriated back there as soon as he was rescued from the German POW camp. I went to London to see him off. He wanted to be in Sydney at the end of the war. When they liberated Singapore, he caught the first flight to search for Glen as he promised.' Sadie shook. 'He never told me what it was like, but I have seen photos of the Jap POWs.' Her teacup rattled in the saucer as she replaced it. 'They kept Glen in hospital for months, but he was still stick-thin when I got him back.'

'How long has it been?'

'He arrived in February.' Sadie turned her head to the window, tears spilling down her face.

'Oh, I'm sorry, Sadie.' Marion rose to comfort her.

'I couldn't cope.' Sadie sobbed. 'Not the way he was. My doctor admitted him to Bracebridge in Lincoln.' Shame clouded her face. She tried to slow down her breathing, a trick she had learned over the last years. 'He came home last week. I shouldn't spoil your happy news, dear.'

'Has my father seen him?'

'No, I thought it best for them not to meet.'

'You've had it so tough, Sadie. I do wish...' She stopped.

'I know what you're going to say. You wish I had let your father help more than he has; finally agree to marry him. He's been good to me, giving me lifts to Lincoln to see Glen, taking me out for a drink afterwards when I was shaking with heartbreak for the strong young man Glen had been.' Sadie choked back a tear before planting a firm smile on her face. 'Alex told me you had met someone although he didn't give me any details. He seeks to spare me sometimes. No, I can't marry him because he wants to care for me. That's not who I am. I have never wanted to be a burden on anyone. I need to concentrate on Glen now.'

'Father still loves you.'

'As I do him, but he doesn't deserve to be encumbered, and I won't allow it.'

'It's just that...' Marion screwed up her eyes.

'What, dear? Spit it out.'

'If there's no hope for you two.'

'There can't be, not with Glen the way he is.'

Marion searched her face, looking for any doubt but finding none. 'I want to ask my father to join me in Colorado. I want him to know his grandchildren.'

Sadie sat still, scarcely breathing. So, this was it. Alex would go. He needed to go. She would encourage him to leave her finally. The last sacrifice she had to make.

'Would you like to meet Glen, dear?' She stood and opened the door. 'He's in the middle room. Come.' Marion picked up her handbag and followed. Sadie paused outside the door and knocked softly. 'It's Mother, Glen. I have a visitor.' She pushed the door open and guided Marion in.

Haunted eyes lifted briefly from the table where he sat studying a complex jigsaw. The cover of the box showed a pretty country garden full of summer flowers and trees. His slim fingers patted the empty plate beside him. Every few seconds he put his fingers to his mouth to lick any invisible crumbs. No expression lit his gaunt face, but his body trembled, and an occasional moan escaped from his mouth. Marion shuddered. Sadie stroked her son's shoulders and gently lifted up his shirt to show Marion before letting it fall and leading her outside the room.

'They say he was flayed with split bamboo several times; the scars allowed to heal and then opened up again and again,' she whispered, softly. 'That and starvation and seeing so many of his friends tortured in different ways, well you can understand, can't you? He's better than he was, a lot better. He learned gardening at Bracebridge; I only wish I had more of a garden for him to manage. I tried to take him out to the seaside, but the crowds upset him, and boys jeered at him when he began to shake, so it's best we stay inside. Take Alex to America with my blessing, Marion. Give him grandchildren and never let them go to war.'

Chapter Thirty-Nine

England -
Cleethorpes, June 1946

He parked outside her house on Saturday morning. She watched him from her bedroom where she was looking out onto a sun-blessed day as the young men kicked a football around on Sussex Recreation Ground opposite, her memories and regrets coinciding, as they so often did.

The sight of him always made her heart leap – this time tinged with more sadness than usual. His impending loss grew acuter with each passing day. Should she even open the door? Half of her wanted to run and hide again, the other to fall into his arms.

He saw her in the window and smiled. Why had he come when it hurt too much? She turned and walked down the stairs to the front door. His shape filled the glass casting a shadow on the parquet flooring. She opened the door, expecting him to stand there and ask to come in but he swooped in and took her in his arms and kissed her.

'Did you think you would get rid of me that easily? Four years I have waited, but now I'm ready to fight for you.'

'But your daughter?'

'I'm fifty-three and not about to be put out to grass on some damn sheep ranch. This town needs men to rebuild it.' His voice softened. 'I want to meet Glen. It's time to meet him, my love.'

'You know I don't want us to be a burden, Alex. I think it best you go.'

'Stop!' He put his finger to her lips. 'Stop running away, damn it. It's time to accept that I am not going anywhere. You're stuck with me, I'm afraid. Come, I have a plan.' He took her hand and led her down the hall to the middle room. 'In here, is he?'

She nodded and stood in front of the door, barring his way.

'He's no longer a prisoner, Sadie, stop hiding him away.' Alex moved her gently aside and entered with Sadie trailing in his wake. Alex's forcefulness was confusing her. It was unlike him.

'Hello, mate.' Alex sat beside her son as he arranged his jigsaw pieces. He took a small chocolate bar out of his pocket. 'I've been saving up my rations for you.'

Glen paused to look at the chocolate and grabbed it, peeling away the silver paper to stuff the chocolate into his mouth. When he had finished swallowing it, he licked his fingers individually with precision and then began licking again.

Sadie couldn't bear to watch.

'You like flowers and gardens, mate?' Alex said, pointing to the jigsaw.

Glen nodded without looking at him.

'Would you like to go and see a real one?'

Another nod.

'Let's go now.' Alex encouraged Glen to stand and led him from the room towards the front door.

His compliance was not unusual. Glen obeyed orders without questioning them. Sadie found that upsetting. She wished her son would rebel as he used to, as he would have before the war. 'Alex, what's going on?' Sadie demanded.

'Trust me. Get your jacket.' He led Glen outside to the car and settled him in the passenger seat while Sadie locked the house.

She felt mutinous but had no option other than to sit in the back. He's taking control, she thought. I have no idea what's happening. A feeling of relief swept through her. It was a glorious day, and she was out of the house. She did not dare leave Glen alone since he had returned from the hospital. Jane shopped for her, but she was beginning to fall into despair in her isolation. Perhaps Glen felt it too.

Alex began to drive and chatted inconsequentially to Glen, who appeared to take no notice. He sat rigid in the seat, waiting for a command or a blow. She hated to think which.

They drove along Clee Road, past the turnoff to Alex's house, past Glen's grammar school, along Weelsby Road and turned left at Nun's Corner towards Laceby.

'Alex, where are we going?' She called from the back.

'Wait and see, not too far now.'

He drove past Nunsthorpe, and when they reached Laceby Village, he turned right and left and right again, she lost track. Eventually, they arrived at a small, run-down farmhouse. He turned into the pebbled drive and switched off the engine.

'What do you think?' He turned around in his seat to look at her.

She shrugged in perplexity.

'Let's get you out, Glen.' Alex said.

Sadie climbed out of the car and opened Glen's door. The scent of roses and honeysuckle hit her. She breathed them in and felt light-headed with the perfume. An ancient wisteria shrouded the greying walls of the house, a few delicate, late blooms still showing mauve against the green leaves. She saw the date 1813 scratched into the wall next to its trunk with some faded letters.

Glen walked to the roses and stuffed his nose into the flowers, looked up and smiled at his mother. The first smile she had seen since he returned. Her heart contracted as Alex caught her hand and squeezed it.

'Let me show you around.' He walked past the house to a side gate. 'Come on, mate; the garden's through here.' He waited as Glen and Sadie walked through to a wilderness of roses, lavender, red hot pokers, faded lilac and ancient apple trees. The scent of newly scythed grass mingled with the headiness of the roses. An old wooden bench sat outside the house with a robin perching on its arm before it fluttered back into the trees.

'Glen! See if you can get the robin to come to you. Here's a slice of bread.' Alex dug into his pocket again and took out a piece of greaseproof paper, offering it to Glen.

Sadie expected her son to stuff it into his mouth, but he didn't. He walked to the bench, took some of the bread and sat perfectly still.

Alex and Sadie watched, silent and unmoving, breathless with uncertainty as the robin hopped from branch to branch, moving closer. When it flew to her son's hand and pecked at the bread before flying off, she began to regain hope.

'Alex, how did you know?' Sadie whispered as the robin returned to Glen's hand once more. Glen sat still, the tension in his shoulders less, the expression on his face relaxed further as the robin ate from his hand.

'I've seen it before,' Alex whispered. 'I had a friend who was shell-shocked. The only thing that helped was being outside in nature. Birds and flowers aren't threatening. They can't harm him.'

'Did your friend get better?' Her eyes beseeched him.

'Better is relative. Don't hope for too much. Hope for a smile, hope for him to say a word now and again, hope for him to sleep without screaming.' Alex stroked her cheek. 'He'll be safe here in this garden; perhaps he will want to work on it when he's a little stronger.'

'What do you mean, Alex? How can he work here?'

'This property is ours, my love. It was going for a song, so I bought it for us. You can help me do it up. I've got builders coming in next week to put in electricity, install a bathroom and board the floors. There's a lovely bedroom for Glen overlooking the gardens. You should see your face it's a picture.' He bent to kiss her cheek.

'How long have you been planning this?'

'For four years, but I found this property the week after your first visit to Lincoln.'

'I don't know what to say. Alex.'

'Say, you'll marry me, woman. Say yes.' He took her face in his hands and kissed her with such tenderness that her breath almost stopped.

'Yes.'

'About bloody time.' He swept her into his arms again and kissed her until she couldn't breathe. 'There's more,' he said putting her down.

'More?' How could there possibly be more? This wonderful man had given her back her son and a future.

'There's stables. Would you like me to buy you a mare as a wedding present? Grooming it will help Glen gain confidence. A horse and a man can only work together when they trust each other. He took her hand and walked towards Glen. The robin had flown away. 'Would you like to see the rest, mate?'

Glen turned his face towards Alex and his mother and nodded. He stood and walked towards Alex and touched his arm, fleetingly. 'Kiwi?' he said.

'Yes, mate, Kiwi.' Alex's eyes welled with tears.

Sadie choked with emotion. Two small achievements in one day and both brought about by a man she had not allowed herself to trust enough. The man she had almost destroyed with her misinterpreted superstition. His wisdom and love cracked open her heart, flooding her with happiness.

'Glen.' She threaded her fingers into her son's hand, and he did not shrink. 'Glen, would you like to live here? You can help feed the birds and grow food, maybe.'

A light flickered in his eyes, and he nodded.

'Good for you.' Alex smiled at Sadie and winked. 'Can you do me a favour, Son? Come to church next Friday and walk your mother down the aisle? You, my daughter and the vicar, no one else, no hassle, I promise. Your mother, well, she's been waiting for a long time for you to do that. It would mean a lot.'

Glen nodded, his fingers tightening in his mother's hand.

The End

Author's Note

For a man who built three thousand miles of railroads, tram systems, bridges, reservoirs and houses, it was surprising to discover so little of Joseph Timms life was documented in public records. That was until I discovered Trove, the Australian newspaper database. With the aid of Trove, I was able to track Joseph's career and was astounded by his energy and activities. It is sad that his eventual misfortune wiped him from history. Most of his achievements have been forgotten leaving narrow-gauge rail lines crisscrossing West and South Australia. Even the Old Ghan which was eventually built by Joseph's brother, Charles, between Adelaide and Alice Springs was replaced because the route chosen was liable to flood.

I began writing these books because so much was forgotten by the family, in England, although not by Australian relatives. Writing this trilogy has been a joy. It has helped us rediscover cousins in Australia whom none of us knew, and I have fallen in love with a country so rich in our family's history. Now we have a new half-great-uncle too, as the story about a second son called Joseph in Broken Hill was given to me by his granddaughter after she discovered my books.

When the children were taken by relatives in 1925, their lives changed irrevocably. In one household they were treated as servants by their aunt. In the other kidnapped by the aunt and their religion changed. Reared without love or family, they escaped as soon as they could. It affected them throughout their lives.

Sadie is less well documented, and her life is mostly fictional. A photograph of her as a bridesmaid, the only image I have. A report of her wedding and her divorce (after her husband's adultery) and a few mentions of her husband's career in Trove gave me the bones to construct a story. I have made him a villain and changed his name. Joseph's fourth wife, we were told was a floozy. Somehow, I doubt that, but once again, I changed her name, and we have a questionable stepmother.

I never met Sadie. If I had, I doubt I would have had the courage to write her story. A rumour from an Australian cousin gave me the story of her first engagement and that the house in Sydney mysteriously ended up belonging to her husband.

Sadie lost two sons in the war, both in the RAF. She told her niece, my mother-in-law, about the hotel landlord seeing her sons in uniform behind her as she searched for accommodation in an unnamed town. It brings tears to my eyes every time I repeat the story.

Jane's son, another Bruce, was found after the war alive. He had been bayoneted in the neck by the Japanese and left for dead in Burma. He was found by the Karen people and hidden. He couldn't help his fingers seeking crumbs off his plate for years after.

No one heard from Stanley between 1939 and the mid-fifties when he returned destitute, from Australia to live out the rest of his life in Cleethorpes, spending a little time every day in his beloved Dolphin. All the time Nibby was alive, Jane refused to talk to him. She softened towards the end. Stanley used to take my husband fishing and told him tales of his life in Australia. My husband didn't believe them. They sounded too far-fetched.

One day, in the late 1970s, a reporter from the Grimsby Evening Telegraph visited the Dolphin looking for a story. The landlord suggested he talk to his oldest regular, Stanley Timms, and a piece was written for the newspaper detailing his life. We read it; made fun of it because it sounded unbelievable. A father who owned an award-winning vineyard and a million-acre sheep station, a friend of the Murdochs and Dame Nellie Melba, a winner of horse races and a member of the CIA in WW2. Not possible, we thought, until he produced his CIA membership card at Christmas dinner. Unassuming, gentle Stanley had spent his war behind Japanese lines as a coast watcher in Borneo. After the war, his forest, the sole remaining piece of Timms property was taken over by the Indonesian government, without compensation, and he was left penniless.

He never told anyone about his war.

The Germans did not capitalise on the butterfly bombs. Their destructive capacity was so deadly and frightening that the government buried the news very effectively. Only a few towns suffered from them.

Through the writing of these stories about Helen Fitzgerald, the convict, Jane Dugmore, the pioneer and her son and grand-daughter, I have learned so much about the human condition. I hold nothing but admiration for a family which takes on the worst that life can throw them and come through as strongly as they have done. Six generations down the line, the descendants I have met are resourceful, hardworking, determined, some entrepreneurial like their great-grandfather, but most of all, loyal and caring. The eighth generation is among us. I hope they learn to be proud of their story.

If you would like to read a book about Grimsby in an earlier century, consider Ranter's Wharf. You may recognise some of the places in an earlier guise.

I hope you have enjoyed this book. Please consider reviewing it on Amazon or Goodreads. Reviews are vital for authors.

Follow me at:
rosemarynoble.wordpress.com
Twitter   @chirosie
Facebook   https://www.facebook.com/RosemaryJaneNoble/

Acknowledgements

Thanks go foremost to my editor, J L Dean, for her help in teasing out and developing the story and correcting the draft. You were a marvel.

Secondly, I must thank my first beta readers, Angela Petch, Patricia Feinberg Stoner, Julie Moten, John Broughton and my son James for their ideas and constructive criticism. To later beta readers for their corrections.

Thanks go to German Creative and Kate Sharp for my cover and to the Noble family for the use of the image of Jane Timms.

I can't forget my husband who has cooked and done most of the housework while I have been tied to the laptop. I promise I will take a break now.

As usual, I thank other members of Arun Scribes and CHINDI authors for their suggestions.

I need to thank my WW2 consultants who lived these times in Cleethorpes, my aunts, Shirley Studley, Pat Basham and Jean Clarke (Vera's niece and daughters). Also, members of Cleethorpes and Grimsby Memories Facebook Pages who are generous with their memories.

Other thanks go to;

The Timms family, collectively for their recollections and generosity in allowing me to tell the tale of their great-grandfather.

Also, to Paula Herlihy of the Yarra Glen District Historical Society and President of the Mount Evelyn Historical Society.

To my dear friend, Gillian Edwards, for seeking out a copy of C E W Bean's, The Dreadnought of the Darling and sending it all the way from Australia. I love that book.

To Robyn Heitmann who offered advice on the chapters set in Adelaide and Johannes Kroonenburg for the chapter in West Australia.

To the staff of Grimsby Reference Library for their patience and help in using the microfiche.

To Alissa Heffernan of St Hubert's Winery for sending me the article from the Journal of Agriculture of Victoria.

To Teresa Carroll for the story of her grandfather. To the Sloans for arranging a visit and taking us to The White House Church (Riverview) in WA.

Finally, to the Trove Newspaper Archive – without which, I could not have written this book.

9 781999 864439